Mills & Boon is
a wonderful sele
best novels f
bestsell

Emma
DARCY

Each volume has three terrific, powerful
stories written by one of the queens of the
genre. We think you'll love them…

March 2014   **April 2014**   **May 2014**

June 2014   **July 2014**   **August 2014**

Emma DARCY

AUSTRALIA
IN BED WITH HER GROOM

MILLS & BOON

Published in Great Britain 2014
by Mills & Boon, an imprint of Harlequin (UK) Limited,
Eton House, 18-24 Paradise Road, Richmond, Surrey, TW9 1SR

AUSTRALIA: IN BED WITH HER GROOM
© 2014 Harlequin Books S.A.

Mischief and Marriage © 1996 Emma Darcy
A Marriage Betrayed © 1999 Emma Darcy
Bride of His Choice © 1999 Emma Darcy

ISBN: 978 0 263 24609 4

010-0714

Harlequin (UK) Limited's policy is to use papers that are natural, renewable and recyclable products and made from wood grown in sustainable forests The logging and manufacturing processes conform to the legalenvironmental regulations of the country of origin.

Printed and bound in Spain
by Blackprint CPI, Barcelona

Emma Darcy's life journey has taken as many twists and turns as the characters in her stories, whose international popularity has resulted in over sixty million book sales. Born in Australia and currently living in a beachside property on the central coast of New South Wales, she travels extensively to research settings and increase her experience of places and people.

Initially a French/English teacher, she changed careers to computer programming before marriage and motherhood settled her into a community life. A voracious reader, the step to writing her own books seemed a natural progression and the challenge of creating exciting stories was soon highly addictive.

Over the past twenty-five years she has written ninety-five books for Mills & Boon, appearing regularly on the Waldenbooks bestseller lists in the USA and in the Nielsen BookScan Top 100 chart in the UK.

MISCHIEF AND MARRIAGE

Emma
DARCY

A2

Dedicated to my beloved husband, Frank, who
shared all the stories of great love with me

CHAPTER ONE

IT WAS A butler's duty, George Fotheringham assured himself, to remind the master of the house of *his* duty. It was a touchy subject, a highly touchy subject, but after this last near fatal incident, the matter had to be raised.

It wasn't that Master Harry was irresponsible. He had a good heart. If Miss Penelope hadn't succumbed to her tragic illness, everything would have been quite different. Nevertheless, the indisputable fact that Master Harry now took life far too lightly could not be ignored any longer. It was three years since Miss Penelope's sad demise. It was time for this frivolous recklessness to stop.

'May I point out, sir, you could have been killed in the avalanche,' George began with portentous emphasis. 'To risk skiing in uncertain conditions…well, it is improvident, sir. It may not be of any concern to you, sir, but there is the matter of an heir to be considered. I wondered if you might give it some thought.'

Harold Alistair Clifton almost sighed. He remembered his cracked ribs in time and eyed his butler wearily instead. 'Sorry, George. I'm not up to getting married at the moment.'

Not up to anything, he thought, staring broodingly into the huge log fire that kept the chill of winter at bay.

The winter of my discontent. Impossible to remove that chill deep within his soul.

Having been rendered immobile with a broken leg, not to mention the damaged rib cage and some internal bruising, boredom was fast setting in. And depression. It had been a bad choice to convalesce at Springfield Manor. It conjured up too many memories of Pen and their last months together when each day had been so precious. Now…he didn't care if he saw another day.

'I wouldn't presume to tell you what to do, sir. I merely propose that you consider possible outcomes,' George persisted, determined on raising Master Harry's awareness of what would result should he die prematurely.

There was no response.

George frowned. He had to focus Master Harry's attention on the future. It was a matter of position and positioning. The agreement between the Cliffton family and his own was extremely significant to George, and to his mind, Master Harry had a solemn duty to fulfil his part of it.

The connection between their two families dated back to the Battle of Flodden in 1513, when Henry Cliffton had joined the Earl of Surrey in fighting the invading army of James IV of Scotland. In a violent melee with the Scottish pikemen, it was George's brave ancestor, Edward Fotheringham, who had saved the life of Henry Cliffton, fighting off the fierce attackers from where the nobleman lay wounded. It was promised then and there, from that day onwards, Edward Fotheringham and his descendants could always find employment in the service of Henry Cliffton and his descendants.

In today's uncertain world with its shifting values, security was not to be scoffed at. George thought of his two sons, fine boys both of them, doing well at school.

They had their expectations, and rightly so. He cleared his throat and pressed his case.

'We do need an heir so that the family traditions can be maintained. An heir, sir, is not so much an obligation, but a duty,' George stated with the gravity due to such an important issue.

The words must have penetrated. Master Harry looked up, cocking a quizzical eyebrow. 'What precisely are you suggesting, George? I doubt that any of my charming female acquaintances would care to have a child out of wedlock in order to ensure that your heirs and assigns have continuing employment for the next few generations.'

George took a deep breath, apprehensive about giving offence, yet deeply conscious of all that could be lost. For centuries, a distinguished line of butlers from his family had served the Cliffton family at Springfield Manor. For that long line of honourable service, and all its concomitant advantages, to be now looking at an uncertain future was unacceptable.

Besides, Master Harry needed an interest, a serious interest that would involve him in a very real sense of continuity again. Having children and bringing up an heir to take over from him would give him a purpose for living.

George played his master card. 'I have taken the liberty, sir, of investigating the Australian branch of your family.'

Harry looked startled, then threw his head back and laughed. 'How enterprising of you, George! Better a descendant of the Black Sheep than no heir at all.'

'Absolutely!' George fervently agreed, the burden of having taken such an initiative considerably lightened by Master Harry's amused response. 'It would, of course, be a preferable resolution were you to marry, sir, if only a marriage of convenience for the purpose of...'

'My sense of duty doesn't stretch that far,' Harry said dryly. 'Don't keep me in suspense. Tell me the fruits of your investigation. Were there any fruits?'

At least he had sparked some interest, George observed with satisfaction. Hope burgeoned in his heart. Master Harry must surely begin to appreciate what had to be done.

'As I recall the story,' Harry mused, 'our Black Sheep was a shameless rake. It was his scandalous affair with the Duchess of Buckingham that led to his being disinherited and exiled.'

'Quite right, sir.' To George's mind, the unworthiness of this branch of the family had to be glaringly evident. 'He was a cad and a bounder. He kissed and told. A disgrace to the escutcheon, sir.'

The point didn't seem to have the desired effect. Master Harry appeared enthused. 'There must be a veritable host of heirs we could call upon Down Under. A hundred years of going forth and multiplying should have produced...' He grinned. 'How many, George?'

'The 1917 influenza epidemic wiped most of them out, sir. One could say we are as much at the end of the line in Australia as we are in Britain. There is a boy, sir. A nine-year-old schoolboy. Such a young child is hardly a safeguard against the ultimate calamity. It will be many years before he can father a child himself, whereas you...'

'But consider, George!' There was a teasing twinkle in Harry's eyes, brightening their blue to a lively hue. 'He's young enough for you to train him up to your standards. You could mould yourself a splendid master who would be everything you wanted him to be.'

George sighed. He had hoped to stir some pride in

Master Harry's direct blood line by using the Australian boy as a spur. There was no doubt in George's mind that Master Harry could have his pick of any number of suitable young ladies whom he had entertained at Springfield Manor in latter years.

'You are not dead yet, sir,' he stated flatly.

'We know not the hour nor the day, George,' Harry replied flippantly. 'Clearly the most provident course is to fetch the boy over here so he'll become acquainted with his inheritance.'

'It is not quite so straightforward as that, sir,' George demurred, deeply vexed at the turn his attempt at subtle pressure had taken. 'The boy has a widowed mother. His father, who was the last direct heir, drowned some years ago. The woman has her own home, runs a modestly successful business and is certainly attractive enough to have formed another attachment. Should she marry again... Well, it will be very messy getting the boy over here.'

'I'll bet you a bottle of 1860 Madeira that I can fetch them here, George.'

Such levity grated deeply on George's sense of propriety. The wine cellar at Springfield Manor was of particular pride to him. One of the finest, if not *the* finest, private cellars in England. Master Harry had to be joking about giving everything up to what had to be an unworthy strain of the family.

'It really would be much simpler, sir, were you to marry and have a decent number of children to ensure a succession of the family.'

Harry grinned. 'Did you get photographs of the boy and his mother, George?'

'There is no family likeness, sir. None at all.'

'The photographs, George.' Harry's curiosity was piqued. 'I want to see them.'

George had a very nasty premonition. He recognised the light of mischief in Master Harry's eyes. He had been witness to it on many an occasion. What followed was invariably mayhem of one kind or another. He had been a venturesome boy and he had become even more dangerously venturesome once the benevolent influence of Miss Penelope's lovely nature had passed away with her.

It had been a mistake to confess to the Australian investigation. It had been a mistake to present Master Harry with any kind of challenge. George knew it was all his own fault when his premonition proved right several hours later.

'Make inquiries about flights to Australia, will you, George? It's summer over there, isn't it? I rather fancy a bit of summer. As soon as I can get this cast off my leg I'll be on my way.'

Master Harry's earlier gloom had completely dissipated. He was in fine fettle. 'Might get in a few days' cricket, as well. Make a note of the dates for the test matches between England and Australia, please, George. If there's one in Sydney, I could take young William with me to watch the game. A nine-year-old should take a lively interest in cricket.' He grinned at George. 'Fine name, William.'

Mischief! That was what he was up to. Mischief instead of marriage. And where would it all end if Master Harry's meddling caused mayhem?

CHAPTER TWO

ASHLEY HARCOURT DIDN'T know that today was to mark the beginning of a completely different phase in her life. Her desk calendar looked the same as usual. It bore no big red letters to give warning of something momentous about to happen. There was no sense of premonition hovering in her mind.

She *was* faced with a particularly nasty piece of work in the person of Gordon Payne, who was sitting in her home office, filling the chair on the other side of her desk and voicing a string of complaints. But she was ready to deal with that. More than ready.

Giving satisfaction was a high professional priority to Ashley. She prided herself on running her employment agency effectively, fitting the right people into the right jobs. But there was a limit, a very definite limit, to how much satisfaction any one person could demand from another.

Ashley had precisely formed opinions on this point. She was twenty-nine years old, had worked hard to build up her own business after being widowed and had dealt with a great many people in a wide variety of situations. Satisfaction in any relationship was a two-way street, a compatible, complementary give-and-take situation.

As she listened to Gordon Payne revealing himself

in his true colours, she silently berated herself for a bad mistake in judgement. The affable manner that had fooled her into misplacing a top quality client with him smacked of the same polished charm that had fooled her into a miserable marriage ten years ago. She should have recognised it, been suspicious of it. Warning signals should have crawled down her spine.

'When I dictate a letter, I expect my secretary to type it word for word, each word spelled correctly,' Gordon Payne ranted on. 'I do not want her assuming she knows the English language better than me. If there is corrections to be made, *I* make them.'

Ashley held her tongue, mentally noting the two grammatical errors in that little speech. Here was another king-size ego who knew everything and could do no wrong! Ashley had been married to one for long enough to have experienced the God complex at close quarters. She had learnt there was no reasoning with it, no appeal that would pierce it, no way to get around it.

In her youthful naivety, Ashley had fallen blindly in love with Roger Harcourt. He had been handsome, always well-dressed, sophisticated in his tastes and strongly athletic, excelling in all competitive sports. Self-assurance had oozed from him, and during their early days together, Ashley had thought him utterly perfect.

Having drifted between divorced and disinterested parents for most of her teens, she had loved the way Roger took charge of everything and told her what was best for her to do. Ashley had interpreted that as proof of his caring for her. She'd had no perception of how tyrannical it could become.

She had thought she was getting love and strength and support and direction in her life when she had married Roger Harcourt.

She had certainly got direction.

She had had such a surfeit of direction from Roger, she doubted she would ever stomach the idea of marriage again. However difficult she sometimes found running her own life and being a single parent, it was still preferable to having her subordination taken as someone else's right.

Gordon Payne was now behaving as though she was subordinate to him, too. 'Run proper tests on these women in future. Don't believe their résumés,' he commanded. 'It's nothing but pretentious twaddle.'

As head of a home construction company—Painless Homes with Gordon Payne—and a member of the local shire council, he was a man of considerable standing in the community. Ashley had thought him a valuable business client, someone who would direct others to her agency if her service satisfied him. After hearing the dismissed secretary's story earlier this afternoon, she had decided then and there to cut him from her files, regardless of cost or consequences.

She was still inwardly fuming over the treatment that this pompous pain of a man had dished out to a young woman whom any sensible employer would cherish. Cheryn Kimball was too good for him. That was the problem.

Cheryn was not only highly qualified in all the areas Gordon Payne had demanded, she presented herself with style and polish and had a natural charm of manner that would endear her to most people. She had been traumatised, reduced to floods of tears by the unjust haranguing and arbitrary dismissal over doing what she believed to be her job.

'And I don't want a woman who talks back at me!' the monster ego raged.

That hit a particularly raw point with Ashley. Roger had felt he had the right to silence her by icily declaring, 'I am the head of this house!' What was she supposed to have been? The tail? The feet running after him all the time? She had discovered, too late, there were only one-way streets with Roger.

Ashley barely stopped herself from glowering at Gordon Payne. What he wanted was a mechanical robot programmed to toadying submission. Yes, master. At your service, master. Whatever you say, master.

The warm indulgence he had displayed towards his previous long-time secretary was explained in Cheryn's report. The woman had been mollycoddling him for the past twenty years. Even though she had retired, she had 'dropped in' at the office each day this week to 'break Cheryn in to the way dear Gordon likes things done,' and deliberately, jealously undermined Cheryn's confidence in her position and abilities.

Just like Roger's mother.

Ashley shuddered.

Roger's mother had considered herself a cut above everyone else since she was supposedly connected to some great line of landed gentry in Britain. Such pretensions had obviously contributed to Roger's sense of superiority. Her condescending manner had been a constant burr under Ashley's skin.

She hadn't wished Roger and his mother dead. She had made up her mind to divorce both of them. The fight for freedom had just begun when fate intervened and released her from the trauma of battling a custody case over William.

Of course, any reasonable person wouldn't have tried to drive across a bridge that was partly submerged by torrential floodwaters. Roger hadn't liked being beaten by anything. He and his mother had been swept away by a force bigger than both of them. They had probably drowned with a sense of outrage that such a thing could have happened.

Now here was this odious man reminding her of all she had put behind her. She wished she could wave a magic wand and give him a taste of servitude under someone like himself. Unfortunately her power of reprisal was strictly limited to a figurative kick out the door.

'I won't be paying your commission until you find me a suitable secretary,' was the predictable ultimatum. 'And I want someone in the office at nine o'clock tomorrow morning to get on with the work. A temporary will have to do until you come up with the right person.'

'I'm sorry you've been disappointed, Mr. Payne,' Ashley said coolly, 'but may I remind you that our contract was for me to supply you with three interviewees with the qualifications you listed. I did so. You chose Miss Kimball. You owe me five hundred dollars, and I expect to be paid.'

'You guaranteed satisfaction,' he answered angrily.

'You specified initiative as one of the qualities you required, Mr. Payne. Miss Kimball believed she was saving you the embarrassment of sending out grammatically incorrect letters. Many employers would value such care, knowledge and attention applied to their correspondence.'

That stung him. 'I tell you she got it wrong!' Gordon Payne's face developed angry red patches. 'When I specified initiative I meant for her to supply me with what I needed, when I needed it, without having to ask all the time. She failed that, too!'

'There is a difference between initiative and mind-reading, Mr. Payne. I do have a reader of tarot cards and a magician in my files, but I don't have any clairvoyants or mind-readers. Not amongst those seeking either permanent or temporary employment. I suggest you try some other agency.'

The red patches deepened to burning blotches. He stood up, using his size to intimidate. He was a bullish figure of a man, short-necked, broad-shouldered, barrel-chested. His rather fleshy features were framed by crinkly brown hair, giving him a deceptively boyish look for a man in his forties. There was a mean glitter in his dark eyes.

'Don't get smart with me, Mrs. Harcourt,' he snarled. 'I hold a position of influence in this town. I could do you a lot of good.'

The threat that he could also do her a lot of damage was left hanging, unspoken but clearly implied.

Ashley was on the petite side, below average height, delicately boned, slim-framed. She achieved what she hoped was a mature and dignified stature by wearing smartly tailored business suits and pinning her long blond hair into a French pleat, but her appearance was essentially dainty and feminine.

Gordon Payne undoubtedly thought he could make mincemeat out of her and eat her for breakfast. What he didn't know was she was one hundred per cent steel-proofed against being bullied into anything she didn't want to do. If he'd looked more closely he might have seen some sign of that in the flintlike directness of her wide grey eyes.

She remained seated. This was her office, her home, her castle, and no-one was going to shift her from the position she had established for herself. 'I appreciate the offer, Mr. Payne,' she said calmly. 'I regret I can't return the favour. I've already done my best for you.'

He pressed the knuckles of one hand on her desk and

leaned forward, his chin stuck out pugnaciously. 'You
don't know what side your bread is buttered on, Mrs.
Harcourt. You have wasted a great deal of my time, with
no satisfactory result, and I expect you to make up for it.'

'How do you suggest I do that, Mr. Payne?'

'By supplying me with temporaries until you come
up with a permanent who's satisfactory to my needs.'

'That was not part of our agreement,' she stated decisively. 'I have advised you that I cannot satisfy your new
requirements and suggested you try another agency. Our
business together is concluded, Mr. Payne.'

He glared at her as though he couldn't believe his ears.

Ashley pushed her chair back and rose smoothly to
her feet. 'I'll see you out.'

'Like hell you will! I haven't finished with you yet.'

He stood his ground belligerently. Ashley had the dis-
tinct feeling he would block her path to the door if she
skirted the desk and made a beeline for it. A physical
confrontation would make him feel superior again. She
stood completely still, hoping to defuse the aggression
emanating from him.

'What more do you wish to say, Mr. Payne?' she enquired blandly.

'I can do you a lot of harm, Mrs. Harcourt,' he
drawled, relishing the prospect of dealing in fear.

'Harm is a two-edged sword.'

'What can you do to me?' he jeered.

The smugness of the man goaded Ashley into a fighting reply. 'I have contacts, too, Mr. Payne. I could make
sure that no-one will ever want to work for you personally again.'

He gave a derisive laugh. 'Money will take care of
that.'

He was probably right. The power of money to corrupt even the highest principles was well proven. Ashley hated Gordon Payne's knowing use of it. The urge to knock him off his cocky perch gathered a compelling force as she remembered all the mean power games Roger had played on her.

Withholding money. Withholding use of the car. Demanding an account for everything she did while he didn't have to account for anything. Let Gordon Payne account for his behaviour, she thought blisteringly, losing all sense of discretion as she went on the attack.

'Money won't restore your reputation,' she asserted cuttingly. 'When Miss Kimball's story shows you up as a fool who doesn't know the English language—'

'I was right!'

The ugly humour was replaced by ugly fury. Ashley didn't care. She remorselessly drove the point home.

'No, Mr. Payne. You could not have been more wrong. You made a clown of yourself by defending the indefensible.'

Naked hatred glittered at her. 'Think yourself a ball-tearer, do you? One of those offensive, insulting females who are so envious of men, they'll do anything to pull them down.'

Ashley's chin lifted in lofty disdain of his opinion. 'You're certainly one of the men who justify the whole feminist movement.'

He sneered. 'I take it you're not a merry widow.' His gaze dropped to her breasts, her waist, her hips, his mouth curling salaciously. 'What you need is a man to get rid of your screwed-up frustrations.'

'A typically sexist statement to gloss over your own inadequacies, Mr. Payne.'

That thinned his fleshy lips and snapped his gaze back to hers. 'Well, we'll see who turns out to be inadequate,

Mrs. Harcourt.' He picked up her favourite Lladro figurine from the desk. 'You have a fondness for clowns?'

She held her tongue, momentarily shocked by the malevolent gloating in his eyes. The wonderful clown he held in his hand was a masterpiece of expression, reflecting the sad ironies of life. Because she had stood up to Gordon Payne, it was about to be destroyed. She could see it coming, could do nothing to stop it and knew her adversary relished her helplessness. The realisation that she had been headstrong and foolish in challenging him came too late.

'I'll enjoy putting you at the centre of a circus, Mrs. Harcourt. I could start by having this home block of yours rezoned as wetlands. Then, of course, there's the licence for this agency. Needs investigation for legitimate practice. A visit from an industrial relations officer. A tax audit...' He lifted her figurine clown to shoulder height, ready to smash it down. 'This is what's going to happen to you....'

Ashley hadn't meant to cry out. She had resolved to suffer the inevitable in silent, contemptuous dignity. Yet an inarticulate croak of protest burst from her throat at the sheer, wanton destructiveness about to be enacted.

'You called, madam?' a very English voice enquired.

CHAPTER THREE

ASHLEY'S GAZE WAS instantly drawn to the office door, which had been thrust open. Gordon Payne turned to look, too, the hand holding the Lladro clown lowering instinctively with the sudden appearance of a witness. They both stared in stunned silence at the totally unexpected vision of the man in the doorway.

He was not your ordinary, everyday person.

Ashley had never applied the word *elegant* to a man before, yet it leapt straight into her mind. Elegant, smashingly handsome and subtly dangerous.

He was tall and lean, beautifully dressed in a three-piece suit that had obviously been tailored for him, the smooth sheen of the blue-grey fabric shouting no expense spared. His white silk shirt had a buttoned down collar, and he wore a gorgeous tie in brilliant shades of blue.

His face was no less impressive, a squarish jawline, high cheekbones, straight nose, a perfectly moulded mouth, rakishly arched black eyebrows over the most dynamic blue eyes Ashley had ever seen. His black hair was thick and mostly straight. It was parted on the left side and swept across his high, wide forehead in a dipping wave.

In his right hand he carried a silver-knobbed black walking stick that tapered to a silver tip. He was not using it for support. He held it well below the knob, and his fingers had the long, agile look that suggested he could twiddle the cane much as Fred Astaire had in dancing routines. Or wield it very quickly as a lethal weapon.

He looked to be in his early thirties, but there was a world of knowledge in the eyes that scanned the scene he had thrust himself into with such timely éclat. He gave Ashley a quirky little smile, as though personally inviting her to relax and enjoy the moment. It was oddly intimate, forging an instant connection between them that embraced both understanding and acceptance that he was here for her.

It dazed Ashley. She had never experienced such a mental touch before. Not from a man. He didn't even know her. They had never met before. She was absolutely certain of that. Yet there was this strange feeling of recognition that he had always been meant to enter her life and play some vital part in it.

'Would you like me to see the gentleman out, madam?' he prompted with all the aplomb of a traditional British butler.

Ashley found her voice. 'Please,' she said gratefully, not caring from whence he had come, deeply relieved that he was offering to rid her of the menacing presence of an enemy she had recklessly made in unbridled and incautious anger.

'Who the devil are you?' Gordon Payne challenged sharply as her rescuer stepped into the room to carry out her request.

'Cliffton, sir,' came the lilting, blithe reply. He actually did twiddle the walking cane. In the flash of an eye it was suddenly resting in both his hands. 'The fortunes of the Harcourt family have been linked to the fortunes of my family for centuries.'

Centuries! Ashley's mind boggled at the claim. Apart from which, she wasn't a Harcourt. She had only married one, and not one that was a high recommendation of the name, either. Nevertheless, she was not about to spoil her white knight's pitch.

'It is both an honour and a pleasure to be of service once again,' he continued, smiling affably at Gordon Payne, who seemed mesmerised by Cliffton's approach. The way he was weaving the cane through his fingers with the dexterity of a magician was definitely having a hypnotic effect.

'May I, sir?' The cane was whipped under one arm like a shillelagh and both hands were out to relieve Gordon Payne of the Lladro clown. 'This piece is more for viewing than touching,' he advised with the air of an art connoisseur. 'If I put it back on its stand, I'm sure you'll appreciate its fine craftmanship better. There's a line and proportion to these things…there! You see?'

Somehow he'd deftly removed the figurine from Gordon Payne's grasp and set it on the desk, positioning it perfectly on its rectangular block and giving the clown's hat an affectionate pat as though it was an old friend.

'Now, sir, if you wouldn't mind, sir.' The cane was flicked into use again, pointing to the door. 'It is time to take your leave of Mrs. Harcourt. I'll see you on your way, sir.'

Ashley could almost feel Gordon Payne bristle as he recollected himself. Cliffton had snatched control from him, and he didn't like it. Not one bit. Yet some animal instinct must have warned him to avoid a trial of strength with the English stranger. He shot a last venomous glare at Ashley.

'You haven't heard the last of this.'

Then he swung on his heel and marched out, not waiting to be ushered or escorted to the front door of the house. Cliffton, however, dogged his steps, ensuring that he left without playing any malicious havoc with her possessions on his way. Ashley trailed after both of them, drawn to watch the end of a scene she now deeply regretted.

Making an enemy of Gordon Payne could rebound very badly on her. He had far more weapons than she did. It was self-defeating to start a fight she couldn't win. Hadn't Roger taught her that, over and over again? If the elegant Englishman had not arrived... Who was he, really? What was he? And why was he here?

She paused in the hallway just outside the office, noticing that he favoured his right leg, a slight limp, reason for the walking stick, yet he executed a smart, skipping sidestep that would have graced any dance floor, beating Gordon Payne to the front door with a deft panache that allowed him to open the door with a flourish.

'Good afternoon, sir,' he said with a respectful nod.

Gordon Payne stopped, stiffened and stared at him, flummoxed at being comprehensively outmanoeuvred. All he could manage was a crude snort in reply. Then he shook his shoulders as though dislodging a monkey on his back, propelled his feet forward again and made his exit from Ashley's house.

Harold Alistair Cliffton closed the door after him on a glorious high of triumphant satisfaction. He had outbutlered George, rescued the fair maiden and polished off the dragon. Maybe he had just found his true vocation in life. Being of service.

On the other hand, Harry suspected his exhilaration had much to do with being of service to Ashley Harcourt. He turned to face her again, aware that she had followed to watch the curtain line of his masterly performance.

The photographs had not done her justice. They hadn't captured the essence of Ashley Harcourt at all. Harry couldn't quite put words to that essence, but it was something that sparked an instant response in him, an excitement, a sense of meeting someone special.

The moment their eyes had met...zing! Like an electric charge. He had felt truly alive again. Grey eyes, completely unlike Pen's soft brown, yet there was something in them that called to him, just as Pen's had. Perhaps a sureness of who and what she was, a belief in herself.

He wanted to know more about her. He wanted to know everything about her. The idea came to him in an inspired flash. Why not keep on playing the butler? It wasn't at all difficult. In fact, he was enjoying the role immensely. It also had a great many advantages.

A butler was in the happy position of always being on hand. Installed under the same roof as Ashley Harcourt, he could get to know her very well, indeed. Harry rather relished the idea of putting Ashley to bed at night and waking her up in the morning with steaming hot...coffee. Like George, he'd be Father Confessor, confidant, adviser, helpmate, on the spot to test the waters for other possible attachments.

It allowed him to thoroughly investigate the situation for getting George an heir for Springfield Manor. This could become an extraordinary exploit that would add to the legends already surrounding his illustrious family—how Harry brought the Black Sheep strain back into the fold!

Alternatively, it might eventuate that young William need not fill the position of heir at all. His mother was beginning to inspire a lively set of other possibilities. He wondered how long her silky blonde hair was when unpinned and flowing free. On a pillow.

Ashley remained rooted near the door into the office, studying the extraordinary man who had erupted into her life with sensational effect. Not only with Gordon Payne. She was acutely conscious of a sense of tingly anticipation, as though she knew intuitively that his startling actions were only the forerunner of more startling actions.

He aimed another quirky smile at her, his bright blue eyes twinkling with unholy mischief. He gestured to the door and commented, 'I thought him a mite touchy.'

Ashley couldn't help being amused. To describe Gordon Payne as *touchy* seemed a masterful understatement. 'I shouldn't have lost my temper,' she said with a rueful grimace.

Cliffton looked sympathetic. 'Touchy people are often aggressive and unpredictable.'

'It was stupid of me.'

One eyebrow lifted in considering assessment. 'Perhaps a tad impetuous, madam. Still, there is an arguable case for throwing caution to the winds and letting fly. Gets a load off the chest, so to speak.'

Ashley could barely stop her mouth from twitching. He was so attractive, so...debonair. Another word she had never applied to a man! Not in real life. Her mind drifted to the Scarlet Pimpernel and she hastily pulled it back to a somewhat frayed level of common sense. Don't forget *dangerous,* she cautioned herself.

'What would you have done if he hadn't let you take the Lladro clown?' she asked.

'Broken his wrist most likely,' came the imperturbable reply. 'Brings to mind the incident with Good Queen Bess,' he mused. 'My ancestor, Hugo, broke the wrist of the Spanish ambassador who presented a gift to the queen, then tried to take it back when she dismissed his king's request.'

Ashley's mind slipped again. Spanning centuries seemed quite normal with Cliffton. 'If you'd done that,' she said, trying to latch onto something practical, 'the figurine would have fallen and broken.'

He grinned. 'Never missed a catch at first slip. I used to play in the first eleven cricket team at school.'

Ashley had no trouble imagining Cliffton being first at a lot of things. But he didn't seem conceited about it. Nor did he emit an air of superiority. Not like Roger. Whatever his abilities, he simply accepted them as completely natural.

Which brought her back to the questions that needed answering. She couldn't let this discussion run on as though they were old and intimate friends. Common sense insisted she had to establish who this man was and what he was doing here.

'I could be a mite touchy, too,' she warned. 'About having a stranger invade my home and eavesdrop on a private conversation.'

'No, no, madam. I would not be so ill-mannered as to enter anyone's home uninvited. Master William let me in.'

'Master William?' She wondered how her nine-year-old son had reacted to being addressed in such a fashion!

'He was playing cricket next door. Has the makings of a fine batsman,' Cliffton remarked admiringly. 'He played a superb hook shot, which I happened to catch before it hit the windscreen of the Daimler that was parked at the kerb outside your house.'

'Oh, Lord!' Ashley breathed, relieved that Gordon Payne didn't have damage to his car to add to his list of grudges against her.

'I explained to Master William that I was on a mission from England and needed to call on you. He told me to wait in the lounge until you were ready to receive me. I was about to enter that room, as instructed by Master William, when a highly unpleasant voice penetrated to the hallway, listing a most unseemly set of threats.'

He put on a mournful face. 'I do apologise for eavesdropping, madam. Most reprehensible of me. It reminded me of a situation that confronted my ancestor, Stafford, with the sheriff of Nottingham over a man called Hood. But right won out in the end, madam. We Clifftons have a way of making things turn out right in the end.'

Ashley was still trying to swallow that story as he went on.

'I must also confess to falling into a trance of admiration at the spirited way you took the gentleman to task. Not a nice gentleman at all, I must say. Then when you cried out…' He shrugged appealingly. 'I thought I could be of service to you.'

'Yes. You were. Thank you.' His voice was wonderfully musical, quite enthralling to listen to. 'What mission?' Ashley asked belatedly. 'Who are you?'

'Butler to the English branch of the Harcourt family.'

He really *was* a butler!

'A hereditary position, madam. I come as an emissary from the last of your Harcourt relatives in Britain.'

Ashley stiffened, snapping herself out of her bemused daze. Roger's mother must have been telling the truth about being connected to a line of landed gentry in England. Although that still did not give her the right to have adopted the attitude of being better than anyone else.

It was an attitude that won no sympathy whatsoever from Ashley. She herself might bear the Harcourt name, keeping it because it was her son's birthright, but it held no sway with her. The reverse, in fact.

'In the current circumstances, your son, William, is

the master of Springfield Manor's only heir, madam, and he would like you both to take up residence at the manor, his country home. I am assigned to help you settle your affairs and expedite your journey to England.'

Typically high-handed, Ashley thought, her backbone getting stiffer by the second. No Harcourt was going to tell her what to do with her life. She had had her fill of that, thank you very much.

Cliffton gave her a smile of such charm the stiffening almost came undone. 'For however long it takes to accomplish that, madam, I am to stay here as your butler,' he declared winningly, 'to serve you and Master William as you will.'

CHAPTER FOUR

FOR AS LONG as it takes...

What monstrous arrogance!

Ashley saw red for several seconds before the brilliant blue eyes of the butler drove the red away. Not Cliffton's arrogance, of course. He was merely carrying out his master's instructions. Although why a man like Cliffton could be content to serve a Harcourt... Imbued with the English class system and centuries of tradition, she supposed, excusing him on the grounds of having been brainwashed from birth.

One thing was certain. She was not going to be carted off to England and suffer the condescension of the gentry installed in Springfield Manor. If William was an heir, he could wait until his inheritance was free and clear of every other Harcourt before considering what it involved and what was best done about it.

In the meantime, Ashley had to decide what to do about Cliffton. Outright rejection of his mission probably meant he would have to return to England to report failure, and she wouldn't see him again unless she followed. That scenario had no appeal whatsoever.

Ashley had never felt so drawn to know more about a person. Cliffton was, without a doubt, the most fascinating man she had ever met, and she didn't want him to drop out of her life before she had the chance to…well, explore possibilities.

He was special. Far too special to be a butler. Maybe a short sojourn in Australia might show him other ways of life that could be far more rewarding than being a butler, yet she could probably only keep him with her if she appeared to be considering the proposition, perhaps needing some persuasion from him to make up her mind.

For as long as it takes…

That suddenly became a highly seductive little phrase.

Taking her years with Roger and his mother into account, Ashley had no problem in reasoning that the Harcourt family did owe her some recompense, and Cliffton clearly didn't mind being her butler for a while. He would be very handy to have around if Gordon Payne decided to carry through on his threats. That could be classed as helping to settle her affairs.

In fact, she could find lots of business that would need settling before she could even consider uprooting their lives and going to England with William. What about William's schooling and leaving all his friends behind? There were many difficulties and obstacles to overcome, and in all good faith, serious matters that would prove quite impossible to resolve in the end. Cliffton would eventually come to see that, and no blame would attach to him for failing to accomplish what was expected of him.

It was only fair to give his mission a chance at succeeding.

Even if it was mission impossible.

Ashley had to smother a huge upsurge of elation at this highly satisfactory conclusion. She lifted a hand to her temple, rubbing at it in a distracted fashion, covering any telltale expression in her eyes as she said somewhat faintly, 'This is all a bit of a shock.'

'Forgive me, madam.' Cliffton was at her side in a flash, gently steering her into the lounge. 'Thoughtless of me to regale you with all this when you've had no time to recover from that nasty encounter. Such incidents do sap one's energy.'

There was absolutely nothing wrong with Ashley's energy. Cliffton's light grasp on her elbow gave it a remarkable boost. She caught a whiff of some tantalising aftershave lotion and wished she was wearing perfume and a more alluring outfit than a business suit. One of the wonderful chiffon gowns that Ginger Rogers used to wear floated into her mind.

At Cliffton's direction she sank into an armchair. He whizzed a footstool under her feet, plumped up a cushion and slid it behind her back for extra comfort, pulled out one of her set of three occasional tables and placed it within easy hand's reach, then straightened up and smiled benevolently at her.

'A cup of tea is always soothing, madam. Or perhaps, since it's after five o'clock, a glass of sherry? Sherry is more fortifying. On the other hand, a gin and tonic can have an elevating effect. I am at your service, madam. If you'll tell me what you'd like...'

Ashley had a mad urge to ask for slippers and a pipe! She sternly reminded herself this was not a game to Cliffton. He was doing what he was trained to do, and her best course, at the moment, was to accept his offer graciously. 'A cup of tea would be lovely. Thank you,' she said with a grateful smile.

He left her before Ashley thought to give directions to the kitchen and where to find everything. Further consideration assured her that Cliffton would have no difficulty finding his way around. This was hardly a butler-size house. The kitchen was at the end of the hallway and was of a fairly standard design. Making a cup of tea did not present a problem.

Finding living quarters for Cliffton did.

Although there were three bedrooms, the third was used for storing William's sporting equipment and housing whatever hobbies had captured his interest. Model aeroplanes and ships took up most of the shelf space, and a work table was currently covered in miniature soldiers, which he was painting in preparation for a replay of the Napoleonic Wars.

A divan bed, shoved against one of the walls, and no cupboard space at all, did not constitute a suitable room for a guest who would be staying longer than overnight. The spare twin bed in William's room didn't present attractive accommodation, either. Which left her room, and it was utterly ridiculous for her to move out and offer the master bedroom to the butler.

It suddenly struck her that she should have asked Cliffton for some credentials instead of accepting his story at face value. The man was a stranger, for heaven's sake! His sheer panache had bamboozled her into being totally unbusinesslike. She had better correct that as soon as he reappeared. Or maybe she should be checking on him right now instead of letting him have the run of the house. What if…

The front door banged open and William came pelting inside, pulling himself to a halt as he caught sight of Ashley through the doorway into the lounge. He looked flushed and excited.

'Hey, Mum! Where's…' He stopped as he took in the cushion at her back and her feet on the footstool. 'Have you twisted your ankle or something?'

'I'm just relaxing,' she said, feeling a flush sweeping

up her neck as though she'd been caught in a compro-
mising position.

'Oh! Okay!' William dismissed the incomprehensible
in favour of imparting the exciting news that had brought
him in. 'You should see the great car Mr. Cliffton came
in. It's a smashing Rolls Royce. The chauffeur said it's a
1987 Silver Spirit. How about that?'

Ashley's mind boggled again. The wayward thought
came to her that it would have put Gordon Payne's nose
further out of joint at seeing a Rolls Royce outshining
his Daimler. Not to mention a chauffeur!

Fortunately William didn't require a reply. Cliffton arrived on the scene bearing the silver tray and tea service
that Roger's mother had given to them as a wedding gift.

'What are you doing with that?' William asked bluntly,
as astonished as Ashley was. Cliffton must have dug it
out of the bottom of the dresser where it had resided untouched, apart from cleaning, for many years.

'Your mother is feeling poorly. I am serving her tea,'
Cliffton replied with unruffled decorum.

William looked wide-eyed at Ashley. 'Are you sick?'

Her cheeks blossomed with hot colour. 'I'm recover-
ing fast,' she answered.

'You don't need me then?' William asked.

'No. I'll be fine in a minute.'

'Right!' William looked relieved and turned quickly
to the butler. 'You'll be staying for a bit, Mr. Cliffton?'

'Yes. I'll be staying as long as—'

'Great!' William cut him off and offered his most appealing face. 'Would you mind if my friends had a turn
at sitting in your car? They wouldn't hurt anything. The
chauffeur could let them in and out. I promise they'll
be good.'

Cliffton set the tray down on the occasional table and

eyed William consideringly. 'How much do you intend to charge?'

William grinned at the quick understanding. 'Only ten cents each. Ten dollars with a photo. Can I borrow your Polaroid camera, Mum?'

'Ten dollars!' Ashley gasped in shock.

'Think, Mum,' her son advocated earnestly. 'This will be a once-in-a-lifetime photograph, a memory they'll be able to pull out of a photo album in years to come to show they really did drive a Rolls Royce. A photo of that value can't go cheaply.'

William always seemed to have a line of inarguable logic for what he wanted to do. 'You said sit in it!' Ashley sharply reminded him.

'If they sit behind the driving wheel it'll look as though they're driving it. I won't actually let them,' he assured Cliffton.

'I am very impressed with the sales pitch,' Cliffton said admiringly.

'So you see, Mum?' William pressed. 'I have to have the camera.'

'William, you haven't received permission about the car, and I don't think…'

'Permission granted,' Cliffton chimed in, his blue eyes twinkling approval.

'The camera, Mum?'

Two against one defeated her. 'Yes.' She sighed, her need to settle various matters with Cliffton more urgent and important than arguing with William over his schemes for augmenting his pocket money.

'Thanks, Mum. Thanks a lot, Mr. Cliffton. I think I'm going to like you.'

He was off like a flash to fleece his friends' pockets.

'Weak or strong, madam?'

Cliffton had the silver teapot poised, ready to pour.

'However it comes,' Ashley answered distractedly. 'You came here in a chauffeured Rolls Royce?'

'It is the customary mode of transport at Springfield Manor, madam. The master wants you to know you'll be given every comfort. Milk, madam?'

'Yes. But surely you didn't bring a Rolls Royce with you from England. Did you?' she added, struck with the feeling that anything was possible with this man.

'I acquired it when I arrived in Sydney, madam. Sugar?'

'No, thank you. I don't think…' Ashley floundered, appalled at the cost of a mission that would certainly— well, almost certainly—be futile. 'You really shouldn't be spending so much on a campaign that might come to nothing,' she burst out. 'A Rolls Royce, for heaven's sake! This seems to be getting quite out of hand.'

'How else can you be shown what to expect, madam?' Cliffton enquired reasonably. 'You haven't tried it yet,' he pointed out. 'I think you'll get to like it. It's quite pleasant and tends to get addictive.'

She was not going to be seduced by a Rolls Royce into becoming a dependant at Springfield Manor. 'I do not need a Rolls Royce,' she stated emphatically. 'And what's more, Cliffton, this smacks of trying to buy my acquiescence to what you want.'

'It is always interesting to test resistance to its limits, madam,' he said with an air of taking up an irresistible challenge.

'Why on earth should you do such a thing?' she demanded. Surely he was taking this mission too far.

'It's in the spirit of my more adventurous forebears who would never take no for an answer.'

Irrepressible, Ashley thought, beginning to appreciate Gordon Payne's perspicacity in retreating from Cliffton rather than taking him on. What could one do in the face of such an unsquashable spirit? And really, did she want to say no to Cliffton? It was only the ultimate no to the Harcourt family that she would have to impress upon him.

'Well, I won't be held responsible for what you spend,' Ashley stated unequivocally.

'The responsibility is entirely mine,' Cliffton agreed. 'Your tea, madam.'

'Oh! Thank you.' In a Royal Crown Derby fine bone china teacup, no less, inherited from her mother-in-law. How much fossicking had Cliffton done in her kitchen? Ashley's whirling mind spun to other concerns, like the possible undermining of her authority with William. 'I don't think you should have let William use the car as a…as a—'

'Money-making venture?' Cliffton supplied.

'Yes.'

'If I may say so, madam, one should never stifle enterprise. In my youth I used to organise frog races. With his entrepreneurial talents, Master William will undoubtedly—'

'Stop!'

'I beg your pardon, madam?'

'You can't call him master. I won't have it.' The last thing she wanted was for William to start thinking he was of a superior breed to anyone else. 'There are no masters in Australia. There are only people, Cliffton,' she added earnestly. 'You must understand that or you won't do any good here.'

'Thank you for your advice, madam,' he said gravely.

'Is there anything else I should know so as not to give offence?'

'I'm not a madam. Madams are people who run brothels.'

'Oh!' The quirky little smile twitched at the corners of his mouth. 'Then that's clearly inappropriate. I shall call you milady.'

'I'm not your lady.' Ashley managed not to say, 'Yet.'

'Mrs. Harcourt?'

She didn't want to be reminded of her marriage to Roger, either, but perhaps it wasn't appropriate to ask Cliffton to call her Ashley at this point. It could wait until she knew him better. She nodded her assent to the name and sipped her tea, trying desperately to collect her thoughts into a properly ordered pattern.

Events seemed to be tumbling over themselves, not giving her time to sort through what needed to be done. And it didn't help to have Cliffton hovering over her enquiringly. Not only were the beautiful blue depths of his eyes enough for her wits to drown in, she seemed to be getting a fixation on the tantalising little tilts and curves of his mouth. She hadn't thought about being kissed by a man for quite a while. The provocative question arose.... Did butlers help put their mistresses to bed?

Ashley was shocked at herself, but a perverse little voice whispered that it had been over six years and she was as normal as the next woman in wanting an exciting relationship with a man, so it was perfectly all right to fantasise what it might be like. Especially with a man of Cliffton's unusual and extraordinary qualities. In fact, she wouldn't be normal if she didn't.

It took an enormous effort of will to drag her mind back to practical matters. 'I think you should show me some credentials, Cliffton,' she said soberly. 'After all, it's asking a lot for me to accept what you're saying off the cuff, so to speak.'

'Quite right! I have the investigative report tracing the family line to young William in my luggage. I shall ask the chauffeur to fetch it in as soon as the photograph session is over. In the meantime, will my passport suffice as a means of identification?'

He removed it from an inner pocket in his suit coat and offered it to her. Ashley put down her teacup, intent on examining whatever solid information she could get about him. It was certainly a British passport, and the photograph unmistakably identified him as Harold Alistair Cliffton. A *very* English name, Ashley thought.

'Harold,' she mused out loud, thinking it didn't really fit him.

'Nobody ever calls me by that name, Mrs. Harcourt,' came the decisive correction. 'Harold is merely a remnant from the Battle of Hastings.'

Yes, it did belong in the realms of history, Ashley privately agreed. She supposed using the surname Cliffton was traditional for a butler, and she shouldn't mess with that formality. Not yet, anyway. However, her curiosity was piqued.

'What about when you were a boy?' she probed.

'I was always Harry.'

Harry. That was better. More lively. She could imagine a Harry organising frog races. A Harry could definitely be as debonair as Fred Astaire.

His date of birth gave her his age. Thirty-three. She suddenly had an awful thought. 'Are you married, Cliffton?'

'No. Unhappily, the woman to whom I was deeply attached died some years ago,' he said sadly. 'As I have no current ties, it was no hardship for me to come away on this mission.'

Free and clear. Ashley was intensely relieved to hear it. Although it did sound as though he had once been very much in love. But that was years ago. And it did demonstrate he was capable of loving someone other than himself, which was all to the good.

'This gives your birthplace as Springfield Manor,' she observed inquiringly.

'As I explained, I hold a hereditary position. Generations of my family have been born at Springfield Manor.'

That wasn't so good. It meant Cliffton had deep roots there. Maybe she shouldn't start something that had little hope of a happy ending. However tempting it was to prolong an involvement with him, it wasn't exactly honest to let him think she was prepared to fall in with the plans made for her and accompany him to Springfield Manor.

Her usual sense of integrity reared its head. She handed him his passport and mustered up the strength to meet his gaze with steady eyes. 'You have rather sprung this on me, Cliffton. I'm sure you think that William and I will be better off living at Springfield Manor, but I've got to tell you that giving up a life of independence goes very much against my grain. It also goes against my grain that I'm being placed in a position of obligation without my consent. I don't like being beholden to anyone for anything.'

To Ashley's surprise, Cliffton looked pleased at this declaration. His eyes positively danced approval. 'I quite understand, Mrs. Harcourt. There is nothing worse than a burden of obligation or the sense of not having a free choice. Believe me, it is the last thing I would put upon you. I merely offer. You decide what you want.'

Put like that, Ashley could find no objection to tasting the waters without committing herself to the whole deal.

'As I see the situation,' Cliffton went on persuasively, 'everyone has personal needs. It is a matter of working out whether or not yours can be accommodated to your satisfaction. I appreciate that this will take time.'

'Yes,' she quickly agreed. 'It will take time. It could be years.'

'As long as it takes,' he reasserted with bland uncon- cern.

'It may never be worked out to my satisfaction,' she warned.

'One can but give it fair trial.'

'As long as that's understood.'

'Absolutely.'

Integrity satisfied, Ashley decided she had to tackle the accommodation question. 'This isn't a big house, Cliffton.'

'It appears to be very cosy and comfortable and prac- tical. You have every reason to be proud of it.'

'Thank you. I wasn't apologising for its lack of gran- deur,' she said dryly. 'I was about to point out we don't have a lot of room. Are you prepared to live with less than you're obviously accustomed to?'

'I was a boy scout. A tent in the backyard will suf- fice,' came the blithe reply.

'No, no, we don't have to go that far.' He was clearly bent on staying with her, no matter what, and Ashley found herself feeling highly gratified by the fact. 'There is a spare bedroom but it is small and rather cluttered. I think you'll have to negotiate with William over what stays and what goes to make room for your things. It's rather complicated with a miniature army of soldiers that are in the process of being painted.'

He grinned. 'I can see your William is a lad after my own heart, Mrs. Harcourt. Perhaps I can help him set up a battlefield. I once did a papier-mâché model for the Battle of Waterloo. One of my ancestors was a key figure in the defence of Hougoumont against the French.'

Cliffton could become the father figure William had been missing all these years, Ashley thought hopefully.

Or was he a soul mate?

Despite Cliffton's mastery of decorum, there was definitely a glint of mischief in his eyes that suggested something wild and wicked lived behind the pose of proper propriety. He was obviously in tune with William's entrepreneurial skills. A hereditary butler was probably in the perfect position to be an opportunist with both his master and his master's guests. Ashley suspected that Cliffton did very well for himself.

Look at his clothes. And the Rolls Royce. Maybe an egalitarian society wouldn't suit him nearly so well. On the other hand, if he was prepared to camp in a tent in the backyard, he was nothing if not flexible.

Since there seemed to be no wrong in accepting him into the house as her butler, at least on a temporary basis, Ashley made her decision with a clear conscience and an exciting sense of adventure. Having a butler would undoubtedly be an interesting and novel experience. When the butler was Cliffton, well, who knew what might happen?

She smiled. 'Is there anything you wish to settle with me before bringing in your luggage?'

He smiled back. 'I believe we've covered everything of present importance, Mrs. Harcourt.'

Ashley could feel his satisfaction and was highly conscious of her own. A two-way street, she thought with growing pleasure.

'Then welcome to our home, Cliffton.'

'Thank you, Mrs. Harcourt.'

How that name grated on Ashley's ears!

'Please be assured I will serve you as best I can until everything is resolved,' he continued.

Happily, she hoped.

'In the meantime, I shall go and survey the sleeping quarters and come to an accommodation with William.'

Ashley came to another decision. 'There is one other thing. In Australia it's quite customary for both employer and employee to call each other by their first names. I'm not even your employer. And since we'll be living in constant proximity, I think it would be more appropriate if I call you Harry and you call me Ashley. It won't, uh, interfere with your duties, and I'll feel more comfortable with it. If you don't mind.'

'Your comfort is my duty,' he replied, giving her a dazzling smile. 'Ashley it is.'

'Thank you, Harry.'

'My pleasure.'

He left her to savour her pleasure, and it was very warm, warmer than anything Ashley had felt for a long, long time.

CHAPTER FIVE

NO SOONER HAD William's friends scattered home for their evening meal than Ashley was faced with some of the wider consequences of accepting Harry into her household.

The telephone rang.

Ashley was slow in answering the call. Harry had insisted on preparing dinner, and William, most uncharacteristically, was helping him. She had slipped upstairs to change out of her business suit and freshen up generally for the evening ahead. By the time she emerged from the bathroom and picked up the receiver in her bedroom, Harry was already on the kitchen extension.

'The Harcourt residence. May I enquire who's calling, please?'

Ashley held her tongue, curious to know how Harry would deal with the caller.

'It's Olivia Stanton. Dylan's mother.'

Ashley grimaced. Olivia was the president of the Parents' and Citizens' Association at William's school, and she had a habit of minding everybody else's business. Her snippy tone indicated a complaint was about to be voiced.

'How do you do, Mrs. Stanton?' Harry's English accent suddenly developed a very plummy tone. 'How may I help you?'

A slight pause. 'To whom am I speaking?'

'My name is Cliffton. I am Mrs. Harcourt's butler.'

'Butler!'

Her astonishment was unmistakable. A butler was a most uncommon personage in Australia, let alone in the Central Coast area of Wamberal. Probably the prime minister or the governor-general had one for official receptions, but Ashley couldn't even vouch for that.

'Did you say butler?'

Olivia Stanton was clearly rocked off her set course.

'I did, Mrs. Stanton.'

'What is Ashley Harcourt doing with a butler? I didn't know she could afford one.'

The rhetorical question, followed by the comment on her financial position, made Ashley realise that Harry's arrival in her life would give rise to enormous speculation and gossip in the neighbourhood. It was a measure of her enthralment with Harry that Ashley found she wasn't overly troubled by this prospect. Let them say what they liked. And they'd certainly do that when they saw him! Her course was set. She was going to keep the butler, no matter what!

'I believe my services are of value, Mrs. Stanton,' Harry answered silkily.

'Well, it is unusual.' Olivia justified her rudeness.

'Perhaps it will start a fashion, Mrs. Stanton. Mrs. Harcourt does run an employment agency.'

Ashley grinned. That was a clever stroke.

'Are you connected to the Rolls Royce that's involved in these outrageous photographs?'

Ashley rolled her eyes, knowing full well that another of William's schemes was coming home to roost.

'It comes with me, Mrs. Stanton,' Harry answered smoothly.

He had solved the problem of accommodating the chauffeur and getting the car off the street by sending them both to a local motel. He dismissed the cost as though it was nothing, assuring Ashley once again that she would not be held financially liable for what he did in pursuit of a successful outcome to his mission.

And the mission had been verified. Harry had shown her the branch of Roger's family tree that had originated from England. It was amazing that so many people had died off, leaving only William as the last of this specific blood line.

'Do you know what use William made of your car this afternoon?' Olivia demanded testily.

'Yes, I do.'

'Are you aware that he is charging ten dollars for the photographs he took?'

'As I understand it, there is no obligation to buy, Mrs. Stanton. If you can't afford the price—'

'I didn't say that.'

'The boys were very happy about the chance of being photographed at the wheel of a Rolls Royce, but if you want Dylan to be unhappy—'

'I didn't say that, either.'

'A once-in-a-lifetime occurrence, Mrs. Stanton, is not something to be belittled. You are, of course, entitled to disagree. I believe William can bear the cost of Dylan being left out of the photo-graphs—'

'I don't want him left out,' Olivia cried, drowning in the string of logic that had flowed from Harry's silver tongue.

'Of course not, Mrs. Stanton. No mother would want her son left out of something so special. Shall I tell William to put Dylan's photograph in the sold pile?'

A died-in-the-wool accomplice, Ashley thought, bemused and amused by his dexterity in handling the most difficult people.

'Yes,' Olivia surrendered weakly.

'Thank you, Mrs. Stanton. Is there anything else? A message for Mrs. Harcourt?'

'No.'

'Then thank you for calling, Mrs. Stanton.'

Killed off with politeness, Ashley thought, as she heard the line disconnect. On the other hand, Olivia was probably dying to get a free line so she could spread the news of Ashley's acquisition of a butler who came with a chauffeured Rolls Royce. It would certainly add a bit of spice to her reputation as a businesswoman.

Fortunately it was no longer a scandalous matter for a man and woman to be living under the same roof together without benefit of marriage. Ashley had no doubt that most of her friends and acquaintances would take the attitude, 'Good luck to you!' while they tried to stifle their envy.

However, she did need to warn Harry not to say anything about their connection to Springfield Manor. That was their private business. Apart from which, it would spoil everything. She didn't want to think about it herself. She simply wanted to enjoy having Harry fix things for her as he'd been doing so beautifully ever since he had arrived.

As on most January days, the heat of summer lingered long into the evening. Ashley zipped herself into her favourite sundress. It was casual enough not to look too dressed up. The polished cotton was cool and the pretty pink and green floral print suited her colouring. The bodice was fitted, with shoestring straps over her shoulders. The full circular skirt always made her feel feminine.

Normally, she would unpin her hair at this time, brush

it out and clip it into a high ponytail to keep it off her neck. Practical it might be, but it didn't look elegant. She effected a more sophisticated casual look by winding it into a loose knot on top of her head. Several strands artfully escaped.

She dabbed on some Beautiful perfume, applied a silvery pink lipstick, slid her feet into strappy white sandals and hoped that Harry would find her more than passably attractive.

The staircase led down to the family room, which was separated from the kitchen by a wide working counter that also served as a breakfast bar. She heard William peppering Harry with questions as she started down. Something about ghosts. William was fascinated with the supernatural.

Harry, however, lost the thread of their conversation as Ashley came into full view on the staircase. His hands stopped tossing the salad he had mixed in a bowl. He watched her descend as though transfixed by her grace and beauty. At least, Ashley hoped that was what was captivating him, and he wasn't simply surprised by the change in her appearance. It was much more heart-lifting to fantasise that he was seeing a woman who attracted and intrigued him.

She was conscious of the full skirt swishing around her bare legs as she descended step by step, conscious of silky strands of hair brushing against the smooth golden tan of her bare shoulders, more intensely conscious of her sexuality than she had been in so many years she had forgotten how powerful the feeling could be. She had given up believing she would meet a man who would trigger such a response in her.

She could feel her whole body glowing under the interest in Harry's eyes, an interest that clearly sizzled with sensual signals as it enveloped all of her, from the loosely draped topknot of her hair to the swell of her full breasts encased in the tightly fitting bodice to the emphasised curve of waist and hips to the dainty slimness of her ankles. All her instincts picked up the knowledge that he found her desirable, and she revelled in the certainty that the strong attraction she felt was not one-sided.

'Oh, hi, Mum! You've interrupted a great story!' William informed her, seeing no reason for the halt in his entertainment.

'Your mother has first claim on my attention, William,' Harry said, quietly but firmly putting her son in his place, his gaze not even slightly wavering from her. His eyes seemed to bathe her with warm pleasure as he added, 'Good evening, Ashley.'

The formal greeting didn't feel like a formality at all. It felt like a promise of wonderful things to come. The gateway to possibilities was open. 'Good evening, Harry,' she returned, giving him a smile that welcomed him to her world.

He had discarded his suit coat and rolled up his shirt sleeves. Ashley noticed that his shoulders didn't need any padding and his forearms were strongly muscular. He was still lean and elegant, but she added physical power to his other attributes, and had little doubt he could fight with more than words, if need be. Harry Cliffton, she decided, was a man with many sides to him. Ashley wanted to discover all of them.

The telephone rang again.

William sighed at this further interruption to the subject that interested him.

Harry took the receiver from the wall phone above the counter. 'The Harcourt residence…'

Ashley walked to the other side of the counter as Harry listened to the person on the other end of the line.

'Just a moment, Mrs. Stanton. I'll see if Mrs. Harcourt is available.'

He held the receiver to his chest as his eyes queried hers.

'Fusspot,' William muttered.

Ashley frowned at him, not approving of disrespect to his elders, although privately she was inclined to agree with him. Olivia Stanton was not her favourite person. Nevertheless, she was a neighbour and the mother of one of William's friends, and it was political to keep on her good side if she wasn't demanding too much. She nodded to Harry and held out her hand.

'Mrs. Harcourt will take your call now, Mrs. Stanton,' Harry announced with marvellous aplomb before passing the receiver to her.

'Olivia—' Ashley tried to inject interest into her voice.

'Ten dollars is a lot of money for one photo, Ashley.'

Olivia hated losing a battle. Flummoxed by Harry, she had obviously decided to shift to another opponent. Having been shown the way to defeat the woman, Ashley took a leaf out of Harry's book.

'What price do you put on your son's smile, Olivia?' she asked sweetly.

Harry's eyes danced pure delight at her. Ashley's heart flipped.

'All right. It's very cheap then,' Olivia conceded, surprising Ashley with such a quick dismissal of the grievance. 'What I was wondering, Ashley, was whether... I'm having my annual neighbourhood party in a week's time....'

This was news to Ashley. She hadn't received an invitation.

'I was wondering if you'd lend me your butler and Rolls Royce for the evening?'

Olivia Stanton had the hide of a rhinoceros. It did make her effective at fundraising for the school, which also fed her self-importance, but this was pure one-up-manship on a personal level, no connection whatsoever with public do-gooding.

'I'm afraid Cliffton is not a lendable commodity, Olivia,' she replied, barely keeping a sardonic edge out of her voice. 'It certainly couldn't be done without his consent. A butler is not a slave, you know. Butlering is a highly respected profession that requires absolute savoir faire and perfect organizational skills, not to mention an impeccable reputation, since he holds such a position of trust.'

Ashley couldn't stop her eyes from flirting wickedly with Harry's as she described his position. She paused for a moment to give Olivia time to swallow all she'd said, then obligingly added, 'I will ask him, if you like.'

'Well, there's no harm in asking, I always say,' came the bull-headed reply.

'Then please excuse me a moment, Olivia. I'll put it to him.' She held her hand over the receiver and grinned at Harry. 'You're already in demand. Olivia Stanton would like to borrow your invaluable services for her neighbourhood party.'

'Don't do it,' William said. 'She's full of herself as it is.'

'That's quite enough, William,' Ashley reproved sharply. He was getting altogether too bold in his opinions. And indiscreet!

'The duties of my profession demand that I stay with you,' Harry stated virtuously.

'Quite so,' Ashley agreed with mock seriousness. She

lifted the receiver to her ear again. 'I'm sorry, Olivia. I'm afraid butler ethics prohibit the lending of a butler. He has to stay with me.'

'Of course, I'd forgotten about that, but perhaps you and he would like to attend as guests.'

Sly vixen, Ashley thought, determined not to fall into that trap. Having established Harry as her butler, to turn up with him as her escort would be tantamount to handing Olivia Stanton evidence that all was not as it should be. After assuming a proper correctness about Harry's professional life, Ashley was not about to cross lines. Besides, she wanted to keep Harry to herself.

'I'm quite sure Cliffton will have me ready for your party in time,' she said with airy confidence. 'When did you say it was?'

'Eight o'clock next Saturday.'

'Lovely! He might even drive me up in the Rolls and park it outside your house for an hour or two.' That would lend some of the status that Olivia desired for her party. 'As it's only a short distance away, I don't think Cliffton will mind taking me there and walking home. Thank you for inviting me, Olivia. I must go now. Bye.'

She hung up on the meddlesome woman and raised her eyebrows in appeal to Harry. 'Would you mind?'

He gave a deeply meaningful look. 'I'll give you anything you want, Ashley.'

It sent a little thrill of pleasure and anticipation cartwheeling down Ashley's spine.

'Great!' William said, his eyes lighting up as he saw an advantage. 'Can we go to Springfield Manor with Mr. Cliffton, please, Mum? All you have to do is say you want to,' he pressed eagerly.

Shock froze all the tingling warmth Harry had ignited. He had got to her son behind her back before she could extract a promise from him not to mention Springfield Manor to William. It was playing dirty, getting William on side against her.

She turned to her son, who was propped on a stool at the end of the counter. He had inherited the blue eyes, the athletic build and the ability to play any sport well from his father, but he had her fair hair and basically her sense of fair play. He never cheated on his deals with his friends, and the fact that he had so many of them testified to the imaginative fun he supplied. She liked her son the way he was. She did not want him reclaimed by the Harcourt family and instilled with values that were not her own.

'Why do you want to go to Springfield Manor, William?' she asked, needing to elicit how far Harry had gone in pursuing his quest and how much he had told William.

'So I can go ghost hunting with Mr. Cliffton,' he answered excitedly. 'I'll be the only boy in the street who has seen a real ghost.'

Ashley felt a deep stab of relief. William still had no idea he was the heir and expected to live at Springfield Manor. No doubt he was already planning how much he would charge the boys to hear a description of a real ghost, and Olivia Stanton would be on the telephone to voice another complaint.

Ashley looked dubiously at Harry. Had he decided an indirect approach through William was his best route to success? 'Are there really ghosts at Springfield Manor? Tell me the truth, Harry.'

'Many,' he replied serenely. 'It was at Springfield Manor that the great bard got the idea for the ghost of Hamlet's father, and Charles Dickens got his inspiration for the Spirit of Christmas Past, the Spirit of Christmas Present and the Spirit of Christmas Future.'

'This has to be fabrication,' Ashley observed sceptically.

His eyebrows lifted in a display of innocence. 'Would I fabricate to you?'

'Probably. To get your own way.'

He looked pained. 'Not at all. You must remember that the winter nights at Springfield Manor are very long and very cold. We spend a great portion of these hours sitting around the fire telling stories.'

William looked fascinated.

Ashley didn't know what to believe. Harry rolled out these stories as though imbued with them, yet she had witnessed how quick he was with clever and manipulative responses to Gordon Payne and Olivia Stanton.

'Don't you have TV at Springfield Manor?' she asked, determined on emphasising the present day instead of the long, historical past.

'There are many sets, but rarely used. Not only are our own stories more lively and less boring than those on the television, it is our belief that families that talk together, stay together.'

Solid principles there, Ashley thought. If true.

Harry sounded so good, looked so good, but was it all a masterly performance to get his own way? Ashley reminded herself he had openly admitted he was a man who would not accept no for an answer. It was as well to keep remembering that. How was she to know if his interest in her as a woman was not merely a ruse to charm, even seduce her into doing what he wanted? Did he consider a widow fair game?

William was already putty in his hands. He had done everything right there, aiding and abetting William in his schemes, filling his head with intriguing myths about Springfield Manor, appealing to the boy in ways that would plant her son firmly at his side in a battle about the future.

'Is this your first trip to Australia, Harry?' she asked, her eyes challenging the twinkling confidence in his.

'Yes, it is.'

'Then may I suggest it's an opportunity for you to learn about a wider range of life than what is incorporated in Springfield Manor. Perhaps you could try to forget that small part of England for the rest of this evening.'

'Aw, Mum,' William protested, 'we were in the middle of a story about—'

'It can keep to another day, William,' Harry inserted smoothly. 'It will hardly be a jolly evening if we bore your mother.' He smiled at Ashley. 'I would love to hear all about your life here.'

He sounded genuine. He looked genuine. He had accepted her block on Springfield Manor with good grace. The rest of the evening should go her way, Ashley thought with satisfaction. Given that he intended to stayed until he succeeded in his mission, she would have plenty of time to find out whether Harry's attraction to her was genuine or not.

CHAPTER SIX

HARRY INSISTED ON serving their meal. Ashley insisted on his joining them at the table. It improved William's table manners no end, and the ham salad followed by ice-cream and freshly cut strawberry mangoes never tasted better.

It was a marvellous evening. Ashley didn't have to do a thing except enjoy Harry's company. In between delving into all the important events of her life as though he was fascinated by everything that had contributed to the person she was now, he cleared the table, whizzed the plates into the dishwasher, cleaned up the kitchen, made and served coffee, saw William off to bed and generally performed all the duties of a housekeeper and parent while making Ashley feel special and extraordinary.

She had never been so pampered, never been the focus of such concentrated attention, never been so appreciated, never had her needs catered to with such charm and finesse. Certainly Roger had never done that. Harry had to be very close to the perfect man, she decided, feeling as intoxicated as though she had drunk a bottle of champagne.

William had not been ignored, either. Harry had generously committed himself to taking him to the Sydney Cricket Ground to watch a day of the test match between England and Australia, since cricket was William's abiding passion at the moment. That was only if Ashley could spare him for a day, which of course she could, for her son's pleasure.

The more Harry committed himself to staying with her and William, the more chance she had of really getting to know him. Ashley had the feeling she could be very happy with Harry Cliffton. He was a giver, a listener, a man who didn't have to prove himself a superior being by reducing women to nothing. Everything he had demonstrated so far put him on a completely different plane to Roger.

Could he be weaned away from his life at Springfield Manor? *As long as it takes*, Ashley thought, deeply pleased that she had a considerable amount of time on her side before any decisions had to be made.

She wandered out to the back veranda while Harry saw William to bed. It was a beautiful balmy night, the sky littered with bright stars, a three-quarter moon beaming enough soft light to take away the darkness, a gentle breeze wafting cooler air in from the sea. The house was only a few kilometres from the beach, and Ashley fancied she could hear the distant sound of surf breaking on the sand.

It was a night made for romance, and Ashley felt her body quivering with the need for it. So many years had been barren of any romance since Roger. She hadn't trusted it, hadn't wanted to invite more disillusionment, hadn't met anybody who attracted her enough to give it a chance.

Would Harry answer that need, she wondered? Would he succumb to more than a professional involvement with her?

The glass door to the family room slid open. 'Can I get you anything, Ashley? An iced drink?'

The caring tone in Harry's voice made her pulse quicken. She flashed him a smile. 'No, thank you. I was just having a breath of fresh air before going to bed.'

'Mind if I join you?'

'Please do.'

He had taken off his waistcoat and tie. His white shirt, unbuttoned at the neck, shone starkly in the moonlight as he stepped out and quietly closed the door behind him. He moved over to the veranda railing beside Ashley and looked at the brilliant sky.

'Where's the Southern Cross?'

Still concentrating on all things Australian, Ashley thought with a twinge of uncertainty. Was he simply being obliging, the ultimate professionalism of a butler? She didn't want duty from him now. She wanted the man, not the man with a mission. She wanted truth, spontaneity of feeling and confirmation that he felt the same attraction she did.

'There it is,' she said huskily, pointing the constellation out to him, willing him to move closer to her.

'So that's what Captain Cook steered by,' he murmured, maintaining a proper distance. 'It's very distinctive.'

'The Polynesian and Portuguese and French navigators also used it, long before Cook,' she informed him dryly, wishing he wasn't quite so focused on English history. She remembered the Harcourt family line he had shown her earlier, tracing it through to William. A spurt of resentment made her ask, 'Why did Roger's great-grandfather leave England to come to Australia if everything's so marvellous at Springfield Manor?'

Harry gave her one of his quirky smiles. 'He disgraced the family with the dishonourable act of publicly revealing he cuckolded a duke.'

'And, of course, the British considered Australia the dumping ground for undesirables.'

His eyes caught hers, searing away their mockery with intense seriousness as he quietly answered, 'It also provided the opportunity to start a new life.'

Was he making a personal statement or simply soothing any ruffled feelings she might have over her country's convict and colonial past?

'That's been true for many people,' she warmly agreed. Although there were some who clung to an old heritage, looking back instead of embracing what a new country offered. Like Roger's mother. 'William is fifth-generation Australian, Harry. I'm seventh generation,' she added, wanting to impress on him that they were well-rooted here.

He smiled. 'What I've admired about the Australians I've met is their attitude of anything being possible for them.'

'Have you ever thought that other things were possible for you?'

'I'm beginning to.'

Hope leapt through her heart. 'Promise me you won't tell William he's the heir to Springfield Manor.'

'I had no intention of doing so.'

'Circumstances can change.'

'Yes, they can,' he agreed without the slightest hesitation, giving Ashley's hope a further boost. 'Though I must say William is a fine lad, Ashley. A credit to you.'

'Thank you.' She smiled on a glorious lilt of optimism. 'He likes you, too.'

His gaze dropped to her mouth. Ashley's skin prickled, reacting to the sudden tension charging the air between them. *He wants to kiss me,* she thought exultantly. But he didn't move. There was a quality about his still-

ness that screamed of iron-willed restraint. Duty and discipline stamping on desire, denying it free rein, Ashley
surmised, and that in itself was exciting, feeling the tug
of war taking place inside him.

She sensed the gathering of purpose. His gaze flicked
to hers, and there was certainly nothing impersonal in the
dark blue intensity of his eyes. She had the uncomfortable feeling that he wanted to scour her soul. Even before
he spoke, she felt herself tensing defensively, knowing
instinctively that he had moved beyond physical attraction to a far deeper need.

'What went wrong with Roger, Ashley?'

The shock of the question set her mind spinning. How
did he know? She had never spoken of the crushing nature of her marriage. Even at the time, pride had insisted
she maintain the public appearance of being happy with
Roger. She had not confided her problems to her parents, let alone anyone else. She had hidden the guilty
relief she had felt when Roger and his mother had died,
accepted the condolences given, and closed the door on
a hard-learnt experience that she never wanted repeated.

'Why should you think anything went wrong?' she
countered, unaware of the guarded tone in her voice, the
retreat from openness in her eyes.

'What people don't say is often more revealing than
what they do say,' he answered quietly. 'You've told me
a lot about your life. Roger Harcourt was your husband
and William's father, yet you did not once refer to him.'

'Roger died seven years ago,' she stated flatly. 'I've
spent far more of my adult life without him than with
him.'

'Happy times usually engender fond reminiscences.'
He shrugged and offered an apologetic smile. 'I didn't

mean to intrude. If it's a sensitive subject... Perhaps you miss him so much it's still too painful to recall.'

'No. I don't miss him,' Ashley confessed bluntly, re-coiling from the idea of letting Harry think she was nurs-ing a long grief that had never been assuaged. 'If he was still alive, we'd be divorced.'

'Why?'

'I guess I stopped hero-worshipping him. I was only nineteen when we married.' Her eyes flashed with irony. 'A pity you didn't come looking for an heir then, Harry. Roger would have leapt at being lord of the manor.'

'He acted that way with you?'

'It had its attractive side for a while,' she acknowl-edged. 'I didn't realise I was supposed to become totally subservient to another person's will.'

'Do you fear that would be expected of you if you came to England?'

'I don't fear it because I wouldn't accept it.'

'It isn't the situation anyway,' he assured her.

'Well, I guess you'd know,' she said lightly, aware that any other judgement by her would be blind prejudice.

'Yes, I do. I'm sorry you had that experience with Roger, Ashley. I hope you don't judge all men by it.'

'If I did, you wouldn't be staying here.'

As soon as she spoke the words, they seemed to hang in the air between them, gathering nuances, laying bare the fact that she thought him special as a man and that being her butler was completely irrelevant. Still he didn't move, and Ashley felt heat creeping up her neck as she recalled the sad way he had spoken of the woman he had loved. Did the memory of her remain in his heart, keep-ing it closed to any other woman?

She turned away and stared blankly at the night sky, fiercely arguing to herself that Harry had brought up

Roger, so it had to be acceptable for her to ask questions that were just as personal.

'What was her name…the woman you spoke of, Harry?'

The ensuing silence shrieked of dredging into deeply private areas. Was it too sensitive a subject? Did he miss her so much it was too painful to recall? They were the words he had used in referring to Roger.

'Pen,' he said at last. 'Penelope.' He gave the longer version of her name a soft, lilting cadence that filled Ashley with envy. It left no doubt in her mind that Pen had been very precious to him.

'How long is it since…' She hesitated, not wanting to sound crassly insensitive to his feelings. 'Since she was with you?'

'Pen died of leukaemia three years ago,' he stated flatly.

Ashley closed her eyes. How awful! Bad enough for death to come suddenly. A long terminal illness had to be grief from start to finish. And afterwards…who could possibly forget it?

'That must have been very harrowing,' she said softly, her natural sympathy overriding her own interests. 'I'm sorry it happened. To both of you.'

He didn't answer. Ashley was acutely aware she had driven his mind into the past. She could feel a great distance between them that had nothing to do with physical space. She waited, although part of her wanted to tear herself away and leave him to his memories. In some strange way, staying with him was like holding a vigil, paying respect to the dead.

'It wasn't like that.'

Ashley barely caught the murmured words.

'After the initial shock of the diagnosis, Pen refused

to allow the situation to become harrowing,' he went on quietly. 'She made each day a celebration of life, finding joy and beauty and pleasure in even the smallest things. There were times when the treatment made her very sick, but she bore it so gallantly....' He shook his head. 'I took it harder than she did. I hated feeling helpless.'

'I'm sure you helped all you could, Harry.'

It wasn't a platitude. Ashley was certain he would have been a tower of strength, supportive, caring, considerate, willing to do anything to make life as easy and pleasant as he could for her. Yet as much as he might have tried to hold death at bay, it was always going to overtake his efforts. She understood his feelings of helplessness.

'I guess her going must have left a terrible hole in your life.'

'She was an adornment to the human race,' he said softly.

How on earth was she going to compete with that? Ashley thought despondently. 'Then you were lucky to have known her,' she said with a burst of envy. 'Not everyone gets the chance to love and be loved by someone so special. Even if it was only for a short time, at least you've experienced it.'

It jolted him out of his reverie. His head turned sharply towards her. Ashley lifted her gaze to his and gave him a full blast of truth. 'Your Pen made part of your life beautiful, Harry. Maybe that makes the loss hard to bear, but you don't carry the sense of having missed out on the best, the sense of an emptiness that has never been answered.'

'Ashley...' His hand swung out, ready to touch. There was something in his eyes...pity? Anguish? She instinctively backed away.

'I think I'll go to bed. I feel cooler now. Good night,

ing if the ice beneath his feet broke. Ashley jolted him into the realisation that he was playing with deep waters.

It behove him to tread very carefully with Ashley Harcourt's feelings. Roger had not been good for her. Harry did not want to inflict any more hurt and disillusionment. He liked her. Very much. She had guts and a firmer grip on self-direction than most of the people he knew. It was wrong to play with the life she had made for herself, yet Harry didn't want to deal himself out of Ashley Harcourt's life at this point.

Nevertheless, he was in two minds about the deception he had so frivolously entered into. He pondered whether he should state his real position as he washed and dressed. He heard William go downstairs and followed him, intent on subtly pumping the boy about the more personal side of Ashley's life.

'Good morning, William,' he started, smiling at the huge bowl of breakfast cereal the boy had helped himself to. 'When does your mother usually wake?'

'Morning, Mr. Cliffton. Mum sets the alarm for seven,' he promptly answered.

Harry had twenty minutes up his sleeve. 'Does she have tea or coffee first thing in the morning?'

'Coffee.' William put his spoon down, deciding to tackle the important question without any beating around the bush. 'Are you going to be my uncle?'

'That's a fairly close blood relation, William. I don't qualify.'

'I don't mean that kind of uncle. I know I haven't got any of those, unless you count step-uncles. Mum's parents got divorced and married other people with kids who are now mostly grown up but we hardly ever see them. And my dad was an only child. I'm not talking about *real* uncles.'

William looked at Harry meaningfully as though he should know the correct import of his question now. Harry didn't care for the flavour of it at all. He found himself recoiling from the idea of joining a queue of live-in relationships that had failed to meet Ashley's needs, then pulled himself up for making unfounded assumptions.

Ashley hadn't struck him as a woman who would lightly invite men into her life. But she *had* struck him as a woman who would kick out anyone who tried to take over.

'Precisely what kind of uncles are you talking about, William?' he asked, seeking clarification before making any judgements.

William sighed, suspecting an evasion. He spelled it out so there could be no misunderstanding. 'Some of the kids at school don't have their dads living with them. Other men move into their houses and live with their mums. Mostly they call them uncle. Rodney Bixell's had three different uncles. He's scored pretty well out of it, too. He got a go-cart from the first, a trampoline from the second and a bike from the third.'

Rodney clearly knew how to play every angle.

'Mum won't let me have a bike until I'm ten because we live on this hill and she reckons it's dangerous,' William continued with obvious exasperation at his mother's judgement on this sore point. There was hope and devious calculation in his eyes as he added, 'Maybe you could talk her into it, Mr. Cliffton. You look as if you could talk Mum into anything.'

Harry had his doubts about that but he hoped it was true. 'Have you had any uncles?' he asked, wanting this point settled unequivocally.

'Nah. No luck yet. That's why I haven't got a bike.

Mum's never even gone out with any guys. So I figure since she let you move in, Mr. Cliffton, it has to mean something.'

'No guys at all, huh?'

William wrinkled his nose. 'She only has boring old girlfriends who don't give you anything.'

Ashley was clearly not into sampling whatever was available. Such complete abstinence was, however, a measure of how gun-shy she was of men in general. Which made her acceptance of him highly intriguing. And flattering. It also loaded Harry with a heavy sense of responsibility. He didn't think Ashley would appreciate the concept of having fun, especially if carried into intimate realms while she was still misled as to who and what he was.

'You're a big improvement, Mr. Cliffton,' William assured him, giving him an encouraging grin. 'None of Mum's girlfriends would think of taking me to a test cricket match.'

'Well, I do happen to like cricket myself,' Harry remarked dryly feeling more of a fraud by the minute. George had already fixed a private box for him in the Brewongle Grandstand at the Sydney Cricket Ground.

'That was a great catch you made yesterday,' William said admiringly. 'It saved a window and a bit of Mum's wrath. She wouldn't have stood back and thought what a fantastic hook shot it had been. She wouldn't have thought of anything else but the broken window.' He paused to let Harry appreciate the different patterns of the male and female mind, then pointedly added, 'I wouldn't mind at all having you as an uncle.'

Was Ashley considering the same possibility? Or did being a butler put him in a different category, someone safe, leaving her in control of what did or didn't happen between them? Would she instantly show him the door if he confessed the truth? He had a strong suspicion she would, despite the attraction he was sure they shared.

'Thank you, William, but I'm here as a butler, not an uncle,' Harry said firmly. 'I think your mother would be very upset if you referred to me as an uncle. It would give people the wrong idea.'

'Oh!' William's face fell. He reconsidered the situation and presented another argument. 'But you are going to stay here for a while. I mean there's the cricket and Mrs. Stanton's party and it would be real good if you took my side on a few things. Like you did yesterday about the photos. Mum gets a bit fussy. Not like Mrs. Stanton. But, you know…she worries about small things that are really okay.'

Harry smiled his understanding. 'Good parents are like that, William. You're very lucky to have a mother who cares so much about your well-being.'

'It can be overdone,' William muttered.

Harry cocked a reproving eyebrow. 'William, I have a lot of respect for your mother. She's achieved a great deal by herself. It couldn't have been easy being a young widow with a young child to take care of.'

'She had me to help.'

'Of course.' Harry smothered a smile. 'That slipped my mind for a moment.'

'But she could do with a lot more help. It would be a good idea if you stayed as long as possible,' William pressed, obviously seeing many advantages to himself in having Harry at hand. 'I'd like to get my soldiers painted and have a few regiments ready to move by next week. Otherwise I can't pretend to be Napoleon.'

'Wouldn't you rather be the Duke of Wellington?'

Harry couldn't imagine William wanting to lead the losing side in any war game.

There was a gleam of pure animal cunning in William's blue eyes as he answered, 'I thought you'd rather play Wellington, Mr. Cliffton, being English and all that.'

William was clearly a master at holding out carrots. Harry was quite a dab hand at it himself.

'Whether I stay or not will be your mother's decision, William. Right now I'm going to make her coffee and take it up to her.' Harry winked conspiratorially. 'Show her what a good butler I am.'

The boy laughed his delight in their mutual understanding. 'That's how I get into favour. Especially when I want something a bit tricky.'

Tricky was definitely the word, Harry thought as he set a tray for the coffee. As William had pointed out, he was already involved here to the extent of taking him to the cricket match and transporting Ashley in the Rolls to Olivia Stanton's party. Letting either of them down after giving his word went against Harry's grain.

He had to maintain the role he had cast himself in until a decision about the future was made, either by Ashley or himself. Confession might be good for the soul, but Harry had little doubt that he would be banished from the household before he could blink if he stopped being the butler. That would not serve the purpose of getting George an heir for Springfield Manor, nor the purpose of getting to know Ashley Harcourt better.

The latter purpose was far more on Harry's mind as he carried the coffee tray upstairs. He had picked a red rose from Ashley's garden and laid it beside the coffee-pot. The romantic touch appealed to him. He hoped it would appeal to her, too. It was wrong that so much of her life had been barren of romance.

He heard the clock alarm go off as he approached her bedroom door and waited until it clicked off before knocking.

'Yes?' A drowsy question.

'It's Harry with your coffee,' he answered.

'Oh!' A pause filled with rustling movement. 'Come in.'

Harry fixed a bright smile of greeting on his face as he opened the door. 'Good morning, Ashley.'

It was just as well he had the words ready to trip off his tongue, because desire hit him in the solar plexus with breathtaking speed, stopping him in his tracks. She was sitting up in bed, a sheet pulled up to cover her breasts but not the two red lace straps that were obviously attached to a very feminine nightie. The pale silk of her hair fell in tangled skeins around the smooth roundness of her bare arms and shoulders. Her face was no less lovely without makeup, and her eyes held a soft, uncertain appeal that pummelled his heart.

Harry knew in that moment it was criminal to deceive this woman in any way whatsoever, yet he was trapped in his own contrived scenario. He didn't want her to reject him. He wanted to take her in his arms, assure her that she was safe with him. He wanted to kiss the slight quiver from her lips, wanted to fill the emptiness inside her with the wonder and pleasure of not missing out on anything. He wanted to give what Pen had given to him.

Perhaps it was another mad impulse, a quixotic urge that could backfire with disastrous consequences. This was not a time for dancing on the edge, he cautioned himself. This was a time for taking things slowly, but his hastily summoned control was severely tested by the sad searching in her beautiful grey eyes. He felt her need and

wanted to answer it. Common sense hammered out that
it was too soon to know if he could.

Keep it light, Harry, he sternly advised himself, pushing his feet forward again. 'William told me you preferred
coffee first thing. Did you sleep well?'

'Yes. Yes, thank you,' she answered distractedly, her
cheeks pinking as she turned to clear some space on the
bedside table for the tray. 'And you? Were you comfortable enough?'

'Very much so.' He set the tray down and proceeded
to pour her coffee. Best to keep his hands busy. It was so
tempting to reach out and touch her hair, feel its silkiness
sliding between his fingers. Her warm, womanly fra-
grance was, fortunately, superseded by the aroma of coffee. 'Bacon and eggs and toast for breakfast?' he asked,
hoping to put her at ease with him.

'I usually have a bowl of muesli. But please help yourself to whatever you're used to, Harry,' she added quickly.

'It's just as easy to cook for two.' He raised a quizzical
eyebrow. She was more composed now. 'Is the muesli a
matter of healthy conviction or a symptom of not wanting the bother of cooking and cleaning up afterwards?'

It drew a rueful smile. 'A bit of both.'

'Well, let the bother be mine. I'm here to serve you,
Ashley, and I want you to enjoy the pleasure of being
served.'

'Then I guess I might as well...once in a lifetime,' she
added with a self-mocking twist.

'It needn't be,' he reminded her. 'It could be your life-
style if you choose to take up residence at Springfield
Manor. Everything should be tried...once in a lifetime,'
he repeated, feeling somewhat exonerated.

She shrugged. 'What would I do with myself there?'

Her eyes flashed derisively. 'In between being waited on hand and foot.'

'Interest yourself in the occupations of others. As you do now. There are estate farms and a village and—'

'I'd be welcome to poke my nose into their business?'

'Helping and interfering are two different things.'

'I'd be an outsider, Harry. A fish out of water.'

'We're all outsiders at one time or another. I'm an outsider here, but that doesn't stop me from getting involved and being helpful and caring. Saying you're an outsider is an excuse for do-ing nothing.'

'Is it your duty as a butler to hand out homilies with coffee?' she asked dryly as he put down the coffeepot.

He flashed her a smile. 'I'm a man with a mission. You can't expect me not to argue my case.'

'You do it very well.'

His eyes held hers. 'I think you could make a place for yourself anywhere, Ashley. Given the desire to.'

Her gaze didn't waver. 'I think you could, too.'

The zest of contest rippled through Harry again. A defiant pride and a will of steel had overlaid the vulnerability that had so touched him when he had entered her bedroom. The simmering challenge in her eyes put him and his beliefs and his heritage on notice that she was not about to be bowled over by any of them. Anything he won from her would be hard earned. But worthwhile.

Harry's blood stirred. 'You'll join me for bacon and eggs?' he asked, pressing for a crack of compliance.

'I'll dance with you, Harry, but don't assume I'll accompany you home,' she answered.

He grinned. 'Then let's make the dance a merry one.'

His feet were light as he exited from her room. Ashley had accepted the game, come what may, and it was fun again. Apart from which, playing the butler wasn't

so deceptive because she would have all that he represented if she came with him in the end.

And more.

CHAPTER EIGHT

ASHLEY PONDERED HER position as she dressed for the day. Harry had reaffirmed his mission, leaving little room for the pipedream that she might be able to keep him in Australia with her. He would go back to England. That was the inevitable reality, and it ill behove her to let it slip from her mind and think other foolish thoughts.

England represented Roger's side of the family. It also represented closer memories of Harry's beloved Penelope. The prospect of taking up residence in Springfield Manor held no attraction for Ashley. Unless Harry overcame all her objections to it.

He had openly declared that he would test her resistance to the limits and he was not inclined to take no for an answer. Ashley wondered how far he would use the tug of attraction to get his own way. He found her desirable. She no longer had any doubt about that.

For several electric moments, when he had first entered her bedroom, she had felt the strong swirl of wanting from him like a physical touch on her skin, a clamp on her heart. He had tried to hide it, tried to ignore it, but it had been still pulsing from him as he poured her coffee. All her senses had been alive to it, treacherously responding to it even as she struggled for the same self-control he imposed upon himself.

But desire wasn't love, Ashley cautioned herself. Desire could be manipulated for purposes that had nothing to do with love. Men and women had been doing that to each other since Adam and Eve. Desire could be a trap that would cost her dear in the end if she succumbed to it. Ashley had been the victim of one man's ego. She didn't intend to ever let that happen again.

Was *winning* uppermost in Harry's mind?

Did he want to be with her as much as she wanted to be with him?

The wise thing to do, Ashley decided, was wait, watch and listen while keeping a good sparring distance from Harry Cliffton. Having settled on this sensible course of action, she headed downstairs for breakfast, confident of holding true to herself despite all the persuasive tactics Harry could come up with.

William was discussing the merits of spin bowling with Harry, swapping reminiscences of the great masters of the art. There was not the slightest hint of being patronising from Harry. They chatted away as equals, and William was very much enjoying the company.

Ashley suddenly felt inadequate as a single parent. It was impossible to be both mother and father to a child, to be the full complementary mixture that answered all needs. Not many people achieved that ideal, she assured herself, dismissing a twinge of guilt at her emotional rejection of her dead husband and her indifference about actively looking for another.

'Hi, Mum!' William greeted her cheerfully. 'I'm going to have bacon and eggs, too.'

Ashley's guilt returned and persisted when the three of them sat down to the cooked breakfast. Like a proper family, she thought, beginning the day together, sharing amiable conversation. Usually William had his cereal and was about his business before she got up in the morning. Her routine was to read the newspaper as she ate her muesli. They only really shared the evening meal, and more times than not the television was on so conversation was mainly limited to ad breaks.

She remembered Harry saying that although there were television sets at Springfield Manor, interesting conversation always took priority over watching programmes. Ashley decided to revise the habits she and William had fallen into. Good communication was important and time should be made for more of it. *Families that talk together, stay together.* Harry was right about that.

'Do you have a busy day ahead of you, Ashley?' he asked.

'Yes.' She explained what had led up to Gordon Payne's visit yesterday and Cheryn Kimball's present predicament. 'Cheryn thought she had a good, secure job and was counting on the income. Given the circumstances, I doubt he'll even pay her what he owes for the week's work. I must try to place her again as quickly as I can. The poor girl was completely distraught yesterday.'

'Can I help you with anything?'

'No. It's kind of you to offer but this is my job and I know how to handle it.'

'You can help me paint my soldiers,' William chimed in, eager to fill in any gap in Harry's time.

'This afternoon,' he agreed. 'Since your mother doesn't need me here, there's a few other things I'd like to do this morning. Reprovision the fridge and pantry, for one. I can't be eating all your mother's food without contributing something.'

'There's no need…' she started.

He smiled, melting the protest on her tongue. 'I want

to. Let me surprise you. It will give me great pleasure to provide a few special meals for you.'

'The kind of meals you have at Springfield Manor?' she asked sharply.

He tilted an eyebrow. 'Is that forbidden?'

It probably made her a closed-minded bigot if she said it was, yet she resented the subtle pressures Harry was applying to undermine her negative attitude to his mission. She forced a smile. 'Please feel free to provide whatever you like. As I understand it, you take full responsibility for the money you spend on us.'

'You do?' William's eyes lit up like Christmas trees. 'Can I come shopping with you, Mr. Cliffton?'

'You might find it boring, William,' Harry warned.

'Are you going in the Rolls Royce?'

'Yes.'

'Then I won't find it boring.'

'You need your mother's permission.'

'Mum?'

Ashley eyed her son sternly. 'You may go, William, but you are not to ask Mr. Cliffton to buy you anything.'

'I promise I won't ask him,' he agreed quickly. A fair bit of hinting could easily be achieved, William thought, his mind leaping to certain shops that could be artfully included in the itinerary.

Ashley retired to her office once breakfast was over, leaving Harry and William to make whatever arrangements they liked between them. She heard the Rolls Royce arrive and hoped William wouldn't find it too pleasant and addictive. They popped their heads into the office to say goodbye, and the house felt strangely empty when they were gone.

Ashley did her best to settle to work. She carefully scanned the Positions Vacant lists in the local newspaper, mentally matching them against the files of her clients for possibilities to pursue. There was nothing that would really use Cheryn's abilities.

She made several telephone calls, scouting employers who had used her agency to find good employees in the past. One of them had a friend who had mentioned a need for an attractive front-office girl with superior secretarial skills. Ashley wasted no time in making the contact and interesting him in the service she could provide. An appointment was made to discuss the matter further, and Ashley hoped it would result in a suitable position for Cheryn.

A few calls came in asking for temps. Ashley had no problem in filling these requirements. She wondered how Gordon Payne was getting on with finding someone to fit his needs and was glad the responsibility was no longer hers. She couldn't, in all conscience, place anyone in such a demeaning situation.

Her gaze drifted to the Lladro clown that Harry had rescued for her, and the scene replayed itself in her mind, pausing over the sense of connection when their eyes had first met. Had it merely been some spark of chemistry ignited by the tension of the moment, or was it an instinctive recognition of fellow travellers on a plane that was subtly removed from other people?

Ashley realised that since her escape from marriage to Roger, she had been content to hibernate emotionally from all other men. She suspected Harry had done the same after Pen's death, withdrawing himself from any close involvement with other women. Had their meeting snapped them both awake, seeding an awareness of needs they had buried? Were they meant to come together or was this encounter simply a turning point in their lives, a spur to reappraising where they had been and where they would go from here?

The realisation came to her that she had been building a *safe* self-containment. Harry tapped a yearning in her for all she was missing out on. Perhaps it was self-defeating to cling to the control she had achieved. Could what she most wanted be gained without risk? What if she was to go to Springfield Manor with Harry....

She shook her head over such impulsive madness. She had only known the man one short day. It was far too soon to consider throwing up everything on the chance that Harry Cliffton was the man to fill the empty places inside her with the satisfaction she craved.

The buzz of the telephone was a pertinent reminder she should be concentrating on work. She picked up the receiver and crisply identified the agency and herself.

'Ah, Mrs. Harcourt... Gordon Payne here.'

Ashley instantly tensed, expecting his demands and threats to be renewed. 'What can I do for you, Mr. Payne?' she said coolly, determined not to lose her temper this time no matter how provoked she was.

He cleared his throat. 'I was out of line yesterday, Mrs. Harcourt. Said things I didn't mean. I'm a man who's set in my ways and I like things to run smoothly, you know?'

'Perhaps mistakes of judgement were made on both sides,' she offered, astonished at the conciliatory tone and happy to meet it halfway.

'Very upsetting. A bad day all round. I regret my behaviour with you, Mrs. Harcourt, and I hope you'll accept my apology.'

Incredulity billowed through Ashley's mind. Roger had never apologised. Maybe she had overinflated Gordon Payne's ego and it wasn't quite so monstrous, after all. 'Thank you, Mr. Payne,' she said, struggling to gather her wits and say something gracious. 'I'm sorry we couldn't have reached a better understanding.'

'I'll put two cheques in the mail today. I presume you'll pass Miss Kimball's on to her.'

'Yes, I will. Thank you. She'll appreciate it.'

'I don't want any trouble.'

'Neither do I, Mr. Payne.'

'You'll have no cause to bring any harassment charges against me. I promise you that.'

Ashley's eyebrows shot up. She hadn't even begun to consider such a means of redress. Even if Gordon Payne had carried through on his threats, how on earth could she have proved he was behind the harassment? People like him always covered their tracks.

'I'd be obliged if you'd assure Mr. Cliffton I've put everything he demanded in train and there'll be no reason to get into litigation.'

Harry?

Enlightenment blossomed.

Harry had overheard the threats. He was a witness. He must have gone shopping for a peaceful and fair resolution to the Gordon Payne problem, as well as food to lead her into temptation.

Images of Harry deftly turning Gordon Payne inside out with clever arguments and putting the fear of messy legal action into him flashed through Ashley's mind. She clapped her hand over her mouth to stifle a wild giggle. She wished she'd been there to watch him run rings around the pompous power monger. It must have been a marvellous performance. A Rolls Royce definitely had the weight to buy more lawyers than a Daimler, and undoubtedly Gordon Payne respected that kind of money.

Having sobered herself enough to speak, Ashley

blithely said, 'I'll certainly repeat the content of this call to Mr. Cliffton.'

'Thank you, Mrs. Harcourt. I won't trouble you any further. Good day to you.'

Ashley put the receiver down and laughed out loud, joy and relief bubbling through her amusement. She felt like dancing. Harry had done it again! The dragon had been slain by her irrepressible white knight. Was it any wonder that she was in danger of falling in love with him? If he kept on righting the wrongs in her world...

But what if he saw it as simply settling her affairs, smoothing the path for her to wind up her business without any hassles before leaving it behind? That was part of his mission, wasn't it? This act of gallantry might not be inspired by any personal wish for her well-being at all.

On the other hand, she was very grateful for the outcome, so why should she quibble about motives? She snatched up the telephone and dialled Cheryn Kimball's number, delighted that she could pass on some good news and brighten Cheryn's day.

Despite the many question marks in her mind, Ashley could not repress her high spirits when Harry and William arrived home from their shopping trip. She heard the Rolls Royce purr to a halt and hurried out of the office to open the front door for them. Harry and William emerged from the back seat, Harry using his silver-tipped walking cane with elegant panache as he stepped out, his beautiful three-piece suit stamping him as a man of class, William following, happily clutching a bag emblazoned with the toy shop logo.

Ashley moved out to the porch, eyeing her son with exasperation. 'William, I told you....'

'I didn't ask, Mum,' he expostulated. 'Mr. Cliffton said we couldn't have a proper war game without model cannons and cavalry. It was his idea. I just showed him where they could be bought.'

'Led him there by the hand, did you?'

'Aw, come on, Mum. Mr. Cliffton doesn't need leading. He's the smartest man I know.' William broke into a run. 'I'll duck upstairs and put these away. Then I can help the chauffeur with the other shopping bags.'

Such virtue was highly suspicious, but Ashley let it pass. She looked at the smartest man William knew and was inclined to agree with her son. Harry's mouth was twitching with amusement as William bolted past his mother. His blue eyes danced with mischief.

'I don't suppose you'd know anything about the cavalry arriving in Gordon Payne's office this morning,' she said archly. 'I got the impression that a few cannons were fired there, as well.'

'I love cavalry charges. Did you know in the Battle of—

'Let me guess. One of your ancestors led it.'

'No. He blew the bugle.'

'As you did with Gordon Payne.'

He grinned. 'It seemed like a good tune to play.'

Ashley couldn't help laughing. 'It worked. The enemy has been routed, and the money is in the mail.'

'A celebratory lunch is in order?'

'It certainly is. And thank you, Harry, both for Cheryn and myself. You're a great bugle player.'

He laughed, and a sweet harmony danced between them, dispelling the defensive reservations Ashley had meant to hold. Harry was a prince amongst men, and there was simply no sense in dimming the pleasure he brought into her life.

They had a positively sinful lunch. Moet and Chandon champagne, cold lobster and an array of exotic salads, plus a selection of temptations from a French patisserie. William made short work of a large slice of chocolate mud cake. Ashley succumbed to an exquisite mille-fleur. Harry produced everything with irresistible flair, and it would have been absurdly churlish to stand on some independent dignity in the face of such treats.

Last but not least, he presented Ashley with a box of Belgian chocolates. 'To help pass the time sweetly in your office this afternoon,' he said with a smile that would have charmed the stoniest heart.

By this time, Ashley's heart was well and truly under siege. She retreated to the safe confines of her office, which was the sensible thing to do, but she couldn't rid herself of the feeling it was a stupid waste of time. How long would she have Harry in her life?

She found it impossible to settle to any productive work. Her mind kept wandering to what she could be doing with Harry—lazing the afternoon away on the beach, showing him some of the scenic beauty spots on the central coast, revelling in his sparkling company.

She wondered how he would look stripped down to a brief pair of swimming trunks. It occurred to her that his skin should be very pale, particularly since he had come from an English winter, yet it wasn't. Where had he got the light golden tan that gave his face and hands such a warm glow of vitality?

Perhaps he accompanied the master of Springfield Manor to the Caribbean to escape the cold. Ashley could well imagine Harry arranging vacations he would find attractive. She suspected he organized quite a lot to suit himself, then used his persuasive powers to make others feel pleased he had gone to so much trouble for them.

A clever manipulator. She mustn't forget that. Underneath all the charm, there burned a steady, relentless and ruthless purpose. He would wear her resistance down until she surrendered to his will. But what precisely was his will? Simply to get William to Springfield Manor for his master? Or did he have some personal desire to have her there for himself?

The doorbell rang.

As she rose from her desk she heard Harry and William come into the hallway from the kitchen. It was a butler's job to answer doorbells, Ashley reminded herself, but she was drawn to the office door to see who was calling anyway.

It was a florist. Harry took receipt of a magnificent bunch of white carnations, thanked the delivery person, shut the door and turned to present them to Ashley as she came forward.

'Wow! Chocolates *and* flowers!' William remarked with unconcealed glee. 'You're doing real good, Mr. Cliffton.'

It drew an ironic smile from Harry. 'They're not from me, William.'

His face fell. He frowned at Ashley as Harry handed her the carnations, two dozen of them prettily set off with sprays of baby's breath. 'Who's giving you flowers, Mum?' he demanded.

Ashley was at a loss to answer until she read the accompanying card. Then she laughed. 'It's a peace offering from Gordon Payne.' Harry must have fired a whole salvo of cannons to wring these expensive blooms out of her erstwhile enemy.

William was not amused. 'Who's Gordon Payne?' he asked in a darkly disapproving tone.

'A gentleman who did some business with me,' Ashley replied, and took the opportunity to deliver an appropriate rebuke. 'He was here yesterday afternoon and but for some very timely intervention, young man, you would have broken the windscreen of his Daimler.'

'Wish I had,' William muttered.

'I beg your pardon?'

Mutiny looked her in the eye. 'I don't want him coming around to our house and giving you flowers. You didn't even tell me about him,' he went on accusingly.

'I'm not in the habit of discussing my business with you, William,' Ashley reproved, taken aback by what was plainly an aggressively rebellious stance.

'If he's sending you flowers, it is my business,' he argued. 'I want Mr. Cliffton to be my uncle. I reckon he'll be tons better than any uncle Rodney Bixell's ever had.' He marched over to Harry's side. 'So I'm telling you right now, Mum. This is where I stand.'

Ashley was stunned speechless. She knew children were growing up rather too fast these days, but to have her nine-year-old son claiming the right to choose a live-in lover for her was a bit much to swallow. Even if he was echoing her own secret fancies.

A flood of embarrassment swept a tide of heat up her neck. She couldn't meet Harry's eyes. What had William been telling him? Or worse, proposing to him? Did he think she was to be had as easily as Rodney Bixell's mother?

Harry, characteristically, took William's declaration in his stride. 'Thank you for your vote, William,' he said with superb aplomb. 'I don't think you need worry about Gordon Payne.'

William looked up, eyes glistening with hope and something suspiciously like hero-worship. 'You mean you'll fight him for Mum?'

'A duel to the death,' he promised, blithely uncaring

that William was taking a personal and not a professional slant on this totally misdirecting piece of gallantry.

Ashley found her voice. 'That's enough!' she snapped, her eyes flashing a fury of pride between the two of them. 'I will not have either of you arrange my life for me.'

'It's my life, too,' William pointed out with irrefutable logic.

'Go upstairs this instant, William,' Ashley commanded, losing patience with him. 'I'll talk to you later.'

She thrust the bunch of carnations at Harry. 'You finagled these. You deal with them. And after you've done that, I want to see you in my office.'

Having seized control out of threatening mayhem and impressed her displeasure on both of them, Ashley strode into the private sanctum where she had always ruled the roost. She slammed the door behind her to drive home the fact that she was the boss here. Her own boss. Those who lived under her roof had better toe her line.

Which was all very well, but as Ashley paced around her office in a ferment of passionate conviction about her own autonomy, an insidious little voice in her mind persisted in questioning what her line was. It was utter hypocrisy to deny that her own desires ran parallel to her son's feelings as to Harry's role in their lives. How, in all honesty, could she reprimand her son for virtually giving her the go-ahead to take what she had been dreaming about most of the day?

But Harry shouldn't have encouraged him to believe there was a chance of him becoming his uncle, going so far as to suggest he would fight any other man for the position. It was wrong, without conscience.

Unless he meant it.

CHAPTER NINE

HARRY STEPPED INTO the office and closed the door quietly behind him. His demeanour was completely unruffled. To Ashley's intense relief he wasn't smiling. Nor was there any amusement twinkling in his brilliant blue eyes. She was so churned up, any trace of a humourous response from him might have triggered a burst of angry frustration.

She realised, after a few fraught seconds, that the tension in the room wasn't entirely hers. His relaxed air was a cloak, another act of self-discipline. She felt the same sense of connection she had felt yesterday, stronger now with their knowledge of each other, pulsing with the need to broaden it, deepen it.

Goose flesh shivered over her skin. Her heart skipped to a faster beat. She faced him defensively across the desk, yet there was no defence in objects or space. His eyes held hers with searching intensity, with indomitable determination, and she stared back, caught in a thrall of desire that would not be repressed, despite the doubts that plundered her mind of any peace.

'Why did you do it?' she asked. 'It wasn't fair to involve William with our...with—' She couldn't find appropriate words.

'He is naturally involved,' Harry answered quietly. 'He is not separate from you, Ashley.'

'But you let him think...' She gestured helplessly.

'That I want to be your lover?' he finished for her.

She nodded, her throat too constricted to speak.

'I do,' he said simply. 'Why should I pretend otherwise?'

She struggled with his apparently open honesty. 'Last night—' she forced the words out '—you spoke of your love for Pen.'

'She was a very meaningful part of my life. I will not deny or hide what I felt for her. But as you yourself pointed out to me, Ashley, that's in the past. You and I occupy the present.'

It was precisely the argument she had comforted herself with last night, but she knew there were other considerations—their backgrounds, the countries they inhabited, the lives they lived...so much to separate them, even if these feelings could be trusted.

'What of the future?' she asked, struggling to decipher what was right, whether to seize the moment or give more weight to consequences.

'Who can foretell the future? At this moment I want you. More than any woman I've wanted in years.'

She wanted him, too. More than any man she had ever met. She couldn't deny it. Nor could she hide it from the blue eyes relentlessly boring into hers, revealing their own naked desire, compelling an unmitigated response from her. Yet how could she give it? How, when there were so many uncertainties plaguing her?

She had a responsibility to herself and to William to make the right decisions, the best decisions. How could she recklessly turn a blind eye to consequences and take what she wanted at this moment, for this moment, simply because she wanted it? She was used to weighing everything, wary of inviting any possible disaster. But if she rejected this...

Harry moved, impelled to take the decision from her, sweep aside her painful uncertainty with action. He knew he was behaving recklessly, gambling that it would all turn out right somehow, but he didn't care. He had to do it, had to know, had to feel. He'd been gambling with death for years and come out alive, if one could call it life.

He hadn't realised how dull everything had become until he had met this woman. She had awakened him, and he couldn't let go of this new exhilarating vibrancy, couldn't let her turn him away, as she might if he didn't act. She had the strength of will to do it if she decided against him. Time was his enemy. Every second that passed was his enemy.

He quickened his pace, closing the distance between them with ruthless intent. The blood was pounding through his veins and he knew the thrill, the primitive excitement of the hunter, the warrior going into battle. The bugle call was ringing in his head and nothing was going to stop him. He would take all before him, carry her away on a journey of discovery that he desperately wanted, that she wanted.

Yes, she did. It was burning through her, too, this need to join with him, to explore the sense of being truly alive, uninhibitedly alive, wantonly alive, awareness driven to the ultimate extreme. It was in the wild turbulence widening and darkening her eyes. It was in the faint tremor of her body as she turned to face him, watching him round the desk, coming to force the admission from her, taking the responsibility for it, changing what had been to whatever would be.

The future held no meaning for him. He would deal

with it as it came. Only now mattered. And now was what
he chose it to be for both of them. That was how it was,
and she didn't back away from it. Nor was she passive.

When he took her in his arms, her hands lifted to his
chest, not to push him away but to touch him, and even
this feather-light touch was like a hammer on his heart.
He could feel a tingling heat spurting through his body,
and it was imbued with the zestful joy and splendour of
life, igniting the lust of the flesh to experience and savour all that bound it to this earth, to this woman who
made the world bearable again, who breathed sweet air
into his lungs and dazzled his mind with hope, with a
promise that it wasn't over for him.

There was more.

He gathered her closer, craving her softness, her femininity, the heart and mind of her, the soul that called to
his from the same pit of loneliness he had known, the pit
where the ashes of dreams resided in a greyness devoid
of the beautiful colours that dreams could paint.

The need to pick up the palette and splash all the bright
primary hues around both of them in wild abandonment
was upon him, irresistible. Let colour fall where it would.
Some of it must stick to them. No more grey. Grey was
emptiness, the void waiting for a new creation, and the
fever to create was too compelling to forgo.

Her hands slid to his shoulders, around his neck, and
her lovely face was lifted to his, the lush curve of her
lower lip tremulously inviting his plunder, and in her eyes
the kindled blaze of hope, the wish, the want, the need
to know, the temptation of the dream of life, to share the
depths and the heights and everything in between with
one who could...who would.

It was a chance, and she couldn't resist it any more
than he could.

He wrapped her more tightly to him. Willingly her soft thighs leaned into the rock steadiness of his, muscles taut with the strength of irreversible need. Her belly pressed over his loins, an enticing cushion of promise for the intimacy within. Her breasts, crested with hard beads of excitement, imprinted themselves on his chest. Her mouth opened under the pressure of his, sweet cavern of sensation, of passion released on a whirlwind of need that swirled from one to the other and fused into a tornado of feeling that swept them up in its tempestuous funnel, away from all worldly things, away from yesterday and tomorrow and the pedantic necessities of getting on with day-to-day life.

Passion feeding on passion, bodies straining to appease the long hunger, hands moving to shed the unbearable barrier of clothes, a totally consuming need to bare all to the desire burning through them, to give all, to take all on the chance that it might prove right, the chance that it would add that precious lustre of true togetherness they both sought, the silver lining beaming from behind the dark clouds, the red-orange-yellow sunburst of golden warmth, the deep calm of blue-green peace.

Their physical surroundings were irrelevant. Behind the desk in Ashley's office they sank to the floor, she pliantly inviting, urgently welcoming, offering the cradle of her womanhood with an utter abandonment of any other care, he needing their mating with an intensity that went beyond all rational thought. *Yes* was the beat of his mind. *Now* was the beat of his body. *Her* was the beat of his heart.

And he plunged himself into the sweet, moist tunnel that would take him to the innermost core of this woman, reaching to the door of her soul, urging it to open with every powerful thrust of himself, wanting to find there the culmination of all he had been blindly searching for since Pen had died.

It came. He felt it begin, the exquisite flowering of ultimate giving to him, the utter yielding of self to the most intimate fusion any two people could achieve, the surrender of every particle of separateness, and it was a wild and exultant intoxicant to him. He moved faster, rushing to meet her climax with his, to share the ecstatic stream of pleasure with her, the essence of life itself mingling, melding, bonding to create the most indescribably beautiful union. He spilled the liquid warmth of his seed into the convulsing heat of her womb, and the blissful perfection of it rippled through them in waves, a wondrous rhythm of togetherness fulfilled and complete.

And they looked at each other, their eyes swimming with the glory of it, their minds dazed that it could be… and was…the possibility, the promise that neither had quite believed in, the chance taken and rewarded, the awareness of its vibrant reality pulsing through them.

She lifted a hand to his cheek, stroking it as though in awe of him or what he'd done with her, and it moved him to kiss her with a surge of tenderness that melted the last of the hard casing that had been around his heart since Pen's death.

'Ashley,' he whispered, and it was a prayer of thanks for being the woman she was, for reaching so far into him that the past had fallen away and he could rejoice in the present because she was here, with him, sharing this moment of revelation, of renewal.

Harry… His name was a throb of sweet exultation in her mind and heart. She couldn't speak it. She felt too much, and his lips were grazing over hers so softly, gently, beautifully, and he was still inside her, filling her with the wonder of all he had made her feel.

What she had known with Roger was a pale thing in comparison, leaving her totally unprepared for such an explosion of exquisite sensation, the sheer billowing glory of it seizing her body, holding it in thrall to the movement of his until that moment…that moment when she was no longer herself but him, too, an entity that belonged to both of them, yet more than either of the two, like an ecstatic star burst that she imagined must have fired the dawn of creation.

It slid into her dazzled consciousness that she wasn't protected against the act of creation that might well be taking place right now with Harry's seed deep inside her, spilled as wildly and wantonly as she had received it. He hadn't thought of it, and she had abandoned all thought from the moment he had first kissed her, abandoned it to the yearning for all she had missed and craved, beyond bearing the emptiness any longer.

What if a child was born of this coming together?

Strange that she didn't care. Perhaps she would care later when the afterglow dimmed, but she doubted it. To know this at least once in a lifetime was worth any price. It was what a man and woman were made for, and Harry had made it happen for her, giving her this precious gift, a memory to treasure no matter what else happened in her life.

He rolled onto his back, carrying her with him, his arms encircling her, hands soothing away what she suddenly realised was a rough prickle on her skin from the carpet. Not once in her marriage with Roger had they ever made love on a floor. She searched for some tiny shock at such uninhibited behaviour and found none. Her office was strewn with carelessly discarded clothes, and she was in a naked, intimate embrace with a man she had known for only one day, but none of it mattered. Only the feeling mattered.

How long would it last? She snuggled her head below his chin and listened to the steady drumming of his heart, weaving music around it, a melody of happy satisfaction she didn't want to end. Let it beat on, she thought, turning now into forever.

Harry lay in contented languor, his fingers weaving through the long, silken strands of her hair, loosed from its pins in the heat of their passion for each other. His senses were drunk with the feel of her, the taste of her, the sight of her, the scent of her. She was beautiful, her skin like satin, her softness more sensual than velvet, her warmth more comforting than any he had known.

He thought of making love to her more slowly, savouring every moment, every nuance of intimacy, but it was better to wait. It was enough to revel in what they had just shared. There was no need to take it further right now.

He should have asked about protection, but he hadn't known beforehand what he was going to do. If she conceived... Harry couldn't stop the smile that spread across his face. A child. His child. An heir for George and Springfield Manor. He almost laughed at the irony of it. So unplanned. Yet if it happened, he would leave no stone unturned to change Ashley's mind about coming to England.

He would enjoy being a father. He enjoyed William, clever little devil that he was. Shock rippled through his mind. They had forgotten William. How long would he wait upstairs before coming to investigate what was going on, before the silence piqued his lively curiosity? If her young son opened the office door, Ashley would be painfully embarrassed, mortified, and she might react badly to the gamble he had taken in pushing for the knowledge they had both wanted.

He sighed, hating to end it, but it was the only sure way to protect what they had shared. He rolled her onto her side so they were facing and gently tucked her tumbled hair behind one delicate ear, giving her time to gather her thoughts as their eyes met in a silent questioning of each other.

Not a trace of regret or hint of recrimination. A brilliant silver shone through the grey of her eyes. He knew it was reflected in his.

He smiled. 'I think we'd better move. You have some talking to do with William.'

'Oh!' She flushed in confusion, horrified at her forgetfulness and what might have ensued from it. She scrambled to her feet in a rush, hunting her clothes in frantic haste.

Harry rose and went to the door, leaning against it to prevent any possible entry. 'There's no cause for panic,' he assured her. 'I'm holding the fort.'

She had already put on her panties and bra, which was a shame because he would have liked to watch her dress more leisurely. She flashed him an anguished look, then all movement was arrested as she stared at his naked physique.

'Do I pass?' he asked, cocking a teasing eyebrow, aware that he was not lacking in any manliness.

She gave a self-conscious laugh. 'I guess you could say you have my seal of approval.'

'You have mine, too.' She had a divine shape, petite but beautifully curved and her bones softly fleshed.

She flushed, her eyes glowing with pleasure. 'I've never been in this kind of situation,' she confessed.

He laughed. 'Neither have I. No style at all. Sponta-neous combustion.'

She giggled, a delightfully girlish sound, shy, nervous, yet rippling with elation. 'I don't think either of us gets top marks for control. Which makes us even.'

'I like being even. I could take a lot of it.'

She didn't demur. Harry felt a zing of elation. She was not going to back off. She wanted more, as he did.

She looked thoughtful as she continued dressing. She finished buttoning and zipping and started gathering up her hair, twisting it into a knot on top of her head. The action lifted her lovely breasts, reminding Harry of how they had felt against him. Desire shot through his loins again, and it took considerable willpower to reduce the surge of blood so that its effect wouldn't be blatantly evident.

She finished pinning her hair in place and gave a help-less shrug as her eyes sought his in eloquent appeal. 'I don't know what to tell William. I don't know where I am myself.'

'As long as I stay here we'll be lovers, Ashley.'

'But you still intend to go back to England,' she said flatly.

'Yes. My place is there,' he answered unequivocally. 'It's up to you to choose whether you'll come with me or not.'

'As your lover?' she asked.

He paused to consider, weighing his answer carefully. 'Let's see what develops between us, Ashley. One thing I can say for certain. I don't intend to be William's *uncle*, so please don't use that term in explaining where we are.'

'So you aim to continue here as the butler,' she said dryly.

He hesitated. Was this the moment for truth? If he

confessed to who and what he really was, would she turn away from him in disgust at his deception? Perhaps feel hurtfully fooled, even over succumbing to the desire that had swept them both into intimacy?

He didn't want to risk bringing any element of change into that. He wanted to know how much more could be built on it, whether it would grow into the magical partnership of souls he craved. He needed more time with her, just as they were.

'I want to be everything to you. I want your every need and desire to be answered by me. If it pleases you to let the established order go on, then so be it.' He gave her a whimsical smile. 'Being a butler doesn't preclude me from being your lover until such time as you decide what you want.'

She slowly nodded. 'We'll need to be discreet. Especially in front of William.'

'That probably would be best,' he conceded reluctantly. 'There's no good in raising his expectations if you know you'll never meet them, Ashley.'

'Me?'

'Yes. You,' he said seriously. 'I won't be an *uncle* for William. I could be a father.'

She looked stunned. 'You're thinking of marriage?'

Why was she so surprised? Didn't she know how special, how rare it was to have what they had just shared together? Maybe not with her limited experience.

'Perhaps we could both think about it,' he said gently. 'I don't even know if you're receptive to another marriage after Roger. There's much to explore and resolve between us.'

She said nothing. Her eyes were slightly glazed, her thoughts turned inward.

Harry decided to spell out the situation as he knew it

would be for him. 'Remember your question...what of the future?'

It snapped her attention to him.

'As I see it, there are two futures for us,' he went on. 'What's between us will either end in a beautiful memory...or marriage.'

She shuddered.

Harry didn't know what it meant. He waited, watching her closely as she came to a decision, hoping he hadn't pushed too far. But it was the plain truth. It would be one or the other.

He would never move in with a woman he couldn't commit himself to. Such an arrangement offended his sense of honour. Nor would he move in with a woman who couldn't or wouldn't commit herself to him. It smacked of second-rate convenience. He had a need for all there could be in a fully committed partnership.

To his intense relief Ashley's mouth slowly curved into a smile, although there was an ironic tilt to it. 'Well, as my butler, perhaps you could bring me a nightcap after William is asleep tonight.'

Pleasure bubbled into a wide grin. 'How fortunate I bought a dozen bottles of champagne this morning!'

'Always so provident, Harry,' she said, her eyes twinkling warmly as she crossed the office to where he stood sentinel at the door for her. She reached up and kissed him, drawing quickly away to discourage a full embrace. 'Thank you. Until tonight, then.'

She left him with that promise, and Harry was content. Eventually he would winkle out all of Ashley's thoughts and feelings. He had another chance tonight. It was enough.

CHAPTER TEN

WILLIAM WAS PRETENDING to be engrossed in painting his soldiers when Ashley entered his bedroom. It was clear that he had said his piece and he wasn't going to unsay it. Ashley had met with her wilful son's passive resistance before.

'I take it that you like Mr. Cliffton very much,' she said dryly, settling onto the end of William's bed.

'He catches on real fast. He doesn't treat me like a stupid kid. He doesn't come the heavy adult. And he knows a lot of interesting stuff. Why shouldn't I like him?' came the belligerent reply.

'No reason at all. I'm glad you do. I like him, too.'

William spun around on his chair, eyes bright with eagerness. 'Then why don't you grab him, Mum? He'd buy us all sorts of great things and he's rich enough to take us to some super places. I bet he'd take me to Seaworld and Dreamworld and...'

'William, he doesn't want to stay in Australia,' she broke in, cutting off his starry-eyed dreams. 'He's here for a while. Then he'll go back to being a butler at Springfield Manor in England, and what he's doing for us now, he'll be doing for someone else over there. He's not really rich. The man he works for is rich.'

'Then how come he's got a Rolls Royce and a chauffeur and can buy anything he thinks of?'

'Because that's what his English boss told him to do while he's here. It's like...well, a holiday for him.'

William's brow puckered. 'Then why is he being our butler?'

It was too pertinent a question for Ashley to set aside. She took a deep breath as her mind flew through what she could say without revealing the real crux of the matter. William could have the tenacity of a bulldog. If she told him he was in line for an inheritance in England, she wouldn't hear the end of it, and what it might do to his ego did not bear thinking about. She fixed on a discreet line and delivered it.

'Over a hundred years ago, a member of your father's family emigrated to Australia from England. Mr. Cliffton's real boss has been researching his family tree and he found out we were very distantly related to him. He sent Mr. Cliffton to learn more about us. In return for living with us for a while, he's being our butler.'

William chewed over this revelation for some time. 'So the Rolls Royce isn't Mr. Cliffton's,' he finally commented.

'He has the use of it.'

'And the money isn't his?'

'Not as I understand it. No.'

'But he is a lot of fun to have around.'

'Yes.'

He eyed Ashley speculatively. 'He likes you a lot, Mum. He cares about what you want and what will please you. And the way he looks at you...'

Ashley could feel her cheeks heating up. Was their desire for each other transparent to her son? Would every look and gesture make a nonsense of discretion? Yet how could she possibly dismiss Harry now? She had to know more. Not to stretch this once-in-a-lifetime experience to its absolute limit would be a negation of the very best life had to offer.

'I bet you could persuade him to stay if you worked at it, Mum,' William said with confident calculation. 'Even if he isn't rich, I'd still like to have him as an uncle.'

Harry's blunt declaration rang in her ears. *I won't be an uncle for William.* Nor for her, either. It would be total commitment—his way—or goodbye and nothing more.

It was all very well for him to make decisions like that. He had had a beautiful relationship with Pen. He couldn't imagine how marriage to Roger made marriage such a fearful step for her.

Why did it have to be marriage or nothing? He hadn't married Pen. At least he hadn't mentioned it. But Pen had been dying. There was a foreseeable end to it, no promise of a future together. No children.

Instinctively she lifted a hand to her stomach. What if she did conceive? Stupid to take risks when the outcome might not be what she wanted. She must do something about that. She had to be sensible.

She caught William's hopeful look and knew she had to dash it. Harry would not be persuaded into being an uncle. He had made that issue decisively black and white. No greys.

'I'm sorry, William. I'm afraid that's impossible. You misunderstood Mr. Cliffton earlier. When he said he'd fight for me, he meant he would protect me from any harm. That's what good butlers do.'

'Oh!' It was a sigh of disappointment. He reconsidered the situation then gave a resigned shrug. 'I guess we'd better make the most of it while we can, Mum, but it's an

awful pity it can't last. It would have been good having
Mr. Cliffton in the family. He makes it better, doesn't he?'

'Yes. Yes, he does.'

Harry painted brighter colour into their lives, excitement and interest and wonderful surprises. Would it always be like that if they shared his world? Could it last?
Or would the shining newness of it wear off? And after
it did, would she be left toeing Harry's line, or the line
the master of Springfield Manor insisted upon, with submission to others' will expected and taken for granted?

She had sworn never to marry again. But was she con-
demning herself to half a life? What she had felt with
Harry just now... Would it always feel so incredibly special with him, so exalting and... She felt her muscles
spasm in an exquisite reminder of the sensations she had
experienced.

Harry could make a great father for William. They
certainly seemed to have struck up a happy rapport. But
the commitment, the complete change of lifestyle would
have long-range effects that were incalculable to her at
the moment. Would she and William ever achieve a sense
of belonging at Springfield Manor, as Harry clearly had?
Deeply and irrevocably.

'Do you miss not having a father, William?' she asked,
concerned that he was feeling the lack of a man to relate to.

He grimaced. 'Yes and no. It kind of depends.'

'On what?'

'Well, it's like mothers. I wouldn't want one like Mrs.
Stanton.' He screwed up his nose to express his opinion
of her motherly attributes. 'And some of the kids have
got fathers who just yell at them, picking on them because they haven't done this right or that right. I figure

I've got it pretty good, really. I mean, as far as mums go, you're definitely the best.'

Ashley couldn't help smiling, even though she knew William wasn't above a little flattery to sweeten her up, thereby slithering out of a deserved scolding.

'Has Mr. Cliffton got that family tree with my father on it?' he suddenly asked.

'Yes. He brought it with him.'

'Can I ask him to show it to me?'

'If you like.' She couldn't deny her son his paternal line. She hoped Harry would keep his promise not to tell William he was the only surviving heir to Springfield Manor.

'Is it okay if I do it now?'

Harry had had ample time to get respectably dressed. She stood up. 'Go ahead. I'm sure you'll find it fascinating with all the stories Mr. Cliffton can tell you.'

'Thanks, Mum.'

He scooted out of the room, his precious soldiers forgotten with the prospect of further dialogue with Harry. Whom he liked enough to have as an uncle even if he wasn't rich.

What kind of husband would Harry make? As a lover he certainly left nothing to be desired.

She left William's bedroom to go to her own, her son's words echoing through her mind. *We'd better make the most of it while we can.*

Ashley intended to do precisely that. Other decisions could wait. As Harry had said, there was much to resolve between them. In the meantime, she would store up beautiful memories.

CHAPTER ELEVEN

THE DAYS SLID by, magical summer days. Even more magical nights. Ashley was loath to bring any note of discord into the happiness of simply being with Harry. She asked no questions about his life in England. It was easy to pretend that was something far off when the immediacy of now overflowed with so many pleasures.

In many ways it was like some idealistic dream, too intoxicating to bring her head down from the clouds. Harry brought gaiety and spontaneity into her life. Inhibitions and planning flew out the window. Over and over again she found herself thinking, 'Why not?' and saying yes to whatever he suggested or initiated.

Their family outings were marvellous fun—a lazy afternoon at the beach, an exhilarating morning spent riding the breeze and the waves in a catamaran, a hilarious evening competing at minigolf, then eating monstrous hamburgers with the works. They picnicked by Somersby Falls and dined on fish and chips at Woy Woy wharf, watching the fishermen and the seagulls.

Both Harry and William inveigled her into sharing their interest in the test match cricket, abandoning work for the day, as she did most days except for following through on absolute-must situations like setting up Cheryn Kimball in the new job she had scouted.

They rode to Sydney in the Rolls Royce, and were ensconced in a private box in the Brewongle Grandstand with a wonderful view of the cricket ground. Drinks were readily available at any time, and a scrumptious buffet lunch was served. She enjoyed watching Harry and William enjoying the game, both of them indulgently explaining the finer points of the batting and bowling to her.

But the nights far transcended the less intimate joys of the days. If their initial coming together had lacked style, Harry more than made up for it, imbuing all that followed with romance. They danced by candlelight and feasted on suppers of strawberries and caviar and lychee nuts washed down by French champagne. Ashley learnt the pleasures of sensuality and for the first time revelled in being a woman, desired, loved, adored and cherished by a man who made her feel she was utterly perfect for him.

When it came to the night of Olivia Stanton's party, Ashley didn't want to go, didn't want to waste the time away from Harry. Nevertheless, the agreement had been made, and Harry took it for granted she would keep her word. He arranged for the Rolls Royce to be standing by to take her in the style Olivia expected, and he and William had their war game all set up to play while Ashley was out.

She felt quite flat-spirited as she dressed, although not to be completely outshone by her mode of transport, she made every effort to achieve an elegant appearance. It was also a matter of personal pride to feel at least equal to Olivia Stanton, who liked to queen it over everybody. Perhaps a touch of vanity entered into it, as well, an underlying urge to show the world, at least her little corner of it, she now knew what it was to be a woman.

Ashley didn't have a wardrobe full of party clothes to choose from. Normally she had no need of them. The only appropriate choice was a black crepe wrap dress that she'd bought for a chamber of commerce dinner.

It had a halter neckline, which she dressed up with gold chains. She fiddled with her hair, achieving a smooth dipping loop across her forehead before sweeping the bulk of it into a soft chignon. A few strands were left curling around her ears, to which she attached long dangly earrings in jet and gold. Her T-bar black suede high heels had been an extravagance—she loved shoes—but they lent a touch of true class.

She applied more make-up than usual, darkening and adding definition to her eyelashes with mascara and deepening her lids with a smoky eye shadow. The black dress demanded red lipstick and a touch of blusher on her cheeks. A dusting of powder took the shine off her nose and added a smooth matt finish to her skin.

An examination of her reflection in the full-length mirror assured her she couldn't look any better. She dabbed some Beautiful perfume on her pulse points, picked up the black Oroton evening bag that had been a gift from Roger so long ago, then went downstairs, still feeling at odds about having to mix with other people when she would much rather stay at home.

It was a measure of how deeply Harry had infiltrated her life. When she had accepted the invitation from Olivia she had felt quite pleased about it. Her social calendar usually ran to lunches with friends she had made through business, or casual barbecues with families who had a child in the same class as William. She was neighbourly and supported community interests, but she wasn't really close to anyone.

It had seemed enough before Harry. She had not been discontent with her life. Being single was a relief after marriage to Roger, and having kept so much to herself for the sake of appearances during the unhappy years with her husband, she had never developed the knack of cultivating bosom friends to whom she might pour out her heart.

She was a good listener, a sympathetic listener, and she thought she was generally liked by others, but no-one really knew her. Not as Harry did. She had told Harry things about herself, thoughts and feelings, she had never told anybody. He had somehow drawn that depth of intimacy from her, and now she wasn't sure if it was good or bad.

It struck home that if she didn't commit herself wholly and solely to him, Harry would leave an enormous hole in her life when he returned to Springfield Manor. In William's, too, she suspected. Perhaps it was time she stopped existing in a wonderful dream and started considering the reality of a future in England. This party tonight might serve to put Harry's influence on her in perspective, bring her feet to the ground.

He and William were in the dining room, their miniature battle lines in place on the table. They were discussing the rules of their war game when she entered, but they broke off their conversation as soon as they saw her.

'Wow, Mum! You're sure dressed up tonight!' William remarked in surprise. 'Is it a special party?'

She shrugged, feeling somewhat self-conscious about her uncharacteristic attempt at glamour. 'I just wanted to look good and feel good.'

'Then you've more than achieved your aim,' Harry said warmly, his eyes agleam with appreciative interest as they skated over her from head to foot and returned to linger on the loosely tied bow at her waist, obviously the key to unwrapping the package. 'Feeling good is important,' he added, his gaze lifting to hers in wickedly innocent inquiry. 'Is there anything I can do to help?'

Her pulse leapt in anticipation of how he would help later tonight. She could feel her body prickling with excitement as she imagined his hands teasing her dress apart, his head bending to...

The telephone rang.

'I'll get it,' William offered, oblivious of the shimmering tension between Harry and his mother. He darted to the kitchen, leaving them together.

'I'm not sure I should let you out of my sight, dressed like that,' Harry murmured, his eyes ablaze with desire.

'Afraid of competition?' she teased, secretly revelling in feeling sexy.

'No. But if the men at Olivia Stanton's party get out of hand, don't hesitate to call in the cavalry.'

She laughed. 'That's never happened to me.'

'Ashley, you're radiating your awareness of your own sexuality. That stirs a man's hormones. All my hormones are rioting over you right now. I have an intense urge to smudge your lipstick and—'

'Mr. Cliffton,' William called excitedly. 'It's for you. Come quick. It's from England.'

'Uh-oh!' Harry grimaced an apology and left her to answer the summons.

Trouble at Springfield Manor? In some trepidation, Ashley followed him into the kitchen, not wanting anything to change now, irresistibly drawn to eavesdrop on his side of the conversation. William handed the receiver to Harry and shamelessly stood by to listen, fascinated by the fact of an international call.

'Cliffton.'

Apparently that was identification enough for the caller. What followed was not exactly enlightening.

'Yes, sir,' Harry said.

After a pause, 'No, sir.'

It had to be his boss at Springfield Manor. Ashley couldn't imagine Harry sirring anyone else. The heat that had been pumping from her heart cooled into a frightening chill. She desperately didn't want any interference to what Harry had started with her and William.

'That would seem improbable at the moment, sir. I have my hands full. Given more time…'

The interruption must have been a very peremptory one because Harry instantly stopped to listen. The reference to time did not bode well.

'I understand, sir.'

A long pause. Ashley felt her whole body tensing with apprehension.

'Arrangements can't be made in a day, sir.'

A brief reply.

'Very well, sir. I'll keep you informed.'

That gave Ashley hope of a longer stay for Harry. However, the ensuing silence was obviously thick with words from the other end of the line. Instructions, orders…

'Thank you, sir. I'll do my best, sir.'

Harry hung up with a heavy sigh and turned to the two expectant faces hanging on his news. He addressed Ashley, a rueful smile accompanying his announcement.

'That was George Fotheringham, the master's voice.'

'What does he want?' she asked anxiously.

'He misses me.'

Who wouldn't miss Harry?

'He says a good butler is irreplaceable.'

He was. Irreplaceable in every sense. Ashley couldn't argue with that.

'Does that mean you can't be our butler any more?'

William asked plaintively, and Ashley sensed her son feeling a pit of emptiness opening before him, just as she did.

'He insists that he needs me at the Manor,' Harry stated in a tone that made it an inevitable reality.

Ashley frantically sought a delaying tactic. 'What about your mission?' she pleaded.

'Yes,' William instantly backed her up. 'You haven't learnt nearly enough about us yet, Mr. Cliffton. I haven't told you any of the stuff Mum doesn't know about.'

'William!' Ashley was distracted by the horrors of misbehaviour this confession implied.

'It was for your own good, Mum, so as not to worry you,' he hastily and piously explained.

'As it happens,' Harry drawled, capturing their attention again, 'Mr. Fotheringham has come up with a solution that he hopes will prove satisfactory to both of you.'

'What?' William asked eagerly.

Ashley held her breath. Her eyes clung helplessly to Harry's. Was he about to reveal the truth about William's position?

His smile had a winning appeal. 'That you accompany me to England for a month's visit at Springfield Manor. All expenses paid, of course.'

'You mean we get to fly on a jumbo jet and...' William raved on, delirious with excitement at the prospect of the great adventure being held out to him. 'Every night ghost hunting...'

A month, Ashley thought dazedly. A month of learning what Harry's life was like. She could put up with any amount of condescension and feeling like a fish out of water as long she could be with Harry whenever he was free. And if she could never feel comfortable with the life over there, the option was open for her to return home.

It was like a miracle, handing her what she needed but not locking her into an irrevocable position.

'Ashley?' Harry asked quietly.

'You can't say no, Mum,' William expostulated, his eyes as big as saucers and his mind whirling with visions of plenty.

No doubt George Fotheringham would be subjected to her son's entrepreneurial skills for the entire month. And since William was his heir… Was this offer a trap to keep them there? She looked uncertainly at Harry.

It was as though he read her mind. 'You retain all authority where William is concerned, Ashley,' he stated unequivocally.

His word was good enough for her. Harry had never done her any wrong. She trusted him. Implicitly.

'Please, Mum. Please, please, please…'

Her relief and joy broke into a happy smile. 'We'd be delighted to accompany you, Harry.'

'Yippee!' William cried in an ecstasy of anticipation. 'I forgive you for all your other wrongs, Mum.'

Done, thought Harry, his answering smile widening to an irrepressible grin. The gamble had paid off. Of course, he'd loaded the odds on his side. The timing and execution of the critical telephone call had been perfect, the outcome reasonably assured with William as dependable an ally as Harry had ever had. Not that the boy was aware of it. He was simply a natural at going after what he wanted with whatever means was available to him. As Harry was.

Good and faithful George could protest and scold as much as he liked, but he would carry out Harry's will. George's sense of service and duty would always prevail, no matter how disapproving he was of the scheme in hand. Not that he should be disapproving. After all, if Harry made everything turn out right, George would have the very result he desired when he had so purposefully reminded Harry of *his* duty.

It was up to Harry to pursue his chosen course with vigour. 'Do you have current passports?'

'You bet we do,' William supplied. 'Mum got them last year when we were booked to go to Fiji, only I came down with the chicken pox and we couldn't go. But just about everyone's gone to Fiji. England will be heaps better.'

William wouldn't have time for much bragging. Harry moved into step two of his new mission, focusing his attention on Ashley. 'I'll see to your visas on Monday and book a flight to London for Tuesday if there are seats available.'

'So soon!' She looked stunned.

'Those are my instructions.'

'But what about my business?'

'We'll attend to whatever is necessary. Everything will be looked after.'

He could see she instinctively recoiled from being rushed, her cautious nature wanting to think it all through. That could invite trouble he'd rather avoid.

'You'll be late arriving at Olivia Stanton's party if we don't move now,' he reminded her, stepping forward to usher her to the front door. 'I'll be back shortly, William.'

Ashley felt her mind was split into at least a dozen pieces, zigzagging off in all directions. As she reached the hallway she gathered enough wits to admonish her precocious son. 'You behave yourself, William,' she said sternly. 'And you are *not* to ask for anything. Do you hear me?'

'Loud and clear, Mum. I promise I'll be as good as

gold. Cross my heart.' He grinned. 'I wouldn't risk not going to England with Mr. Cliffton.'

And that was the crux of it, Ashley thought wryly as she accompanied Harry to the Rolls Royce. William was getting totally out of hand. He needed a father. But was Harry any different to her son? Everything seemed to be suddenly out of hand. She didn't feel in control of anything any more.

Harry saw her settled in the front passenger seat, wanting her beside him. As he rounded the bonnet to the driver's side he felt the exhilaration of having crossed another critical line. Not only had becoming lovers exceeded all his hopes and expectations, he had successfully put in place the process of moving Ashley to his home ground.

It had niggled at him all week that not once had Ashley questioned him in any practical sense about his life. A woman who was considering him as a husband surely would. It had seemed to him she was satisfied with collecting beautiful memories while Harry had progressed to absolute certainty about what he wanted.

It was possible that she saw a visit to Springfield Manor as a chance to fill a treasure chest of memories, but it was a step towards him, a step towards the future he could give her. Surely she would see that what he offered was entirely different from the life she had suffered with Roger. He couldn't lose now. No way. She wanted him. And they were great together. No doubt about that.

Ashley didn't look at him as he slid into the driver's seat and started the engine. She appeared deep in private thought. Not worrying, he hoped. He drove slowly, considering how best to make his next move.

'Do you always do what Mr. Fotheringham tells you to?' she asked.

It was a tricky question. Harry didn't want to lie to

her. Soon, very soon, he would have to lay out the truth, but that was better done in England when she was under his roof. He could more easily counter a negative reaction there. He chose his words with as much care as he had in explaining George's telephone call.

'We tend to come to an agreement, Ashley. I did tell you that George Fotheringham's family and mine have been connected for centuries. Since the Battle of Flodden in 1513. There is a line of respect kept by both sides and an affection and indulgence that comes from long familiarity.'

'A sense of belonging,' she murmured.

'Yes.'

'That must be…comforting.'

'You can share it, too, Ashley. You and William.'

She made no reply to that. She pointed ahead. 'There's the house. The one where people are out on the front balcony.'

The Rolls Royce was definitely on show, Harry thought with a flash of irony, but status symbols were totally irrelevant to what was on his mind. The driveway to the Stantons' double garage had been left clear, and he drove the Rolls into it for Ashley's convenience. He switched off the engine and turned to her, reaching over to take her right hand and hold it.

She looked at him, her eyes mirroring a fearful uncertainty, but she left her hand in his, perhaps needing the comfort of the contact. Without hesitation, Harry gave her one rock-solid certainty to hang onto.

'I want to marry you, Ashley. Will you think about that while you mix with your friends tonight?'

'Harry…' It was a breathless little gasp as though he'd punched the air out of her lungs. Her eyes widened wonderingly.

'Don't answer me now. I just want you to know,' he said with quiet seriousness. To imprint it firmly on her mind, he repeated, 'I want to marry you.'

CHAPTER TWELVE

THE NEXT FEW moments were a blur to Ashley. The trip to England, Harry's declaration on top of it followed by him playing the chauffeur, stepping out of the car to open her door for her and see her safely onto her feet... It was all happening too quickly for her. Now he was leaving her at this meaningless party to go home and play a war game with her son, and she didn't have wits enough to stop him, to say she didn't want him to go and leave her here alone.

She stood, stupidly speechless, watching him close her door and move to the driver's side, decisive in all his actions. He entered the Rolls, switched on the engine, reversed out of the driveway, and Ashley felt deserted in no-man's-land.

But, of course, she wasn't. People were watching. People were waiting. People who had made up her world before Harry had swept into it. It was probably a good idea to remind herself of what she was leaving behind before she left it to go to England with Harry, before she made decisions that would affect the rest of her life. And William's. She turned and walked up the steps.

'Ashley! You're looking marvellous!'

Olivia Stanton pounced the moment Ashley stepped onto the broad balcony that fronted the house and gave sweeping views of the sea. Her beady, black eyes were avid with curiosity. She was a tall, robust woman, overpowering in her manner. She grabbed Ashley's upper arms and bestowed a cheek-to-cheek greeting as though they were bosom friends.

'And your butler!' she said in Ashley's ear. 'What a prize! So gorgeous, and I'm sure very obliging.'

She'd had a good view of Harry as he'd helped Ashley out of the Rolls. Everyone here had undoubtedly cast an eye over Ashley's highly unusual acquisition. Olivia drew back and gave her a knowing smile.

'I've never seen you so glowing.'

He wants to marry me.

Ashley dragged her mind off the overwhelming thought and found an appropriate response. 'You look quite superb yourself, Olivia.' The flowing tunic and wide-leg pants in accordian pleat were of some expensive silky material, and its brilliant turquoise colour was clearly meant to outshine everyone else. 'That is certainly your colour.'

She laughed, preening. 'I adore bright colours. But, of course, you're still young enough to wear black and men do find it sexy. I daresay having a man like your Cliffton around the house must be quite exciting.'

'He does make a difference,' Ashley replied, letting Olivia interpret that any way she liked, not really caring what anyone thought. Somehow what had happened with Harry had made her feel quite apart from these people, as though they didn't count in her life any more.

He wants to marry me.

Olivia's husband came forward, pressing Ashley to take a glass of his especially concocted New Year punch from the tray he carried. He was a big man who'd been highly successful in real estate. He enjoyed showing off, and the exotic-looking punch with a piece of pineapple and a cherry attached to the rim of the glass had the same attention to detail as everything he did.

'Thank you, Geoff. I hope it doesn't have too much of a kick,' Ashley said, obliging her host.

He laughed merrily. 'What's life without a few kicks? I bet you enjoy riding around in that Rolls.'

'It's very comfortable.'

'A Silver Spirit, isn't it?'

'So William tells me.'

'Enterprising boy, your William,' Geoff Stanton said approvingly. He grinned. 'Must get it from his mother. Enterprising of you to take on a butler of such class, Ashley.'

'It's certainly been interesting.'

He boomed another big laugh, his eyes sweeping over her in male speculation, obviously seeing her in a totally different light than he had previously. Ashley wondered if his hormones were stirred. Did her new knowledge of herself really show, as Harry said, or was Geoff Stanton's imagination running riot?

It didn't matter. What she felt with Harry superseded everything else.

He wants to marry me.

She wanted to say yes, yet she also wanted to find out what lay ahead, what new turning points she might be faced with. It was good that she and William were going to England. She needed to see what life would be like at Springfield Manor.

'Ashley! Over here!'

It was Sonya Bixell, Rodney's mother, calling and beckoning her to join the group of people she had gathered around her at the other end of the balcony. Rodney's third uncle, a very muscular gym instructor, was prominently at her side.

Ashley excused herself from the Stantons' company and made her way to Sonya, smiling at the outré image she always affected. Her hair was dyed a deep burgundy and highlighted with wide blonde streaks. She wore a purple and green outfit and was bedecked with the arty costume jewellery she designed and made herself. Her penchant for taking and discarding lovers was put down to her artistic temperament, and she was such a bright spark, her company was always welcome.

'Darling! I'm a cocktail of admiration and envy.' Sonya waggled her eyebrows as no-one else could. 'What a move up in the world! A butler and a Roller! How did you do it?'

Ashley grinned. 'I didn't really do anything. They simply arrived. And I thought, why not?'

'Why not, indeed? A man like that doesn't happen very often. I'd have snapped him up, too.'

'Come on, Sonya,' the muscle man protested. 'Not in front of me, please.'

'Take heart, dear boy!' She patted his hand. 'I never poach on my friends.'

He gave Ashley a droll smile. 'Handcuff him to you, Ashley.'

'Uh-uh! Bad move,' Sonya advised. 'That would mean she was handcuffed, too. Keep your freedom, Ashley.'

'Not everyone is a free spirit like you, Sonya,' one of the other women said. 'I like being married.'

'Thank you, darling,' her husband purred.

All marriages weren't bad, Ashley thought.

'Well he is the father of your children,' Sonya conceded indulgently. 'Rodney's father left me holding the baby, and that experience was quite enough for me. Having more kids is not on my agenda.' She grinned at Ashley. 'I bet William's enough for you, too.'

She had thought so, but would she really mind if Harry wanted a child...children? If she married him.

'That boy of yours is something else,' Sonya went on, 'taking photos of his friends in the Rolls, then selling them at ten dollars a pop. Has he got your butler twisted around his finger?'

'I think Cliffton has his measure,' Ashley said slowly. She had the strong impression Harry was always one step ahead of both of them. Her wayward son wouldn't be able to get away with quite so much if Harry was her husband. From what William had let drop earlier this evening, some closer supervision was called for. What *was* the stuff she didn't know about?

The conversation flowed onto other topics. She half listened to the gay repartee, more observing the people than hearing what they said. Were they happy with their partners? Did economics and family ties keep them together or did they have a very real emotional commitment?

She couldn't go down Sonya's track. Not with Harry. Besides, she didn't have the temperament or inclination for a life of changing partners. All or nothing. Harry was right about that. Until he had swept into her life, *nothing* hadn't seemed so bad. Now... Well, she would make her decision in England.

Her gaze drifted to the huge living room beyond the glass doors that opened to the balcony. It displayed the very latest in modern furnishings, no expense spared, and display was definitely the key word. The Stantons' home was by far the most impressive in the neighbourhood, and Olivia took great pride in the sophisticated decor. Children were not allowed to play indoors, a matter of some disgust to William.

Ashley wondered what Springfield Manor was like. Such an old place was probably full of precious antiques. She hoped the grounds would be large enough to divert William from playing where he shouldn't. Ghost hunting could become a costly sport if he wasn't careful.

She was startled to see Gordon Payne amongst the guests in the living room, then realised it wasn't unlikely for him to be friends with Geoff Stanton. Building project homes and dealing in real estate went hand in hand. With all that had followed from the delivery of his two dozen white carnations, she had forgotten to send him a thank-you note. Much as she still disliked the man, Ashley decided it was diplomatic to acknowledge the gift.

She waited until she caught his eye then moved purposefully towards him. Surprisingly he detached himself from the group around him and moved to meet her, ensuring a private little chat.

'Mrs. Harcourt,' he greeted with dry formality. 'Quite the little show stopper tonight.'

Crass, Ashley thought, but she put on a polite smile. 'I wanted to thank you for the flowers. It was a generous gesture, Mr. Payne.'

He smirked. 'Pure politics, Mrs. Harcourt. That so-called butler of yours went to the minister of local government on your behalf and was creating trouble for me. Obviously I had to find means to protect myself.'

Alarm jangled through Ashley's brain. This odious man had something up his sleeve. 'What have you done now?'

'I have connections in London,' he boasted. 'I had them investigate your so-called butler and find out precisely who and what he is.'

'There's nothing sleazy about Harry Cliffton,' Ashley declared hotly, hating Gordon Payne's snide manner.

'No? Well, let me tell you—'

A loud commotion distracted both of them. Dylan Stanton came pelting into the living room, dripping blood from his nose and mouth and bawling for his mother and father. To Ashley's horror, William was at his heels, blood dripping from a cut over one eye, but totally undeterred by the wound. He grabbed Dylan's T-shirt and rained blows on his shoulders.

'Stand and fight, you snivelling coward!' he yelled.

'Boys! Boys!' Geoff Stanton shouted, plowing towards the fray as guests shrank from it.

'Oh, my God! They're bleeding on my carpet!' Olivia shrieked.

'He broke my nose, Dad,' Dylan cried.

'William!' Ashley gasped.

'I'll break more than that before I'm through with you, you little creep,' William snarled, grabbing his hair and putting a headlock on Dylan with his other arm. 'You take back what you said about my mother or I'll throttle you.'

'It's true!' Dylan croaked, his arms flailing in an effort to fight William off. An elaborate vase of flowers was knocked from a coffee table, crashing in a mess onto the floor.

'Dirty liar!' William muttered fiercely, unabashed by the chaos being wrought around them.

'Stop it, William!' Ashley commanded, pushing forward to try to pull him off the other boy.

'He said bad things about you, Mum. He's gotta take them back.'

'You young ruffian!' Geoff Stanton roared, reaching them first and tearing the two boys apart.

William stumbled, crashing into the coffee table.

Glasses of punch went flying onto a white leather couch, the sticky orange liquid splashing over the cushions and dripping onto the floor.

Olivia screeched. 'It's going to stain. They're ruining everything!'

'Someone get towels!' Geoff snapped.

Ashley reached William and helped him up, relieved to see that the cut near his eyebrow was more a slight split that an open gash. He would end up with a black eye, but of the two boys, he had sustained by far the less damage.

'There's not that much blood,' William said, eyeing the carpet judiciously. 'There would have been a lot more,' he declared without regret, 'if I could have held him down a bit longer.'

'Oh, William!' Ashley cried despairingly. 'How could you?'

'I did it because I love you, Mum.' He glared murder at Dylan, who was now cowering behind his father. 'He said you had the hots for Mr. Cliffton. He reckoned being a butler was just a fancy name for being like Rodney Bixell's uncle.'

'It's true!' Dylan jeered from the safety of his father's back.

'It is not. Let me at him, Mum,' William demanded in a fury, struggling to free himself from her hold.

'My mum saw them in a clinch through your living-room window late one night,' Dylan claimed triumphantly.

Ashley's heart sank. Dancing by candlelight. So much for discretion.

'Your mum couldn't see out of a paper bag,' William yelled.

'This is an absolute disgrace!' Olivia cried, seething

with outrage at the despoiling of her perfect house. 'Have you no control over your son, Ashley?'

'What was your son doing out at this time, repeating your tattle to William?' Ashley retaliated. While she didn't approve of fighting, her son had stood up for her. Loyalty deserved loyalty.

'He knocked out one of my teeth,' Dylan wailed.

'Yeah, and I've got it right here.' William pulled a bloody tooth out of the back pocket of his shorts and displayed his gruesome trophy with defiant pride. 'It's gonna cost you to get it back, too.'

Ashley went into shock.

Not so Olivia. 'You little savage! You should be sent to a reform school.' She looked around wildly. 'Someone call the police.'

No-one moved. No-one had gone to get towels to clean up the mess, either. No-one wanted to miss one second of this horror show. It was too deliciously fascinating to all the non-participants. Surreptitious glances flashed from neighbour to neighbour as they wondered what quality of moral direction was being given to their children with what was going on about them. Were they all above reproach?

'Now, Olivia, let's not overreact,' Geoff Stanton demurred. 'I'll take Dylan to casualty at Gosford Hospital straight away. We'll see an orthodontist.'

His wife was aquiver with rage. She pointed an accusing finger at William. 'He has assaulted and maimed our son, wrecked our living room—'

'I'll pay for all damages,' a calm voice interposed, and all heads turned towards it.

The crowd from the balcony parted for Harry to step into the limelight. As far as Ashley was concerned, it was a very timely entrance. She needed all the support she could muster. Her white knight had come to her rescue again, and her heart danced a tune of sweet relief.

A buzz went around the guests as Harry surveyed the scene with his usual charismatic panache, unruffled, assuming authority as though it was naturally his, handsome, debonair, a class act that focused every eye on him. He targeted Olivia first.

'Mrs. Stanton, I regret that I was unable to stop this little fracas. The boys were already fighting when I arrived at the Harcourt residence. On seeing me, your son ran off, with William in hot pursuit, both of them racing through the backyards of several houses, climbing over fences which I, with a recently injured leg, had to negotiate with restraint. Neither boy heeded my calls.'

'My son has a broken nose and a smashed mouth. He needed his mother,' Olivia said haughtily. 'He was simply coming home.'

'After he went to *my* home to stir *my* son,' Ashley pointed out, determined that William not be blamed for everything. 'People intent on causing trouble often get more than they bargain for.'

'How true!' Harry agreed, and blithely related one of his stories. 'It reminds me of the time when Cromwell sent his Roundheads to pillage the village near Springfield Manor. One of my ancestors, Richard by name, resented this intrusion upon his peaceful life. He organised an ambush that pillaged the Roundheads, separating them from their weapons, their clothes and their teeth. They were sent back to Cromwell with the message that he'd better find men with more bite.'

Stunned silence.

Harry gave Geoff Stanton a man-to-man smile. 'I'm sure you understand that an offensive act invites retaliation. Quite primitive, of course, but it is in all of us.'

Ashley suddenly realised that Harry was subtly showing his bite. He was not only defending William's action, but prepared to go to battle on her behalf. Her heart fluttered. Harry was a formidable slayer of dragons.

Geoff Stanton was obviously weighing his response to this challenge. He enjoyed showing off but he was not a stupid man.

Olivia exploded. 'How dare you walk in here and patronise us! What kind of butler ethics is this supposed to be? Just taking over as though—'

'He's an imposter, Olivia,' Gordon Payne inserted loudly. 'He is not a butler. He's never been a butler. And he's never likely to become one,' he added derisively, strolling forward to stand by Geoff Stanton and revel in the reaction to his startling disclosure.

'He is so, too,' William rebutted.

'For you, William,' Harry said quietly. His vivid blue eyes burned intensely into Ashley's. 'And for your mother.'

'A con man,' Sonya Bixell breathed. 'Oh, poor Ashley! He looks so good and sounds so good—'

'I knew it!' Olivia crowed. 'Why would a real butler come here? You've been suckered in, Ashley.'

'She has not!' William denied fiercely, flinging his arm protectively around Ashley's waist. 'My mum is the smartest woman in the world. Mr. Cliffton is real good to her. He—'

'Happens to be one of the richest men in England,' Gordon Payne drawled, enjoying the shock value of this new revelation. He warned his friend, 'And that's a lot of muscle, Geoff. To put it in a nutshell—Harold Alistair Cliffton, landed gentry, upper class, owner of an ancestral manor with attached farms and a village.'

It had to be a mistake, Ashley thought numbly. Yet

Harold Alistair Cliffton was the name on Harry's passport. How many Harold Alistair Clifftons were there in England? And Harry wasn't denying it. Harry wasn't laughing as though it was nonsense.

'The art gallery in his home is alone worth millions,' Gordon Payne went on. 'Cliffton has carried on the family tradition of being a highly enterprising financier, and his personal fortune is calculated in billions. A bit of a gambler, but his reputation is that of always being one step ahead of the market. They say he has the Midas touch.'

'I never deal in gold,' Harry said dryly.

Ashley could feel the blood draining from her face. It was no mistake. Harry wasn't the butler from Springfield Manor. He was the master. Master of so much her head whirled at the enormity of his possessions. His power.

He turned to her, his eyes blazing with compelling inner conviction. 'In fact the only gold I want is right here. And I will not have it tarnished in any way whatsoever.'

He swung to Olivia. 'Mrs. Stanton, I'd be obliged if you told your gathered guests what you did see that led to the scurrilous allegations you made in front of your son.'

Olivia went red. 'I won't let you bluff me, no matter who you are. You were holding Ashley in an embrace.'

'We were dancing. There is nothing reproachable in that, Mrs. Stanton.' Harry cast a slow, quizzical glance around the room. 'Is there anyone here who wishes to put some other interpretation upon two people enjoying a dance together?'

It was a mildly spoken question, but simmering behind it was a sword, ready to cut off any head that presented itself. Ashley didn't think anyone was in doubt about that. Despite his air of languid elegance Harry emitted a power that was all the more mesmerising for being understated.

Not a word was so much as murmured.

Ashley noticed that Sonya Bixell looked absolutely entranced. She had a preference for the muscular type, and Harry was displaying a new dimension of muscle that clearly fascinated her.

'Perhaps I should mention that if an action lies for defamation, I'm prepared to exchange the names of our legal advisers,' he went on smoothly, turning to Olivia. 'You have nothing more to say, Mrs. Stanton?'

Geoff Stanton forestalled any reply from his wife. 'I don't believe Ashley would do anything to, uh, compromise her, uh, spotless reputation.'

Harry bestowed another smile on him. 'Thank you. Mr. Payne omitted to relay that I also have a reputation for righting wrongs. I wouldn't want that overlooked.'

He paused to let it sink in, then swung to Ashley and held out his hand to her. 'The car is waiting outside. Are you ready to leave now?'

'Yes,' she said huskily.

She put her arm around William's shoulders, hugging him close to her, not only to inhibit any further outbursts or mayhem from her son as they walked across the room to Harry, but also needing to hang onto the one known constant in her life. Whoever Harry was, whatever he was, he was providing the quickest avenue of escape from this dreadful scene, and she was not about to delay that, no matter how confused she felt over his real identity.

He took her hand in his, warm, strong, comforting. 'Good night to you all,' he said pleasantly.

'You'll pay for this,' Olivia shot at him. She had been upstaged and forced to swallow a public reprimand while seeing her son and husband beaten into submission. The humiliation of it all was a dreadful blow to her self-blown authority.

'I would pay anything for Ashley and William, Mrs. Stanton,' Harry replied. 'Do enjoy the rest of your party.'

Even in her fury she recognised that Harry couldn't be touched. She turned her venom on Ashley. 'Don't think I'm going to forget this. You'll pay, too. And this wretched boy of yours.'

Ashley's chin came up in defiant pride. 'Then you'll need a long arm, Olivia. William and I are going to England with Harry.' She paused, then tossed off the perfect exit line. 'He wants to marry me.'

CHAPTER THIRTEEN

THE ROLLS WAS once more parked in the Stantons' driveway. To Ashley's intense relief, they reached it without further incident, Harry seeing her into the front passenger seat while William scrambled into the back. Harry had them on their way home in a matter of seconds.

As soon as the Stantons' house was behind them, William could repress himself no longer. 'Have you really got billions, Mr. Cliffton?' he asked in a tone of awe.

Clearly, the offense he had taken at Dylan's slurs on his mother had been superseded by the vista of a fortune that even his enterprising mind found beyond his imagination. Ashley empathised with his sense of disbelief, but she could not condone such point-blank curiosity about someone else's private affairs.

'William, you mustn't ask personal questions like that. It's bad manners.'

He sighed. 'Sorry, Mr. Cliffton.'

Harry sighed, too. 'Wealth isn't everything, William. It sometimes gets in the way of more important things. Like people seeing you as a person who has the same needs and feelings as themselves. And the same sense of loneliness and isolation.'

It was true, Ashley realised. One never really thought of wealthy people being vulnerable to anything but their own excesses. Yet when Harry had revealed how much Pen had meant to him, how much he missed her, how empty his life had become, Ashley had listened with heartfelt sympathy, never doubting the depth of his feeling.

As though Harry was tuned in on her thoughts, he softly added, 'All the wealth in the world doesn't have the power of commanding life and death in those whom you love.'

Ashley caught her breath at the underlying pain in those sad words. Was Pen truly in the past for him? He had seemed really happy this week, but he hadn't said he loved her. Did he want to marry her because he had found in her and William some kind of panacea for his loneliness?

'Mum and I see you as a person,' William claimed, having digested the sense of Harry's remarks. 'Is that why you pretended to be a butler with us?'

'Partly,' he answered.

He glanced at Ashley. She could feel his eyes raking her profile, feel his concern about what she was thinking, but she wasn't ready to make any comment yet. Not in front of William. She stared steadily ahead, trying to calm the turmoil inside her. There was a lot to deal with.

'Mostly it was to persuade your mother to let me stay with you,' he added quietly.

Even if he had to camp in a tent in her backyard, Ashley remembered. His desire to stay could not be doubted.

'Because you wanted to get to know us?' William inquired further, working through the situation with commendable logic.

'Yes.'

Ashley wondered if she had been hopelessly gullible in swallowing his butler masquerade. She had wanted to believe it because Harry...was Harry. The desire to keep him with her had been very strong.

His reluctance to reveal his wealth and position was understandable. She had been prickly enough about Springfield Manor and the style of life it entailed. How she would have resented his true situation, assuming he had come to lord it over her and William! She would have shown him to the door in a fury of pride and fierce independence. And she would have missed out on all that had followed.

'Mum, is it true that Mr. Cliffton wants to marry you?' William asked, unusually cautious in putting the question.

'He said so,' Ashley replied, feeling wary herself about being too definite on anything to do with Harold Alistair Cliffton.

'Is it true, Mr. Cliffton? You want to marry Mum?'

'Yes, I most certainly do.' Nothing hesitant about that.

There was the audible release of a long breath from the back seat. Then, on a patently hopeful note, came the question, 'Have you said yes, Mum?'

'It's not a decision I want to rush into, William,' Ashley answered curtly. When it came to turning points in one's life, becoming the wife of a billionaire from the English landed gentry was like having the whole world swing on its axis.

'But, Mum, all you have to do is say yes. Just say yes! Please say yes!' William was off the back seat and hanging between the two front ones, urging her consent. 'Please, Mum, it would be so good for us. You wouldn't have to ever work again or worry about how much things cost. And you'd be free to—'

'Please sit down, William!' she said sharply, hating his reference to money.

He ignored her, all pumped up to fight for what he wanted. 'Look how great it's been this week, like being a real family, and you not stuck in the office all day—'

'William, your mother told you to sit down,' Harry cut in with quiet but firm authority. 'I think you've said enough for now.'

For once in William's life, discretion was the better part of valour. He sighed and retreated, although he had made clear which way his vote had been cast. There could be no conflict about William's future, Ashley thought with considerable irony. It was a tribute to the respect Harry had earned from William that the obedient silence from the back seat was maintained until they arrived home.

'Straight upstairs to the bathroom, William,' Ashley ordered as they entered the house. 'That cut needs to be cleaned and attended to.'

'Would you like me to do it, Ashley?' Harry asked.

'I'm used to it,' she said dryly. 'A pot of coffee wouldn't go astray. I'll be down as soon as I've seen William to bed.'

'Bed!' It was a squawk of protest. 'What about our war game?'

'The war games are over for the night,' Ashley declared very firmly.

'But I didn't do anything wrong, Mum. Dylan Stanton deserved what he got.'

'I want some private time with Harry, William.'

'Oh! All right then.'

Apparently he was prepared to keep the peace for what he hoped was the greater good. He didn't even attempt any further persuasion on the marriage question. Like a docile lamb he suffered Ashley's ministrations in the bathroom, standing still as she cleaned away the blood, then applied antiseptic cream and a butterfly closure to the cut. He swallowed two pain-killing tablets, changed into his pyjamas and settled himself in bed without any protest.

The eyelid below the cut was quite puffy and beginning to discolour. Ashley felt a fierce rush of maternal love as she bent to kiss her wounded warrior son good night. He had fought for her against the scuttlebut and gossip amongst her neighbours. She wondered how bad it had been. What wasn't known had probably been invented. She hoped they felt ashamed of themselves.

Perhaps William's fight tonight had put an end to it. If not, Harry's threats of legal redress would certainly have them thinking twice before opening their mouths again. She smiled. Her two protectors, both of them using the power at their disposal on her behalf. While she still felt confused about Harry's motives, she knew her son's were absolutely pure.

She dropped another kiss on his forehead. 'Good night, William.'

'I love you, Mum. I want what's best for you,' he pleaded softly.

'I know.' She gently stroked his hair. 'I love you, too. When we go to England…then we'll know what's best. Go to sleep now.'

She was committed that far. Maybe she was committed all the way. But there were some things she had to find out first, and she needed the truth now, the absolute truth.

Harry was in the kitchen. He poured two cups of coffee and set them on the counter as she came downstairs, waiting until she reached the family room before looking at her. His face was grave, tense. His eyes had the

intensity of lasers, searching hers for some hint of what
she was feeling.

'Should I start with an apology?' he asked.

Her legs felt like water, but she walked steadily to the
kitchen counter and drew out one of the stools to sit facing him. She settled on it and pulled her coffee closer
before speaking.

'Are you sorry for anything?' she asked with credit-
able calm.

'No. I'd do it all again to have what we've shared this
week.'

Well, that was ruthlessly honest, Ashley thought. She
lifted her gaze to his, determined on knowing all she
needed to know. 'What about your stated mission? Is all
of that true?'

'Yes. Except I was the one who wanted to meet you.
George Fotheringham is my butler at Springfield Manor.'

Ashley took a deep breath. This was a big question.
'Can't you have children, Harry?'

He looked startled, then somewhat bemused. 'I've always assumed I can. There's no reason I know of to think
I can't. Why do you think otherwise?'

'Why come for William?'

He gave her a rueful smile. 'Because George was nagging me. Since Pen died I hadn't formed any suitable
alliance for the purpose of procreation, and he was disturbed that the family line might come to an end. That
would leave his family unprovided for.'

'So we were the means of letting you get on with your
life without any further nagging from George.'

He shook his head. 'It was more a case of getting on
with my death until I met you, Ashley. That was what
was really worrying George. When I broke my leg in a
skiing accident, he instigated the search for an heir. He

handed me William in an attempt to blackmail me into conducting my life sensibly.'

She had to smile. 'He doesn't know you very well, does he?'

Harry's responding smile was more a wry twist. 'He does, actually. His need for me to do my duty blinded him to the possibility that I might embrace the Australian connection.'

'Then he's not too happy about us.'

'He will be. If you'll marry me, Ashley,' he said seriously, his eyes blazing with his desire for that outcome.

'And have your children?' she asked, wondering if this was the crux of everything.

The challenge, the uncertainty in her eyes made him pause. Very gently he asked, 'Is that the problem? If you can't have any more children, Ashley, please don't think it's an impediment to our marriage. We can have so much together. More than I ever hoped was possible for me. I hope that's true for you, too.'

'Oh, Harry!' She could barely speak over the choking lump in her throat. Tears blurred her vision. The knots in her stomach started unravelling. He wanted to marry her simply for her, for them to have each other. Maybe she wasn't as perfect as Pen had been for him, but she had given him a reason for living. And he was so good to her!

She barely saw him coming before she was swept off the stool and into his embrace, his arms wrapping her tightly to him. 'Ashley, my love,' he murmured tenderly. 'Can't you feel how much I want you?'

My love?

'I can have children, Harry,' she blurted out. 'But you didn't once ask me about protection.'

His chest heaved and fell, his breath feathering her ear. 'I wanted whatever you wanted, and in the end it had to be your choice. Any man who's as much in love with you as I am would want to share his child with you. That's natural and normal.'

'You decided so soon?' she asked incredulously, lifting her head to see his expression.

A whimsical little smile curved his mouth. His eyes softly pleaded for her understanding. 'Ashley, when you've been in a desert, you know when you've struck an oasis. And you don't want to leave it. Ever. You want to drink from it as deeply as possible. But if you don't want another child…'

'I didn't say that,' she quickly demurred. 'I wanted to be sure I would be more to you than the mother of your heirs.'

'The only mother I want for my heirs is a woman I love, Ashley. The loving comes first. And if children are born of that love, well and good. If not, we still have William. I'll adopt him.' He suddenly grinned. 'That boy needs a father.'

She laughed, joy bubbling up to dissipate the last little shadows of doubt. 'Do you think you're up to the challenge?'

'I must confess I could never resist a challenge. Will you take the chance and marry me?'

'I don't know what's expected of a billionaire's wife, let alone—'

'There are only two requirements.'

'What are they?'

'Love me.'

How could she not love him? He gave her everything she had ever dreamed of in a partner for life. 'And the other?' she asked.

'Let me love you. No restrictions. No restraints. Let me shower you with all the love I want to express in all the ways I can think of, because we only live once, Ashley, and we must make the most of every moment while we can.'

'Yes,' she agreed, knowing he was thinking of Pen, but it didn't matter because he was thinking of her, too, and the love he had in his heart for her was the present and the future.

'Is that the yes I want to hear?'

'Yes,' she said with a commitment she carried to his lips.

It was a kiss that released all the tension of the evening and replaced it with a wondrous welling of emotion, flowing from one to the other with every touch, every breath, every beat of their hearts. The ultimate two-way street, Ashley thought, and knew she would give Harry however many children he wanted, because deep down in the roots of his being, his ancestry and the long-held heritage at Springfield Manor meant a lot to him.

Happy and confident that everything was settled to their mutual satisfaction, Ashley decided that Harry could do with a bit of chiding for his lengthy masquerade. 'And just when were you going to tell me the truth about yourself, Harold Alistair Cliffton?'

'On my home ground.' He grinned. 'I always play the advantage.'

'You thought Springfield Manor would sway me?'

'No. It simply kept the ball rolling my way until you were ready to acknowledge you didn't want a life without me.'

'Well, it should be interesting to meet George,' she mused.

'Why?'

'Because he started it all, didn't he? We wouldn't have

met except for George. One could say it's a classic case of the butler did it.'

'I think it was I, pretending to be the butler, who did it,' Harry said, cocking one eyebrow in wicked humour.

Ashley laughed and wound her arms around his neck, swaying against him teasingly. 'Let's see if you can do it again.'

'What a splendid idea! I think I'll start with this little bow at your waist…'

'Wait!'

'You have some better idea?'

'No, but after the stands you and William took tonight, we should pull down the blinds.'

CHAPTER FOURTEEN

GEORGE FOTHERINGHAM WAS exceedingly pleased with himself. It had been his initiative that had inspired Master Harry to go off on such a fortuitous venture. Producing the Black Sheep with the Australian heir had, indeed, been a master card. Although one could not underestimate the drawing power of the accompanying photographs.

George had them on the table in front of him, trophies, one might say, of his astute judgement. Miss Ashley was a fine-looking woman—intelligence in her eyes, character in her face—and her feminine qualities were more than presentable. As a wife for Master Harry, George had no doubt she would do him credit. And the boy was proof that she was fertile. Such a relief to be sure of that. Poor Miss Pen... But thankfully that was in the past now.

Springfield Manor was going to be a happy place again. The whole staff had brightened up with the prospect of Master Harry bringing home a fiancée. And the boy. A child did liven up a home. George nodded approvingly at the photograph of William. He looked a bright young spark. George fancied he discerned a family likeness there, a certain set about the eyes. Amazing how genes could pop up generations down the line.

Mischief and mayhem.

George frowned. Now why had those words slid into his mind? Master Harry was about to embrace marriage and fatherhood, both of which had a sobering influence on any man. Unseemly antics were definitely at an end. Life at Springfield Manor was about to enter a new, productive cycle.

The telephone rang. George had been waiting for the call. He felt his heart lift in anticipation as he picked up the receiver. It was the expected message.

Cook and Mrs. Fotheringham were conferring in the kitchen, and several maids were standing by for further orders when George emerged from the private sanctum of the butler's pantry. He clapped his hands to gain the appropriate respectful attention, then made his announcement.

'Ten minutes, everyone. Spread the word. Ten minutes. And mind that you're all tidy.'

Ashley thought she was prepared for it. Twenty-six acres of gardens and parkland, Harry had told her. He didn't know how many rooms there were in Springfield Manor—George or his wife, the housekeeper, could undoubtedly tell her—but only part of it dated back to the thirteenth century. It had been added to by various ancestors. One of its features was a domed tower by Christopher Wren. The whole of the inside had been thoroughly modernised by Harry's parents, who had drowned in a ferry disaster in the North Sea.

The manor was set in a wooded valley of the Southern Cotswolds, and there was trout fishing in the river. A heated swimming pool and an all-weather tennis court provided other outdoor leisure activities. Inside, a well-stocked library, a billiards room and a solarium were places of interest to guests. William would like the minstrel gallery, where quite a few ghosts had appeared over the years.

George would be able to tell her how many staff were employed. It was George's responsibility to see to maintenance and the efficient running of the household. For all practical purposes, George ruled the manor, and he was excessively proud of it.

Ashley took a deep breath as the Rolls turned through a massive stone gateway. This was what Roger and his mother had wanted but didn't know how to achieve, coming back home to England. She wondered if they somehow knew that William, unbeknownst to him, was achieving their ambition, about to receive all the benefits that had been lost so many generations ago. Although Ashley would make sure it didn't go to his head!

The two-hour trip from London had flown by, and Springfield Manor now lay straight ahead of them. It was a mind-boggling sight, huge, like three or four mansions joined together. Apart from the domed tower, most of it was two storeys high, plus the attic area under the steep roofs from which rose a forest of chimneys. The spacious lawns leading up to it were as smooth as bowling greens, and behind it was woodland with immense, majestic trees that must have been growing since King Arthur was a boy.

In front of the manor a long line of people stretched out from what was clearly the main entrance. 'Uh-oh!' Harry sighed. 'George has decided this is an occasion. Consider yourself welcomed and honoured, Ashley. You're to be greeted by everyone on the staff. At least, all those who are readily available.'

'I count twenty-seven,' William said helpfully. He had always been good at numbers.

'What do I say to them?' Ashley asked, nervous at

the prospect of meeting so many people at once, people who would be eyeing her in the context of future mistress of the manor.

Harry smiled at her. 'Don't worry. They're predisposed to think you're the best thing that could happen to them. George will lead you down the receiving line and make the introductions. Smile, say hello, repeat their names and answer any remark made with something friendly. You've probably done it thousands of times when meeting prospective clients. It isn't any different.'

His confidence boosted hers. All the same, she was very glad they had stopped over in London for a few days to shop for suitable clothes for the English winter, even more glad that Harry had insisted on buying them for her, steering her straight into designer outfits.

Her burgundy-coloured overcoat was elegantly tailored, and Ashley adored the matching suede boots and the perky hat with its smartly curved brim. For the hat to sit properly she had to wear her hair down, which Harry preferred anyway. She glanced at the dazzling diamond on the third finger of her left hand and decided to leave both gloves off. The fabulous engagement ring Harry had given her definitely reinforced her position as his future wife.

She gave her son a quick check before the Rolls came to a halt. William looked astonishingly smart in a double-breasted navy overcoat, white shirt and tie and long trousers. It was cold enough for him not to demur at wearing such unaccustomed clothes. Besides, Harry was similarly attired, and Harry could do no wrong in William's eyes. Not in the present propitious circumstances.

The chauffeur opened the door for Harry, who then helped Ashley out of the car. William followed under his own steam. A buzz of excitement ran down the greeting line at first sight of them.

A most impressive figure of a man stepped forward from the head of it. He was taller than Harry, broad-shouldered, barrel-chested, black-suited and enormously dignified. He looked to be in his fifties, although his benign face was relatively unwrinkled. Beneath the iron-grey eyebrows that matched his iron-grey hair, a pair of bright brown eyes bestowed approval.

'Welcome home, Master Harry,' he intoned, as though it was a highly portentous occasion.

Harry gripped his hand. 'Well done, George,' he replied with a tinge of amusement. 'May I present Ashley Harcourt, my fiancée, and her son, William. Our butler, George Fotheringham.'

'I'm delighted to meet you, George,' Ashley said, offering her best smile and her hand, which was quickly and warmly enveloped.

'Your coming is a pleasure that has been much looked forward to, Miss Ashley. We at Springfield Manor will do all we can to make you feel comfortable and at home.'

'That's very kind.'

'And your son, too, of course. How do you do, young William?'

'I'm fine, sir,' William replied, shaking hands without so much as batting an eyelash. Ashley was proud of his good manners until he piped up with, 'How many ghosts have you seen in the minstrel gallery, Mr. Fotheringham?'

'Not now, William,' she reproved.

The butler raised his eyebrows at Harry.

'Runs in the family, George,' he answered. 'It didn't die out on the other side of the world. No rest for you, I'm afraid.'

'What didn't die out?' Ashley asked, bewildered by the understanding the two men obviously shared.

George looked at her with rueful resignation. 'Mischief and mayhem, Miss Ashley. It has been the lot of the Fotheringhams down through the centuries, since the Battle of Flodden in 1513, to rescue Master Harry's family line from the mischief and mayhem they have invariably indulged in and brought upon themselves. If Henry Cliffton hadn't stirred up the Scottish pikemen with insults about what was under their kilts…' He sighed. 'So it has always been, Miss Ashley.'

'Look at it this way, George,' Harry blithely invited. 'It's another challenge for you. You'll be in good training by the time Ashley and I produce the patter of little feet.'

'Master Harry,' said George very dryly, 'I cannot recall ever being *out* of training.' He waved to the waiting line. 'Shall we proceed, sir?'

Ashley was introduced to George's wife, Alice, the head housekeeper, who organised and supervised all the cleaning, the meals and whatever services family and guests required. Then came innumerable maids, valets, footmen, the head gardener, the under-gardener and so on. Ashley committed as many names as she could to memory and hoped that the staff's obvious goodwill towards her would stretch into good-natured patience when she made mistakes.

In the next few hours, Ashley was introduced to the style of life at Springfield Manor. It was luxury to a standard she could not have imagined. Gordon Payne's appraisal of the private art collection was probably a modest one, and she had certainly been right about antiques. Everywhere she looked, they graced rooms and hallways alike.

The furnishings were nothing short of fabulous, satins and silks and velvets and brocades. There were huge marble fireplaces, oak panelling, painted ceilings, wonderful Persian carpets. She was dazed by a multitude of splendours.

A maid was assigned to take care of her personal needs. Her luggage was unpacked for her. Lancombe toiletries were provided in an ensuite bathroom that even contained a spa bath.

George presided over the serving of a gourmet lunch and an exquisite afternoon tea. The latter was lingered over in a wonderful sitting room in front of a huge log fire. Floor-to-ceiling windows looked out over a rose garden hedged by ornamental shrubs. Darkness gradually shrouded the view, the winter night falling quite early.

Ashley went up to her bedroom to have a rest and change before dinner. She stripped off her arrival clothes, enjoyed a long spa bath, then, leaving only a dim table lamp on, she stretched out on the luxurious four-poster bed to relax for a while and adjust herself to becoming used to the riches around her. It seemed incredible that this was going to be her life from now on.

She wondered if William could be dissuaded from staying up all night in the minstrel gallery. It was unlikely, with Harry and George aiding and abetting him and the whole staff adopting a light-hearted approach to the coming adventure.

A movement caught her eye. She turned her head in time to see a figure materialising through the heavily carved door that led into her bedroom. She blinked in sheer disbelief. But her eyes weren't playing tricks with her.

The insubstantial figure quickly took on more solid form, a woman, a young woman dressed in a long button-through skirt, blouse and cardigan, all of them oddly colourless. She was painfully thin yet her face, framed by short soft wavy hair, had an ethereal beauty, and her eyes seemed to glow as though lit by some otherworldly vision.

Slowly and warily, Ashley pushed herself into a sitting position, hardly daring to accept that a ghost had appeared in front of her. But what else could the woman be? And Harry had said there were ghosts at Springfield Manor.

The woman smiled at her. And spoke. 'I'm sorry if I gave you a fright. I should have knocked. But one gets so used to walking through walls and doors. Indeed, I wouldn't know how to tap on your door even if I wanted to.'

Ashley wished William was here to see this.

'Your William is in the kitchen,' the ghost said with a tinkling laugh. 'I've been down there listening to the gossip about you. I wish I could have been at Olivia Stanton's party. It must have been a wonderful scene.'

'William's telling them about that?'

'He kept Dylan Stanton's tooth and he produced it with the air of a master magician playing his ultimate trick.'

'Oh, no! He couldn't!'

'Don't worry. Everyone loved it. I think another legend has been born, with both William and Harry as the heroes.'

She could be right about that, Ashley thought. After all, it couldn't be much more outrageous than some of the other legends she'd heard about the family.

'Besides,' the ghost went on, 'they're dying to hear all about your romance with Harry, and William is earning favours with every tale he tells. There's no harm being done, believe me.'

Ashley released a shaky breath. She didn't know

ghosts could read minds, too. It was disconcerting, to
say the least. 'Who are you?' she asked.

'Penelope. Harry told you about me in great detail.'

'Yes. Yes, he did. I'm so sorry…'

'It wasn't to be,' she said sadly.

'Have you…' Ashley swallowed hard. 'Have you appeared to Harry?'

'No. That would have made things worse for him. I
desperately wanted him to meet someone like you whom
he could love as deeply as he's capable of loving.'

'You don't mind?'

'I'm happy for you both. Very happy. I've been waiting all this time for it to happen. It's a great relief to me
now that it has.' Her smile was strangely luminous. 'And
the baby makes it perfect.'

'What baby?'

'You're pregnant, Ashley. If you want to check it out,
I can recommend a local medical practitioner, Dr. Jekyll.
He lives in the village in Mr. Hyde's cottage. He was so
good to me during my illness. He'll take every care with
both of you.'

Ashley shook her head in bemusement. She let the
Jekyll-Hyde connection float over her head. Nothing
about Springfield Manor and its environs was going to
surprise her any more. She honed in on the important
point. If she was pregnant, it must have happened when
she and Harry had first made love together.

Penelope nodded. 'Yes. I'll leave you now. I just
wanted to meet you and satisfy my curiosity. And assure you there's nothing to fear from Harry's memories
of me. They no longer have the power to hurt. Love has
no boundaries. Love holds no restrictions, only those
self-imposed by people. Harry loves you. Never doubt
it, Ashley. He loves you.'

'You don't resent that I'm going to have all the happiness that was once rightfully yours?' Ashley asked.

Penelope's smile held no reservations. 'In my condition strange things happen. I will have that happiness in ways you cannot possibly understand.'

'You don't mind my being pregnant?'

'The bringing of life to Springfield Manor is the greatest joy of all.'

The sincerity in her voice convinced Ashley that this was rightly so. 'You're so unforgettably beautiful,' she couldn't help saying.

'So are you. Don't be alarmed. I can assure you through means that I cannot reveal that I will not interfere with your future happiness. In fact, in this part of the universe it works quite the opposite way. If you ever need help or someone to talk to, I'll come to you, Ashley. I want us to be friends.'

'Yes.' Ashley was not about to disagree with that.

'It's very simple really,' Pen explained. 'My love for Harry now joins yours.'

Ashley didn't see her dematerialise. She was there. Then she had passed through the solid oak door and was gone. Ashley wondered if she'd dreamt the visitation, but how could she have when she was sitting up in bed wide awake? She pinched herself to make sure. It hurt. Either she was having hallucinations or it had actually happened. Well, there was one way of finding out.

Ashley dressed as quickly as she could. She left her bedroom and went to Harry's. He was sliding his arms into a gorgeous teal blue jacket as she entered. He grinned at her, his eyes dancing wickedly. 'You beat me to a visit.'

She dithered. Should she let sleeping dogs lie?

The twinkle faded as he frowned. 'Is something wrong, Ashley?'

There could be no harm in it. Penelope had told her so. If ghosts could be believed. Besides, ghosts needed to be laid to rest, as well. 'Do you have a photograph of your Pen, Harry?'

'Yes.'

'May I see it?'

The frown deepened. 'Ashley...'

'Please?'

He shrugged off his concern. 'If you wish.' He went to a bureau drawer and drew out a framed photograph. 'This was taken towards the end. Pen was very thin by then.'

Ashley took one look and knew she hadn't hallucinated. 'Yes,' she said. 'That's her.' The same beautiful face and soft wavy hair. Even the same clothes, although they were coloured in the photograph.

'Mum! Mum! Where are you?' The call from William was loud, breathless and excited.

She quickly handed the photograph to Harry and hurried to the wide corridor that ran the length of this bedroom wing. 'I'm here, William.'

He came pelting out of her bedroom. 'Mum! Guess what? I saw a ghost. And I wasn't even hunting for one.'

'Where?' she asked sharply.

'Downstairs. I was having a look at all the old stuff in the great hall and I saw her zap straight through the doors into the sitting room.'

'Her? A woman with short, wavy hair?'

'Yes. But she was definitely a ghost, Mum. The doors were closed. I chased after her but when I went into the sitting room, no-one was there.'

'Are you sure?'

'No kidding, Mum. It was a ghost. I'm going to find Mr. Fotheringham. He might know who she is.'

He was off again just as Harry joined her outside his bedroom. 'What was that all about?'

'A ghost in the sitting room.' She flashed a look of entreaty at Harry. She wanted his belief. 'It was Pen, Harry. She's saying goodbye. She came to me about half an hour ago.'

He searched her eyes for several tense moments, then accepted her statement without equivocation. 'Let's go down to the sitting room. She liked lying on the chaise longue by the windows, watching the roses bloom and the daffodils in flower on the lawn. Nature's sunlight. She loved the sunlight. She always brought light wherever she was.'

That was where they found her, right at the far end of the room in a soft glow of light. She rose from the chaise longue and turned to them both, more ghostly than before.

'It's all right, Harry,' she softly soothed. 'I'm not here to haunt you. I never wanted to.'

'Why now, Pen? Why didn't you allow me to see you sooner?' he asked gruffly.

'I wanted you to let go, Harry. You had so much more of life to live. Your grief kept me here,' she said sadly, then slowly a smile grew, glowing with the most incandescent benevolence. 'Your happiness…your love for Ashley and hers for you…releases me from the chains of your grief. My soul is now free to soar. I wish you and Ashley every happiness in the world. Don't waste it. Never waste it.'

She began to fade.

'Pen…' Harry reached out to her.

'It's loving that's life, Harry. Loving…' It was barely a wisp of sound, a wisp that shimmered for a moment, then disappeared.

The ensuing silence was fraught with swirling emotions.

'Loving,' Harry murmured at last, and slowly drew Ashley into his embrace. 'We must never let anything get in the way of loving, Ashley.'

'No. We never will, Harry. Pen told me something else, too.'

'What?'

'She advised me to see Dr. Jekyll in the village.'

'There's nothing wrong, is there?' he asked anxiously.

'No. Something very right. Pen said I was pregnant, Harry. I'm only two days overdue. I can't be certain. But Pen was quite definite that we'd made a baby.'

He smiled. The smile grew into a grin, then a chuckle, then a burst of happy laughter. 'I hope you're pleased, my love, because I can't help feeling I'm the luckiest man on earth.'

'And I'm the luckiest woman,' Ashley said fervently.

A long way away, their kiss was sensed, a pure bonding of souls, an explosion of joy and love, and the being who had been known as Penelope was content.

The thought came to Ashley that for all the years she and Harry lived at Springfield Manor, a vase of roses or daffodils would be placed beside the chaise longue in the sitting room.

There was a knock on the door. William rushed in, followed more sedately by George. 'Any ghosts in here, Master Harry?' George inquired.

'Not at the moment, George.' He smiled at William. 'It will have to be the minstrel gallery tonight. Eric the Red might pay us a visit if we're lucky.'

'Indeed, yes.' George tactfully gathered William under his wing. 'Come. I shall show you the fireplace where

Eric the Red split the mantel with his axe. Quite an exciting ghost, Eric.'

'Before you leave us, George...'

'Yes, Master Harry?'

'The bottle of 1860 Madeira we discussed before my trip to Australia. I think you've earned it, George.'

'How gracious of you, Master Harry!'

'And tell your good wife that a June wedding date is out. We'll be having the wedding much sooner. As soon as it can be suitably arranged, in fact.'

'I shall certainly drink to that, Master Harry.'

A self-satisfied smile played on George's lips as he ushered William out of the sitting room to give the happy couple some private time together. A duty well done, he thought.

Then, with intense pride, he added... And, of course, the butler did it.

The *Times*
Personal Column
Births

Cliffton—On 14 October to Ashley and Harold, a fine son, Edward John, at 8:10 p.m., and a beautiful daughter, Emily Louise, at 8:20 p.m. A brother and sister for William.

* * * * *

A MARRIAGE BETRAYED

This book is dedicated to Sachiko Ueno, who came from Japan to meet me and whose all-time favourite book is *The Wrong Mirror*

CHAPTER ONE

IN EVERY life there are turning points, some brought about by conscious choices, others caused by sheer accident. When Kristy Holloway broke her trip from London to Geneva for a one-night stopover in Paris, she had no idea that Fate was about to deliver a major turning point from which there would be no going back. Ever.

The stopover was not a considered decision, nor part of a deliberate plan. Kristy acted on impulse, a sentimental impulse. A nostalgic tribute to Betty and John, she told herself, easing the guilt of going to Geneva to do what she would never have done while her adoptive parents were alive.

They were both gone now, beyond any sense of hurt or betrayal, and their love remained in her heart, swelling into a prickling of tears as she stepped out of the taxi and stared up at the stately façade of the Hotel Soleil Levant.

The Renaissance architecture was very impressive, as befitted one of the most prestigious hotels in Paris with its privileged position between the Avenue des Champs-Elysées and the Tuileries. Even the lowliest room available in such a place as this would undoubtedly make a significant hole in her carefully calculated finances, but Kristy brushed aside any concern over cost. A remembrance of two people she had dearly loved was more important than money.

Over forty years ago, Betty and John Holloway had spent their three-day honeymoon in the Soleil Levant. The once-in-a-lifetime extravagance had formed a romantic memory which Betty had related to Kristy many times. The stories had been poignantly recalled when she had come across the old postcard in John's effects, a snippet of memorabilia he'd cherished.

Laying the past to rest...that was what this stopover in Paris and her trip to Geneva was all about. A last treasured memory of the people who had brought her up as their daughter, then her quest to find out, once and for all, if there were any records of her real family at the Red Cross Headquarters in Geneva.

She had been letting herself drift since John's death, feeling without purpose or purposefulness. It was time to take control, do something positive, settle the restlessness inside her, the yearning she couldn't quite identify. The future stretched ahead but she couldn't put any shape to it. Not yet.

It would always be possible to pick up her nursing career again, somewhere down the track. She didn't want to go back to it right now. The long time spent helping John fight his losing battle with cancer had been a deep, emotional drain on her. She felt she had nothing left to give in that area, not for a while, anyway.

As for a man in her life...no prospects there since Trevor had given up on her, frustrated by her commitment to John's well-being. Too many broken dates to sustain a relationship. Not that Trevor had been the love of her life. She didn't know precisely what that felt like, only that her experience with men hadn't produced it.

She had regretted losing Trevor's pleasant companionship but in the face of John's illness, on top of the grief over Betty's death…choice hadn't really entered into it. She'd owed her adoptive parents too much to even think of not giving John all the support and solace she could.

So here she was, twenty-eight years old, no family, no partner, career on hold, nothing important or solid enough to hang her life on.

The hotel in front of her was certainly solid, she thought with ironic humour. Sighing away her reflections, she crossed the sidewalk towards the entrance doors and encountered the first unnerving little incident that made her wonder if the stopover impulse had been foolish.

The doorman finished chatting to a stylish couple emerging from the hotel and caught sight of her approach. The benevolent expression on his face changed so abruptly, Kristy's feet faltered. A sharp scrutiny slid into puzzlement, then startlement with an edge of disbelief, which swiftly built into utter incredulity and outright shock.

Was it her clothes? Kristy wondered. Admittedly her blue denim jeans and battle jacket were hardly sophisticated garb, and her comfortable Reeboks were somewhat the worse for wear, but surely they constituted a kind of universal uniform amongst travellers these days, acceptable practically anywhere. On the other hand, the canvas carryall she was toting did not convey an aura of class and this was a very classy hotel.

Kristy swiftly reasoned that as long as she could pay for her accommodation, there was no reason for anyone to turn her away. The glazed look of disbelief in the doorman's eyes had to be a reflection of his snobbery. She decided to disarm him with a friendly smile.

Her smile was definitely her best feature, though Betty had always raved on about her hair. Its particular shade of apricot gold was rather rare, and there was a lot of it, bouncing around her shoulders in a cascade of unruly waves and curls. Her face was not nearly as spectacular, although she had always thought it nice enough. Her nose and mouth were neat and regular—nothing to take exception to—and her eyes were a very clear blue, which a lot of people remarked upon, probably because the colour was such a sharp contrast to her hair.

The doorman, however, was not disarmed by her smile. If anything, he looked thoroughly alarmed by it. Kristy decided her next best option was to impress him with his own native tongue.

"Bonjour, Monsieur," she greeted him sweetly, demonstrating her perfectly accented French. It was her one real talent—a natural gift for languages, enabling her to fit in easily wherever John's army postings had taken them.

"Bonjour, Madame."

No enthusiasm in his response. A very stiff formality. Kristy didn't bother correcting the *Madame* to *Mademoiselle*. The man was clearly uneasy with her presence, turning aside quickly to summon a bellboy who hurried forward to relieve her of her bag. At least she wasn't being rejected.

The door was punctiliously held open for her passage into the lobby. She would have liked to tip him, proving her worthiness as a guest, but the doorman clearly disdained accepting anything from her, his attention fixed with some intensity on the reception desk. Shrugging off the uncomfortable sensation of being considered riffraff, Kristy moved on into the lobby.

The bellboy carrying her bag whisked past her, heading straight for the check-in. One of the clerks stationed at the desk seemed to be alerted by something behind Kristy. Then his gaze shot to her and the jolt on his face gave her further pause. It wasn't so much disbelief this time. It looked like absolute horror. What was going on? Why was she causing this odd reaction? Was she really unacceptable in this hotel?

It made no sense to Kristy. However, if she was going to be turned away, she was not going to be entirely done out of her trip down nostalgia lane. She'd come here to feel, as best she could, what Betty had felt forty years before. A belligerent determination halted her feet and sent her gaze sweeping slowly around the grand lobby.

Bathed in a soft golden haze...magical. Those had been Betty's words, and they were still true, even after all this time. The yellow glow in the light seemed to beam off the walls, covered in their richly veined Siena marble. The floor was a gleaming chessboard of marble tiles, just as Betty had described, and the sumptuous chandeliers overhead added their lustrous effect.

The atmosphere of opulence had not been over-stated. Intent on observing everything, Kristy gradually realised the sense of richness—even of greatness—was reflected by the beautifully dressed and elegantly shod guests scattered through the lobby. No-one in common jeans. Not even designer jeans. As for scuffed Reeboks, Kristy suspected the people around her wouldn't be seen dead in them.

She didn't fit in here. That was the plain unvarnished truth. Betty and John had undoubtedly worn their best honeymoon clothes at the time of their stay. Coming to this hotel was not supposed to be an act of impulse.

However, it was done now and she didn't really have to fit, Kristy assured herself. All she wanted was a room for the night. That would complete her mission here and she saw no reason why it shouldn't be achieved. Once out of sight she wouldn't present a problem to anyone. Besides, there was nothing wrong in pursuing a sentimental whim.

The bellboy was standing guard over her bag at the reception desk. Both he and the clerk who'd been alerted to her entrance were keeping a wary eye on her. Kristy hated feeling unwelcome, but these people meant nothing to her. The fantasy of a forty-year-old honeymoon had a much stronger call on her than their approval.

Refusing to be intimidated, Kristy fronted up to the desk, noting how the clerk, a tall thin man with a receding hairline, positioned himself to be in direct line to serve her. He was obviously the senior man on duty. No doubt he always took charge of *difficult* guests.

"How can I help, *Madame*?"

Studied politeness, Kristy thought. He didn't want to help her at all. The crease of concern on his brow and the trace of anxiety in his voice telegraphed a wish to get rid of her as fast as possible.

"I want a room for tonight. Only the one night," she answered with pointed emphasis, hoping such a brief stay would win his toleration. At least he couldn't fault her French, she thought, having mimicked the exact modulation of his voice.

He hesitated, uncertainty flicking over his face. "We have a suite...."

Kristy looked him in the eye. He had probably surmised she couldn't afford an expensive suite. "I want a room. A regular room. For one night. Are you saying you can't accommodate me?"

He seemed to take fright at her assertive challenge, perhaps sniffing the possibility of an unpleasant scene. *"Non, Madame,"* he answered hastily. "A room can be arranged."

"Your cheapest room," Kristy spelled out so there was no mistake.

His eyebrows shot up. His face dropped. *"Oui, Madame,"* he choked out.

He pushed across the registration form and Kristy filled it in, feeling she had won a minor victory over petty snobbery. Why the staff here was automatically addressing her as *madame* was a puzzle, but she shrugged it off as irrelevant. She was *in*. That was all she cared about.

Having written down the information required and signed her name, she handed the form back. The clerk started to glance over it. Kristy could have sworn his eyes actually bulged as he took in her particulars. Probably stunned to discover she was an American, not French at all.

Nevertheless, that didn't explain why he then became quite agitated, shoving the form under the desk as though it was contaminated and passing a room key to the bellboy with fussy officiousness, gesturing pointedly to the elevators.

The bellboy set off smartly with her key and bag, but the clerk's manner had irked Kristy. A streak of stubborn pride emerged, prompting her to loiter in the lobby. She didn't like being pushed around, or viewed as disposable garbage. Her independent spirit insisted she ignore such pressures.

Her gaze was drawn to a couple seated behind a low table, conversing quietly but with the kind of animation that was distinctly French. The woman was a striking brunette, superbly groomed, and wearing a black and white outfit that had to be the creation of one of the top Parisian designers. She gave *chic* a new meaning.

Her companion was even more striking, the perfect image of aristocratic elegance. He was handsome in a distinctly Gallic way: a high intellectual forehead, a slightly long but very refined nose, a firm imperious chin, and an extremely sensual mouth. He was clothed in tailored perfection, his dark grey suit encasing a body that conveyed grace, virility and vitality.

Something about him tugged at her, as though she should know him, yet she was sure she'd remember if she'd ever met him before. The feeling caused her to study him with keener interest.

His black hair was sleekly styled, as though he knew he needed no flamboyance to distract from the fine sensitivity of his face. She imagined him having a deep appreciation of art and music and good food and wine. The quizzical arch of his brows suggested he would take pleasure in questioning everything, and the dark dancing brilliance of his eyes seemed to promise he missed nothing.

There was passion in the slight flare of his nostrils, a worldly but not unkind cynicism in the faint curl of his beautifully moulded mouth. He was in his mid-thirties, Kristy guessed, with the mature authority that came with many years of being successful at whatever he did.

She found herself envying the woman who was with him. They had to be celebrating something. A bottle of champagne rested in a silver ice bucket on the table and two flute glasses of gleaming crystal were at hand. *Their* honeymoon? she wondered, and felt a sharp inner recoil from the thought.

The man suddenly bestowed a brilliant smile on his companion and Kristy caught her breath as his attraction took a mega-leap. She was riven by a fierce wish for that smile to be directed at her...only her...which shook her so much she wrenched her gaze away.

The bellboy was shuffling impatiently by the elevators. She hadn't asked for his services, Kristy thought irritably. As a guest in this hotel, she had every right to move at her own convenience, not his. No doubt the couple she'd been watching did as they pleased, assuming it was the natural way of things. She looked back at them with a burst of burning resentment that was quite alien to her normal nature.

What happened next was inexplicable. Had she somehow shot a blast of negative force across the lobby? The man must have felt something hit him. His head jerked, attention whipping away from his companion and fastening on Kristy with such sharp intensity, her heart contracted. He started to rise from his seat, his face stricken with...what? Surprise...astonishment, shock...guilt...anger?

His hand flashed out in aggressive dismissal. It struck the glass nearest to him. Over it went, rolling towards the edge, splashing fluid across the table. He moved instinctively but jerkily to grab it and the whole table tipped. Ice and shards of crystal splattered over the chessboard floor in a spreading foam of spilled champagne.

Momentarily and automatically his gaze left Kristy to follow the path of destruction radiating out in front of him. A totally appalled look flitted over his face. Yet his gaze stabbed back at her, dismissing the mess, projecting some savagely personal accusation at her, as though this was all her fault and she knew it as intimately and certainly as he did.

It made Kristy feel odd, as though time and place had shifted into a different dimension. Her pulse went haywire, pumping her heart so hard her temples throbbed. Vaguely she saw the woman leap up and clutch the man's arm, commanding his attention. Then a hand touched her own arm, jolting her out of the strange thrall that had held her. It was the clerk from the reception desk.

"Your room, *Madame*," he pressed anxiously. "The bellboy has the elevator waiting for you."

"Oh! Yes. Okay," she babbled, momentarily forgetting to speak French.

She forced her legs to move away from the embarrassing scene. It wasn't her fault. How could it be? She was nobody here. She didn't know the man and the man didn't know her. She must have imagined that weird sense of connection.

The bellboy was holding the elevator doors open for her, the canvas bag already deposited in the compartment. His head shook dolefully over the mess in the lobby behind her as she stepped past him.

"An unfortunate accident," she offered by way of glossing over the incident.

"*Un scandale,*" he muttered, smartly stepping into the elevator after her and releasing the doors, shutting them both off from whatever was now happening in the lobby. As he pressed the button for her floor he added on a low note of doom, "*Un scandale terrible!*"

CHAPTER TWO

WHAT melodramatic nonsense! Kristy thought, determinedly blocking irrational impressions out of her mind and switching it onto a sane, sensible level.

Such an accident might be uncommon in this grand hotel, but staff would be snapping into action, cleaning away the mess fast and efficiently, sweeping it out of sight, out of mind, as though it had never been. Breakage and spillage hardly constituted a terrible scandal.

She decided not to offer any further comment as the elevator travelled up to her floor. Clearly she and the bellboy were not on any common wavelength. Besides, she was still shaken by the sheer force of what she'd felt coming from *the man*.

She had never experienced anything like it. Perhaps a culmination of grief, stress and fatigue had affected her nervous system, throwing her emotions out of kilter. Even the impulse to come here now looked foolish. Certainly ill-considered, given her reception by the staff. Or was she putting too much emphasis on that, too, blowing niggly little feelings out of proportion?

As for the man who'd triggered such a vivid range of emotions…was there such a thing as *knowing* someone from another life? She shook her head in wry bemusement. Perhaps it was this hotel making her fanciful…Betty's and John's honeymoon hotel. Her strong fixation on the attractive foreigner must have coloured her perception, making her see things differently to the actual reality.

The woman he was with could have said something to upset him. Then he'd probably found Kristy's staring at him offensive, especially when he'd knocked things over. No one liked having witnesses to an embarrassing scene. It was stupid to read any more into the incident than that.

The elevator stopped. The doors opened. Having recollected herself, Kristy stepped out, resolving not to be flustered by anything else on this one-night stopover in Paris.

The bellboy ushered her into a room which had no pretensions to being the least bit cheap. Her heart quailed a little at the price she might have to pay for it tomorrow, but then she sternly told herself she was here to soak up and enjoy the atmosphere and ambience around her. Cost was to be discounted.

She searched her handbag for a few coins to tip the bellboy. It was a futile exercise. He scuttled away with a rapidity which was startling. Apparently official courtesy ended at the door, now she was safely tucked away from causing any public displeasure.

Sighing away her vexation at being treated like some second-class citizen, Kristy set out on her own tour of the accommodation she had insisted upon. At least, she was on her own here. She wouldn't bother anyone and no-one would bother her.

The bedroom was lovely. The colour scheme of off-white, beige and brown, smartly contrasted with black, was very stylish and Parisian. It was also too modern to have been in place forty years ago. Reason told her the furnishings had probably been changed many times since Betty and John had stayed here, but she was sure they had been just as delighted with their room as she was with hers. Of course, being in love had probably made it even more delightful.

The marble bathroom was utter luxury. Kristy could well imagine Betty revelling in what she would consider the height of delicious decadence. Sumptuous plumbing was not a feature of the third-world countries where John had frequently been posted throughout his army career. Not that Betty had ever complained about primitive facilities, but whenever they had returned to "civilization", it was a well appointed bathroom that defined "civilization."

Kristy was moving to unpack and settle in when a quiet rap on the door drew her attention. She opened it to a distinguished-looking gentleman in a pinstripe suit. His cheeks were full, well-fed and although he was no taller than Kristy, which put him at barely average height for a man, he exuded an air of benign authority.

"*Madame,* a word with you," he appealed softly.

She flashed him a smile. "And you are…whom?"

He returned her smile. "A good jest, *Madame,*" he replied with a jovial little chuckle.

Kristy wondered what the joke was.

"May I come in?" he asked, gesturing an eloquent appeal to her good nature.

Kristy frowned over the request. A stranger was a

stranger in her book, especially one who acted strangely. "What for?" she demanded suspiciously.

He made an apologetic grimace. "This room... there has been an error. If you will allow me to re-arrange..."

"Oh!" She instantly slotted him into place. He was management. Had he come to tell her this room wasn't the cheapest available, or was she going to be thrown out of the hotel after all?

He laced his hands together, revealing some anxiety over her possible displeasure. "A most unfortunate, regrettable error..."

Kristy stared back stonily, wondering whether it was worth the effort of making a fuss. If all the staff had a down on her, her stay here could be made too unpleasant to persist with it.

"I must..." the voice of authority continued affably, "...if you'll forgive me...insist you vacate it."

Kristy felt herself bridling and struggled to remain calm. She could stand her ground, perhaps even demand compensation for the hotel's error, but was it worth fighting about? As much as she despised snobbery, there was not much joy in bucking a system which remained immutable no matter how many little victories could be scored against it. At least she hadn't unpacked, so she didn't have to suffer the humiliation of repacking.

"Please allow me, *Madame*, to escort you to somewhere more suitable...uh...to your needs," her ejector said with exquisite politeness. It was a very civilized way of putting her in her place.

"You are a master of tact, *Monsieur*," Kristy said dryly.

He completely missed the irony edging her words. He positively preened, beaming his appreciation of her compliment. "We have—may I say it—a worldwide reputation for tact and...uh...understanding. Thank you."

"This place you wish to escort me to...I hope it is cheap, *Monsieur*," Kristy said with blunt directness. There was no onus on her to play with subtleties. "You see, I don't have a lot of money..."

"Say no more, *Madame*. Discretion. Appeasement. Understanding. With my experience..." He spread his hands in a gesture that embraced a whole world of discretion and appeasement and understanding.

"In that case," Kristy said decisively, "I may as well get going right now. If you will excuse me, I'll just collect my bag." She didn't want the services of another bellboy, not in this hotel.

"*Non, non, Madame*. Allow me to carry it for you."

It surprised Kristy. She would have thought it was beneath his dignity to act as her porter. In a tearing hurry to get her out of his hotel, she thought with bitter cynicism.

She stepped back, waving a careless invitation for him to enter. He collected her canvas carryall while she retrieved her handbag. Coming here had been a silly daydream, Kristy told herself as they vacated the room. The past was gone and could never be truly recaptured. At least she'd seen the place. In the circumstances, that was quite enough.

The manager led her along the corridor. He only went a short way before putting down her bag and producing a set of keys which he flourished as though he was St. Peter about to open the portals of heaven. Kristy did a swift rethink. He couldn't be throwing her out of the hotel after all, so this must be a cheaper room.

He unlocked the door before them, swung it open like an impresario, and eloquently gestured Kristy forward. "*Madame*, your room," he announced with almost smug satisfaction.

Kristy took several steps, saw what was in front of her, and stopped dead. Was this some kind of joke? To take her out of a room and lead her to what was clearly a luxurious suite had to be the height of perversity when she had made such a point of revealing a very real need not to be extravagant.

"I can't afford this," she protested.

The manager looked offended. "*Madame* is our guest. Of course *Madame* is not expected to pay for anything while she is our guest." His voice had a touch of outrage at her failure to understand *his* understanding.

"I think," said Kristy forcefully, "there is some mistake."

"*Madame*…uh…Holloway…" He gave another little jovial chuckle and added a conspiratorial wink. "The mistake has been rectified."

He marched into the huge sitting room—complete with a conservatory and a private terrace—and into a dressing-room where he deposited her canvas carryall, thereby emphasizing her accepted status here. Kristy watched him doubtfully, certain there had been some ridiculous mix-up. On the other hand, he had called her by her own name although why he persisted with *Madame* was beyond her. He could not have failed to notice she wasn't wearing any rings.

"Are you sure this is the right place for me, *Monsieur*?" she asked, feeling the need to get this pinned down to something concrete.

He beamed supreme confidence. *"Certainement."*

Kristy gave up. She didn't need the stress of sorting out this madness, or getting a room in another hotel. This was some management bungle and they could pay for it. She'd made her terms absolutely clear, and after all this hassle, no way was she going to be shifted again.

"One last thing, *Madame* Holloway…"

"Yes?"

The manager went to a door on the other side of the sitting room, took a key from the flourished key ring, and inserted it in the lock. "For your use only," he said solemnly.

Kristy looked at him blankly. What did he mean by that?

He gave the key a dramatic twist. "Unlocked," he said. Then he turned the key the other way. "Locked," he said. "I will leave it to *Madame*'s discretion."

"Monsieur…" Kristy expostulated, totally bewildered by the whole sequence of events.

"Say no more. Say no more. Tact. Diplomacy. Understanding. We know all these things."

He withdrew the key from the lock, came across

the room, and pressed it into her hand. It was too much for Kristy. Altogether too much.

"*Monsieur...*"

"Enough. You are our guest. You pay for nothing. If this...er...delicate situation can be fortunately resolved...uh...please remember me."

And so saying, he bowed his way out of the room, leaving her with another of his jovial little laughs, to which he seemed addicted.

Of one thing Kristy was absolutely certain. There was some mistake here of gigantic proportions. It was equally clear it was someone else's mistake. She had nothing whatsoever to do with it.

She frowned over his parting words...*this delicate situation*. What was he referring to? She didn't have a clue. It just seemed that ever since the hotel doorman had laid eyes on her, the world had shifted out of kilter.

Discretion said she should get out of here as soon as possible. Retreat. Retire before some ghastly disaster occurred. *Un scandale terrible!*

The over-the-top thought evoked a burst of somewhat hysterical laughter. Which suggested, after she'd sobered up again, that her nerves were in a bad way. The experience of this hotel was definitely not soothing, as she had anticipated it would be. The depression of being totally alone hit her again, whispering that her trip to Geneva would probably be a failure, too.

The energy that had driven her to this journey drained away. Let the hotel management discover its mistake, she decided listlessly. There was no need for her to pre-empt any action. She had tried to protest, to explain, to set the situation straight. None of this was her fault. No doubt she would receive another visit soon and everything would be resolved properly, so there was no point in unpacking her bag.

Meanwhile, she had this key in her hand. Kristy eyed the interconnecting door which could be locked or unlocked with the burning-question key. Maybe the answers, or some answer to this *delicate situation*, lay on the other side of the door. It was none of her business, of course. On the other hand, she had somehow got involved.

She thought of Pandora who opened the lid of the box which let loose all the troubles of the world. Curiosity was a terrible thing and it could be very dangerous. Better to let it go and not risk adding more trouble to trouble.

Kristy set the key down on a coffee table and turned her back on it. She walked out to the private terrace, deciding she might as well enjoy all this luxury while she could because she couldn't see it lasting for long. This was not the place for her and that key could only lead to something even more out of bounds.

The view was the kind which sold postcards; the Eiffel Tower, the Arc de Triomphe, and the Place de la Concorde, all spread out for her to admire and wonder at the genius which had planned such a magnificent vista. Kristy, however, could not concentrate her mind on it. A sense of restlessness drove her back into the sitting room.

The key kept drawing her gaze. It had a powerful

fascination. Caught on a seesaw of temptation, she almost leapt out of her skin when a knock came on the door. But it wasn't on *that* door. It was on the one which led in from the corridor.

They've discovered the mistake, she thought, relieved that she hadn't surrendered to the curiosity which would have led her into a very awkward indiscretion.

Anticipating a return of the manager, she was surprised when a maid entered, bearing an elegant vase of long-stemmed roses. It was placed on the table beside the key. I'm getting in deeper, Kristy thought. She weakly thanked the maid who withdrew without comment.

Her inner tension moved up a notch when a second knock came. It heralded another maid who carried in a bottle of champagne and an artistically arranged platter of fruit. Kristy stared at both offerings as though they were deadly poison. Why was she such an honoured guest? What was behind all this?

A third knock brought a third maid bearing gift boxes of *eau de toilette* and soaps.

It was as good as a birthday, Kristy thought ruefully, except she wasn't enjoying it. Impossible to shake off the feeling that the gifts were connected to *that* key. She eyed it balefully. Would it unlock the door to the mystery of why she was here and suddenly being treated like royalty? Maybe she should find out what she could before she became even more entrenched in this weird situation.

She picked up the key.

I'll take just a little peep, she thought.

It's none of your business, her mind chided.

Yes, it is, another part responded. I'm already in this up to my neck. I didn't ask to be involved but I am. I definitely am. And I've got every right to find out.

She listened to the other side of her mind in case it wanted to pull her back behind the safe cautious line.

No response.

The argument was perfectly sound.

After all, the manager had left the decision in her hands, and she wasn't doing anything wrong. She did have every reason to take a little peek into the room beyond *that* door. She had been invited to unlock it at will.

Her fingers closed tightly around the key as her legs moved forward. Determinedly ignoring the burning feeling in her palm and the apprehensive hammering of her heart, Kristy reached the door, fitted the key to the lock and turned it with a swift decisive twist. Then taking a deep breath to calm her leaping nerves, and telling herself she was acting positively and purposefully, she opened the door.

She half-expected some monster to be on the other side but there was no reaction to the door's opening. No sound. No movement. Nothing. Taking courage at finding no repercussions to her initial trespass, Kristy pushed the door fully ajar. It revealed another sitting room, similar to hers.

She stood motionless for several seconds, listening intently. Still no sounds of occupation. No signs of occupation, either. She took the first step over the threshold. The need to find some answer to this extra accommodation urged her on.

The click of a key in a lock made her freeze halfway across the room. She stared in horror at the door which gave access to the corridor outside. Her throat constricted, her heart thumped in wild apprehension as the door opened. Her eyes widened in shock as she instantly identified the man who stepped inside.

It was the man from the lobby, the man who'd transfixed her with his knowing eyes, the elegant aristocratic man who had inelegantly broken up the romantic interlude with his companion, creating *un scandale terrible*!

Kristy's mind dazedly registered the fact that he did not look shocked at seeing her. He actually smiled at her, but it was not the brilliant smile of pleasure that had lit his face for his companion in the lobby. It was a cold cynical curl of his lips, a knowing little smile. Whatever knowledge was behind it gave him no pleasure at all.

He shut the door without a word, without a crack in his composure. Everything in his manner projected he had anticipated her being here.

Yet how could he?

And what could he know about her?

A sense of weird unreality gripped Kristy, holding her in tense waiting for what would come next.

CHAPTER THREE

"So!"

It was a sibilant hiss that seethed with explosive emotion. Kristy instantly realised his composure was a facade, and it was not only his voice that revealed how brittle the façade was. The dark eyes were not dancing with amusement. They glittered with a primitive ferocity...anger, pain, blistering accusation.

"What do you have to say for yourself?" he demanded, repitching his voice to a tone of sardonic mockery that didn't quite disguise an undercurrent of barely leashed savagery.

It was a beautiful voice, rich and male and mesmerisingly coloured by the emotion it projected. Kristy had to shake herself out of her appreciation of it, focus on what was being demanded.

He probably thinks I'm some kind of thief, she thought, and frantically searched her mind for the best way to explain her presence. An attempt at appeasement came up as top priority.

"Je regrette..." she began tentatively, but got no further.

"You're *sorry*?" Incredulity resonated around the room. The dark eyes swept her with scathing contempt. "You're sorry," he repeated jeeringly. He tilted his head back and rolled his eyes at the ceiling. *"Bon Dieu!* You have a thousand things to explain and all you can say is you're sorry." His derisive laugh had an element of wildness that sent chills down Kristy's spine.

She darted a look at the interconnecting door, measuring her line of retreat.

"Oh, no, my precious darling!"

The endearment held no affection whatsoever. The tone of venomous purpose whipped Kristy's gaze back to him. He was moving swiftly to cut off her escape route and the aura of violence he emanated was quite enough to hold Kristy absolutely still. She didn't want to provoke him any more than he was already provoked by her presence here.

"You will not leave until I'm satisfied you have explained…everything…to me," he promised her, a threat underlining every word.

Kristy swallowed hard. Her whole body seemed to be vibrating with electric tension and it was difficult to make her mouth work. But speak she must. "It's very simple really," she began.

It seemed to provoke the man even more. "Simple!" he interjected, his eyes blazing dark fury. He moved closer to tower over her. "Two years! Two long lonely bitter years! And all you can say is *you're sorry*? And it's *simple*?" His voice literally shook with outrage.

Kristy's mind whirled with confusion. What did two years have to do with anything? "I don't know what you want to know," she rushed out in the hope of getting some direction from him since he didn't like anything she said.

At least it had a calming effect, Kristy thought with

relief. The blaze of fury banked down to a simmer which still looked dangerous but was temporarily under control. Then he smiled at her. Somehow the smile was as chilling as his derisive laugh had been. It spelled disaster if she put a foot wrong.

"Did you come here in the hope of hearing words of love from me?" he asked in a soft jeering tone.

"Certainly not," Kristy replied incredulously. The idea was absurd. Why would she expect to hear endearments from a stranger?

One black eyebrow rose in mocking challenge. "To tell me that you love me?"

Kristy could hardly believe she was hearing this. She didn't know the man. What kind of woman did he think she was? A boldly enterprising callgirl on the make, slipping into his room to set up a chance?

"That's ridiculous!" she protested.

He laughed. "How true!" The dark eyes burned more intensely into hers and his voice lowered to a purring throb. "Was it to seduce me into making love to you? To feel my body caressing yours in the way you most enjoy?"

"No! Absolutely not!" Kristy cried, terribly disconcerted by the effect his suggestive words had on her pulse rate.

Her reply seemed to incense him. "Then I will tell you what I think," he seethed. His mouth curled around the words as he spat them out. "You are a cowardly sneak! Your effrontery in presenting yourself here is unbelievable! You are shameless, heartless, gutless..."

Shock paralysed Kristy's mind for several seconds.

Then a tidal wave of outrage swept through her, lifting her hand, propelling it with furious force. It struck his face so hard it snapped his head back. It left reddened weals across his cheek, and Kristy's eyes burned with savage satisfaction at the sight. Never had she felt so angry in her life.

"Keep your slanderous words and thoughts to yourself!" she hissed, ready to fight tooth and nail if he so much as tried to insult her again in such an offensive fashion.

He had no right. All she had done was trespass into his room, and she had been given a key for that purpose anyway. She couldn't see how any blame for that could be attached to her. She did not deserve such abuse and no way in the world would she tolerate it.

The dark eyes flared with violent passion. She met them with blue ice, defying him to do his worst. The clash of will and turbulent emotion somehow seeded something even more disturbing. Kristy was conscious of a shift inside herself, an uncoiling of a need, a desire, an awakening tingle in her blood that she had never felt before.

She did not know this man.

Yet something inside her did. Or seemed to. Some subconscious recognition she was at a total loss to explain. The feeling was even stronger now than it had been in the lobby, spurring with it a fiercely primitive urge to have what he'd put into her mind. She found herself literally craving to know what it would be like to feel his body caressing hers.

Suddenly the searing dark eyes were like magnets, dragging on her soul. A sense of deep intimacy pulsed between them. She had a compelling urge to reach up and touch his cheek, to tenderly stroke away the hurt marks she had inflicted. She only just managed to check what would have been an insane move, given the situation.

Kristy didn't understand herself at all. How could she be so enthralled by the man, when what was happening now was hardly a promising beginning for anything? She had never struck anyone in her whole life until *he* had stirred her into it.

An appalled horror descended on her. She was a nonviolent person. Words, not fists, had always been her creed. Ever since she had entered this hotel, things had started swinging out of normality.

Was it Alice who had stepped through the looking glass and into another world?

Kristy was beginning to feel the same thing had happened to her. She took a deep breath and tried to regain some sanity. How could there be any sense of intimacy between this stranger and herself? She had to be imagining it. His talk of love and lovemaking must be triggering wild offshoots from the need to belong to someone, somewhere.

Yet, as though they *were* somehow acutely attuned to each other, she sensed a similar withdrawal from him, the automatic reaction to shock and disbelief, needing time to pause and take stock, to reassess. His face tightened. His mouth thinned into a grim line. The dark eyes narrowed to gleaming slits.

Kristy thought about apologising, but since this whole scene had erupted from her initial apology, it didn't seem like a good idea. Besides, he had been as much in the wrong as she was. Pride insisted she concede no fault in what she had done, but explanations were certainly due.

"Monsieur..." she started again.

"Don't call me that!" he snapped angrily.

Whatever I say seems to get me into trouble, Kristy thought. "Very well," she agreed, wondering what else she could call him. "There is an explanation...."

"I shall be interested to hear it," he snapped again. "I shall be fascinated to hear how you explain yourself," he went on, his voice gathering a stinging contempt. "Every word will be a priceless pearl to my ears. I shall assess it with intense appreciation for its worth."

Which set Kristy back on her heels because her explanation didn't make much sense to her, and she doubted it would make sense to him either. However, the truth was the truth. "I have this key...." she began slowly. "The manager gave it to me...."

That was as far as she got.

He took hold of her shoulders and shook her in furious impatience. "You are *incredible*! Totally incredible!" he seethed.

Kristy realised that what he was saying was true. Her explanation was totally incredible. But this man was teetering on the edge of being totally out of control and she didn't know what to say or do. "Please..." She couldn't call him *monsieur*. "...take your hands off me," she begged.

He laughed with arrogant disdain, but he released her and dropped his hands to his sides. "You think I cannot do that?" he taunted, his eyes flashing bitter derision. "You think I have to touch you? That I cannot help myself?" He bared his teeth in a scornful sneer. "I can do it. See for yourself!"

"Thank you," Kristy breathed in deep relief.

Violence did breed violence, she thought. She shouldn't have slapped him. Strictly words from now on, she promised herself.

As though he had come to the same civilized conclusion, he stepped back from her in haughty rejection, a cold pride stamped on his face. His aristocratic bearing was very pronounced as he strode around the room, releasing his inner turbulence in sharp angry gestures and bursts of scorn.

"You are nothing," he hurled at her. "Nothing at all! Not a speck of dirt. Utterly insignificant. Meaningless."

Kristy steeled herself to remain cool, no matter how hotly this man stirred her blood. In actual fact, what he said was a fairly accurate description. To the world at large, she *was* a nobody. There was no-one left who cared whether she existed or not. Besides, agreeing with people's ideas was a better way of placating them than disagreeing with them.

"I realise that," she said calmly.

Her answer brought him to an abrupt halt. His brow creased in puzzlement. The dark eyes stabbed at her in suspicious re-assessment. "You realise that?" he said slowly, watching intently for some telltale reaction from her.

"Certainly," Kristy said with assurance. Why should she mean anything to this man? They were complete strangers.

He sauntered towards her, ruthless purpose stamped on his face. "I'll prove how worthless you are."

"You don't have to prove anything of the kind," Kristy cried in alarm. She didn't want him to shake her again.

"Where have you been for the last two years?" he bit out savagely. "What have you been doing? Why did you move out of my life without so much as a word of warning or excuse?"

Understanding began to dawn in Kristy's mind. For some reason this man thought she was someone else. Enlightenment grew in rippling waves. The hotel staff, from the doorman to the manager, had thought she was someone else. It was the only explanation that fitted the facts; all the odd reactions she had been getting from the staff which she had set down to snobbery, the accident in the lobby that *had* happened because this man had caught sight of her, the bellboy's proclaiming it *un scandale terrible*, the manager with his strange manoeuvrings and talk of discretion.

This certainly loomed as a very *delicate situation*!

The tantalising question was...who was she supposed to be? Who did they all think she was? And why couldn't they see she wasn't who they thought she was?

"Answer me!"

He was towering over her again, commanding her attention. Kristy pulled her mind out of its whirling flurry of activity and concentrated on what was most immediate. Somewhere, sometime, there had to be an explanation of what was happening. In the meantime, Kristy thought, it was imperative to answer this man's question truthfully and with a calm composure. Her heart gave a nervous little flutter as she looked up into the darkly demanding eyes.

"I was in San Francisco most of the time...."

"So! You did go with the American!" he threw at her. "Yes...I can hear it in your voice. Damn you for the conniving cheat you are!"

"I'm not a cheat!" she hurled back at him in fierce resentment.

"You think you can get to me again? After what you've done?"

She hadn't done anything! Except use the key that had brought her into this room. However, before she could expostulate, his hand lifted and curled around her cheek. Kristy flinched away from the touch but it was an ineffectual movement. He tilted her chin up, bent his head, and his mouth crashed onto hers.

The shock of it left her momentarily defenceless. His hand slid into her hair entangling itself in the thick tresses and binding her to him as forcefully as the arm that scooped her body hard against his. Then an explosion of sensation robbed her of any thought of resistance.

His mouth possessed hers in a frenzy of passion, igniting a response that rushed into being, spreading through her like wildfire, an uncontrollable force, taking her over, thrumming to a beat of its own. Heat pulsed from him, suffusing her entire body, exciting an almost excruciating awareness of hard flesh and muscle imprinting themselves on her. His kiss plundered and destroyed her previous knowledge of what a kiss could be, arousing a compulsive need to cast

all limits aside and plummet into more and more enticing levels of melding together.

The break came as swiftly and as shockingly as the
enforced connection. He tore his mouth from hers.
His hands encircled her upper arms, holding her away
from him as he stepped back. Dazed by the abrupt
withdrawal and still helplessly churning with the sensations he'd stirred, Kristy looked at him in blank
incomprehension.

His dark eyes glittered with malevolent triumph.
"You see?" he said, removing his grasp, lifting his
hands away as though the touch of her was distasteful
to him. "I feel nothing for you. Absolutely nothing."

It was a barefaced lie.

He was not unaffected by her, nor what had passed
between them. His breathing was visibly faster and
even as he swung on his heel and turned his back to
her, Kristy was recalling all too acutely the burgeon-
ing of his erection, proving he had been physically
moved. Besides, how could such passion be generated
out of nothing?

Though that raised the thorny question of how
could *she* have been so deeply affected when ostensibly there was nothing between them but a misunderstanding. Worse, a case of mistaken identity! A
painful flush scorched up her neck and burnt her
cheeks. He had been abusing another woman, while
here she was, deeply shaken by a vulnerability she
couldn't explain.

Nevertheless, explanations were in order. In very
fast order, too, given the volatile nature of feelings
running riot here. She had to correct his conviction

she was someone he had known before. That was at the heart of this whole wretched mix-up.

"The reason there is nothing is because there was nothing in the first place," Kristy said shakily.

He whirled around, his face contorted with furious resentment. His eyes stabbed black daggers at her. "Don't make a fool of yourself by stating the obvious."

Still hopelessly unsettled by the turbulence he'd aroused, Kristy couldn't stop her own temper from flaring. "You're deliberately trying to provoke me!"

He did not deny it. He made no reply at all but his eyes kept accusing her of dark, nameless crimes.

Kristy struggled to get herself under control. "What has happened is quite simple," she stated once again, determined to make him listen, no matter what he said. "You see…"

"I know what has happened," he cut in emphatically.

Kristy let the interruption fly past her. "…you're making a mistake about me. You think I'm someone else.…"

He gave a cynical laugh.

"I'm not the same woman who…"

"No. Most decidedly not. As far as I'm concerned, you've been dead for the last two years. I wish you were. It would be better if you were dead."

Kristy almost stamped her foot in frustration at his refusal to listen. "Will you give me one chance…"

"Absolutely not," he bit out with venom. "No more chances. You don't deserve any chances."

They were talking at cross-purposes. Trying to explain the true situation was obviously a futile exercise. His mind was set on one idea and he wasn't in the mood to listen to her.

"Fine," Kristy agreed with some asperity. Since he was not open to reason, it was best for her to give up and walk away. "Please excuse me. I'm going back to my room."

He waved a disdainful dismissal. "Do that."

"And locking the door." So he couldn't storm after her.

"Good!" He looked satisfied.

"I'm leaving Paris tomorrow." That gave him a deadline if he could calm down enough to hear her side of this crazy business.

"Excellent!"

Kristy burned over his intransigence. "I'm never coming back," she declared.

That should finish it for him, she thought. He could consider her dead forever. For some reason, that hurt deep down inside her, but she steadfastly buried the hurt. If it was what he wanted, this meeting with him definitely had no future. Best for her to forget it had ever happened.

His eyes narrowed suspiciously, as though he didn't believe her. "What do you want from me?" he demanded.

Kristy's chin lifted in proud rejection of him and all that might have come of this encounter if he could have accepted that things were different to what he thought they were. "Nothing!" she declared in snapping defiance of his suspicions about her. "Absolutely nothing!"

Having delivered the most affirmative exit line she could think of, she swung on her heel and strode for the interconnecting door. She had her hand on the knob, ready to sweep the door shut behind her when his voice cracked out again in harsh command.

"Wait!"

She'd had enough. She'd done her best. He wouldn't listen. He was only upsetting her further and further. So she did not wait. She did not so much as glance back at him. With her head held high, she marched into the suite she had been given and swiftly shut the door on him. One firm twist of the treacherous key and the lock clicked into place.

And that, thought Kristy, was that!

CHAPTER FOUR

KRISTY steamed up and down the luxurious sitting room, totally unaware and unappreciative of her rich and elegant surroundings. Her mind was in a ferment. What an aggravating man! What a positively infuriating man! Interfering with her life just because he thought she was someone else, turning her inside out with his confusing words and actions, making her feel things she had never felt before!

It wasn't fair!

He wasn't fair!

None of what had happened since she had arrived here in this damnable hotel was fair!

Kristy felt like picking up things and throwing them. Her gaze balefully targeted the vase of roses. But *he* would not have ordered them. *He* hated the woman he thought she was. No, the vase of red roses was the hotel management's idea to help the resolution of a delicate situation. Except it wasn't delicate! It was downright hopeless!

Why did they all think she was someone else? Why?

Kristy marched into the marble bathroom and examined her reflection in the mirror there. It was a most uncomfortable feeling to think there was someone else who looked exactly like her. Was there such a thing as a perfect double? She had heard of movie stars who had look-alike stand-ins, but they weren't perfect doubles. Surely a man who had been her double's lover would see some differences if there were any, even though it had been two years since he had been with her. A close resemblance might fool hotel staff, but a lover of intimate acquaintance?

Kristy stared at her reflection in bitter frustration.

Who are you there on the other side of the mirror?

Why did you walk out on him without a word?

I would not have done that.

I'm different from you. I'd never do such a heartless thing to someone who loved me. Or was it wounded pride on his part, losing a possession he'd believed was his. Either way, you must have been a callous creature to dump him like that. But why can't he see I'm different?

Her hand lifted to trace her features. Was every line exactly the same? The shape of her face, her mouth, her nose, her eyes? And what about colouring? Were her eyes exactly the same clear blue? The blue of cornflowers? Was her hair precisely the same unusual shade of apricot gold? How could it be so? Surely it was impossible. Yet…how else could he make such a mistake?

Kristy shook her head in pained bewilderment. The whole thing was a nightmare. She wrenched her gaze off her reflection in the mirror and left the bathroom. She paused in the dressing-room, eyeing her canvas carryall.

She should pick it up and get out of here. It was the sensible thing to do. Get out of this suite, out of this hotel, right out of this nightmarish situation. Then she would be just herself again, on her way to Geneva, precisely as she had planned before letting herself be sidetracked by a sentimental impulse.

On her way to Geneva…

Kristy's heart stopped dead as her mind performed a double loop. Her mission was to search the Red Cross records for some trace of the family she had lost twenty-five years ago. What if she hadn't been the only survivor of the earthquake? What if she had a sister—*an identical twin sister*!—who'd also survived? Or who hadn't even been in the same place at the same time?

Family—real family!

Her stilled heart burst into rapid pumping.

The answers she wanted might be right here. With the man in the suite next door. Having a twin made more sense out of everyone's conviction she was someone else. If it was true.

Her mind whirled, struck by the set of eerie coincidences…*the man who knew* staying in this hotel, being actually in the lobby when she had entered for the first and probably the last time in her life… Betty and John bringing her here after their deaths…an impulse…guided by feelings for the very people who might have inadvertently separated her from a twin sister.

Kristy rubbed at her forehead. It ached, as did her heart, carrying the burden of too many thoughts and too many feelings. There was only one way to sort them out. She had to talk to the man again, whether he wanted it or not. Besides, he probably needed a resolution as much as she did.

Too agitated to wait for a longer cooling-off period for him, Kristy headed for the dangerous door again. Nothing was going to put her off her purpose this time, not insults, not threats, not even physical abuse, though she didn't believe he'd try that again.

She knocked to give him warning, then twisted the key in the lock and thrust the door open. *"Monsieur..."* she called commandingly, determined not to be deterred from asking the questions that had to be asked and answered.

No reply.

She stepped into his sitting room and called again, shooting her gaze around as much as she could see of his suite. It appeared as empty as when she'd first entered and there was no response to her call. She waited, riven by dreadful tension. Perhaps he was in the bathroom. She listened hard. No sound. There was an empty feel to the place, not even a remote sense of his strong presence.

Kristy stood blankly for several minutes, robbed of her purpose and at a total loss what to do next. He wasn't here. She didn't know his name. The hotel management was so hung up on discretion, it was most unlikely they'd just give it to her. Apart from which, since the mix-up was still in force, they'd probably think such an inquiry was another little *joke* on her part.

Her best course, she finally decided, was to wait a few hours and see if he came back. It was midafternoon now. If he was occupying this suite, he'd probably return to it to change for dinner. On the other hand, he might have washed his hands of her and gone off with the beautiful brunette.

It was a depressing thought.

Kristy brooded over the strong pull he'd had on her, then sternly told herself he wouldn't want to have anything to do with the twin of a woman who'd dumped him. Maybe they shared the same chemistry. That would help to explain the extraordinary feelings he stirred in her.

Despondently she returned to her suite, relocking the connecting door. She needed his name, but that could wait, too. If she failed to make any further contact with him today, she would tackle the hotel management tomorrow morning, argue her case, and demand co-operation. No way would she countenance losing this link to a possible sister.

Having been through so much emotional upheaval, Kristy tried to steady herself down. She unpacked the few things she'd need from her carryall, took her toilet bag into the bathroom, freshened up, then remembered she hadn't eaten any lunch. Her stomach felt like a bag of knots, but some sustenance was in order if she was to face another confrontation with the man.

The complimentary platter of fruit beckoned—easily digestible food within reach. Kristy still felt she had no right to it, any more than she had a right to this suite. However, it was paramount she stay here, close to any useful development from the current impasse.

That need made up her mind for her. She selected a bunch of grapes and wandered out to her private terrace, hoping the view might provide some distraction for a while. Idly, and without any sense of appetite, she popped grapes into her mouth as she watched the traffic and people traversing the Place de la Concorde below her. Eventually she was left with an empty stalk in her hand and belatedly realised she hadn't tasted anything. But she was calmer and was beginning to feel hungry.

She returned to the sitting room and selected a peach, intent on enjoying the taste of something. It was halfway to her mouth when there was a knock on her door. Her heart gave a kick at the thought it might be *him*. But surely *he* would knock on the interconnecting door, not the one facing the corridor. She replaced the peach, took a deep breath, and determinedly set herself to remain in control, no matter what!

Having reached the door, Kristy cautiously opened it only far enough to identify her visitor. A bellboy and two maids carrying large boxes were lined up in the corridor outside. The boy held out a small silver tray on which lay an envelope from hotel stationery.

"A note for you, *Madame*," he said, eyeing her with avid interest.

The maids' faces were lit with curious speculation as well. *The delicate situation* was still very much alive as far as the hotel staff was concerned, Kristy thought in vexation.

"*Merci,*" she got out between her teeth, and picked up the envelope. To refuse it could only exacerbate whatever gossip there was, and Kristy could not deny she was curious to see its contents. Was the note from *him* or the manager?

An idea struck. "Do you know my name?" she asked the boy, hoping her perfect double would be identified. A name would help as a starting point to unravelling the mystery.

"*Oui, Madame.*"

"Then what is it?" Kristy demanded.

The bellboy looked at her suspiciously. His eyes turned wary. Uncertainty flitted over his face. "Everyone knows it is...uh...Madame...uh... Holloway."

Discretion above all, Kristy interpreted, and deduced she would get nothing further out of him. He knew the other woman's name all right. Kristy was certain of it. But undoubtedly he had had instructions and would stick to them to the letter. His job probably depended on it.

Quelling her frustration, she slit open the envelope and withdrew a single sheet of notepaper, aware that the action increased her involvement in this murky affair but driven to learn whatever she could about it. Her gaze instantly homed in on the signature which dominated the middle of the page.

Armand.

No hotel manager would sign a Christian name. The note had to be from *him*. And his name was Armand. Armand what? Armand who? Kristy fiercely wished she wasn't so ignorant of the basic facts of this mess. She glared at the bellboy and the maids who knew more about it than she did, then ignored them as she dropped her gaze to the top of the sheet to read what *he* had to say.

"There are matters to be resolved."

Kristy's heart leapt with hope. Surely this meant another chance to talk. Her eyes skated to the next sentence.

''To keep a further meeting between us both impersonal and as civil as possible, I suggest we meet in Les Etoiles for dinner. Eight o'clock.''

Tonight. On neutral ground. Kristy breathed a huge sigh of relief. He wouldn't make a scene at dinner. Not on public view. It was the opportunity for her to ask all the questions she could think of.

Her eyes skipped on to the next line—

''Should you not attend, be assured I will hound you off the face of the earth until I do get these matters resolved.''

Kristy almost laughed out loud. His threat had no teeth whatsoever. In fact, if *he* should not attend, *she* would be the one hounding him. However, his words did reveal an intensity of purpose which she couldn't dismiss quite so easily. He was affected by her—or her double—very deeply. She had best tread very cautiously at this proposed meeting.

There was a postscript underneath his signature— ''P.S. I have taken the liberty of providing you with appropriate clothes. Make no attempt to shame me in public again or your cause will suffer commensurately.''

Which explained the boxes being carried by the maids. So much pride, Kristy thought. Deeply wounded pride. However high-handed it was—supplying her with what he considered suitable clothes— refusing to accept them would not get her where she wanted to be. She could swallow her own pride in this instance. Probably the only way to get into the arena of his choice was to wear them. The means to an end.

She lifted her gaze to the bellboy. "Do you know a place called Les Etoiles?" she asked.

He looked startled by the question. "*Oui, Madame. It is the premier restaurant here in this hotel.*"

Of course. Top class. Kristy flashed the bellboy a smile to gloss over her ignorance. "So it is."

The boy and the maids looked at her as though she had lost her sanity. Which she probably had, Kristy thought. But there was no turning back from the speculations stirred by Armand X's behaviour, especially since it was echoed by the behaviour of the hotel staff. She had to pursue the *double* issue, regardless of where it led and how it was done. She had to know.

She waved the maids with the boxes into the suite. They deposited these in the dressing-room. Kristy noted the maids were different from those who had brought the other things, earlier in the afternoon. The hotel staff was obviously sharing the delicate situation around. No doubt it was enlivening their day. She ignored their surreptitious glances at her as they made their departure and closed the door on this latest visitation.

The new development spurred Kristy into further cogitation on the circumstances which were now presenting a clearer picture. Armand X had to be someone important and influential for the staff at the Soleil Levant to be so anxious to please and appease him. He might even be a public figure whose good reputation was at stake. *Un scandale terrible*, the bellboy had said, and maybe it hadn't been a melodramatic exaggeration. Obviously there was a lot more to this delicate situation than Kristy could possibly guess at.

Another shock awaited her in the dressing room. The boxes were emblazoned with The House of Dior. It proved a couple of things straight away. Armand X's name had to pack one mighty big punch to get The House of Dior sending garments at his command, and he had to have the wealth to back it up.

It all added up to *power*.

And she was a nobody with nothing and no-one to back her up.

A little shiver of trepidation ran down her spine. How dangerous were the waters she was about to wade into?

She stared at the famous designer name.

Was she getting in too deep here?

What power did she have?

Only the truth, and she mightn't get to the truth held by her powerful antagonist if she didn't accept his terms. She took a deep breath and lifted off the lids of the boxes.

The contents were awesome—a black crepe dinner dress with a plunging V neckline, beaded shoulders, and a narrow skirt which was artfully draped away from a dropped V waistline; a beaded evening bag to match; elegant high-heeled shoes; the finest of fine black silk stockings; a French corselet of black lace which was so sexy it was sinful.

The whole lot had to have cost him a small fortune, yet Kristy suspected the cost was meaningless to him—a trifle that bought him his way. Simple expedience. The image of his companion in the lobby flashed into her mind. The beautiful brunette had definitely been wearing couturier clothes. This was what he was used to.

Nevertheless, as afternoon wore into early evening, Kristy couldn't help brooding over the fact that her double—her possible twin—must have worn such clothes. Had they been supplied by Armand X or did she belong to a wealthy family? If she'd been gone without a trace for two years, it seemed doubtful there was family. A man of power could surely have found her through them.

Would there be nothing for her at the end of this journey?

More *nothing*?

No...at least she'd have knowledge, information she hadn't had before.

Hoping for this much, Kristy set about getting ready for the fateful dinner. She soaked herself in a long, relaxing bath, carefully applied what make-up she had which best complemented the dress, and brushed her hair to shiny bounciness.

Putting on the black lace corselet and silk stockings made her feel like a courtesan, prompting the question of what exactly had been her double's relationship with Armand X? A sexual one...that was certain. And very passionate. She remembered his kiss, then wished she hadn't. It made her feel shaky inside and somehow increased the bleak emptiness of her life.

Her hands trembled as she eased herself into the black crepe dress. She wondered what had been done with the chic companion? Not that it was any of

Kristy's business, but she imagined the brunette's day had been totally spoiled by the *scandale*.

Were they in love, as she had sentimentally speculated? For some reason, Kristy didn't want to think so now. Besides, she couldn't see how Armand X could be so deeply affected by the supposed return of her double if he now loved someone else. Surely there had been more than pride stirring his passions in their last encounter.

The dress fitted her perfectly. Too perfectly. Kristy's height and figure made her a fairly standard size twelve—along with thousands of other women— so maybe the law of averages was on her side. Nevertheless, she felt slightly discomfited by the uncanny fact that her size had been judged exactly right. It suggested that she and her double shared the same body shape as well as everything else.

Kristy picked up the shoes. Not her feet, she thought, stifling a queer sense of panic. They couldn't possibly have the same shaped feet. There was no way these shoes could fit perfectly. Even identical twins had little differences. Surely life brought them out over the years and there'd been twenty-five years of separation with very different paths taken along the way.

She eyed the elegant high-heeled pumps assessingly. They looked about the right size for her but they were sure to pinch or rub somewhere.

She bent down and placed them on her feet.

They fitted perfectly.

They could have been handmade, specifically for her.

A weird feeling hit the pit of her stomach. She and her double *were* exactly the same. As much as she'd like to discover a sister, the feeling of being cheated of her own individuality washed through her in sickening waves. It was as though someone had performed some ghastly sleight of hand at her expense. How could anyone else be made *exactly* like her?

Kristy's mind ran feverishly over the possibilities. What if Armand X would not believe she was someone else? Was her passport sufficient proof? He might argue it was forged but it was all she had to identify herself, and the American Embassy would run a check on it if necessary. She hastily transferred it from her luggage to the beaded evening bag, ready to produce if her word was questioned.

It suddenly occurred to her The House of Dior must have a record of all her double's measurements. These things had not been sent on a potluck basis. Kristy was quite sure that the houses of top Parisian couturiers did not work that way. Which meant her double must have had an account there.

Her mind buzzing with questions about her possible twin sister, Kristy turned instinctively to look at herself in the mirror. The effect of the clothes gave her a reflection she was not used to. It was as though she had crossed over to the other side of the mirror and become the woman she didn't know, the woman Armand X was expecting to sit down to dinner with.

If he clothed you like this, she asked the image who was her, and yet not her, what kind of life did you lead with him? What was so wrong with what you shared with him that you left and never once looked back in the last two years? Are you still alive out there somewhere? What happened to you? Were you really bad? A heartless, gutless, shameless cheat?

Did she want to know and own a sister of such suspect character?

A little shiver of premonition ran down Kristy's spine. Perhaps carrying on with this dinner arrangement was a step into more madness. It might not resolve anything. And then…what then?

Armand X knew it all…or thought he did.

She was not going to change her mind now.

It was five minutes to eight.

Time to step through the looking glass and find out what was on the other side.

CHAPTER FIVE

KRISTY arrived at the entrance to Les Etoiles at precisely eight o'clock. Armand X was not there. Her inner tension moved up several notches and fed a fast-growing wave of angry resentment. *She* had complied with his instructions. *He* had specified the time. Giving her the courtesy of punctuality was the least he could have done in these supposedly scandalous circumstances.

She saw the maître d' hurrying across the dining room to attend to her. No doubt he had been primed to the delicate situation as well. Kristy nonchalantly sent her gaze roving around the premier restaurant of the Soleil Levant, pride insisting she not look put out at having to stand here alone.

The setting was pure eighteenth-century grandeur. The walls were at least five metres high and covered in superb tapestries, varieties of marble panelling, and ornate mirrors. The ceiling was delicately painted with clouds and decorated with gold leaf. The chandeliers lent their golden glow to the finely set tables and magnificent arrangements of flowers.

It was a fabulous room, and Kristy did have the assurance that she was appropriately dressed for it. On the outside she knew she looked the epitome of high class. On the inside, she was a mass of shrieking nerves, so much so she almost jumped when Armand X suddenly appeared at her side.

"My apologies for keeping you waiting."

Kristy stared at him, totally dumbstruck as her heart performed sickening aerobics in her chest. She had thought him striking when she had first set eyes on him, but in a formal black dinner suit, he was breathtakingly handsome.

"Don't!" he commanded harshly.

"Don't what?" she asked, feeling swallowed up by the intensity of his gaze.

"Pretend I mean anything to you but money."

His bitter cynicism jolted her out of the magnetism he emitted. "These clothes were your idea, not mine," she snapped, arming up to fight the implication she had set out to take him for a ride.

He instantly proceeded to disarm her, offering a dry whimsical smile. "And may I say how well they suit you. But I'm sure you know that. Your beauty hypnotised me...kept me immobile...while I watched your arrival here."

Kristy had never thought of herself as beautiful. It had to be the clothes. Which belonged to her double. He wasn't really seeing her—Kristy Holloway. He was seeing the other woman.

He took her hand, lifted it to his mouth, brushed his lips over the back of her fingers. Kristy felt a tingle of heat under her skin. He was confusing her very badly with this sudden switch in his manner. It was too much more than just *civil*, especially after the flash of bitterness. She'd almost prefer the honesty of this afternoon's passionate rage.

"My arm," he said, prompting her out of her daze as he offered it.

She took it, her heart fluttering into more frantic action as his strong masculinity somehow became forceful, swamping her with a sense of weak femininity. She wasn't a weak woman. She had never been weak. So why did her bones feel as though they were dissolving? It had to be the strange duplicity of the situation, she reasoned frantically.

The hovering maître d' apparently saw their linked arms as his signal for affirmative action and made a ceremony of leading them into the restaurant to their table. Kristy prickled with the awareness of being watched. Surreptitiously, and with the best of good manners and breeding, *every* eye turned towards them. Kristy became extremely conscious that it wasn't just Armand X drawing the attention, it was more the fact that *she* was with him.

What had her double done? Was she a notorious woman in this highly privileged society? Was she guilty of more than thumbing her nose at Armand X's attractions by disappearing without notice? Had he been accused of doing away with her? What was the point of this harmonious public display tonight?

They were seated.

A wine waiter was instantly on hand to pour them a glass of champagne.

Armand X lifted his glass in a toast. "To a better understanding," he murmured, his dark brilliant eyes projecting the intimate knowledge that Kristy simply did not have.

"I'll drink to that," she replied with considerable

irony. A sip of wine was just what she needed. Her mouth and throat were as dry as the Navajo desert.

It was not until she put the glass down again that she saw the satisfaction on his face, the glitter of triumph in his eyes. The realisation came to Kristy that the apparently friendly toast was all part of the show she had become an unwitting party to.

It did not take much thought to work out this whole sequence had to do with pride—Armand X's pride. If she had not turned up, he would not have been seen waiting alone. If she had not worn the clothes he had provided, he would not have made his appearance beside her.

His gallantry—complimenting her, kissing her hand, offering his arm—undoubtedly demonstrated he could rise above any situation, however delicate it was. He was not only as handsome as the devil, Kristy thought, he had the pride of Lucifer as well.

"I've passed muster for you, have I?" she mocked, her own pride insisting she let him know she was not taken in by his act.

His eyes hardened. He gave a Gallic shrug of his shoulders. "You staged your scene in the lobby. Did you not expect me to redress that humiliation?"

"I didn't expect anything from you," Kristy replied truthfully.

"So you said." His mouth curled into a cynical little smile. "Your arrival at this time, however, is too opportune for me to believe you have no expectations."

"So tell me what you do believe," Kristy challenged, hoping to pry something revealing from him.

He did not like being put on the spot. He wanted to run this scene his way. He delayed an answer, rubbing his chin reflectively as his eyes watched her with wary intensity. Finally he said very slowly, "I mistook you for Colette. Which I think you intended to begin with. For impact purposes."

Colette.

At last her double had a name! And he realised *she* was a separate entity! Relief swept through Kristy in a tidal wave. She didn't have to prove anything. But there was still the task of finding out what all this meant and plumbing the possibility of Colette's being her sister.

It was going to be tricky. He might close up like a clam if she revealed her total ignorance of the situation. Why would he help a nobody who meant nothing to him?

"So you now know I'm Kristy Holloway, not Colette," she slid back at him.

His eyes burned with black resentment. "The likeness is perfect, as I'm sure you're aware. I will not apologise for my behaviour since you deliberately stirred it."

Kristy bit down on her tongue. The vehement denial that threatened to leap off it might close doors she wanted opened.

"However, I now concede you did attempt to establish your true identity," he stiffly granted.

"May I ask what finally convinced you?" For her own sense of self, she wanted to know the differences.

He grimaced, vexed by the error he had made.

"You used your left hand in closing the door. An awkward action to my view that instantly struck me as wrong."

It had been natural to her, automatic, especially in her distressed state. She remembered him calling, "Wait!" Impossible for her to have guessed the significance of the call. She hadn't known her perfect double was right-handed.

"And when I kissed you..." His deeply set eyelids lowered, thick black lashes veiling his expression. "...the way you responded...that also was different."

Kristy swiftly swept her own lashes down, but she was unable to quell the squirmish tide of heat that flooded her body. "It did not seem significant to you then," she tersely reminded him.

He shrugged. "I was aroused by other issues."

Oh, sure! Kristy thought savagely, still far too alive to his sex appeal and the intense vulnerability his strong physical presence tapped in her. Futile feelings, where he was concerned, and there was certainly no future in them. She fiercely wished they'd just go away. She needed all her wits about her to dig information from him.

"So on that basis you're prepared to accept I am who I say I am," she dryly concluded.

He gave a short laugh and relaxed back in his chair, still eyeing her narrowly. "Not quite as easily as that. I ascertained from the senior desk clerk that you filled out your hotel registration form with your left hand. And I had the passport number you'd given checked through the American Embassy."

Power, wealth and influence...hard to beat, Kristy

thought flippantly. "So the hotel is now aware of the mix-up, too," she commented.

"The management is, though be assured the current arrangements will remain in place." His mouth curled. "You will not be required to pay for anything."

Her chin went up. "I'm perfectly prepared to pay for the cheapest room. Which was what I asked for."

He made a dismissive gesture. "You accepted the suite…"

"Under protest!"

"…and you accepted the clothes."

"Because you made it clear this meeting depended on my doing so."

"Of course. The meeting is what you came for, is it not?" he countered derisively. "To fight Colette's battles for her?"

Kristy barely stopped herself from spilling out the truth. She took a hard pull on her temper, armoured herself as best she could against his goading, and coolly stated, "In your own words, *there are matters to be resolved.*"

"With absolute finality." His eyes glittered intense resolution. "Make no mistake about that, Mademoiselle Holloway."

Finality would be reached very fast, Kristy reasoned, if she let slip she had no knowledge of the woman who incensed him so much. "Why do you think I'm here to fight battles?"

"Because I shall give you one on everything you ask of me on Colette's behalf. Which I am sure she anticipated and why she sent you in her place." His mouth thinned in contempt. "Too gutless to face me herself."

"You are quite intimidating," Kristy acknowledged.

It evoked a wry smile. "Not to you. You're a fighter. Another difference. But as I've been given to understand, this is usual with mirror-image twins, one personality more positive than the other. More aggressive. Stronger."

Mirror-image twins... There seemed to be no doubt in his mind about her relationship to Colette, and the phrase described her own speculations on her double. But was it true? Did he have proof?

A waiter arrived and presented them with menus. He remained at the table, ready to help them with their choices. Kristy glanced down the lists, totally disinterested in food. She picked out the wild mushrooms as an entree and the roast beef as the main course—simple fare and easy to eat. Armand X did not discuss his choices with the waiter, either. They gave their order, their menus were taken and they were left alone again.

There were several seconds of silence as he gazed at his wineglass, pushing the stem of it around between his index finger and thumb. "I didn't believe in you," he said, raising weary, self-mocking eyes. "I thought you were a figment of Colette's imagination. A wish. A need."

She knew about me? Kristy was so startled by this revelation, she almost gave the game away in her eagerness to learn what Colette had known. She leaned forward, a host of questions rushing through her mind, but he forestalled her, offering more.

"It's quite a twist…being faced with the reality," he went on. "Your name was Christine. Colette called you Chrissie. How did that get to be Kristy?"

Kristy's stomach contracted. He was no longer speaking of her as a figment of Colette's imagination but a real person he knew about.

"An American couple adopted me," she answered. Had she called herself Chrissie? A three-year-old, not aware of her full name? "I guess it was their choice."

"You didn't remember your name?"

"Not that I recall. I was very young."

"Four years old," he remarked critically.

Four? John and Betty must have misjudged her age. Or maybe she wasn't the Chrissie Colette remembered. Uncertainty racked her again. "I was in a coma, on life support machines," she said slowly, trying to sort out the truth. "When I woke up, I had no memory of before."

He frowned. "You were assumed dead, buried by the earthquake."

Dear God! This was a link she could not gloss over! His mention of the earthquake stretched coincidence too far. She really did have a twin sister who remembered her. Kristy suddenly felt sick. All these years they could have known each other, been with each other…lost. Irretrievably lost.

"I was buried for five days," she said flatly.

"Five?" he repeated incredulously. "How did you survive?"

"I don't know. John said it was a miracle."

"John?"

"Holloway. He and his wife, Betty, adopted me. They're both gone now."

The increased sense of loss tore through her, giving rise to a huge lump of emotion in her throat. She reached for her wineglass, fighting back a prickling of tears. A few cautious sips of champagne helped to clear the blockage to speech. Extremely conscious of Armand X's silence, she felt pressured to offer more on the subject of her survival.

"John was in the U.S. Army," she started jerkily, then paused to muster a coherent explanation. "In those days he headed a special rescue task force, posted to disaster sites. At the time I was found, it was believed there were no more survivors and bulldozers were already moving in to stabilise the area, knocking down unsafe structures."

The near-crushing of her unconscious self brought back the horror of the story, the nightmares it had set off through her childhood, the fear she couldn't control. She shook her head, wishing she hadn't been reminded of it but compelled now to complete the explanation.

"John told me I was in a protected pocket, uncovered as other material was pushed aside. There was water from a broken pipe within reach of my mouth. It was thought I must have been conscious and drank from it at some time," she finished quickly. "After I was freed from…from the hole…I was airlifted to a hospital in Tel Aviv."

"Why Israel?" he queried. "The earthquake was in Turkey, near Ankara."

His placement of the earthquake sealed her connection to Colette beyond any possible doubt. "The hospitals there were already overcrowded. I needed special treatment. John arranged it. He saved my life," she recited, knowing the story by heart.

"So that was how you were missed," he mused, shaking his head. "Colette never really accepted you were dead. She said she felt you…alive…somewhere. I put it down to the fact the rest of her family was wiped out and it was too much loss to accept."

No family? All gone except herself and Colette? But at least there *was* someone, she swiftly consoled herself. The sense of aloneness was wrong. Who could be closer to her than a mirror-image twin—the other half of herself?

"And she was right," he went on, flashing her a darkly ironic look. "Did you feel the same?"

Kristy hesitated, searching for the truth of what she had felt. "I had no conscious memory of her. No conscious memory of anything before I woke up in the hospital and only vague memories of that period. But I did feel very strongly that some part of me was…lost. I've always felt that."

Which was why she had been going to Geneva.

There was nothing to find there now, no real family left except Colette, and Armand X had more recent knowledge of her sister than any records in Geneva.

"Well, I trust Colette is a happier person now for having found you," he commented acidly.

Kristy stared at him, painfully conscious of the awful gap of knowledge between them. Should she confess her ignorance now? His expression was neither inviting nor receptive. A hard, cold pride was stamped on his features. His dark eyes were not emitting black fury but she sensed a blackness of heart in those windows to his soul. His *giving* so far had been inadvertent. She doubted there was any intention to give more than he had to.

Impatient at her apparent reluctance to reply to his comment, he tersely added, "If not, she has only herself to blame."

"Is that so?" Kristy put in testingly. Despite being unaware of what had transpired between this man and her twin sister, her sympathies were instinctively stirred on the side of her own flesh and blood. "I notice you have consoled yourself with another woman."

His mouth thinned. "Colette's jealous suspicions over Charmaine were totally unwarranted at the time. Totally!" he repeated fiercely.

"Oh, really?" Kristy challenged, instantly seizing on how vehemently he protested and recklessly pursuing the point. "Was I mistaken in observing a strong attraction between you and your companion in the lobby?"

"It has been two years!" he retorted.

Kristy's own envy of his relationship with the beautiful brunette fed the urge to defend her twin. There had to be a reason why Colette had walked out on Armand X and as far as she was concerned, the reason had the name, Charmaine. Her eyebrows lifted in arch mockery.

"The smoke of ignition precedes an actual blaze, *Monsieur*. Having seen the two of you together, I have no difficulty in imagining there was enough smoke around for Colette to smell for herself.''

Hot slashes of colour highlighted his aristocratic cheekbones. ''She has fed you neurotic lies.''

''No. I knew nothing of Charmaine before today. I simply observe, *Monsieur*.'' And from her observation he was as guilty as hell!

It threw him for a moment, but he came back fighting. ''Then you have no cause whatsoever to justify Colette's actions with such spurious conclusions.'' He was angry now, very angry, his eyes glittering daggers at her.

Which only served to deepen Kristy's suspicions. He was far too attractive for his own good, without a doubt arrogantly confident with women. The way he had kissed her this afternoon—just taking as he willed—demonstrated how cavalier he was with his passions. Kristy burned again at the memory, hating how deeply she had been aroused by him—a man who was currently involved with another woman. Fidelity obviously meant nothing to him!

''So what reason do you have in your mind for her leaving you?'' she sniped.

''The American!'' he hurled back.

''What American?''

He hesitated, clearly discomforted by her questioning this point. In a flare of frustration he said, ''They left on the same day.''

''Is that the only connection you can tell me?'' she shot at him incredulously.

''There were other circumstances,'' he snapped.

''How convenient!'' she drawled sarcastically.

"Tell me, *Monsieur*, did you smell the smoke? Did you see them leave together?"

The black fury was back in full force. "I did not have to see them leave together. They departed on the same day. Without so much as a word to me. Explain that, *Mademoiselle*!"

"I don't have to explain anything, *Monsieur*," Kristy retorted. "I know nothing of the American you speak of."

Maybe she was being irrational, taking her sister's side, but this man riled all her most primitive instincts. In attacking her twin's integrity, it felt as though he was attacking hers and she wouldn't have it! There was something very wrong here—she felt it very strongly—and she was not going to accept her twin was to blame for everything. There were always two sides to a break-up.

Certainly her denial gave him pause for thought. His eyes narrowed. "If you have come to see if a reconciliation is possible, let me state unequivocally your mission is futile."

The fire had been replaced by ice.

Kristy held her gaze steady on his, refusing to flinch from the deep-freeze tactic. "I have seen that for myself, *Monsieur*," she replied, wondering how much blame for her sister's flight could be laid at Charmaine's door. She could see, in her mind's eye, the other woman's possessive clutch of his arm in the lobby.

His hand sliced the air, putting a decisive end to that issue. "I am agreeable to discussing the legal arrangements for a divorce. I suggest you proceed on that basis,'' he bit out.

A divorce?

Colette was his *wife*?

Shock paralysed Kristy's thought processes on that one totally unanticipated fact. This man was married to her mirror-image twin sister. He was her husband. Not a spurned lover. Her husband.

He leaned forward, glaring at her, and she could feel an intense violence swirling through him, barely contained behind the tension of fiercely controlled flesh and muscle.

"And let me spell out right now, she will never, *never*, get custody of our children. She left Pierre and Eloise with me and that's exactly where my son and daughter are going to stay...*with me!*"

CHAPTER SIX

HER twin was not only Armand X's wife, but the mother of his two children!

And she had deserted all of them!

Without a word of warning beforehand and without any communication afterwards. Absolute silence from her for two long years!

No wonder there had been shock all around at her supposed reappearance...from the doorman onwards, being greeted as *Madame,* then the *scandale terrible* with Armand X in the hotel, romancing another woman. Everything fell into place and it was not good. Not good at all. The hotel manager's description of *delicate* was a masterpiece of tactful understatement.

So appalled was Kristy by the situation, words completely failed her. There was no defence for a mother who walked out of the lives of two small children. They had to be small. Colette was the same age as herself—twenty-eight. No, twenty-nine by her husband's reckoning. Her son and daughter would surely be under ten years old, younger still when their mother had disappeared.

What mother could do that? How could she become so alienated...not to care what happened to them...not to want to even hear about them? Kristy knew she herself would be incapable of walking away so totally. It seemed inhuman...heartless.

Heartless had been the word Armand X had used this afternoon. *Heartless, shameless and gutless.* Kristy had to agree it looked that way...yet why would a woman who had experienced her own traumatic loss as a child visit the same feeling of bereftness on her own children?

She was still puzzling over this when a waiter arrived to serve their entrees. The plate of wild mushrooms had no appeal whatsoever to her churning stomach. Not wanting to draw attention to her dilemma, she picked up her knife and fork and pushed the food around, cutting off the occasional small piece, managing to swallow a few bits.

Her mind kept circling what she now knew of Colette, trying to find excuses for what she had done. Could she have had a nervous breakdown, lost her mind and memory? What kind of pressures had she lived with? What kind of life did Armand X lead?

Neurotic lies, he'd said. *Neurotic* suggested her twin was off balance. If she wasn't a fighter by nature, as her husband had implied in comparing her to Kristy, maybe everything had become too much for her. And she'd had no family to turn to for support.

The emptiness of that reality wrenched at Kristy's heart.

Am I too late to help?

She had to find Colette. Nothing more could be answered until she did. Somewhere her twin sister was in need. Armand X didn't believe that but Kristy did. In her heart, she couldn't believe anything else.

"Lost your appetite?"

The sardonic comment focused her attention on
him. There was a gleam of savage mockery in his
eyes. He thought he'd put her in a hard place with no
room to manoeuvre and she was wilting under his
relentless stance. The marriage was over. Custody of
the children was his. All that remained was to settle
visiting rights—if any—and a division of property.
He had it figured that money was all she and Colette
were interested in.

He couldn't be more wrong.

But how to begin? How to pursue finding a woman
he'd given up on? He had thought *she* was the answer
to the problem of his missing wife. He needed an
answer if he wanted to put Charmaine in Colette's
place. Oh yes, he *needed* an answer as much as Kristy
did. Which was why he'd gone to such lengths to
ensure he got one, even threatening to hound her off
the face of the earth if she didn't co-operate in getting
these matters resolved.

She set down her knife and fork, and feeling more
sure of her ground now, had no hesitation in admitting
the truth. "You're right. I have no appetite at all." A
glance at his plate showed he'd had no such trouble.
"At least one of us has done justice to the food," she
added, wondering with some irony how well he'd
manage the next course.

"Perhaps it is because I have justice on my side,"
he taunted.

Kristy decided not to contest that point, though she
inwardly rejected it. She met his gaze squarely and

asked, "Do you have any doubt that I am your wife's mirror-image twin sister?"

"There can be no doubt. Apart from the evidence of my eyes, and everyone else's…" He glanced derisively around the dining room. "…the details of your background affirm the fact."

She nodded. "I believe that, too."

He raised his brows quizzically. "You thought, perhaps, you would need papers to prove it to me?" He gestured a waiver of any such necessity. "*N'importe.* I accept your credentials to speak for Colette."

Kristy scooped in a deep breath and took the most direct path to the future. "I cannot speak for Colette. I have never met my twin sister. I had no knowledge of her existence until you gave it to me, *Monsieur.*"

The stark statements hit him like blows. His head jerked. Then his whole body seemed to steam forward, eyes blazing. "*Sacre bleu!* What is the purpose of these lies? What can you hope to gain by them?"

Kristy barely stopped herself from recoiling. As it was, her heart skittered in fright. But there was no changing the course she'd chosen and she could not be intimidated out of it.

"Only the truth," she answered with direct simplicity.

He made a scoffing noise and sat back, eyeing her with icy disdain. "A delaying tactic will not earn you anything, *Mademoiselle.*"

The cold waves of bitterness coming from him sent a shiver down Kristy's spine. She steeled herself to go on. There was no going back. The turning point had come and gone much earlier today.

"I apologise for misleading you, *Monsieur*," she said with genuine sincerity, keeping her voice quiet and hopefully sympathetic. "I had no idea what I was dealing with. From all that has happened to me since I arrived at this hotel, I could only surmise I was some other woman's perfect double. I am here with you now because I had a very great need to resolve the mystery."

His mouth thinned. His face was stiff with disbelief.

Her eyes did not waver from his, steadily projecting a plea for understanding. "You were very hostile to me. The staff evaded answering any questions they considered sensitive."

She lifted her hands, touching the beaded black dress, trying to demonstrate how strange her position was. "These clothes, shoes, fitted as though they were made for me. It was as though I had somehow crawled into some other person's skin. I wanted to know who I was supposed to be."

She paused, hoping to push home the dilemma she'd found herself in. Then she quietly asked, "Wouldn't you...if you were me?"

There was a long, tense, assessing silence. Kristy felt her explanation was being dissected, measured piece by piece against the conversation which had preceded it. When he finally spoke, his voice was sharp with suspicion.

"Why do you defend a woman you profess not to know?"

It was difficult to express her feelings, but knowing she had nothing but the truth to give in reply, Kristy did her best. "You convinced me she was my twin sister. I felt...bonded to her cause. I didn't know about the children. How could I? But I had seen you with the woman in the lobby and..."

That electric sense of intimacy which had struck her...the fierce wave of possessiveness...jealousy... had it been some kind of psychic link with her sister's feelings...invested in him and somehow echoing out to her? It had been so strong, so unexpected, unwarranted in any ordinary circumstances.

"And what?" he probed harshly.

Kristy shook herself out of the disturbing reflection and searched his eyes for a trace of the sense of connection to her. Something moved in those dark unfathomable depths and her pulse quickened. "I felt I knew you," she said softly. "Even though I was sure we'd never met, I felt...."

"I thought you were Colette," he snapped and whatever he'd *felt* was instantly shielded from her view.

"Of course," she sighed and sat back, trying to untangle the mess of her emotions. There was no denying he affected her, on more levels than she cared to examine now she knew he was her sister's husband. Any kind of intimacy with him had to be shut down. It could never be right.

The waiter came to remove the plates. Their glasses were topped up with more champagne. Kristy's chest felt so tight, the moment the waiter departed, she reached for her glass, hoping the champagne might relax her tightly strung nerves. Having swallowed a few sips, she loosened up enough to construct a peace-offering smile.

"I don't even know your full name. Armand…what?"

He was observing her keenly. "Dutournier," he briefly replied.

"Colette Dutournier." She rolled the name off her tongue, wishing she could conjure up the person.

"What brought you to this hotel today?"

He was still suspicious of her, but more guarded in his expression than downright distrustful. It was on the tip of her tongue to say *an impulse*, catching the words back as the idea flashed into her mind that there might have been other forces at work, pushing the impulse—forces beyond her normal understanding. Commonsense insisted he would think her mad if she tried that thought on him. Best to stick to plain facts.

"My adoptive parents honeymooned in this hotel. They've both passed on now, John…very recently." Sadness dragged a husky note into her voice. "I came here out of a sentimental memory of them…before I went on to Geneva in the hope of finding some record of my real family."

"*Bon Dieu!* You, too?"

They were startled words from him and they startled Kristy, as well. She watched, inadvertently holding her breath as some deep inner conflict warred across his face. Was it guilt? Finally realising she was waiting for an explanation, he visibly controlled himself.

"In the last months of our marriage, Colette spoke several times of going to Geneva," he said with an air of intense irritation. "On her behalf, I had already had a search of the records done. Nothing pertinent was found. She accepted the results of the investigation at the time...."

He paused, frowning heavily. "Just prior to her leaving, it seemed she chose not to believe them. She kept saying if she went herself..." He made a sharp, negative gesture. "I had no patience with it. I told her to go and satisfy herself, but then she'd go off the idea, apparently preferring the torment."

Which proved to Kristy her sister had not been in a strong state of mind, though she had yet to find out why. "Perhaps she did go when she left you. Did you look for her there?"

"Of course," he answered tersely. "There was no trace of her in Geneva. No trace of her ever having been there. Police inquiries came to nothing. Private investigators were unable to pick up any trail at all. Some missing people, I was informed, do not wish to be found."

"Did she leave by car?" Kristy queried, finding it difficult to accept there was nothing to follow.

"Yes. The car was not found, either." Frustration edged his voice. "Colette was not capable of planning such a comprehensive disappearance herself. It had to be the American."

"Two people disappearing without trace?" Kristy shot at him incredulously.

"Do you think I did not make every effort to find them?" came the fierce retort.

He would, she quickly reasoned. His own pride would have demanded it. And cost would not have been a factor. Nevertheless, it still seemed unbelievable that no clue to their whereabouts had been found. There had to be something.

"Two years and nothing...until you," he said with intense frustration. "And you have nothing for me, either."

Kristy was feeling frustrated herself.

"July the fourth they left," he went on. "Your American Independence Day." He picked up his glass of champagne in a mock toast, his eyes savagely derisive. "To your mirror-image sister, *Mademoiselle*, who made her independence total!"

Kristy was beyond responding, her mind having seized on the date of her twin's disappearance, connecting it, collating it with the experience of her own near death on the very same day two years ago. *The same day!* The doctors had been unable to explain it. She'd always enjoyed good health. She had no medical history that could account for what had happened to her. Nothing like it had occurred before or since.

She'd been at the hospital, on her nursing round. She remembered stopping at the shock of something thumping into her heart, then the sensation of falling...fear ripping through her...screaming in her head...endless falling...a sharp premonition of

death...cold washing over her...drowning in cold...
unable to breathe...terrible pain in her chest...
choking...

She'd been told afterwards she had stopped
breathing. A fellow nurse had revived her with
mouth-to-mouth resuscitation. She'd been put into a
hospital bed and kept under observation while various
tests were run. Nothing wrong with her heart. No
damage sustained. No sign of epilepsy. No answers
for what had happened to her.

The answer was in the time, not in her at all. The
certainty of it gripped Kristy in a haze of devastating
horror. Colette...disappearing on that day...and nothing of her since...nothing because there was nothing!

"Mademoiselle..."

The note of sharp concern tapped on the edge of
the haze. Through a blur she saw the man sitting
across from her lean forward, one hand lifted in urgent expostulation.

"Are you unwell?"

It was difficult to focus on him, to wrench her mind
out of the pit of loss that engulfed it. Colette's husband. But he wouldn't care. No loss to him. It was
what he'd wished. He had Charmaine now. The marriage was over. Gone...like Colette.

"Tell me what is wrong!"

He was commanding her to give him the answer...the sickening, terribly simple answer to why
her twin had deserted her husband and children and
never looked back. She could feel tears gathering be-

hind her eyes, a surge of grief thickening her throat.
Best to speak now. Get it over with.

"Your wife...my sister...is dead, *Monsieur*. I
know it...because I felt her die...on the fourth of
July...two years ago."

Tears swam across her vision. She gripped the table
to hold herself steady as she rose to her feet. "Please
excuse me," she choked out. "I cannot bear to be
with you."

CHAPTER SEVEN

ARMAND Dutournier was on his feet before Kristy took a step from the table. She turned quickly, blindly, stumbling slightly in her haste to get away from him. Her legs felt shaky. She was trembling.

Before she could even start to make good her escape his arm was around her waist, tucking her close to him. "No!" she cried in painful agitation.

"You need my support," he insisted.

In a way he was right. She didn't have the strength to break free of him. She couldn't even see straight. Everything was wobbly and the dining room was a minefield to walk through. Her exit could be strewn with disaster.

He didn't want another scene. That was why he was beside her, holding her, guiding her. But she hated it, hated his power seeping through her, generating a sense of togetherness that was horribly false. Her sister had been innocent of the crimes he'd heaped on her head. He should have known that. This closeness with him was all wrong.

The maître d' intercepted them. "*Monsieur*, can I be of service?"

"*Mademoiselle* is not well. If an elevator can be summoned ready..."

"*Oui.*"

She was deftly steered out of the restaurant. If the

manner of their departure drew attention and gave rise to more scandalous gossip, Kristy neither knew nor cared. This wasn't her life...not the hotel, its patrons, the class image of designer clothes, the man at her side. Her life had just been emptied again, in the worst possible way.

An elevator was held open, waiting for them. As they stepped into it, Kristy elbowed herself away from Armand Dutournier and shrank back against the far wall of the compartment. "I can manage on my own," she asserted, glaring at him through a veil of tears.

He pressed the button for their floor. The doors closed them in together. "You cannot expect me to walk away from the claim you have just made, *Mademoiselle*," he stated quietly. "As distressed as you may be, I have waited too long for news of my wife to release you from my company until I am satisfied that what you say is true."

"I can't prove it," she burst out, hugging her midriff to hold in the pain his presence caused her.

"I want to hear the circumstances of your knowledge," he said, his tone and manner exuding relentless determination.

Kristy swallowed hard. The elevator was on the rise. Soon they would arrive at the floor of their suites. She was not going to let him into hers. Desperately she focused her frayed mind on what few facts she had.

"It happened at about eight o'clock in the morning, San Francisco time. There was an initial impact, then a falling. She fell a long way. Into water, I think. It was very cold. It felt as though I was drowning. That's all I can tell you.''

The elevator was slowing.

"Look for a car accident that matches the time,'' she advised shakily. "Measure the distance on the road to Geneva. A place where a car could have gone off the road and fallen into deep water.''

"Why Geneva? If she was with the American...''

"I know nothing of the American,'' she cried, hating the slur of infidelity on her twin's character. "Geneva...because she must have been thinking of me. *Me*...'' Her voice shook with the vehemence needed to correct his blindness to the real situation. "How else could I have felt...''

A gush of tears filled her eyes. She pushed herself off the wall as the elevator doors opened and rushed past him into the corridor.

"You are going the wrong way, *Mademoiselle*.''

Kristy stopped, mentally cursing her faulty sense of direction, hunching her shoulders as she struggled to hold back sobs. She fumbled with the beaded evening bag, finally succeeding in extracting the key to her suite, more by touch than sight.

"How can I believe this?'' he demanded, his voice torn with uncertainty. "Every road accident which occurred that day was checked. And more.''

She swiped the tears from her cheeks, took a long deep breath, let it shudder out, squared her shoulders and swung around for the walk in the right direction. "If the accident wasn't reported and the car is in deep water in an inaccessible spot, why would it be found?'' she flung at him, striding hard to get past him to her door.

"That's a great many ifs,'' he argued.

"Maybe you don't want it found,'' she sliced at him as she came level to where he stood.

He caught her arm, forcibly holding her. "What do you mean by that?''

The words tumbled from her mouth in fierce bursts, resentment spilling over. "Finding Colette might raise questions you don't want to answer. It might upset your pat little story about her disappearance. What if the American is not with her in that death car?''

"I want the truth,'' he declared vehemently.

"Do you?'' she wildly challenged. "How will you justify yourself then, knowing she was a woman in torment and not the heartless, gutless, shameless creature you called her?''

"You do not know how it was,'' he bit out, his eyes flaring fury at her judgment.

"Well, let me tell you, Monsieur Dutournier, I don't believe for one moment my twin would desert her own flesh and blood. Her family. Not having been through what we both went through as children. And you, her husband, should have known that.''

He flinched at the sheer violence of her conviction. Kristy instantly seized the advantage of his distraction and wrenched free of his grasp.

"I didn't believe it at first,'' he hurled after her as she fled to her door.

Kristy shook her head. "She would have died before doing that. And she did. She did.''

Tears flooded her eyes again. She couldn't work

the key. The wretched thing wouldn't go right and Armand Dutournier was looming up beside her, merciless in his persistence. He took the key from her, literally snatching it out of her hand.

"Let me go!" she almost screamed in frustration.

"*Non!* Not until we have an agreement."

Confusion spilled into frantic protests. "What do you mean? I've done all you said. There's nothing left to agree on!"

"You will come to Crecy with me tomorrow. You will help me seek the truth."

Commands, not appeals.

"I can't tell you any more. I don't know any more!" she cried bitterly.

He was immovable. "If there were lies told...if Colette was maligned...I will find the truth with you, *Mademoiselle*. You will be seen as taking Colette's place..."

"You want me to pose as your wife?" Kristy protested in horror. "I won't!"

"That is not what I'm asking. It is not possible anyway," he retorted, and there was a slight shift in the ruthless purpose in his eyes, a deep uneasy acknowledgment of her as he muttered, "you are you." His face tightened into steely resolution. "Nevertheless, the shock of your resemblance to Colette... I want to see what will eventuate."

Kristy found herself in turmoil again. How could he affect her after all she now knew? "Why should I help you?" she cried, more in self-torment than in denial of his plan. "My sister is dead. For all I know, you contributed to her state of mind that day."

"There are the children," he said quietly. "They are your family, too. Do you not want to know them?"

The children…Pierre and Eloise!

Dear God! She *did* have family…a niece and nephew. She wasn't alone in the world. Colette had left behind two precious lives and they were part of herself, as well.

Motherless children…

The thought both tore at Kristy's heart and filled it with a bright and shining purpose. She was their aunt. She could be like a mother to them, love them, protect them, take care of them. If *he* would allow her to…their father.

Kristy's focus on Armand Dutournier suddenly gathered an urgent intensity. "Where is it you want me to go with you?" she asked warily.

"To my home—the chateau at Crecy, near Bordeaux."

A chateau, no less. She had certainly been right, thinking him aristocratic. "The children are there?"

"Oui."

Of course. Since he was romancing Charmaine in Paris, he wouldn't want the children hanging onto him, Kristy thought viciously. "Who is looking after them?" she asked.

"The chateau is a family holding. My mother is there, as well as my brother and his wife, and my sister. Naturally we have staff."

Naturally. Kristy's heart sank. The children probably had a nanny. But she was their aunt, the closest person to their mother they could have. "I could stay for a while and get to know the children?'' she appealed, unable to keep a note of yearning out of her voice.

He nodded. ''They should know their mother's side of the family, as well as mine,'' he said fairly.

Kristy let out a long, grateful sigh. ''It means a great deal to me. Thank you, *Monsieur*.''

His mouth twitched with irony. ''Then at least I have performed something which is right to you.''

It was disconcerting. Kristy wanted to hang onto her hostility. He hadn't done right by her twin sister. She was sure of it. Yet he still exerted this strong pull on her.

''Tomorrow, you said,'' she reminded him brusquely.

''I am eager to get started on another investigation. The sooner these matters are resolved, the better,'' he stated grimly. ''If you would join me for breakfast in the suite adjoining yours tomorrow morning, we could make appropriate plans.''

The suite where he'd kissed her! Kristy instantly clamped down on that thought. It was totally, totally inappropriate. ''What time?''

''Is nine o'clock convenient?''

''Yes. Good night, *Monsieur*,'' she managed stiffly, keeping her eyes trained on his, all too aware of the sexual power of the body he had imprinted on hers this afternoon.

''In the circumstances, it is best you call me Armand. I am your brother-in-law,'' he dryly reminded her.

''Very well. Armand,'' she repeated, telling herself

there was nothing intimate in calling him by his first name. He was family too...by marriage to her sister.

"And you will not object if I call you Kristy?"

"No. That's fine," she agreed, feeling her skin prickle at the soft sensual roll his voice gave to her name.

"For the sake of the children I would like us to be...in harmony."

Her heart turned over at the soft appeal in his eyes. "I won't try to alienate them from you, if that's your concern," she said, struggling to ward off his strong attraction. Charm was just another weapon to get his own way, Kristy fiercely told herself.

"To present a united front is what I want, Kristy, but we will talk of this tomorrow. Forgive me for holding you here against your wishes. I will hold you no longer."

He unlocked the door for her, handed her the key, and stood back with a slight bow, giving her free passage.

Kristy bade him a quick "Good night." It was a blessed relief to enter her suite and close him out...at least physically. It was impossible to close him out of her mind. He was too entangled with her twin's life and death.

The tears welled and spilled as she hastily divested herself of the clothes he'd insisted she wear...clothes befitting the twin of his wife. All for public show...for his pride. He hadn't stopped to think how she might feel in them with their close connection to Colette.

She put everything back in their boxes. Maybe they

could be returned to the House of Dior. She didn't want them. Feeling an aching need simply to be herself again, Kristy donned the silk kimono wraparound Betty had bought her in Japan. It was comfortable. It belonged to her. *He* had nothing to do with it.

Drenched in misery over all the years she might have shared with her twin sister—irretrievably gone—Kristy wandered out to the sitting room, brooding over what might have happened if she had been on hand to support Colette before the fatal car trip to Geneva. Why had Fate played such a cruel hand to both of them? Taking too much, then giving too late.

The interconnecting door between the suites caught her eye and she stopped, staring at it. This afternoon it had been a tempting door to an intriguing mystery. Now she knew better. It was the door to Colette's world. And tomorrow morning she would be stepping into that world.

What would really be there…on the other side of the mirror?

CHAPTER EIGHT

THEY were on their way. It was over five hundred kilometres from Paris to Bordeaux, Armand had told her, so Kristy concentrated on relaxing, knowing she had to share the enclosed space of the Citroen with him for several hours.

It was not going to be easy. They had been in conflict all morning and she still didn't feel right about what he'd forced upon her. But for the children she would never have given in to his demands. Getting access to them was her top priority and it was best done with the approval of their father. He knew it, too, and Kristy couldn't help seething over the power he'd so ruthlessly wielded.

She plucked fretfully at the soft suede of her new trouser suit. This didn't represent her. It wasn't her at all. She wanted to be in her denim jeans and battle jacket, familiar comfortable clothes. She didn't want to be a copy of her sister. Though Armand had denied that aim, his insistence that she wear designer clothes smacked of it.

The moment she'd walked into his suite this morning, he had started. "You cannot wear such clothes at Crecy."

"I haven't got much else with me," she had explained reasonably.

"I shall order clothes for you and have them brought to the hotel."

"You will not! I'll go shopping for myself."

"That will take too much time. There are various houses that have Colette's sizes…"

"I am not my sister."

That, at least, had given him pause, seeing the fierce light of rebellion in her eyes. "I will have a selection of clothes sent. You can choose what you like."

"I can't afford designer clothes."

"I shall pay for them."

"I won't accept that."

"Do you want to come to Crecy to meet your sister's children?"

"You know I do."

"Then you will come on my terms, Kristy."

He was totally relentless on that point. Kristy had finally snapped, "Fine! Tell your designer houses I like colour. Blues and greens—especially lime green—and lemon shades. It's a waste of time sending me black or neutral tones."

Again he'd paused, the tension between them explosive before he'd given way to her stated preferences. Kristy had been ready to fight to the death on that issue, inwardly recoiling from the black he'd chosen last night, and remembering Charmaine in her chic black and white outfit. She was not going to look like *her*, either.

At least she'd won that argument, Kristy thought with grim satisfaction, glancing down at the clothes she was wearing. The long-sleeved blouse and trouser pants were royal blue and the matching vest and belt had clever turquoise and green inserts which gave the outfit an eye-catching attraction. Nothing neutral about this choice. Her shoes matched it, too, suede shoes dyed royal blue with swirls of green.

She now had a whole new bagful of such clothes—all at Armand's expense. How it was worth the enormous cost to him she had no idea and no longer cared. Let him have his own way, as long as she got what really counted to her. Pierre and Eloise were more important than any amount of money.

"Tell me about your life, Kristy," Armand suddenly invited.

They were out of Paris, driving through the countryside, with a lot of time to fill in. Kristy didn't mind recounting the main events of her life, the countries she'd lived in through John's various postings, the odd schooling she'd had because of their many moves, how she'd caught up on her education when they were finally based in the United States, then choosing a career in nursing.

"Is there no man in your life?" he eventually asked, shooting her a sharply probing look.

Probably wondering how long she'd want to stay at Crecy with the children, Kristy surmised. "Not at the moment. John was so ill during his last months, I had no time for anything but nursing him," she explained.

"It must have been very difficult," he said sympathetically.

"I didn't begrudge any of that time."

He nodded. "You are a very caring person."

The words were accompanied by a smile that scrambled Kristy's mind and stirred a host of treacherous yearnings in her heart. She found herself fiercely envying her sister's intimacy with this man, envying Charmaine. He was so lethally attractive when he wanted to be. Even when he wasn't trying, the tug was still there. Nothing seemed to block it.

"How is it you speak such perfect French?" he queried, and Kristy was intensely grateful for the distraction from her wayward feelings.

"As I said, John spent several years in the Philippines. We used to go to Nouméa for vacations."

"Ah, New Caledonia."

"Yes. French is spoken there. I found it very easy to pick up and I kept an interest in the language. Studying it. Betty bought me tapes. And I have been to France before. Paris and Provence."

"When was that?"

"Ten years ago."

"Before I married Colette," he muttered.

Before anyone of consequence might see Kristy and question her identity. If only their lines had crossed then…a sense of bereftness tore at her again.

"You were born French," Armand remarked. "You would have heard it spoken in your infancy. Perhaps that was why you had a quick ear for it."

This was news to Kristy. "You haven't told me what happened to Colette after the earthquake," she prompted, wanting to know all she could of her twin's life. Might they have run across each other in Paris or Provence?

"Your family was touring Turkey together," he

started, frowning as he recalled the facts he knew. "Your father and mother with the two of you, your father's brother and his wife—no children—and your father's parents. They were camping near the village where the earthquake occurred. Colette and your aunt were rescued alive one day afterwards. Apart from you, the others were found but they had not survived."

"Why wasn't I with them?"

"Your aunt said you were lost in the chaos. Everyone panicked."

Kristy wished she could remember. "What was my family name?" The name she'd been born to...

"Chaubert."

Christine—Chrissie—Chaubert. Christine and Colette.

"Do you know my mother's and father's names?" she asked, eager for more knowledge of her real family.

"Marie and Philippe."

"What of my mother's parents? *Her* family?"

"She had none. I understand she was Irish. An orphan. Philippe had met her in the Peace Corps."

An orphan like her daughters, Kristy thought sadly.

"Your aunt adopted Colette and brought her home to France," Armand went on, supplying the information he could give. "Her name was Odile and she could not have children herself, due to injuries she sustained in the earthquake. Eventually she married a vigneron—a widower with grown-up children— Auguste Deschamp. His vineyard is near Bordeaux.

Odile saw Colette married to me, but died two years afterwards.''

Another loss. ''Was Colette close to her stepfather or his children?'' Kristy asked, wondering if those connections could have been helpful to her sister.

''Auguste was kind to her, but not close. His sons were much older than Colette. They were not really part of her life.''

No one for her twin to confide in then, Kristy concluded. She had been right last night. Colette would have felt very alone. Though she shouldn't have with Armand's family all around her, living under the same roof. Clearly there had been an estrangement with Armand—and the fault behind that was very murky—but what of the other family members? Had no one befriended her?

Well, she was going where she would find out, Kristy thought, embracing an even stronger sense of purpose. It wasn't only the children who would get her attention at Crecy. Something had been very wrong there for Colette to feel driven to go to Geneva, especially since her husband had told her there was nothing to be found.

In a valiant attempt to ignore the disturbing presence of the man beside her, Kristy watched the beautiful countryside they passed on this route through the Loire Valley to the heart of the Cognac country. As lovely as the scenery was, her mind kept turning to their destination and what she'd be faced with.

Wine was Armand's business, and it was undoubtedly very very profitable to live as he did. When she'd asked about Crecy this morning, he'd explained it was a village, next door to the chateau, housing a whole court of craftsmen to work the vineyard and tend the wine. Carpenters, painters, bricklayers, mechanics, gardeners, tilers, electricians, plumbers, and farmers; all lived there with their families.

The chateau itself, unlike many chateaux in the district, had always been lived in by some branch or other of Armand's family, going back to when it was built in the first decade of the nineteenth century. It served not only as a home for the Dutournier line, but as a centre of entertainment for special occasions.

Wealth, power, very high social status, pride in his reputation and his heritage…Armand exuded it all. His family undoubtedly would, too. Had Colette felt intimidated by it, crushed by it? Kristy vowed she wouldn't. She had a place there as the children's aunt. The poor relation, maybe, but still an important relation.

Poor…she frowned over that description, wondering if Armand had insisted on the designer clothes to wipe out that image, to actually help her fit in more easily. Was it a kindness or did he have some other stronger motive? *The shock of your resemblance to Colette*…he had said last night. What did he expect that to evoke? From whom?

I'm being used, she thought.

Nevertheless, it did get her into the lives of Colette's children.

And no way would she allow herself to be abused!

It was late afternoon when the Citroen turned into the tree-lined driveway which led to the superb stately mansion which was the Chateau Crecy-Dutournier.

Kristy was prepared to expect a certain amount of old grandeur, but the building still took her breath away.

It stood in the middle of a park which, while not on the same scale as that at Versailles, had a similar elegance with its expanse of lawns lined up with pools and fountains, and the precise formality of its gardens. The chateau was three storeys high, and fronted by a magnificent flight of steps leading up to a central portico supported by four gigantic columns. The architecture featured the precise and splendid symmetry so dearly loved by the French.

Armand halted the car at the steps.

"I have arranged that you meet the children first." He gave her an intimate look of understanding. "As I am sure you are eager to do."

"Yes," she agreed in a strangled voice, her heart thumping hard as the connection between them seemed to deepen, tearing at her very soul.

He alighted from the car and Kristy took a deep, deep breath as he strode around to her door. *The children,* she thought frantically, trying to get her mind focused entirely on them...her twin's children...her very own flesh-and-blood family. *His, too,* came the unsettling truth. She had to share them with him. And what else?

She shied away from taking his arm as she stepped out of the car and deliberately kept distance between them as they mounted the steps. Even so, she was more physically aware of him than she had been of any man in her entire life.

And she was about to enter his home, live under the same roof. How on earth was she going to hold distance between them in the days ahead, with those dark knowing eyes continually drawing on something inside her she couldn't control? There was no way she could trust that sense of intimacy.

One of the great doors was opened for them as they reached the portico. A woman dressed in black, grey-haired, past middle age, and very conscious of her dignity, stood by to greet them.

Armand smoothly took charge of introductions. "Thérèse, this is Mademoiselle Holloway. Thérèse is in charge of the staff at the chateau and will oversee your comfort during your stay here, Kristy."

"Welcome, *Mademoiselle*." It was formally said but no amount of formality could hide the shock and curiosity in the woman's eyes.

"Thank you," Kristy replied, wondering what Thérèse had thought of her twin.

"The children are in the main reception room, *Monsieur*, with your mother," she announced.

"Ah, my mother is receiving, is she?" Armand said very dryly.

"It is her wish, *Monsieur*."

"So it begins," he murmured mockingly. "Lead on, Thérèse."

Caught up in the undercurrents of this little interplay, Kristy didn't object when Armand took her elbow and steered her forward, following Thérèse to a set of double doors to the right of the great entrance hallway.

"A united front," he muttered close to her ear. "I am counting on that, Kristy."

It was more a taut command than a reminder of what he wanted of her presence here. Did he see his mother as an antagonist, Kristy wondered? Did he suspect *she* had contributed to Colette's unhappiness here? If so, having driven away one twin, she would hardly welcome the other.

Kristy steeled herself to meet and defy opposition as the doors in front of them were opened. They entered a vast and fabulous room. She had an overall impression of elegant antique furniture, tall windows, brocade curtains, paintings in ornate gold frames, beautiful lamps and chandeliers, a richly patterned carpet overlaying a polished parquet floor.

The shock that hit her killed any detailed observation of the magnificent furnishings. On a sofa facing the door sat a woman whose commanding presence might have riveted Kristy's attention, but for the children who sat on either side of her.

The boy looked so much like Armand it was impossible not to see the father in him, and the girl was the image of herself as a child: clear blue eyes and a silky mop of apricot-gold curls...her twin's daughter, but she could have been Kristy's own.

Her heart turned over.

She truly did have family...no longer a yearning, a hope, a dream...*real family*...right here in front of her...in touching distance.

Both children stared at Kristy, seemingly as transfixed as she was. Did they remember their mother? Probably not. The boy looked to be only five or six, the girl three or four. Two years had passed since their mother had gone out of their lives, but there would be photographs of Colette they had surely seen.

Kristy wasn't aware of the long, tense silence. Time stood still for her as thoughts and feelings tumbled through her. Then the boy moved, shifting off the sofa, planting his feet firmly on the floor, his little face determined on taking some initiative. Just like his father, Kristy thought, a leader, born and bred.

"You look just like *Maman*," he declared. "Papa said you did."

Instinctively Kristy gave him an encouraging smile. "I am your mother's twin sister," she explained. "Your Aunt Kristy from America."

"Did *Maman* go to America?" he asked.

"I'm sorry, Pierre. I don't know where your mother is," she gently replied. "I didn't know about you until your father told me." She held out her arms in an inviting gesture. "I want to know you very much. I hope you want to know me, too."

He nodded, eyeing her assessingly. "*Maman* used to hug me a lot," he informed her.

Did he miss the warm and comforting show of affection? Kristy's heart instantly went out to him. He might look like Armand but he was also Colette's child, her firstborn. "I would love to hug you, too, Pierre."

His face lit with pleasure. He gave a little skip then hurtled across the room towards her. Kristy bent to scoop him up. He perched happily in her arms, flinging his own around her neck and pouring out a torrent of words.

"Eloise doesn't remember *Maman*. She was too little when *Maman* got lost. I am glad that Papa has found you, Aunt Kristy, because now Eloise will know what *Maman* was like." He gave her a wise look, sharing how difficult it had been. "I told her…"

he said, stressing the importance of having imparted knowledge of their mother. "...but now *you* are here, she will know."

Kristy hoped so, yet she herself had so little information of her sister. Was looking like her enough for the children? Just being here, assuring them their mother had been *real*?

Pierre looked at his father for approval. "That is good, is it not, Papa?"

Armand, his face softened with loving indulgence, reached out and ruffled his son's hair. "Very good, Pierre. Now come to me so that Eloise can get a hug from her Aunt Kristy, too."

The little boy went readily into his father's arms. No lack of affection there, Kristy thought, and quickly turned her attention back to the little girl who had slid off the sofa but was still hanging shyly by her grandmother's knee.

"Eloise..." Kristy called softly, holding out her hands in invitation.

The big blue eyes lifted to her father and brother, wanting reassurance from them.

"Come on, Eloise," Pierre urged impatiently. "Look at her hair. It is the same colour as yours. Just like *Maman*'s. I told you so."

Very much the leader, Kristy thought, as Eloise's gaze lifted to her hair. The little girl's hand went up and touched her own gleaming curls, apparently fascinated by the comparison. Kristy decided to take the initiative in the hope of encouraging her, walking slowly towards the child, keeping a warm smile fixed on her.

"Does Pierre tell you what to do all the time, Eloise?"

The little girl gravely nodded.

"But you don't always do what he says."

A shake of the head.

"Would you like to tell me what you want to do?"

The head ducked down shyly.

Kristy crouched down beside her. "Is it all right if I tell you what I want to do?"

A slight nod, big blue eyes peering up through thick lashes.

"I'd like to hold you like your Papa is holding Pierre. Would you like that, too?"

A big breath for courage, another look at Kristy's hair, then finally a nod.

Kristy swept her into her arms and stood up, hugging the child against her shoulder, barely holding a strong wave of possessiveness in check. Eloise reached up and felt her hair, running it through her fingers. A smile of delight lit her face and at last she spoke.

"Everyone dark, like Pierre and Papa. Now I've got someone like me."

A poignant sense of loss hit Kristy again.

Like your mother, she wanted to cry.

And most probably like your Irish grandmother who died in the earthquake.

And we'll never know either of them.

But at least they now had each other, and no one was going to part them in this life, Kristy thought fiercely. Not Armand, not Charmaine, and not the grandmother who, Kristy was suddenly, skin-pricklingly aware, was watching her, silently weighing up the situation.

Both Armand and his mother had let the scene run, neither of them making any personal acknowledgment or pushing an introduction. This struck Kristy as odd now. Conscious that her own intense concentration on the children might have appeared rude, she turned quickly to the woman who would nominally be her hostess while she was at the chateau and nodded respectfully as she greeted her.

"Madame Dutournier..."

She had the kind of handsome face that could be forty or sixty years old, although the streaks of white in her black hair indicated she had no vanity about age. Her eyes were grey and cold, untouched by any of the emotion of this meeting. A formidable woman, used to wielding power and authority, Kristy thought, and one who would not be easily influenced from what she considered right. Yet she had not demanded the normal politeness of an introduction, nor chided her son for not giving one.

She inclined her head slightly and a dry little smile curved her mouth as she returned the greeting. "Mademoiselle Holloway..."

"Satisfied, *Maman*?" Armand's voice broke in, hard and challenging.

She stood up, tall, regal in her bearing, casting a mocking look at her son. "You surely did not expect me to ignore your arrival with such a guest, Armand. I will leave you with the children now, as you wish. Their nanny is waiting in their quarters."

"Thank you," he mocked right back.

She looked back at Kristy, the grey eyes quite chilling in their lack of any warm welcome. "We will talk at dinner. It should be an interesting evening."

Kristy met her gaze unflinchingly, her own eyes clear and direct. "Thank you for your forbearance, *Madame*," she returned politely, determined not to be intimidated.

One strongly arched eyebrow rose in surprise. "The mirror image is only skin deep, I see. But, of course…" Her gaze switched to her son. "…you bring more than one surprise in Mademoiselle Holloway, Armand."

"Until this evening, *Maman*," he returned commandingly.

She nodded and swept out of the room without another word.

Kristy wasn't sure what was going on between them. Her only certainty was Armand Dutournier was determined on having his way, and that included establishing a relationship between his children and their new aunt, for which she was intensely grateful.

As for the rest, it could wait.

Tonight would come soon enough.

For now, these two beautiful children were hers.

CHAPTER NINE

IT WAS both a huge relief and pleasure to Kristy that the children continued to accept her uncritically. They were excited about showing off their quarters to her, especially the playroom where she had to see and admire all their treasured possessions; toys, books, a railway set with three different trains, a doll's house and every bit of furniture in it...

The nanny, Jeanne, presented no problem, either, seemingly pleased Pierre and Eloise now had an aunt who was eager to spend time with them. She was a young woman and had only been at the chateau for the past eighteen months—no help as far as telling Kristy about her twin—but she had established a good rapport with the children. They liked her.

Armand stayed with them and it was more than evident he was not a distant father. Eloise happily climbed on his lap. Pierre basked in his approval. Kristy had to concede her sister's children were not in any way neglected, which made it difficult to press a need for her own presence, except in so far as she was *like* their mother.

She was extremely conscious of Armand watching how she responded to the situation and knew intuitively he was poised to step in if she made what he might consider a false step with his son or daughter. Strongly protective...smotheringly so with her sister?

Kristy wondered. More and more she *needed* to know why their marriage had gone wrong.

A maid brought in the children's nursery tea and Armand smoothly directed their leave-taking. "Your Aunt Kristy needs to rest now. She has been on a long journey and I have yet to show her to her room. You will see her again tomorrow."

"In the morning, Papa?" Pierre asked eagerly.

"Yes. In the morning," Kristy promised, determined on seizing as much time with them as she could.

She kissed them both before accompanying her host whose air of benevolence encouraged her to assure herself he was not against her plan. Nevertheless, she checked with him as soon as they were out of the nursery.

"I hope you don't object?"

"Not at all." A warm pleasure simmered from his eyes. "You are very good with them."

It instantly kindled her warmth. "They're so lovable."

He averted his gaze as he dryly remarked, "They do not connect well with everyone."

"To whom are you referring? Not their nanny," she said with certainty.

He did not answer immediately, escorting her to a staircase which led up to the next floor before commenting, "I chose Jeanne myself."

The grim satisfaction in his voice prompted Kristy to ask, "They didn't like the nanny chosen by Colette?"

"Colette did not choose. My mother did. She

thought the children needed a firm routine and discipline. At the time I bowed to her judgment.''

"Why not your wife's?'' Kristy sliced in pertinently.

He sighed. ''Colette was suffering from postnatal depression after giving birth to Eloise. She was not interested in making decisions.''

Kristy knew from her nursing experience that postnatal depression could not be lightly dismissed. Another contributing factor to her twin's state of mind? She brooded over this as they ascended the stairs side by side, finally asking, ''Didn't she care at all who was looking after her children?''

"At a later date, yes,'' he answered heavily. "But nothing seemed to please her then. I believe now I should have given more weight to her complaints. It might have made a difference…''

His voice trailed off. Was he regretting his failure to extend more understanding to her sister? Somehow Kristy found herself less ready to cast Armand as a villain, having seen his caring manner with the children. Nevertheless, impatience was not the way to handle depression.

"It wasn't until six months after Colette had gone that Pierre told me he hated his nanny,'' Armand went on. "I had been busy with the investigation and…'' He paused, shaking his head. "Too late then to repair whatever damage she'd done with Colette.''

At his mother's instigation? Kristy wondered. An intimidating mother-in-law and an intimidating nanny could be very undermining in any woman's domestic situation, especially if she felt she couldn't count on her husband's support.

"Pierre is now less rebellious and Eloise not quite so fearful," Armand concluded, satisfaction returning to his voice. "I think your coming will also be beneficial to them."

Kristy had every intention of making it so. At least she and Armand were in agreement on that point, which gave her a foothold in this very foreign household. She decided then and there that no one else would force her off the ground he'd given, not for any reason whatsoever.

They were now on the floor above the nursery quarters. Armand opened a door and ushered her into the room which had apparently been assigned to her since her bags were laid along an ornate stool at the end of the bed.

And what a bed! A huge four-poster draped and covered in a rich burgundy silk with tasselled decorator cushions piled across the headrest. Lovely rosewood antique furniture decorated the room, wing chairs upholstered in a embossed velvet, cream mixed with burgundy and gold, an elegant dressing-table with mirrors that reflected the whole room, a secretaire, tables with bowls of flowers and paintings of flowers... Kristy stood quite entranced with the overall effect.

"The doors on either side of the bed lead to your own personal bathroom and dressing-room," Armand instructed.

Luxury on a grand scale, Kristy thought, swinging slowly around to take in every exquisite detail of her surroundings. Another door on the opposite wall to the bed drew her notice. "Where does this one lead?" she asked.

"To my suite," came the matter-of-fact reply.

Her heart instantly started skittering. This position needed confrontation here and now, she fiercely told herself, turning to face him. "You're putting me in a suite that adjoins yours?" She could hear her voice climbing nervously.

"You need not be concerned about it," he stated coolly. "The door has a lock."

"Is there no other guestroom in this huge chateau?" she queried, her mind pulsating with the certainty she would find his proximity disturbing, lock or no lock.

"This was Colette's. I thought you would like to feel...close to her," came the quiet, almost gentle reply.

Her stomach contracted. How could she be close to her twin without being close to him, too? She felt...trapped...confused...horribly uneasy. "Why did you have separate rooms?" she asked, driven to question everything. "Is this how a marriage is conducted in your world? Through a door that can lock the other person out?"

His face instantly tightened. "It was not my choice," he bit out.

"Then why was it hers, Armand? What did you do to alienate your wife?"

"You go too far!" he snapped.

"I didn't know truth had a limit to it," she challenged, uncaring of *his* sensibilities when hers were smarting so painfully. "What truth are you seeking in bringing me here? Only what suits you?"

Pride warred with his need to have her as his ally. "Colette insisted on separate rooms after the birth of Eloise. She did not wish to be disturbed by me, and out of consideration for her wellbeing, I did not press what I wanted."

"For how long, Armand?" Kristy pushed. "I am aware of the effects of postnatal depression but you said she did start caring about the children again. She must have recovered enough to care about you, too."

He threw up his hands and began pacing around. "She convinced herself I was having an affair with Charmaine." He glared at Kristy. "It was not true. And I will not have you accuse me of it. It was not true," he repeated emphatically.

Undeterred, Kristy put the obvious question. "Then why did Colette convince herself of it?"

"Perhaps it was easier to direct her energy into jealousy than doing something positive about our marriage," he flared.

"There had to be some cause," Kristy argued.

He paused in his pacing. His shoulders squared, his chest visibly expanded, and she sensed a harnessing of ruthless power. Her skin literally tingled under the burning gaze he turned to her.

"Yes…" It was a venomous hiss. "I now believe there *was* cause. And having you here with me may well help me uncover it."

Alarm speared down Kristy's spine. "What do you mean…*here with you*?" Did he have some secret agenda for having her in this bedroom suite adjoining his? Her heart beat erratically as suspicion overrode his supposed consideration for her need to know more of her sister.

His mouth curled sardonically. "Having the twin of my wife at my side…and in my private quarters…does produce a rather piquant situation that some people may find disturbing."

She found it disturbing. "I'm not sure I like this," she blurted out, gesturing agitatedly at sumptuous furnishings that suddenly felt like a gilt prison.

"Part of our deal, Kristy," he stated, a ruthless edge to his voice. "You have what you want, do you not? Free access to the children, right in their home?"

The pointed reminder of his power to deny her that access as easily as he'd given it to her, forced Kristy to bite down on her tongue. Tension screamed along her nerves as he very deliberately closed the distance between them, impressing his authority with arrogant confidence. His gaze remained locked on hers, exerting his will, transmitting a force that would not be denied.

"You have convinced me that twins can feel the same things, so you may feel what your sister felt in this household," he said, and those riveting eyes were tunnelling into her soul again, forging the connection that went beyond her understanding.

Was she to serve as a spy, reporting how others reacted to her, or was it enough for him to observe that for himself, with a more heightened perception than he'd applied in the last months of his marriage?

"Though there is a fire in you Colette never had,"

he added softly. "And that is the difference which will make a difference to all that is important to me."

The deeply personal note thumped into her heart. Kristy was so mesmerised by his overpowering closeness she didn't grasp the full significance of what he was saying, only that he did see her as being different from her twin, which sent a sweet shiver of relief through her.

Then his gaze dropped to her mouth and she knew—knew with heart-squeezing certainty—that he was thinking of how she had responded to the kiss which he had declared meant nothing to him. Except it hadn't meant nothing. Desire had stirred in him, as it stirred in her now…a wave of yearning spreading down from her stomach, peaking her breasts, mashing every bit of commonsense out of her mind.

Her senses took on a life of their own; her eyes clinging to the shape of his mouth, examining the sensual curve of his lips; her nose inhaling the faint scent of masculine cologne and finding it seductive, her ears filling with the thunderous beat of her pulse, her hands itching to reach out and touch, her mouth tingling with the remembered taste of him.

It was he who broke the dangerous enthralment, an uncharacteristic gruffness edging the rich tone of his voice. "Whether you like it at this moment or not, your place is here, Kristy. It has to be so."

She wrenched her gaze up to his, though still too dazed by the strength of her own feelings to gauge his. "Why does it have to be so?" she croaked, her throat hopelessly dry.

One eyebrow arched. "Do you not think Fate has dealt us both a new hand?"

"You seem to be mixing it up with the old."

"That was yesterday. Today…" His eyes glowed with an almost hypnotic brilliance. "…today I know better."

"Well, I don't," she protested.

He gave a low little laugh. "You'll see soon enough. The family will be gathering in the salon at seven-thirty. It will be formal dress for dinner. If you require the services of a maid—unpacking, any refreshment you'd like—there is an intercom by your bed which will connect you to the staff quarters."

Kristy struggled to regather her wits. "I don't know where the salon is."

"I will escort you. Expect my knock on your door at seven-thirty."

"Which door?" She glanced nervously at the one connecting their suites.

"The door by which we entered," he said dryly. "And by which I'll now leave you."

It was difficult not to feel slightly foolish as she watched him walk away from her. He hadn't really done anything that could be considered…inappropriate…yet the sense of being somehow at risk with only one wall between where he slept and she slept was too strong for Kristy to ignore. He invaded her space in a way no other person ever had, evoking an intense vulnerability. She found herself fiercely wishing the circumstances were different, that he had never belonged to her twin, that he had never…

"Has Charmaine ever occupied these rooms?"

The question shot out of her mouth, jealously accusing, and she had the awful, blood-curdling sensation that her twin might have spoken the same words in the same way.

He was on the point of making his exit, the door already opened. In what seemed like excruciatingly slow motion, he looked back at her, his dark eyes uncomfortably piercing. "No. And never will. As long as *you* stay."

He left her with those words ringing in her ears, gathering echoes of many shaded meanings. The locked door that linked their suites tugged at her mind, tugged at her heart, tugged her into staring at it. She had unlocked the one at the hotel and that action had propelled her into this life on the other side of the mirror...this room which had been her sister's.

As long as you stay...

Did Armand intend that she take her sister's place...with him...on the other side of *this* door?

CHAPTER TEN

KRISTY stared at her reflection in the mirror, one part of her fascinated by the difference designer clothes could make, another part worrying if she'd chosen wrongly. She hadn't tried on any of the clothes Armand had had sent to the hotel. Time had been short, and she hadn't really cared what she picked out, as long as it wasn't black or white or neutral.

Now seeing herself in this Herve Leger violet silk evening gown, she wasn't sure it was her at all. The shoestring straps and the artfully pleated bodice somehow combined to emphasise a cleavage that looked more voluptuous than her bosom usually did and the colour seemed to give the expanse of exposed flesh a shimmering luminescence.

The dress hugged her whole figure, the wider ringed pleats around the skirt highlighting the curves of waist, hips and thighs, making her look very curvy indeed, and very sensually feminine. Provocatively feminine.

Then the high-heeled strappy silver sandals added considerable length to her legs and since the skirt ended well above her knees, the shapeliness of her legs was very much on show, too. If Armand wanted her on display, this outfit was certainly displaying her, but if he wanted her for some more *personal* reason, was she playing with fire wearing this dress?

Her heart leapt as his knock reverberated through the door. Too late to change now. Besides, the other gowns he'd insisted on buying were probably just as revealing in their own unique styles. With slightly tremulous hands, she picked up the little silver chain evening bag and took several deep breaths on the way to the door, hoping to calm her skittering pulse.

The impact of him struck harder than last night when she had known virtually nothing about the man. He stood back from her door, not only stunningly handsome in his dinner suit, but eyeing her with an approval that was more than warm. She was instantly aware of a very male appreciation of how she looked, as well as a simmering exultation in her having fallen in with his plans...whatever they were.

All Kristy could think about was her sense of being on the edge of a situation that pulsed with danger. Could she trust Armand Dutournier? Had he told her the truth about himself and his marriage to her twin? The truth about Charmaine? How did he intend *using* her tonight?

"Do not be afraid." His words fell softly, curling around her heart. "I will be at your side, supporting everything you say and do."

She wasn't afraid of *his family*! This man had been her sister's husband. She wasn't sure if it was right to feel how she did about him. "A pity you didn't do it for Colette," she replied sharply, more from her own inner confusion than a wish to blame.

"A grave error on my part," he admitted.

Was that regret in the dark depths of his eyes?

"I do not intend to repeat that mistake with you,

Kristy,'' he added, again in that soft seductive tone that suggested far more than his words did.

''You'd better tell me the names of those I'm to meet. They've slipped my mind,'' she said briskly, setting out along the corridor, studiously avoiding touching him.

He listed them off but the information floated past her agitated mind, her own thoughts circling the question…if *he* wasn't entirely to blame for Colette's need to find support she could trust, who was?

Finally she blurted out, ''Who do you think made my sister so unhappy with her situation?''

They reached the foot of the staircase with still no reply from him. Kristy shot a querying glance at him. He was frowning but he instantly caught her look and relaxed his expression into one of intimate challenge.

''You'll be the next target. Those who wanted Colette estranged from me, will undoubtedly act in a similar way to you. I'd rather not prejudice your judgement with my suspicions.''

Her…the target. A simple, ruthless plan. On the surface.

Then he smiled and softly added, ''I'm counting on your feelings, Kristy.''

And the certainty zapped through her mind there were many layers to his plan with herself as the target of all of them. She didn't know what to do about this. She really didn't. The attraction was there, tugging at her all the time, and he surely knew it. How long would he hold back from acting on it? And what did he intend to get from her?

She was in such turmoil, she didn't notice where

they were walking. Armand paused at a set of double doors, taking the handle on one of them. "The family salon," he murmured, a gleam of predatory anticipation in his eyes.

Kristy's heart was thumping madly as he ushered her into another room with opulent furnishings, though slightly less formal than the reception room off the entrance foyer. Here there were three chesterfield sofas, upholstered in a cream silk, delicately patterned with pink and green. They were grouped around a low, cream marble table, beautifully streaked with pink, and a similarly patterned marble fireplace stood in ornate glory on the fourth side.

Two of the sofas were occupied, the third obviously designated for her and Armand, who suddenly slid an arm around her waist, coupling them more physically than Kristy was prepared for. His hand rested lightly on the curve of her hip, its heat seeming to burn through the thin fabric of her gown, and his body pressed close to hers, stirring all her senses again.

"You have met my mother..." Armand started the introductions as he drew her to the corner space between the chesterfields.

The grande dame of the chateau, quietly elegant in a black and grey gown adorned with a large diamond brooch, was seated at the far end of the sofa across from the table. She nodded acknowledgment, her eyes shrewdly assessing Kristy's appearance and her son's alignment with her. Then with a thin little smile, she offered, "Your sister always called me Yvette. You are welcome to do so."

It was a surprising concession, almost a welcome, though there was little warmth in it. "Thank you," Kristy replied, unable to discern any active hostility and deciding that caution from the older woman was reasonable in the circumstances. She offered her best smile as she added, "And please call me Kristy."

"Next to her is my sister, Stephanie," Armand went on.

No smile there. Stephanie looked to be in her early thirties, very sophisticated with her thick black hair cut in a short bob and her almost angular thinness poured into a dramatic dress featuring glittery red and black zigzags. Dark eyes glowered at Kristy under straight black brows and red lipstick emphasised pouting lips.

"Well, well, another Colette," she drawled, then cocked an eyebrow at her brother. "Wasn't one enough for you, Armand?"

The lash of outright hostility was stunning. Kristy held her breath, waiting for Armand's *support*.

"Some civility would not go amiss, Stephanie," he coldly rebuked.

She returned a venomous glare. "What civility did you show Charmaine, dropping her cold for the twin of a woman who didn't care to be a wife to you?"

It was a reasonable argument, Kristy acknowledged, wondering what Armand had done about the beautiful brunette.

"My relationship with Charmaine is none of your business."

Complete shut-out on that subject!

"She's my friend," came the hot retort.

"Yes, and I've been wondering how much more she is to you, Stephanie."

Kristy's mind boggled. Things were getting very personal here, but his sister had started the personal line.

Patches of angry red highlighted Stephanie's cheekbones. "If you're suggesting…"

"I suggest nothing. I just remember how often you invited Charmaine here and how long she stayed with you during the months before Colette left."

That Charmaine had not been here at *his* invitation was news to Kristy. Welcome news, but she had no time to think about the relief she felt.

"She's my best friend!" Stephanie declared. "And you let her down, humiliated her…" She turned a glare of furious contempt upon Kristy. "For what?"

"For family," Armand replied calmly. "Unlike you, Stephanie, I put family ahead of friendship. Might I remind you that Kristy is my children's aunt?"

Yvette Dutournier reached out and closed her fingers authoritatively over her daughter's arm, silently commanding a halt to the outburst of feeling. "Kristy is also Armand's guest, Stephanie," she chided. "His wishes should be respected."

The younger woman's mouth thinned in seething resentment. She made a dismissive gesture with her free arm and with biting condescension, conceded, "While I am critical of my brother's timing on my *best friend's* behalf, I'm sure I'll find it interesting making your acquaintance, Kristy."

"As it will be making yours," Kristy returned equably, aware that nothing she said would change the other woman's hostility towards her position here. Nevertheless, some conciliatory remarks were called for so she added, "I'm sorry my coming has upset anyone. That was not my intention."

"And it is of no real consequence," a deep voice assured her. The man on the sofa facing the fireplace surged to his feet and moved forward to offer his hand to Kristy. He was shorter, more solid than Armand, and his black hair had a definite curl in it that he tried to subdue. His facial features were similar, yet not quite achieving the same fine elegance. He was also years younger, younger than Stephanie, Kristy surmised.

"I am Lucien, Armand's brother," he pressed, clearly anxious to reduce the awkwardness that had been stirred. "Welcome to Crecy," he added warmly as Kristy gave him her hand.

It was clear her presence did not displease him and he was pained by the scene his sister had created, darting an apologetic look at his brother, pleading no part in it.

"Thank you, Lucien," Kristy responded with a grateful smile. "I did so want to meet the children."

A smile flashed back at her. "They are delightful, are they not?" He gestured to his wife. "Please excuse Nicole from rising to greet you. As you can see, she is expecting our first child soon."

"Please…stay comfortable, Nicole," Kristy urged, extending her smile to the heavily pregnant woman on the sofa Lucien had vacated. "I'm very pleased to meet you."

''And you, Kristy,'' was returned with a tentative smile.

She was a very pretty young woman with wavy dark hair softly framing an endearing face that invited friendship. Kristy sensed she would have liked to say more but Stephanie's hostility was intimidating in this small family circle. Nicole would be living with Lucien's sister for a long time, while Colette's twin was a much more uncertain element.

''Sit down, Kristy, Armand,'' Lucien urged, eager for activity that didn't spotlight his wife. ''Let me get you drinks. What will you have?''

He kept up a stream of bright inquiries about Armand's trip to Paris. Kristy sat on the sofa facing Yvette, Armand next to her, facing Stephanie. They accepted glasses of champagne. Kristy observed that Yvette's hand had been removed from her daughter's arm and the older woman sat in self-contained silence, prepared to watch and await developments. Stephanie remained silent, as well, but it was clearly a seething silence, biding her time. Nicole, playing it safe, didn't look at anyone except her husband.

Eventually there was a pause in the conversation between the two men and Yvette took the opportunity to draw Kristy out about her life. The questions were put with a faultless show of natural interest and Kristy answered them with all the confidence of having nothing to hide. Only when she came to talking about her career did Stephanie break in.

''A nurse?'' She said it as though it was a lowly profession, unworthy of respect or pride.

Determined not to be stung by such undeserved

contempt, Kristy deliberately turned a smile to Lucien's wife. "Yes. And I've worked in a maternity ward so I'd be happy to chat with you over any concerns you might have, Nicole."

The younger woman blushed. "How kind!" she murmured shyly.

"I had no idea nurses were paid so highly," Stephanie drawled. "That is a Herve Leger gown you're wearing, is it not?"

"Yes, it is," Kristy affirmed without blinking an eye, instantly determined on not explaining how she'd got it.

"And very beautiful she looks in it," Armand purred beside her, causing her heart to palpitate alarmingly.

"Thank you, Armand," she flashed at him, only to find his gaze slowly traversing the length of her body in blazingly obvious admiration.

It jerked Stephanie to her feet. "Time for dinner," she snapped.

"Yes, it is time for dinner to be served," Yvette agreed, rising more regally from the chesterfield.

They led off towards a set of doors at the end of the room. Lucien helped his wife up and they followed. It seemed to Kristy Armand deliberately waited for them all to precede him before he moved, and since he was the mover and shaker in this meeting with his family, she waited, too.

When he stood and captured her hands to draw her up with him, it was executed so quickly and lithely, Kristy found her arm firmly tucked around his in formal escort mode in a matter of seconds. She told herself there was no point in protesting the physical link he seemed determined on displaying. These were *his terms*, however much they disturbed her. Besides, they would be sitting down again soon enough.

The dining room they entered was furnished to blend harmoniously with the family salon, pale green and cream and peach tones contrasting with the highly polished wood of the table and the gracefully carved chairs. While Kristy was totally unused to such a high style of living, at least she was coming to expect it in this chateau so it no longed dazed her.

The setting for six featured sparkling silver and crystal and the family members had already moved to their places, Lucien and Nicole on the far side of the table, Yvette at one end, Stephanie taking the chair next to the other end so that the obvious place left for Kristy was between her and Yvette, given that Armand sat at the head of the table.

However, he did not escort her there. "Stephanie, I wish to have Kristy seated next to me during dinner," he stated in a tone that brooked no opposition.

Stephanie rounded on him in fierce aggression. "She is not your wife, Armand, and I have the right to this chair."

"My partner has the right to that chair, and I choose to put Kristy in my wife's place tonight. Now please move down."

It was an order, not a request, and it was chillingly obvious that Armand didn't care what tensions he stirred with it. He was going to have his way.

For a moment, Kristy thought she saw a flash of naked hatred towards her brother in Stephanie's eyes.

Was there a fierce sibling rivalry between them? But the challenge that hovered briefly in the air was suddenly dissipated by a shrug and Stephanie gave up the disputed chair, moving towards the one adjacent to Yvette's.

"I do not understand you, Armand," she said mockingly. "If I were Kristy, I'd feel uncomfortable about taking over my twin's place."

Which was a direct strike on Kristy's heart.

"I mean it as an honour, which I feel my wife's sister deserves," Armand answered blandly, performing the courtesy of seeing Kristy seated before moving to his own place at the head of the table. He cast a smile around the company as he sat down. "And I have every confidence Kristy is, and shall always be, her own person, not her twin." The smile beamed on her with such a glow of admiration and approval, Kristy barely stopped herself from squirming.

Was she a pawn in some power game, or did he mean what he said? Impossible to tell, as yet, and it was a welcome distraction when a manservant led in a couple of maids to start serving dinner and attend to filling glasses with wine. The first course was a variation of vichyssoise soup, accompanied by freshly baked crusty bread rolls.

Kristy didn't attempt to eat the roll, afraid of splattering flakes of crust over the magnificently set table. The last thing she wanted was to draw critical attention to herself. Until Stephanie spoke...

"Perhaps you are more like your twin than you realise, Kristy. Colette didn't eat rolls, either," she said snidely, then used her sharp teeth to bite into her own.

"Actually, I prefer to have my soup first, roll second," Kristy replied offhandedly. "I guess everyone's eating habits vary."

And she made a point of doing just that, rankled by the thought that Stephanie might have had a repressive effect upon her sister. Besides, why should she be inhibited by the luxury around her? These people weren't.

The first course was cleared away. The men discussed the quality of the wine. Nicole plucked up the courage to ask Kristy more about her nursing career. The time between courses was passed pleasantly enough. The main dish was, Armand informed her, a local specialty, *entrecote bordelaise*, prepared with shallots, red wine and seasonings, and accompanied with steamed vegetables.

Kristy did the fine food justice, sensing Stephanie was storing up a pile of spite to deliver at any opportune moment. She wasn't sure yet if this was on Charmaine's behalf or whether it was part and parcel of some deep antagonism towards her older brother. If it was the latter case, Colette had undoubtedly been a target of disfavour, as well. Which put Kristy in a fighting mood.

The staff deftly removed plates and placed platters with a selection of cheeses on the table. They had no sooner departed the dining room than Stephanie opened fire, pretending harmless curiosity.

"You didn't tell us how you came to be in Paris, Kristy, coincidentally at the same hotel as Armand."

"It always amazes me what a small world it can be, running into people one would never expect to meet," Kristy mused before answering, "I simply chose to have a one-day stopover in Paris on my way to Geneva, and that hotel had a sentimental appeal to me. The people who adopted me had honeymooned there."

"Geneva," Stephanie drawled with a sneer in her tone. "Well, if you'd gone on there, you might have found Colette, instead of settling for her children."

Kristy bristled but forced herself to remain calm. She couldn't prove her sister was dead and she wasn't about to lay her feelings out for this woman to scorn. "Armand assured me he'd already carried out a thorough investigation there."

"True," Stephanie carelessly conceded. "And on second thoughts, I'd consider it more likely you'd run across her in your own country, tucked cosily away with her American lover."

Kristy stiffened. No way was she going to accept her twin being maligned. Her whole being revolted against it. She turned a very steady gaze upon the detractor beside her. "Nothing you, or anyone says, will convince me my sister would desert her children and run off with a lover," she stated categorically.

"How very narrow-minded!" Stephanie mocked. "You remind me that Colette had an inability to face facts, too."

"Like the facts you fed her, Stephanie?" The words flew off her tongue before she could catch them back, shot from a deep basic instinct that rose strongly in her twin's defence.

Stephanie laughed in her face. "What's this? Does it suit your purpose to put blame on others, finding scapegoats for what your sister did?"

"Just precisely what did my sister do?" Kristy quietly challenged, freed of normal politeness by the personal attack on her integrity.

A scathing look lingered on her, then was thrown at Armand. "Don't tell me you didn't tell her!"

"Kristy considers her sister has been very falsely judged," he coolly replied.

"How convenient!" Stephanie jeered. "So how does she explain Colette's exit with the American?"

"Are you quite sure you saw them leave together?" Armand inquired, his voice taking on a silky edge that sent a shiver down Kristy's spine. There was danger in that question. She didn't know how or why, but she felt it very strongly.

His sister reacted aggressively, snapping, "I told you I did."

"Yes...and he was your friend, too, was he not? It was you who invited him here, along with Charmaine, your very best friend."

Kristy's mind buzzed with the implications. Was Armand suggesting some kind of conspiracy involving Stephanie, Charmaine and the American man...all of them against Colette?

Stephanie's chin lifted in proud disdain. "Not a friend. Simply an amusing acquaintance."

"Whom you haven't seen since."

"I would have told you if I had."

"Yes, of course." He left the words hanging for a moment, letting them reek of doubt, before he blandly added, "Might I remind you Kristy had no part in whatever happened with Colette."

"*She* brings it all back," came the swift, resentful retort.

For several moments the air seemed to swirl with violent currents and Kristy knew intuitively that her sister had had a deadly enemy in Stephanie Dutournier.

"Armand is right," came the quiet, authoritative voice of his mother. "Kristy played no part in our memories of the past. It is not fair...."

"But this is so interesting, *Maman*," Armand drawled, still in that silky, dangerous tone. "Anyone might think Stephanie was the hurt party in my wife's apparent defection." His gaze pinpointed his sister again. "Strange...I don't recall you feeling hurt at the time. Not even for me."

"We all hurt at your wife's total incapacity to carry off the role of your wife," she shot at him, her eyes a black scornful blaze. "You were well rid of her and it's about time *you* faced *that* fact!"

The callous judgment was too much for Kristy. *"Well rid of her?"* She heard her voice climb with outrage, and her body climbed too, right out of her chair so she could glare her own contempt down at the brutally mean woman seated beside her.

Armand's own words spilled from her lips. "You shameless, heartless creature! My sister was ill and in need of support, and your answer to that is you're *well rid of her*? Or did you go further, Stephanie, and plot to get rid of her, chopping away at her self-esteem, making her feel her position here was getting more and more untenable?"

"Just who do you think you are?" came the haughty riposte. "You don't know a damned thing about Colette's failures to rise to any occasion. All she was good at was running away."

"Stephanie…" Armand roared, rising to his feet.

"Face facts, Armand," she hurled back at him, standing to defy him.

"Oh, I shall, Stephanie. Believe me, I shall." His voice throbbed with threat. "Like *the fact* Colette's car was found today."

Shock speared through Kristy and everyone else from the startled gasps emitted around the table.

Armand gave no pause for comment. He prowled around the table behind Lucien and Nicole, aiming his words ruthlessly and relentlessly at his sister. "Like *the fact* it went over a cliff two years ago and the investigators can place the day of the accident on the day my wife left here to go to Geneva."

He clapped his hand on Yvette's shoulder as he passed. "Odd that my wife didn't see fit to mention her destination to you, *Maman*? Or did you keep *that fact* to yourself?"

Conflict was written on his mother's face as she started to reply, "Stephanie said…"

"Ah yes, Stephanie said…" Armand cut her off as he proceeded to his sister's shoulder, clamping a hand around it as he bent his head to her ear. "But I now have *the fact* Colette was alone in the car. Not with your American friend, Stephanie. Not with anyone."

He picked his hand off her and moved to Kristy,

encircling her shoulders with his arm. "And Colette was not running away at all. She was running *to* the one person she felt would support her whatever the circumstances. To the twin she never believed was dead. And she was right!"

He tightened his hug of her shoulders, leaving no doubt whatsoever where his support lay now as he threw down the final gauntlet. "*That fact* is right here in front of you—the living mirror image of my wife— and let me tell you it's going to be right in front of you for as long and as often as Kristy wants to be with her sister's children, because it is the only thing I can do for Colette now and it is what she would have wanted."

CHAPTER ELEVEN

THE silence of appalled reflection seemed to stretch for a long time—Colette dead—not guilty of betraying her marriage—not guilty of anything but seeking the help she hadn't found within these walls.

For Kristy the proof of her own inner convictions hit hard. She hadn't doubted her feelings, yet the physical evidence of the accident revived them, making them more starkly true. There was no joy, no triumph in having her reading of the situation vindicated, just a deeper feeling of desolation.

"Why was the car not found until now, Armand?" Lucien asked quietly.

"There had been an accident in the same place a week previously. The safety fence had not been mended. Tyre marks and other evidence were attributed to the first accident, and the car was in deep water, not visible from the road."

So simple—the explanation when it was spelled out, yet Kristy knew the two-year disappearance had eaten into Armand's soul, twisting any trust he might have had in her twin. All so wrong...wrong...

"How did it come to be discovered now?" Lucien asked.

Armand's sigh whispered through her hair as she felt his chest rise and fall. His voice held a soft empathy with her pain as he answered, "Kristy told me where to look. She experienced a strong psychic link to a sense of falling and drowning on the day Colette left here. She gave me the time. It was only a matter then of calculating the distance.''

"How extraordinary!" Nicole murmured.

"And did your psychic link tell you what happened to Colette's American companion?" Stephanie demanded in harsh scepticism.

Kristy was jolted out of the dark swirl of emptiness inside her. She stared at the face of Armand's sister. It was ugly with vicious meanness, a meanness that had surely stolen Colette's peace of mind to feed a greedy, pitiless soul. Kristy had met her kind before…the joy takers, she'd privately christened them…those who puffed themselves up by leeching the joy out of others. She'd always replied to such meanness with laughter, to take the sting away, but she couldn't laugh tonight. She could see Colette in the car…alone…

"He was not Kristy's twin, Stephanie," she heard Armand shoot back at his sister in a hard cutting tone. "And we only have your word for it that he got in the car with her. He is not there now."

"Then she must have dropped him off somewhere," came the pat reply, eyes glittery in her determination to paint Colette in a bad light.

A false light, Kristy thought, hating the impugning of her sister's character.

"Hardly consistent with their being lovers," Armand savagely mocked. "As you suggested to me."

Yes, the joy takers were wonderfully sly with their nasty suggestions.

"It answered the question of why she wouldn't share your bed with you," Stephanie sliced back maliciously.

Sly and clever.

"Oh, I tend to think that is now answered by your having suggested to Colette that Charmaine and I were lovers," Armand countered.

Of course. A consistent pattern of demolition.

Stephanie laughed. "Trying to make yourself out to be lilywhite, Armand?"

"No. Just establishing how my marriage was betrayed, Stephanie. And it wasn't done by Colette, nor by me. Do you have anything to say, *Maman*?"

Were mother and daughter two of a kind?

Yvette's handsome face seemed to have aged, looking tired with too many years. She shook her head with slow weariness. "Only that I'm sorry Colette died as she did, Armand."

No lasting venom there.

"Well, I'm not sorry and I won't say I am," Stephanie declared scornfully. "As far as I'm concerned you're a bunch of hypocrites."

"Now, see here…" Lucien began to protest.

She ignored him, swinging a black, scathing look on Armand. "You especially. And all because you now fancy another version of Colette. Until *she* doesn't live up to what you want, either."

Kristy tensed. The most effective nastiness had a grain of truth in it, a grain that kept working under the skin, hurting, hurting, hurting…

"Stephanie…" Yvette attempted to call her daughter into check again.

"Designer clothes won't make a pearl of her," she continued to jeer. "Any more than they did Colette."

Armand's arm was around Kristy's right shoulder but nothing was holding her left arm. Before she even knew what she was doing it lifted and swung. The clap as her hand connected with Stephanie's cheek was more shocking than anything that had preceded it. This was open violence. Honest violence, Kristy fiercely told herself, and heartfelt words poured straight after it.

"My sister is dead. And you…" Her gaze targeted the woman who'd so contemptuously belittled both Colette and herself, then swung around each person around the table. "…all of you…"

She pulled away from Armand to stand by herself, completely by herself. "…you had my sister in your keeping, as I never did. And who of you listened to her? Who of you cared for her? Who even saw she was a person in need? Who tried to answer her need? You had her here…and you lost her on me before I could find her."

Tears gushed into her eyes. "She's gone. And I'll never get to know her. And all you can do is argue over who did what. No caring for her…no caring…"

She backed away from them, repelled by the hard emptiness in this room, the lack of giving that had driven her sister away to her death. She had a blurry vision of Stephanie with a hand nursing the struck cheek and didn't regret the action…not at all. One slap didn't begin to equal a thousand malicious little cuts.

"Kristy…" The deep velvet throb of Armand's voice, his hand reaching out to her in appeal.

Her heart contracted but she shook her head. "You didn't tell me. You used me."

Yvette stood up. "There is a time for truth," she said heavily, as though that justified everything.

"Look for truth within yourselves," Kristy cried. "I know my truth. I know it…and it breaks my heart."

She spun around then, putting them all behind her. Out of the dining room, through the family salon, into a maze of corridors…she didn't consciously know how to get back to her room…Colette's room. Some homing instinct took over. She had to hold onto the banister of the staircase, her legs quivered so much. At last she was there, closing herself into another place of emptiness.

What use was the luxury that surrounded her? What consolation had it been to Colette in all the lonely hours she must have spent here? How many times had she looked at her reflection in the mirror on the dressing-table and spoken her own deep yearning for her lost other half…Chrissie…Chrissie…?

So vivid was the image in her mind, the call to her soul, Kristy's feet automatically took her to the same dressing-table, the same reflection. Her tears dried up as grief gave way to a different wave of emotion…a fierce love and loyalty and desire to do all Colette would have wished of her. A vow gathered force in her mind.

I will do you justice.

I will demand respect for both of us.

Stephanie will not succeed in undermining my position here with your children. I will stand and fight for what I believe is right for them.

Against Yvette, too, if necessary.

And Charmaine will never get Armand. Stephanie's best friend...never will I let them win over you!

As for Armand...

The deeply felt resolution wavered into painful uncertainty.

Where does he fit, Colette? Why does he get to me the way he does? Is it right or is it wrong?

A knock on her door cut into the maelstrom of thoughts and feelings. It was an unwelcome intrusion. She didn't want to see or talk to anybody and she certainly wasn't going to apologise for her behaviour. Let them all think what they liked and say what they liked. But not in front of her. Let them step over the line she'd drawn and she'd face them down every time.

The door opened.

Armand stepped into the room.

Anger spurted over the mad inner leap of response to the power of his presence. "I didn't invite you in."

"I wasn't sure you'd found your way back to this suite," he said quietly, his eyes raking the taut defensiveness of her stance.

"You see I have."

He nodded, but he didn't go. He shut the door behind him. "The call about the car came just before we were to go down to the salon. I had intended waiting until after dinner to tell you. I'm sorry I allowed Stephanie to goad me into a public announcement before telling you privately."

"It suited your purpose," she accused harshly.

"I did not anticipate the attack coming quite so openly."

"It might be as well for you to remember next time you set me up as a target, this target shoots back."

"I don't think anyone is left in any doubt of that, Kristy," he said gently. "Your firepower is formidable."

A self-conscious flush burned her cheeks. Had she gone too far? More in pain than in certainty, she cried, "You deserved it. All of you."

"No. Not all," he corrected, but still gently. "Lucien was never anything but kind to Colette, though he did not have much time for her during her last year. He was courting Nicole, who barely knew Colette at all. She and Lucien have only been married for fifteen months."

"So I did them an injustice." She closed her eyes and shook her head, rueing her indiscriminate attack.

"Do not be concerned. Both Lucien and Nicole would be in sympathy with what you said."

Aware of his soothing voice coming closer, Kristy snapped alert, her nerves jangling at his approach. "I have never slapped anyone before I met you and your sister," she threw at him in anguish over the changes being wrought in herself. "What is it with you people?"

"Both of us violated your sense of self, Kristy, and

that sense of self is now entwined with Colette. You did what you had to, in defence of both of you.''

Entwined with Colette...

She shivered. Did his understanding go so far? Further?

Suddenly he was standing behind her, his hands gently rubbing the goose flesh on her upper arms. Heat flowed from his touch, sending electric tingles through her bloodstream and rendering her bones insubstantial. Defensively, almost desperately, her fingers gripped the chain of the little silver evening bag she held in front of her, needing something solid to hang onto.

''Did you love her, Armand?'' The words sounded as though they had been scraped from her throat...raw...needful...

There were several painful heartbeats of time before he answered and she felt his fingers digging unwittingly into her soft flesh, wanting...what?

''Yes. I loved her. But not enough. I know that now. Not enough.''

She heard the aching regret in his voice and remained silent.

He released her and moved restlessly around the room, tormented by memories she had no knowledge of. She remained still, watching him in the dressing-table mirror, intuitively aware she was there for him, yet linked to the life he'd shared with her twin.

''She was so beautiful...yet there was an elusive quality about her...like a fey child...not quite of this world.'' He paused by the bed, stroking one of the silk cushions. ''It entranced me,'' he murmured. ''I wanted to hold her, keep her safe, clothe her in riches, lay the world at her feet…''

He expelled a long breath and left the bed, shaking his head. ''I was caught up in some mad romantic idyll and it didn't work that way. I failed her because I didn't understand that what I wanted…wasn't in her…and it was up to me to make up for it.''

He was speaking his truth. Kristy didn't doubt it. The conflict between expectations and realities was written on his face. Then frustration emerged, his hands opening and clenching as he recalled other failures.

''That last year…after the birth of Eloise…she just kept slipping away from me. I couldn't reach her. She kept erecting barriers between us, turning in on herself.''

He suddenly strode across the room to the connecting door between the two suites, unlocked it and flung it open. He whirled to face her, one arm outstretched to his room. ''I tell you, my door was open to her, Kristy! It wasn't me who locked it.''

Not Colette, either, she thought sadly. More a combination of forces that neither of them had found a way of breaking through.

He dropped his arm and came towards her, gesticulating with jerky movements, a man beaten out of the control he had been unable to assert. ''She didn't want me in her bed. She avoided any closeness. Even with the children, she'd put them between us to guard herself from me. Yet in her eyes…there was a reproach…as though I'd caged her in a place that was unbearable…and I swear to God I never meant to!''

His voice was riven by the passion of deep pain and it poured from him, crashing through Kristy in tumultuous waves as he closed the distance between them.

"Every time she looked at me like that, I wanted to hurl the barriers aside."

He snatched the silver bag from Kristy's hands and threw it away.

"I wanted to sweep her into my arms and crush all resistance to me."

He enacted his words, except it was Kristy he held, her heart hammering against his chest. Like a steel clamp he kept one arm around her as he lifted the other and thrust his fingers through the mass of her hair to her scalp.

"I wanted to drive all the doubts and fears out of her mind and put back her trust in me. But always…" His eyes burned into hers, transmitting a terrible tearing uncertainty. "…always there was this aura of fragility about her, so I told myself to wait…and wait…"

His hand raked back through her hair and captured her cheek and chin. "You spoke of Colette's need…and I don't deny it. But what of mine, Kristy?" he fiercely challenged. "Will you deny I had a need, too?"

She couldn't. It was so palpable. Not only did she feel it encompassing her, permeating every cell of her body, the pent-up force of it was mind-spinning.

"Then you came," he went on, his voice throbbing with mesmerising power, his fingers fanning her lips, compulsively touching, wanting. "…a different

Colette…pouring out to me the very things I failed to draw from her. And all I can think of is how long I've waited for this…wanted this…and I can't wait any longer!''

His hand slid back into her hair, fingers weaving, capturing, forging a strong, unbreakable bond, tying her to him irrevocably as his mouth took and invaded hers, passionately seeking, wildly determined on drawing from her all he had craved.

And even as Kristy recognised the source of his need—the anger and frustration that drove it—her own anger and frustration demanded an equal release. Why did it have to be this man—her twin's husband—who tore at her so deeply? Was the sense of intimacy with him a tantalising echo from Colette or…

The ravaging explosion of sensation in her mouth fired a tempestuous assault on his. There burst through her such a raging, rampant desire to know the truth of him, of herself, of everything, it smashed the divisive reservations in her mind, it crushed any reason for inhibitions, it swamped her entire being with a clawing intensity that would not be denied.

A kiss was not enough. She'd had that from him, and he'd denied being stirred. No denial now and he was very definitely stirred, flagrantly stirred, his arm sliding down to lock her against his rampant arousal, wanting the sensation of the soft give of her flesh to his aggressive hardness.

And she revelled in it, revelled in his strong maleness, the heat of him, the power, the taut pressure of his muscular thighs and the wanting he couldn't hide, deliberately inflaming it with a provocative slide of her body, seductively female, exulting in her own power.

Oh, yes, no denying she excited him. And he excited her, too. Fiercely. He wrenched his mouth from hers and burned a trail of kisses down her throat, seizing on the hammering pulse at the base of it, making her heart pump faster, and she wanted to do the same to him. More. She wanted to own his heart, make it pump only for her, bleed for her, die for her.

As he dragged one of her shoulder straps down with his teeth and proceeded to graze his hot mouth over the heaving curves of her breasts, she tore at his bow tie, pulled savagely at his shirt fastenings. *His* flesh should be exposed, too. It wasn't fair that he could take what she couldn't.

He raised his head, eyes glittering into hers, their darkness ablaze with feverish lights. She didn't know what he saw in hers, only knew she was consumed by the challenge of meeting him on equal terms, whatever that comprised, wherever it took her.

As though asserting who was master, he suddenly bent and scooped her off her feet, hoisting her against his chest and shoulder. "Not here...not here," he muttered, barging straight for the door leading into his suite.

Somewhere in the recesses of Kristy's raging mind she understood what he meant and it was right. There were to be no haunting shadows touching this. He was taking her out of the room Colette had staked as hers alone, the non-sharing room.

Beyond the door it was dark, and the darkness suddenly seethed with the pulsing heat of their bodies, moving, clinging, driven, and every one of his fast, purposeful footsteps carried an urgent beat of now, an overwhelming, compulsive *now*.

There was no gentle release from his forceful clasp. He tipped her onto a bed, soft slippery satin under her skin, and his hands dragged down her body, clutching her breasts, filling his hands with them, moving them under the pleated silk of her bodice in what seemed like an agony of longing, then sliding to her waist and hips, a sensual revelling in the feeling of her feminine curves, the very real woman she was.

He pushed up her skirt and in a fast, frantic, hauling movement, stripped off everything beneath it, ripping off her shoes in the process. The swift naked exposure stirred an exultant wave of anticipation, driven to even higher extremes as he hurled off his own clothes and came to her, lifting her bare legs around him, looming over her, all dominant aggressive male, and everything female in Kristy yearned to meet his wanting, meet it and meld with it.

His breathing was fast and harsh, hers so shallow it was almost nonexistent. She reached out and raked her fingers down his body, scraping his nipples, causing a flexing and contracting of flesh and muscle. He cried out and her ears rang with the raw sound of it, an animal groan that hissed into a growl, acted on with instant, volatile force as he drove himself inside her, a swift, deep thrust of explosive possession, and her flesh convulsed around him in greedy delight, loving the sense of fullness he gave her, the sheer incredible wonder of encompassing him, holding him, and she heard herself cry out but it was a word, not a sound, and the word was "Yes..." A mad, shrill beat of pure elation.

No sooner was it uttered than he scooped her up from the bed, his arms winding around her, hugging her tightly to him as he rocked back on his heels, holding her across his thighs. Instinctively she wrapped her legs around his hips, linking them to lock him to her, and she cradled his head as he buried his face in her hair, breathing it, tasting it, all the while rocking her from side to side in a fierce ecstasy of possession. The sense of being pinned to him, both inside and out, held Kristy in such deep thrall, it was as though his mind was linked to hers, too, flooding it with a rhythm of need which was unstoppable.

He found the zipper at the back of her dress, pulled it down, dragged the straps from her shoulders, bared her breasts, and devoured them, arching her back over his arm as his hot hungry mouth drew on each breast in turn, and she felt her nipples distending, thrusting forward to gloat in the feast of sensation, the pleasure of it so sharp, so intense, Kristy didn't care what he did as long as he kept doing it.

Somewhere the sense of challenge slipped away from her. Control lost any meaning. There was no purpose, only feeling, and it was impossible not to give herself up to the spasms of exquisite excitement that quickened into long rolls of it undulating through her.

Her legs went limp, sagged, energy all focused on where he was taking her and it was almost unbearably sweet...the prolonged plunder, the intimate invasion, the constant moving in on her, the revelling in feeling, touching, tasting, having more and more.

He paused long enough to whip her dress over her head and be completely rid of it. She was glad it was gone, leaving her free to feel all of him next to her, nothing coming between them. He carried her down to the bed again, slid an arm under her hips, and started another rhythm, back and forth, back and forth, a fast delicious pummelling that drove Kristy to aid and abet it, arching and writhing to capture all the fantastic ripples of excitement that flowed from it.

And sometimes he stopped deep inside her and bent his head to kiss her, soft and sensual, relishing the taste of her giving, or passionately urgent as though he could not bear anything of her to escape him.

But the control he'd taken upon himself slipped away, too, and need reigned supreme, consuming both of them as they plunged into the final mating ritual, a long climactic scream of all of him totally concentrated on all of her, meeting in a fast and furious reaching for the pinnacle of fulfilment, him spilling into her in a consummation of all that had been given and taken, the absolute release and satiation of need for each other.

It came in a burst that shattered both of them, a wild fusion that exploded into tidal waves of sensation, draining all their energy yet soothing the drain with billowing flows of wonderment at the primitive power of it, the deep intimate intermingling of coming together like this.

It should have been enough but it wasn't for Armand. Nothing seemed enough for him. He pulled her with him as he rolled onto his side, nestled her body against his, caressing her skin, stroking her hair, luxuriating in every sense of having her beside him, naked, available, responsive.

Kristy was beyond resisting anything he wanted of her. The compulsion to know and experience all of him still held absolute sway. It was like a dream, a dance, an intense pas de deux, and wherever he led she followed, caught up in the intimate interweaving he orchestrated, moving to his will. He did not speak. Nor did she. And only when the dream slowly drifted into sleep did the dance end.

Was it entire unto itself?

Did it have any continuance?

Had it held any meaning beyond the need of the moment?

Kristy's sleep was not disturbed by these questions.

They lay in waiting for when she awoke.

CHAPTER TWELVE

THE unaccustomed heaviness of an arm flung across her waist stirred Kristy into consciousness. Awareness of where she was and who lay beside her followed with heart-jerking speed. Her eyes flew open. It was still dark, not a dark that incited reckless behaviour but a dark that harboured too many unknowns for Kristy's comfort.

How long had they slept? How much time had passed since Armand had carried her into this room? How far away was morning and what would tomorrow bring? Most critical of all…was what they had done good or bad, and what would the consequences be?

Kristy's mind see-sawed frantically between the rightness of action or non-action in these delicate circumstances. The temptation to stay precisely where she was with Armand was strong. She wanted this intimacy to continue, to explore it further, but she wasn't clear on what basis it could or would continue. What if Armand had been simply working through a kind of exorcism of all his frustrations from his marriage?

It wasn't just the two of them. Colette suddenly loomed large in this darkness. As much as Kristy wanted to believe it was she alone who had inspired such intense wanting, she wasn't sure, and the more she fretted over it, the less sure she became.

They had both been off balance last night, affected deeply by the material evidence of Colette's death, an irreversible loss that had left a hole in their lives which had somehow incited a primal need for the emptiness to be filled. But was it filled, or was she fooling herself with a fantasy of intimacy that wasn't truly real?

One way or another they would have to face each other in the morning. Was it better to stay here...to see...to know?

Or was that too...naked! Too confronting when neither of them might be ready to examine what had transpired between them, let alone make decisions on it.

There had been no sober judgment in what they'd done, more blind, irrational instinct driving them into an answer which may well not be an acceptable answer in the cold light of day. In which case, it had to be glossed over because there were the children to consider. She couldn't allow her position with them to be shaken.

Better to have time apart for reflection before looking at this unconsidered plunge into intimacy, Kristy decided. The feeling gripping her heart was of this being far too big and too important to risk having it looked at without a lot of consideration.

The command came swiftly and decisively...go now while Armand was still asleep. Buy time.

Very slowly and gently she eased herself out from under Armand's arm, pushing a pillow into her place so his subconscious wouldn't register a shift from her. With her heart fluttering anxiously at the thought he might wake, she crept around the bed and collected her clothes, aided by the lamplight coming from the open doorway to Colette's suite, then tiptoed to her sister's private sanctuary.

It was a huge relief to reach it, a relief to close the door behind her. She stared down at the key on her side, wondering if she should use it. Did she want to lock Armand out? A locked door would almost certainly represent to him a decisive end to intimacy, another comprehensive shutting out.

She wanted honesty between them, a door that could be opened if he wanted to open it. She had nothing to hide. Not even her body after last night. Though she wasn't feeling heated right now. Quite chilled, in fact. Having deliberately left the door unlocked, she hurried to the dressing-room, put her clothes away and donned the T-shirt nightie she usually slept in. She strapped on her plastic Swatch watch, too, noting the time—3:27.

As reluctant as she felt about climbing into Colette's bed, it was the only sensible course to take at this hour of the morning. Having moved the decorator cushions aside and turned down the bedclothes, she switched off the lights and slid between the sheets, settling herself as comfortably as she could.

For a while she felt very uneasy about having slept with her twin's husband. Then she remembered her vow and reassured the spirit of her sister with the thought...*better me than Charmaine*. On that conscience-soothing conviction, Kristy drifted into sleep again.

She didn't wake until almost ten o'clock. Shocked to see what time it was, she scrambled out of bed, then didn't quite know what to do with herself. What was the daily routine at the chateau? Too late, she imagined, to attend a family breakfast table. She could probably call for something to be brought to her, but lingering here didn't appeal.

Her eyes targeted the door she had closed but not locked last night. It was still closed. It was up to Armand to seek her out, she decided, not the other way around. Her place was with the children this morning.

Having decided it would be no hardship to wait for lunch for something to eat, Kristy showered in the ensuite bathroom, tidied herself up, then deliberately chose to dress in her own clothes; jeans, T-shirt, battle jacket, Reeboks. As far as she was concerned, Armand had achieved his purpose with the designer outfits he'd insisted on buying and she saw no reason to dress up like anyone else.

First and foremost she was herself, and if superficialities meant more than character to Armand and his family, too bad! She was not going to fit herself into some acceptable mould to win their good opinion. It hadn't worked for her twin anyway. They would just have to take her as the person she was. No frills. Besides, she definitely didn't want Armand mixing her up in his mind with Colette. He had to be sorted out well and truly on that point.

She found the nanny alone in the nursery quarters,

tidying up the rooms. "Good morning, Jeanne," Kristy greeted her. "Where are the children?"

"With their father in the garden, *Mademoiselle*." She pointed the direction. "They always play outside at this time if the weather is fine and Monsieur Dutournier wanted to be alone with them."

"Oh!" Kristy shifted uneasily, not knowing what to do with herself now. "I don't wish to intrude…"

"Non, non, Mademoiselle," Jeanne anxiously assured her. "Monsieur Dutournier said to be sure to ask you to join them if you came. Please…you will be welcomed. The children are very happy you are here."

Kristy took a deep breath. Armand certainly wasn't ducking *a morning after* confrontation and there really was little choice about facing it herself. She was here primarily for Colette's children, and Jeanne was already opening the door for her to go to them.

Kristy thanked her and found the way to the play area. This was a wide expanse of lawn, hedged for protection and probably to keep the soccer ball Pierre was kicking from straying too far. A white aluminium table and chairs were set on a gravel path along one hedge line and Armand sat there watching the children. He was not dressed for play. The dark suit he wore looked very, very sober.

Eloise was pushing around a plastic trolley filled with brightly coloured blocks and it was she who saw Kristy first, her little face lighting up with delight.

"Aunt Krissie!"

She released the trolley and charged across the lawn towards Kristy as fast as her short legs would go. Alerted by his sister's call, Pierre left his ball and ran to catch up with her but Eloise won the race and giggled breathlessly as Kristy lifted her up to give her a hug.

"Aunt Krissie mine!" she crowed down to her brother, and tugged a tress of Kristy's hair to prove it.

"She's my aunt, too," Pierre argued, "and her name is Kristy, Eloise, not Krissie."

"Krissie," she repeated, not getting her tongue around the "t."

"It's all right, Pierre," Kristy assured him, bending down to encompass him in a hug. "Your mother used to call me that when we were both little, like Eloise."

"Papa told us *Maman* has gone to heaven and can't never come back," he told her gravely.

"No, she can't, Pierre, but we will always remember her, won't we?" she softly replied, her heart cramping as she realised Armand was watching, gauging how she was handling this information.

Pierre nodded. "It is easy to remember *Maman* with you here, Aunt Kristy."

"Papa said *Maman* is an angel," Eloise said happily. "And she found you for us, Aunt Krissie."

"Yes, I think she did," Kristy agreed, barely negotiating a lump in her throat.

Whatever Armand thought of last night, he was still keeping his word about her staying with the children for as long as she liked, and making her feel very specially welcomed, as well. Certainly what he'd said to his children had dispelled Eloise's shyness with her, and eased the knowledge that their mother was forever lost to them. As a kind and caring father, she couldn't fault him. But where did this leave her in his personal picture?

Trying to keep her inner tension under control, Kristy gently released the children, brightly asking, "What games are you playing?"

They chatted enthusiastically to her as they strolled across the lawn. Pierre was practising to be a World Cup soccer player. Eloise was going to set out goals for him with the plastic blocks in her trolley when she found the right places. Kristy was acutely conscious of Armand having risen from his chair, waiting by the table, observing her progress, listening to her conversation with his children, feeling...what?

That was the big question. It loomed so hugely in Kristy's mind that when he directed Pierre and Eloise to go on with their game while he talked to their aunt, she stood absolutely tongue-tied, watching the children skip away instead of looking at him. Despite the defensive armour of her own clothes, she felt every bit as naked as when she had left him in the early hours of this morning.

"I hope you can forgive me for what I demanded of you last night, Kristy," he said quietly. "I have no defence. No excuse."

She closed her eyes, wanting to shut out his words, hating them.

"I cannot take it back," he went on.

She couldn't bear it. She flashed him a look of fierce challenge as the plain unvarnished truth shot from her tongue. "You didn't rape me, Armand."

For a moment his eyes seemed to dilate, the pain

in them expanding to something more complex. But Kristy barely caught a glimpse of that expression before his brows and lashes lowered. "I wasn't sure how much I forced my...my own desires. When I woke and found you gone..." He heaved a long, ragged sigh. "...it was not a good moment."

"It was not a good moment when I awoke, either," Kristy offered wryly.

"But you are not..." He hesitated, his face riven with conflict as he searched for the right words. "You do not feel...badly used over this?"

"It happened," she said quickly, not wanting to bear his guilt, either. "It involved both of us, Armand."

His lashes lifted enough for her to see a burst of intense relief. "Then you do not hold it against me."

"I think we can put it down to the heat of the moment," Kristy said evenly, cautious about committing herself too much.

"Yes," he agreed. His eyes searched hers with urgent intensity. "I do not wish you to feel uncomfortable with me, Kristy. Or...unsafe."

Her own lashes dropped as she thought of the door she had left unlocked. Obviously he hadn't tried it or he'd know safety was not a priority where he was concerned. "I don't suppose the same circumstances will ever arise again," she muttered with considerable irony.

"Not the same...no," he said decisively. "I regret I must leave you now. There are certain official things to be done, you understand. Regarding Colette's...death."

"Yes, of course."

"I could not go until I had assured myself you were all right. That you did not feel…you could not stay."

Her gaze shifted to the children. "I have two very important reasons to stay, Armand."

"I am glad that is so," he said with such deep warmth Kristy felt her skin starting to flush.

For you…or for them, she wanted to ask but couldn't bring herself to voice the words.

"I'll be away most of the day," he informed her. "If there is anything you need or want…"

"I'll be fine here," she quickly assured him.

"Then I shall take my leave and hope to see you this afternoon."

She risked a look at him, needing to see if the hope was genuine. Perhaps he caught her uncertainty. His eyes instantly blazed with a conviction that pinned her gaze to his. "You are important to all of us, Kristy," he softly declared, his voice seeming to roll through her and wind around her heart.

Then he stepped aside and called the children to him, explaining he had to go now and they were to look after their aunt and be good for her. Which they eagerly promised.

He cast one last glance at her before he strode off, a dark searing glance, projecting a determination that would be satisfied, whatever it took.

It left Kristy with the torment of more questions. What *did* Armand want of her? What importance did he think she had to his family? The children she could certainly do something for, but the rest of them?

Time would tell, she told herself, not that it was

much consolation for her current inner misery. Still, at least Armand had cared enough to wait on her appearance this morning, to assure her she was *safe* from a repetition of last night's mad passion.

Except it hadn't been mad to her.

And she wished she could feel it all over again.

If only she could be certain *she* was the woman Armand wanted.

CHAPTER THIRTEEN

FOR the rest of the morning, Kristy concentrated on the children, throwing Pierre's ball back to him, conspiring with Eloise to plant the plastic block goal posts with a smaller distance between them to test Pierre's skill, and generally having fun with them.

They took breaks for drinks and both children filled Kristy in about their lives. She learnt they viewed *Grandmère* as a great lady whom they respected. *Tante* Nicole was nice. She often gave them sweets. *Oncle* Lucien was very good at games. Jeanne, their nanny, was clearly their favourite person, except for Papa whom they loved and hero-worshipped.

They did not mention Stephanie. Kristy concluded Armand's sister ignored the children and subsequently they didn't relate to her. Which was all to the good, in Kristy's opinion. She didn't want Stephanie blighting their self-esteem.

Eventually, Jeanne called them in for lunch. Kristy would have shared their meal in the nursery but for the arrival of Thérèse, the head of staff, who brought an invitation from Yvette Dutournier for Kristy to join her for lunch in the conservatory. Thérèse would conduct her there if *Mademoiselle* was agreeable.

A royal summons, Kristy thought, and decided she might as well deal with Yvette now, since there was little point in putting it off. Neither of them was about to shift their ground, and if she was to spend much time here, a working relationship was best established with Armand's mother. But no way was she going to sit down with Stephanie.

"Am I the only guest?" she asked Thérèse.

"*Oui, Mademoiselle.* It is a private luncheon."

"Fine! Then I take it *Madame* would not expect me to dress up for it."

"It is as you wish, *Mademoiselle.*"

Armand had not commented on her clothes, no doubt an irrelevant triviality compared to the more weighty things on his mind. Kristy briefly pondered the politics of this meeting with Yvette, deciding not to kowtow to other people's standards without good reason.

"I'll accompany you now, Thérèse."

The woman nodded, discreetly sticking to a no comment policy.

Kristy was given a mini-tour of the chateau, enough to get her bearings, as she was conducted to the conservatory. The chateau was built in a U-shape. Armand's and Lucien's apartments were contained in the same wing, Yvette's and Stephanie's on the other side, and the centre held the public entertaining and communal rooms. Corridors were all logically planned for easy linkage between areas.

The conservatory was at the back of the main body of the building, its ceiling and outside walls paned with glass, allowing in light and sunshine to nurture the mass of exotic plants and ferns in equally exotic pots and urns and hanging baskets. Artfully placed in open areas were cane lounge groupings and tables and chairs. One relatively small table was set up for lunch and Kristy was pleased to note it only had two placings.

Where Yvette was concerned, her trust was in short supply. The understanding between mother and daughter had been all too evident last night, though Stephanie had defied Yvette's cautionary admonitions. An older head, she thought, but not necessarily containing a different perspective or a kinder nature.

Despite her private reservations, Kristy was surprised at finding Yvette by a birdcage, trying to coax two colourful lovebirds into talking back to her. It was an oddly human touch, not in keeping with a formidable character.

"*Madame…*" Thérèse interrupted her.

"Will she come?" Yvette asked without looking around.

"I have come," Kristy answered, refusing to feel daunted by the older woman's immaculate appearance; the elegant dark green suit and perfectly groomed hair.

Yvette's head jerked around, her gaze swiftly encompassing Kristy's casual clothes and the rubber-soled shoes. "I heard only Thérèse's footsteps," she explained. "I do beg your pardon, Kristy." She offered a wry smile, no hint of criticism in her expression. "I half-expected you to refuse my invitation."

The self-deprecating honesty was also surprising, recalling the words she'd spoken last night—*there is a time for truth*. It prompted Kristy to say, "I wanted to hear your view of Colette."

"Of course." She sighed and waved a dismissal to

her head of staff. "Thank you, Thérèse. Tell Henri we are ready to be served."

Once they were alone, Yvette gestured to the table and they walked towards it. "I am sorry for your loss, Kristy. To have been separated from your twin sister so young and missed so much and come too late…" She shook her head. "In your place, I think I would feel what you expressed last night."

Conscious of having done Lucien and Nicole an injustice, Kristy decided to be generous. "It was a somewhat intemperate outburst, and I apologise for any offence given."

"You had every justification for acting as you did," came the quick, firm reply. "Your feelings were not spared, neither by Stephanie nor Armand. And I was at fault, too, for caring too much about the problems your presence inevitably raised."

She gave Kristy a rueful look. "There is an old saying…let sleeping dogs lie…which is what I've done, and I saw last night how wrong I was. The dogs might sleep for a while, but given a prod, they spring up and bite just as savagely as they ever did."

Kristy frowned. She wasn't sure if Yvette was referring to her children or the circumstances of their family life. She waited until they were both seated at the table, then asked, "Would you mind telling me why Stephanie is so hostile towards Armand?"

A weary resignation settled on her face. "Armand is the firstborn and a man. Stephanie has always resented the fact she is neither. And there is nothing I can do to change that. We are born what we are."

"And Colette? Why did she hate my sister?"

Kristy pressed, wanting to understand the forces that had been arraigned against her twin.

Yvette frowned. "I don't see it as personal as that, Kristy. Whoever Armand married was going to displace Stephanie as the one to follow me in being the chatelaine of this estate. It infuriated her that Armand chose Colette whom she saw as totally inadequate for the role."

"Was she?"

Yvette paused to ponder. "I don't think it mattered," she answered slowly. "Armand would have carried her. For him, just having Colette as his wife was enough."

Strange how deeply that hurt. She'd wanted affirmation that her twin had been loved by the man she'd married, yet now...

"Did *you* think she was inadequate?" she blurted out, trying to block the painful confusion the thought of Armand's love stirred.

The grey eyes met hers very directly. "At first. I tried to help her with what I considered her responsibilities as Armand's wife. I thought with guidance she could be shaped, but the more I tried to guide, the more Colette shrank from me, and I finally realised her personality was so different from mine, I was doing her a damage by persisting. It wasn't that I withdrew my support, Kristy. It wasn't that I didn't care for Colette. It was clear I made her feel inadequate, so rightly or wrongly I left her to herself." She gave a wry shrug. "I cannot change who or what I am, either."

Kristy mulled over Yvette's position in her twin's

life. Being a mother-in-law was probably never an easy role, and the life of the chateau was a factor Colette had obviously never come to grips with.

"What did you see as her personality?" she asked.

Yvette's mouth twitched. "As different from yours as chalk is to cheese. It would have been impossible to have this conversation with your twin."

"How so?" Kristy persisted.

She frowned. "There was an ethereal quality about your sister...as though...not quite of this world."

Armand had described it as "fey."

Yvette shook her head. "I always found her elusive. She led a very sheltered life before coming here. Perhaps too protected." She paused, a shrewd appraisal in her eyes. "Unlike yours, Kristy, which seems to have given you the confidence to take on anything."

Kristy refrained from comment. She'd always faced what had to be faced but much of it had not been easy...like facing Armand this morning. Coping was more true of her than confident.

Her silence prompted Yvette to add, "You mustn't think Colette was always unhappy here. Until she had Eloise, I think she cocooned herself in a life with Armand which was quite a happy one for both of them."

"Postnatal depression can be quite a serious illness," Kristy said sharply, not wanting to be reminded of that love. "And the nanny you hired was unsympathetic," she added, wondering if Yvette might be spreading snow on the past.

The older woman winced. "I had hoped she would provide stability. It's true I misjudged the situation."

"And Stephanie capitalised on it," Kristy bored in relentlessly.

"Yes. I believe now she did," came the weary acknowledgment.

Kristy started looking for holes in Yvette's exposition, wary of completely trusting her. "Why does Stephanie want Charmaine in Colette's place if she'd hate any wife Armand took?"

"Stephanie has always dominated Charmaine," came the matter-of-fact reply. "I think she saw her friend as a way of winning over Armand, working through his wife to set up whatever she wanted. But that will not happen now. It's over."

Was it? Stephanie hadn't struck Kristy as the kind to give up easily and the question of Charmaine's place in Armand's life had still not been completely laid to rest. "How can you be sure?" she asked.

Yvette eyed her curiously. "Don't you realise what a catalyst you've been?"

She'd certainly smashed a few misconceptions, Kristy thought with grim satisfaction. The phrase Yvette had used came to mind. "I woke the sleeping dogs?"

"Every one of them," she answered dryly. "And there's no going back."

Another turning point.

"Stephanie left Crecy this morning," Yvette went on, her tone flattening out. "She knows now she must find a life for herself, apart from Armand's. He will not suffer her interference again."

This was news! "He banished her from the chateau?" she queried, wondering if it had happened before he'd come to her last night.

Yvette nodded. "It is for the best. Best for both of them. But I lose my daughter." Her grimace was laced with sadness. "It can be very difficult, being a mother."

"I'm sorry," Kristy said impulsively, empathising with the pain of having to choose between two of your own children, not that she had any sympathy for Stephanie. "You must have seen Charmaine as an answer that was workable, too."

She sighed. "People compromise when they cannot get all they want. But that does not mean they are happy with their compromises. I'd prefer to see all of my children happy."

"Lucien and Nicole seem happy," Kristy offered in consolation.

"Yes." Yvette smiled with genuine warmth. "Lucien was always my joy. Armand, my pride." The smile twisted. "Stephanie, my trial. So it is with children. Yet I love all three and wish the best for them."

Which was fair enough, Kristy privately conceded. She wasn't a mother and might never get to be one, but she could see how different Pierre and Eloise were and she resolved to nurture harmony between them.

Henri arrived, wheeling in a traymobile with a selection of salads which he served at their direction. Kristy carried on an amiable conversation with Yvette throughout the meal, both of them moving to less sensitive subjects. It wasn't until the table had been cleared and they'd been served with coffee that she voiced her underlying thoughts.

"I appreciate very much your being so open with me, Yvette," she said softly. "Especially in circumstances where you, too, are feeling a painful loss."

"I don't think it's all loss for either of us, Kristy. I wanted you to know I am not against you. And to be completely truthful...Armand insisted I prove it, to both of you."

"Armand...ordered this luncheon between us?" Kristy couldn't keep the incredulity out of her voice.

"I did fail to answer Colette's need," Yvette said regretfully. "And I gave in to Stephanie's needs too much. I should not have tolerated the American. He was nothing but a freeloader, handsome, charming, too ready to please." She paused a moment, as though gathering herself to reveal more, then bluntly stated, "Stephanie paid him to disappear when he did."

"You knew this?" Kristy stared at her in total shock. For Yvette to let Armand believe...

"Not then," she quickly corrected. "I didn't believe he was Colette's lover but I had no proof to refute Stephanie's account of that day. So I let it stand...until last night."

"Armand knew this last night?" How could he not have told her?

"No. I told him this morning. I spoke to Stephanie privately, late last night. I went to her apartment and confronted her with my suspicions." She shook her head, her eyes slightly glazing as she recalled the scene. "Stephanie accused me of silently collaborating in her scheme to discredit Colette. She believed I would have approved of her paying the American. It was all so…so twisted against Armand…how she could have thought I'd agree with her…"

*There is a time for truth…*but what painful, terrible truth!

"I realised then how blind I'd been," Yvette went on sadly. "Blinding myself, excusing it with always thinking of Armand as the strong one. But he has needs, too." The grey eyes sharpened again, meeting Kristy's with direct resolution. "It is right that I now answer them."

Yes, it was right, Kristy thought strongly, yet to ask his mother to bare her soul like this…to someone she barely knew…did Armand have the right to demand so much? "I'm nothing to you," she couldn't help pointing out. "A virtual stranger."

"You are not nothing to Armand, Kristy. Nor to his children."

You are important to all of us.

"He shouldn't force what he wants on others," Kristy muttered, relieved that the question of the American had been cleared up, but feeling Armand should have told her instead of insisting his mother do it.

Surprisingly, Yvette smiled. "Do not be concerned. Armand had just cause for his demand. And this luncheon together has given me the chance to unburden myself of many things. I'm glad you came to it."

Kristy found herself smiling back. "Then I am, too."

But well after their meeting had broken up, the

words "just cause" kept echoing in Kristy's mind. It seemed to sum up everything Armand had done from his first sight of her at the hotel, if she looked at it from his point of view.

Though it didn't quite cover making love to her as he had. There had to be other answers, but there was nothing she could do about the aching need to know them until Armand came back.

CHAPTER FOURTEEN

"PAPA!"

Pierre went hurtling across the nursery sitting room to grab his father first. Eloise didn't try to compete. She stayed in the circle of Kristy's arm, content with her aunt who had been leafing through the baby album Colette had kept of her daughter, evidence that depression had not stopped her from loving her child. Which had made Kristy's heart heavy, and Armand's entrance did not make it any lighter.

She looked up at him, the man who had married her twin, who had fathered her children, who had just come from seeing to the formalities required to make her death official, and she felt sick over wanting him for herself. But she couldn't help it. He stood there, looking back at her, and it was as though he knew and shared her feeling.

"Papa," his son called again, demanding full attention.

Armand dropped his gaze to Pierre.

"Did *Maman* tell you she was going to heaven in the note?"

Armand frowned. "What note was that, Pierre?"

"I remember her writing it the day she left us. She gave it to Nanny Marchand and said it was for you."

Kristy's heart clenched. Colette hadn't left without

a word. It had seemed so unlikely she would, and here was the proof.

Armand crouched down, his face tightened to urgent intent. "Are you sure, Pierre? Nanny Marchand didn't give me any note."

"That's 'cause *Tante* Stephanie took it from her. She asked Nanny if *Maman* had left a note before going away and Nanny gave it to her."

Pain...even across the room Kristy could feel Armand awash with it. The effort made to push it away from his son was visible.

"Ah, that note," he said with forced lightness. "No, she didn't say she was going to heaven, Pierre. She said she was going to find your Aunt Kristy. I don't think she knew she had to go to heaven to do that."

"And become an angel," Pierre concluded, nodding his understanding.

"Yes. A beautiful angel who will always care for us," Armand assured him.

Kristy's eyes filled with tears. She bit her lip, swallowed hard and fought back the rush of moisture, inwardly screaming at herself...not in front of the children!

"Now I want you and Eloise to stay here with Jeanne," Armand went on. "I've come to take your Aunt Kristy for a walk."

"Can't we go, too?" Pierre asked plaintively.

"Not this time," was the firm reply.

Kristy shut the baby album, handed it to Eloise, and ushered the little girl over to her nanny, grateful to have any excuse to relieve her choked emotions.

Armand took control of settling the children with Jeanne, then he was steering her to the door which took them outside to the grounds.

Kristy thrust her hands into the pockets of her denim battle jacket, put her head down and walked, automatically following Armand's choice of direction but keeping herself rigidly to herself, knowing he also needed personal space to work through this final coming to terms with what had really happened on July the fourth, two years ago.

No desertion by his wife...the wicked malice of Stephanie, wanting him to believe the lover scenario, even though the lie would have come unstuck once Colette had returned from Geneva...except she never did return...and Stephanie had let the lie fester all this time, feeding him Charmaine as balm for the wound.

But the wound had never closed, never stopped festering, and the pain from it had poured out on Kristy in those first meetings at the hotel...the pain of a love betrayed...a marriage betrayed. Not pride. Public pride, perhaps, but pain had been uppermost. He had loved her twin. And he'd been robbed of her last words to him, the last words that would have told him there was no betrayal.

"I will not allow Stephanie to ever set foot here again!" he declared with bitter passion. "There is no way she can justify any of this...what I went through...with her knowing all the time..."

There would be no softening on his sister's banishment and who could blame him?

"You spoke truly last night, Kristy. It is Stephanie who is shameless and heartless. You were right all along…about everything…even to the note I never got.''

There was no pleasure in being right. Her understanding encompassed so much more now…the train of events…the people involved…why they did what they did…or didn't do. She had not been involved in the passions and personalities that had fashioned this tragedy, yet she was inextricably linked to it now, and all she could feel was a terrible sadness. There was no fixing it, only a going on from it, and she wasn't sure Armand was prepared to do that.

''I think your mother has done her best to atone for her mistakes,'' she said quietly.

''So she should,'' he retorted with harsh vehemence. ''Without your coming she'd still be protecting Stephanie, letting her get away with murder.''

Murder…premeditated destruction. Kristy couldn't really refute the idea, given Stephanie's intent to kill Armand's marriage, but she didn't like to think of it as attached to her twin's death. That was not planned nor intended, and had inadvertently frustrated the scheme to get Armand married to Charmaine.

''Colette's death was an accident, Armand,'' she gently reminded him. ''I hope you can let my sister rest in peace now, knowing she never meant to do you wrong.''

Her soft words must have pulled his thoughts from other directions. She sensed him reconcentrating his mind in the silence that followed, was suddenly conscious of the crunch of their feet on the gravel path, and could feel his thoughts weaving around her with a tension that stretched her nerves.

"Can you forgive me for doing her wrong?" he asked, his voice strained with tormenting doubt.

"There was no intent," she answered as she saw it. "I think it's more a case of forgiving yourself, Armand. I think we all have a need for answers and we try to find those that will make sense of what we know…or what we think we know."

"That's very generous of you," he said in quick relief.

Not generous, she thought, just honest. It was easier for her, not having been fed lies that hit at her insecurities, easier for her to look at the whole and see the parts that made up the picture. She hadn't been here, feeling the shifts in Colette's and Armand's world, being personally affected by them.

"But for you I would never have known," he murmured on a heavy sigh.

"Oh, that works both ways, Armand," she said wryly. "But for you *I* would never have known. And it was…is…important to me."

"I know."

A little shiver crept down her spine as the tug of intimacy got to her again. In a defensive rush, she asked, "Have you made arrangements for Colette's burial?"

He stopped and pointed towards a stand of magnificent old pine trees. "See the chapel beyond the trees? It belongs to the estate and was built at the same time as the chateau. It has been used by generations of my family for christenings, marriages and funeral services. Colette will be laid to rest in the family cemetery behind it."

It felt right to Kristy that her sister would be given a place of belonging to a sense of history, a sense of family. Somehow it echoed Kristy's own deep desire to have solid ground beneath her feet, ground that wouldn't shift. No earthquake. No chaos. Peace.

Her gaze drifted over the beautiful parkland they were walking; wide green lawns and wonderful trees, planted to a pattern that showed them off, such old established trees, giving the sense they'd been there forever. My sister will be here forever, too, she thought, and I'll always know where she lies.

"I'm glad you're bringing her home," she murmured. "It is where she would want to be...near her children...and you."

"You, also, Kristy." His voice throbbed with deep conviction. "Colette wanted to be with you, too. What I said to the children about their mother being an angel taking care of us..."

He paused, as though uncertain of how she felt about it.

"I thought it was a very comforting idea, Armand," she assured him. "It made them feel good instead of them dwelling on their loss."

"I was thinking of it in regard to us, Kristy, that she wanted us to come together," he said on a lower, more intimate note, and suddenly everything within her quivered with fearful anticipation.

She didn't want Colette linked to their intimacy, yet how could she not be? Her twin was an integral part of both their lives. On the other hand, Armand might not be referring to what had happened between them last night. Just because that memory of "coming together'' was consuming her, didn't mean it had the same powerful draw on him.

"I'm not sure I understand what you're thinking, Armand," she asked, trying to sound calm and reasonable.

"Do you not wonder how it came about that you appeared at the hotel when you did?"

She turned sharply to him, her eyes searching his with swift intensity. "Surely you don't believe…'' She shook her head at the fanciful notion that Colette in some angel mode had directed their meeting. "I told you how I came to be there, Armand," she reminded him forcefully.

"But you do not know why I was there with Charmaine," he said as though it had important meaning.

She frowned, not liking the idea Charmaine had any importance whatsoever. "Does it matter?"

"The timing was…uncanny. I had decided I would accept what Charmaine had been offering me for a long time. It did not seem to concern her that I was not in a position to offer marriage and the idea of an accommodating lover was very tempting." His mouth curled self-mockingly. "You could say I set the scene…and you walked into it, Kristy."

The images flashed into her mind again…the two beautiful people leaning towards each other, the champagne, the sexual promise hovering between them…possible honeymooners, she had thought, and instantly hated the idea, hating it irrationally yet so strongly.

Armand was right. The timing was…uncanny.

Had Colette somehow led her there to break Stephanie's final triumph over Armand's marriage, to prevent the consummation of betrayal? Were there forces at work beyond any human comprehension? Who could possibly know? All Kristy could truly lay claim to was she had been on her way to Geneva, adrift from everything that had previously made up her life.

At a turning point.

As Armand had been with Charmaine.

Coincidence… Fate… Kristy dragged her mind off other mysterious paths and focused it on what was knowable. "So you and Charmaine did not become lovers."

"And never will be." His eyes said *not after last night with you*. "I called on her after we parted that first evening and apologised for having allowed any kind of relationship to develop between us, because I'd realised by then it couldn't be right."

Relief swept through Kristy.

He had finished it with Charmaine. Finished it with Stephanie, too. Did that wipe the slate clean?

"Well, I'm glad that's clear-cut to you," she said, yearning for something more positive towards herself.

"It was clear-cut from the first jolt of seeing you."

Kristy's heart sank. "Because you thought I was your wife," she muttered, dropping her gaze to hide the savage disappointment.

"No. It was more than that. There was a power in you that drew me on more strongly than anything I'd felt before. I tried to deny it. I tried to dismiss it. In the hotel room I kissed you in anger because it was something I'd never felt coming from Colette and it shouldn't have been happening, given the circumstances I'd come to believe.'' He paused then softly added, ''And you kissed me back, Kristy.''

He left those words hanging for her to comment on. She couldn't find a clear thought in her head let alone her tongue. Her whole body was churning between wanting to believe him and fear that she might be misinterpreting what he was saying.

''Why did you kiss me back, Kristy?''

His voice curled around her heart and squeezed. She closed her eyes, desperate to hide her vulnerability, unable to trust the need she felt coming from him. Then she felt the tingly warmth of a hand tilting her chin and the physical contact fired her brain. One clear bolt of decision scattered all the muddled feelings—*no compromises*!

Her eyes snapped open and blazed into his as she answered him, the words tumbling out in a fierce, challenging stream. ''Because you touched something in me I couldn't control. Because when you kissed me, I simply couldn't help kissing you back. And it had absolutely nothing to do with Colette. Nothing! I didn't even know I had a sister at that point, let alone an identical twin.''

She wrenched her chin out of his light grasp, her eyes flaring intense protest. ''If you think Colette is somehow angelically guiding my response to you, please keep your hands off me and never touch me again! Because I am *me*, Armand. Not Colette. And I will not allow you to fantasise having your wife again through me.''

He looked shocked. "Is that what you think?"

His shock fuelled the fire. "What am I supposed to think? You dressed me in Colette's clothes…"

"No! *You* chose them. And if you're not wearing them because of what Stephanie said…"

"*This* is me!" She whipped her hands out of her pockets and raked her fingers down her jacket and jeans. "*This* is what I am, *who* I am!"

"What you are is inside you, Kristy," he argued.

"Well, you were inside me last night, Armand, and you didn't know the difference," she hurled at him.

"Oh, yes I did!"

"Don't lie! It was your sexual frustrations with Colette that you worked out on me last night. I know this. I know it because this morning you asked me to forgive you for forcing your desires, which you didn't force at all…because I *wanted* you. And God help me, I even left the door unlocked, so you'd know I still *wanted* you!"

Her reckless statement lit an exultant triumph in his eyes that shocked Kristy. She backed away from him. "Don't you dare think I'll accommodate you again!"

"Accommodation has nothing to do with it," he declared, stepping after her, emanating relentless purpose.

She held up her hands to ward him off. "I will not share a bed with you and my sister."

He kept coming. "Your sister is dead."

She pushed against his chest. "You think she's an angel."

He grabbed her hands and planted them on his shoulders. "If she is, she wanted us to be together."

"Stop this!"

"No!" He wrapped his arms around her and pulled her in to him.

She strained against him, frantically crying, "You loved Colette."

"But you excite me beyond anything I've ever known."

"That's not the same."

"I don't want it to be the same. Why would I when it's so much more?"

"More?"

"You don't tug on my heart, Kristy. You grab it." One of his hands slid up into her hair, grabbing hard. "You don't appeal to my mind, you possess it."

Her protests died. Her hands stilled. Was it true? His eyes were dark whirlpools of emotion, sucking her in to his inner world as his voice rang more and more deeply through her ears.

"You don't dance lightly on my soul. You claim it so completely I know I'd be forever incomplete without you."

Dear God, yes! It was what she felt.

"And my body doesn't want to protect you. It wants yours with an intensity *I* cannot deny or control."

He kissed her. And she felt all that he'd said pouring through her, filling her mind with the awesome power of his passion for her, seizing her heart and making it pound with the pleasure of it, stirring surges of excitement that pulsed into every cell of her body, and there was a joy in her soul that billowed over everything else…the joy of recognition, of intimate certainty, of feeling complete.

She believed him.

And kissed him back.

CHAPTER FIFTEEN

FOUR months on...

The wedding party spilled from the banquet hall, through the grand foyer to the reception room where Yvette had waited with the children when Kristy had first entered this chateau. Nothing seemed formidable to her now. Family and guests were bubbling with goodwill, and Kristy stood at Armand's side, brimming with the happy confidence of being his bride in front of everyone and knowing how truly they were husband and wife.

She spied Lucien carrying in his new son, eager to show off his firstborn to the guests, and Nicole hurrying across the room to chide him for bringing the sleeping baby from the nursery.

"Lucien is in trouble," she remarked laughingly to Armand.

He grinned at his brother. "No. He's just an irrepressibly proud father and Nicole will forgive him anything."

Which was true on both counts.

It was easy to forgive where there was love, Kristy thought, and wondered fleetingly if Stephanie would ever come to know that. Kristy hoped she would. It was a cold, comfortless world where there was no compassion.

Pierre, with Eloise in tow, weaved around a waiter

carrying a tray of glasses filled with champagne and confronted his father with a clear sense of mission. "*Papa*, Eloise wants to know if we can now call *Tante* Kristy *Maman*."

Kristy's heart turned over. The little girl was looking up at her adoringly. She didn't remember her real mother, only knowing that Kristy was her mirror image, and the bridal finery had probably made her look like an angel to Eloise.

Armand crouched down and scooped both children up in his arms. "Well," he drawled indulgently, "I guess that's up to Kristy." He turned to her, his dark eyes dancing in hopeful appeal. "Do you want to be the mother of this bold son of mine and this awe-struck little flower girl who happens to be my precious daughter?"

Two little faces beamed at her expectantly and what else could Kristy do but step forward, hugging and kissing them both and saying they already felt like her children and they could call her *Maman* if they wanted to?

Whereupon they both chorused the word with such delight and satisfaction, Kristy could not feel she was taking anything from her twin, but giving what she felt was right...the mother love Colette would have given them.

It was a poignant reminder of the vow she'd made on that first fraught night here...caring for the children, justice for her sister, the winning of respect, the clearing of the past and how it had been darkened for Colette.

And there was no doubt left in her mind about what was right for Armand. For herself, as well.

He put the children down and they skipped off to tell *Grandmère* their special piece of wedding news. Yvette, who was chatting to a nearby group of friends, bent to listen to them, then bestowed such a warm smile of approval on Kristy, there was no doubting what she felt, either.

Yvette had become a supportive friend. She had never been an enemy. And she no longer took the strength of her older son for granted. Perhaps she had learnt it wasn't enough to love silently. Certainly their relationship had grown warmer over the past few months.

"We'll have to be leaving soon, if we're to make it to Paris at a reasonable hour," Armand warned, glancing at his watch.

Paris tonight—where she would truly be *Madame* at the Soleil Levant—then the flight to Tahiti tomorrow for their honeymoon. They would fly back via San Francisco, stopping there to tie up the last loose ends of John's estate and choose what possessions she wanted to keep before returning home to France for Christmas.

"I'll go and change now," Kristy decided.

"Want my help?" Armand's eyes twinkled wickedly.

"Tonight," she promised with a glowing smile. "Stay here with the children, Armand."

The urge to be alone for a little while was strong, yet Kristy didn't know the reason for it until she was almost ready to leave. Having removed her wedding dress and veil and donned a royal blue suit, she was putting on the matching hat when her gaze fell on the bridal bouquet she'd set down on the dressing-table, and the thought came...her twin had once carried a bridal bouquet, too.

There was no hesitation. Time was not as important as this. Kristy picked up the flowers and made a private exit from the chateau. She walked to the chapel where her sister had been married, where her sister's children had been christened, and from where her sister had been buried. But it wasn't the place to lay the flowers.

She skirted the chapel and entered the cemetery behind it. A new headstone had been erected. Not white marble like the rest. Kristy had insisted on a warm, red-brown granite slab, the inscription lettered in gold.

Colette Dutournier
beloved wife of Armand
mother of Pierre and Eloise
twin sister of Kristy
Rest in Peace

Gently, Kristy laid the sweet-smelling bouquet in front of the headstone and her mind and heart filled with all she wanted her sister to hear and know.

"We have come together, Colette. Not in the way either one of us wanted it to happen, but I do feel close to you. I love Armand and your children, and will always hold their memory of you safe. As you would have wanted to be remembered. I hope I have done all you might have asked of me. And if you are an angel, looking down on me now, please give me your blessing for a life I might never have had but for you calling to me. I am here...your Chrissie...for you, too, and I always will be.''

A quiet peace seemed to seep into her soul as she turned away and a smile of contentment curved her lips. When she lifted her gaze, there was Armand at the cemetery gate, waiting for her. Had he somehow sensed she would come here...this man who was her soul mate?

''It felt right,'' she explained, gesturing back to the bouquet resting on her twin's grave.

They had promised each other there would never be any locked doors between them, nothing hidden, nothing kept to themselves.

He nodded to her now, an understanding in his eyes that had no need for explanation. ''The gift of love. It's what you've brought to all of us, Kristy,'' he murmured, drawing her into his embrace.

''Oh, I'm selfish enough to want it returned,'' she teased happily.

He laughed. ''I shall think of many ways to show you it is...in abundance.''

They kissed, revelling in the flow of intimacy which was such a constant joy to both of them. Then with Armand hugging Kristy close, they left the cemetery together, in perfect harmony, walking towards their future.

BRIDE OF HIS CHOICE

Emma
DARCY

For Pearl Grant, with much love and appreciation
for having shared my books with me from the
beginning, for giving me the confidence to write
what I do and, most of all, for being my friend

CHAPTER ONE

THE plane touched down with barely a bump. Leigh Durant unclenched her hands and opened her eyes. She was back. A safe landing...though the nerves still knotted in her stomach proclaimed there was little else that would be *safe* about this trip.

From her seat next to a window, she noted the rain forecast for Sydney was certainly accurate. The view of Botany Bay was obliterated by wet darkness.

It was a dark and stormy night...

The cartoon character Snoopy, sitting on his doghouse with his typewriter, always started his stories with those ominous words. Leigh wondered if she was starting a new phase of her life by coming home or simply ending the one that had started the day she was born, twenty-four years ago.

Ever since the media had broken the news of Lawrence Durant's fatal heart attack, she'd started hoping her long, lonely exile was over. Yet she wasn't sure of anything where her family was concerned. All she knew was the man who had so cruelly dominated their lives was dead. And Leigh wanted to see him buried. Buried beyond any possible redemption. After that...

Well, she'd try to ascertain if it was possible to forge a new relationship with her mother and sisters. They might not want anything to do with her. It had been six years since she'd been part of their world...six years since she'd run away from the hell of knowing she didn't belong to it and never could while ever Lawrence Durant lived. It might be that none of them would welcome her back…and the hole of emptiness in her life would never be filled.

Leigh instinctively fought against the prospect of that bleak outcome. There had to be a chance. Lawrence was no longer there to influence their behaviour towards her…the daughter who wasn't *his* daughter, the cuckoo he'd hated having in his nest. Her mother and sisters were free of him now. Surely she could be re-united with them, if there was any fairness at all in this world.

The plane came to a halt. Leigh released her seat-belt and rose with the other passengers to retrieve her hand luggage. She was stiff and tired and did a bit of stretching to ease her cramped muscles as they waited in line to disembark. It had been a long trip—yesterday's flight from Broome to Perth, the stopover there to buy suitable clothes, then this afternoon's flight from Perth to Sydney, right across the Australian continent. It would be good just to get out of the plane.

The passengers moved slowly down the aisle towards the exit door. Leigh had worked her way up to being level with the first-class seats when her gaze fell on a discarded newspaper. The photograph of a face caught her eye and her heart contracted.

Richard…Richard Seymour.

Before she even realised what she was doing, the newspaper was in her hand and she was staring at the current image of the man who'd haunted her teenage years.

"Move on!" someone called impatiently.

"You're holding us up, Miss," the man behind her said more politely.

"Sorry," she gabbled, her face burning as she hurried forward and shot into the disembarking tunnel, still holding the wretched newspaper. She wished she could drop it and vowed to do so the moment she reached the first litter bin inside the terminal.

Richard Seymour...

She'd read about him in various articles relating to Lawrence Durant's shock death...the man who was now in charge of the vast financial empire, steadying the ripples on the stock exchange...the man groomed by the great tycoon to take over from him...Lawrence Durant's protégé and right hand. But none of the articles had been accompanied by a photograph.

It was seeing his face again that had got to her, releasing a flood of the ambivalent feelings he'd always stirred. Stupid! she savagely berated herself. One thing was certain. If this was the start of a new phase in her life, *he* wouldn't be featuring in it. There was no reason for him to ever mix with the Durant family again. He now had what he wanted, the top spot with no one to answer to except the shareholders.

A furious energy coursed through her as she entered the airport terminal, spotted a rubbish bin and strode straight over to it, ridding herself of the photographic reminder of a man who wasn't worth thinking about. Of course she would see him at the funeral tomorrow. Richard Seymour could hardly miss that. But no-one could force her to have anything to do with him. Not any more. Lawrence Durant was dead.

It was still raining when she stepped out of the terminal. Luckily she didn't have to queue for a taxi-cab. There were plenty waiting. She ran to one, jumped into the back seat, hauling her bag with her, shut the door and gave the address of her hotel to the driver. He zipped off into the line of traffic and Leigh tried to relax.

Impossible task. She stared broodingly out at the wet street, a zigzag of lights reflected in sheets of streaming water. *A dark and stormy night…*was it an omen? Should she have stayed in Broome, keeping the past pushed behind her? Was she on a totally hopeless mission?

No point in not going through with it now, she stubbornly reasoned. She was here. Tomorrow she would go to Lawrence Durant's funeral, see her mother and sisters, and their attitude towards her would determine if she had a place here or not. One day was probably all it would take to settle her future course. At the very least, she wouldn't be left wondering for the rest of her life.

CHAPTER TWO

NOTHING had changed…

Leigh stood in the grand reception room of the Durant mansion, feeling the same oppressive sense of being utterly worthless as she had as a teenager, as a child. It was as though she'd moved back in time and all she had escaped from was swamping her again; the insecurities, the rejections, the fear of not fitting in, the despair of not belonging.

It should be different now, she fiercely told herself. Lawrence Durant—*her father* for the first eighteen years of her life—was dead. Surely his repressive, tyrannical force had died with him, leaving her mother and sisters free to follow their own inclinations instead of kowtowing to his rule. Was it too soon for them to realise he was truly gone? Hadn't the funeral today brought that home to them?

Conversation at the chapel service had naturally been limited. The shock of seeing her after so long an absence might have caused a loss of words, too, but why were they avoiding her now, ignoring her presence, leaving her completely alone? If they would only show her a glimmer of welcome…

Feeling hopelessly ill at ease amongst the crowd of notable people who filled the reception room, paying their last respects to a man who'd wielded wealth and power, Leigh felt a jab of hopeful relief on seeing her mother detach herself from one mourners' group and move away, unaccompanied. She moved quickly to intercept her, touching her arm to draw attention.

"Mother?"

Alicia Durant shot her youngest daughter a brief, impatient glance. "Not now, Leigh. I must get back to Richard."

It was the barest pause, a frowning acknowledgement, so devoid of warmth it made Leigh shrivel inside. She dropped her hand and watched with a sense of wretched helplessness as her mother made a beeline towards the man who already had the undivided attention of her four sisters.

Richard Seymour...the heir apparent of Lawrence Durant's financial empire, presiding over the great tycoon's funeral and this ostentatious wake in the family mansion. She'd refused to even glance at him at the funeral. Looking at him now brought an instant resurgence of her old hatred of him.

He was still everything she wasn't and never could be...what Lawrence Durant had wanted of his fifth child...the shining son to carry on from him. Except the fifth child his wife had delivered was Leigh, another daughter by another man, a total reject who'd never shown any attributes worth the slightest bit of notice, apart from disapproving notice. Cruel notice when comparisons were made to Richard Seymour, the chosen one.

He certainly shone in every department—looks, brains, personal charisma. The aura of power and success and confident purpose literally pulsed from him. Leigh deliberately turned her back on him, telling herself none of this mattered any more. She no longer had any reason to hate Richard Seymour. She'd made her own life away from everything Lawrence Durant had ever touched, and had only come to his funeral out of a sense of closure to that miserable part of her life.

And to see if she meant anything to the rest of her family...her mother and sisters.

It was self-defeating to let these old feelings get to her today. She no longer wished to be something she wasn't. It had taken her a long time to become her own person—six struggling, lonely years—and Richard Seymour could not affect that now. If she could just show her family that she'd come of age, more or less, and that things could be different...

Leigh heaved a sigh to relieve the painful tightness in her chest. Her mother and sisters were probably dancing attendance on Richard Seymour out of habit. The king is dead. Long live the king. Except Richard was not family, so Leigh didn't really understand their fixation on him. He couldn't rule their lives as Lawrence Durant had. Not with the same iron hand and surely not with the same cruel judgement of crime and punishment.

Maybe when the wake was over and all these people who had to be impressed were gone, there would be a better opportunity to re-unite with her family. She'd give it a chance anyhow, one concerted effort to mend the bridges she'd broken in fleeing from the unbearable ex-istence she'd led in this house.

Meanwhile, there seemed little point and no pleasure in hanging around the edges of this crowd, forced to chat to people who could only see her as a curiosity. She made her way out to the back patio which was not in use, due to a gusty wind which would undoubtedly dis-comfort most guests.

It didn't worry Leigh. She wasn't wearing a hat and she didn't have a fancy hairstyle that could be ruined.

The thick mass of her almost waist-length hair could be untangled with a brush when she went back inside.

She wandered over to the steps leading down to the gardens which were terraced to the water's edge, and paused to look out over the much prized vista of Sydney Harbour. Last night's rain had gone but it was a grey winter day, no warmth or sparkle anywhere. Even the boats seemed to be hurrying to get to their destination.

She thought of the seaport of Broome, high up on the coast of the other side of Australia where there was constant heat, turquoise waters, and "hurry" was a foreign word—a different life a long way from this city. But had she really made her home there or was it still a refuge?

"Leigh…"

Her head jerked around at the unexpected call of her name. Nerves already shredded by being virtually ignored by her family were instantly on edge. Richard… Richard Seymour…seeking her out for attention? He was so closely entwined with Lawrence Durant in her mind, fear clutched at her heart, making it skitter until defiance surged to the fore.

She wasn't a teenager trapped in this place any more. She was an independent young woman, twenty-four years old and well established in another life away from here. There was nothing she could be threatened with, nothing anyone could hold over her head, and she'd learnt to cope with all manner of things.

She stood tall and straight and still, forcing herself to stare coolly at the man who had been a figure of torment to her in the past. Her mind was a total blank on why he'd bother with her at this point in time. What business with or interest in the black sheep of the Durant family could he possibly have?

Not once in the past six years had she asked for or tried to claim a single thing from the Durant holdings. So why on earth would Richard Seymour leave his admirers and follow her out here? She had to be totally irrelevant to his life.

"...you're not leaving, are you?" he demanded more than inquired.

He looked concerned, which confused Leigh even more. "Why would you care?" she asked in bewilderment.

He strolled towards her, a whimsical appeal in the smile he constructed for her. "I haven't had a chance to talk to you."

Leigh instinctively bristled at the projection of charm. He hadn't attempted to charm her in the past. Why now? What was the point? "I wasn't aware we had anything to talk about," she blurted out.

It didn't stop him. Her nerves screwed up another notch. She didn't want him with her. He brought back too many memories...painful, bitter memories of hopes dashed and dreams turned to dust.

"You've been gone a long time," he remarked casually as he closed the distance between them, making her very conscious of how tall and aggressively male he was.

The perfect tailoring of his dark mourning suit gave him a polished veneer but Leigh wasn't fooled by it. Richard Seymour was a hunter in the same mould as Lawrence Durant. For some obscure reason he was hunting her at the moment and her heart was quivering, still reacting to the old fear of being pounced upon.

Somehow, she summoned up an ironic smile. "Did

you want to welcome me home?'' No one else had and she certainly didn't expect him to.

He was quite sickeningly handsome up close. The photograph in the newspaper hadn't done him justice, missing the compelling vitality he'd always emitted. He had to be thirty-four now and definitely in his prime. His clear tanned skin gave his face a healthy glow. His hair, not quite as black as hers, had an attractive wave which some hairstylist had made the most of. His nose was strong and straight and his mouth perfectly balanced. Although his jaw line was rather squarish, the firmly defined chin lent even more strength to his features.

Despite all this impressive framework, it was his eyes that drew and dominated, piercing blue eyes, all the more compelling for being set off by thick black lashes and arched eyebrows which carried more than a hint of arrogance. They scanned her expression with too sharp an intelligence for Leigh's comfort.

''Have you come home?'' he asked in a soft lilt that sent a shiver down her spine.

All the defences she could summon shot into place. He was not going to get to her. She couldn't— wouldn't—let him. With the most determined deliberation Leigh could manage, she adopted a careless air.

''Only to test the waters again. They seem rather cold at the moment so I thought I'd take a walk in the garden while the VIPs are attended to.'' She threw him a dismissive little smile as she added, ''If you'll excuse me...'' then proceeded down the steps.

His voice followed her. ''Do you mind if I accompany you?''

It wasn't so much a shiver this time. Her spine literally crawled with a tangled mass of unresolved feelings, but nothing good could come of pursuing any of them with Richard Seymour. That time was gone...gone...gone! He might look like hero material but he hadn't been a hero when it counted to her, when she'd wished he'd charge in like a white knight, smiting her father and rescuing her. Such foolish, teenage yearnings!

She squared her shoulders before glancing back at him. "You'll be missed," she pointed out, mocking the importance everyone else placed on his company.

"You're the person I want to be with," he said with a directness that jiggled something deep in Leigh's heart, deep and dangerous to her.

"Not a good choice," she quickly parried.

"It's mine. I don't allow other people to make my choices for me."

There was purpose written in his eyes, undivertable purpose. As much as Leigh wanted to defy it, she knew he would not be turned away. A ruthless hunter always caught up with what he was hunting.

Did he think she'd come home to make trouble for him? Did he see her as someone he might need to pin down and neutralise so his takeover from Lawrence Durant was absolutely smooth? A black sheep could be unpredictable. After all, why turn up at the funeral after six years of non-communication?

Knowing herself to be a total waste of Richard Seymour's time, Leigh decided no harm could come to her from one brief cross-examination from him. "Fine!" she agreed, then, determined to show she wasn't disturbed by the prospect, she added, "I do admire people who have the strength of character to make their own choices."

He smiled. "So do I."

Leigh felt a very definite punch to the heart. His smile seemed to link her to him, as though they were co-conspirators in complete tune with each other. Leigh instantly rejected the idea, but she still felt shaken by it. Richard Seymour was not the man she'd wanted him to be and she wasn't about to be tricked into thinking differently.

He ran appreciative eyes over her as he headed down the steps. "You're looking good, Leigh."

"Thank you." She dragged out the memory of the last time he'd commented on her appearance, instinctively defending herself against the flattering power of his compliment. "As opposed to looking anorexic, I presume."

He'd accused her of it after one of Lawrence's ritual Sunday lunches, which she'd been unable to eat, her stomach too screwed up to accept anything. Although she had been dieting, her non-consumption of that meal had nothing to do with losing weight.

Richard shrugged. "Believe it or not, I was worried about you at the time. You were far too thin."

"And you put it so kindly. *Anorexia might be a way of taking control of your body but it won't give you control over anything else,*" she quoted.

His eyes locked onto hers again as he reached her side at the foot of the steps. "I thought you needed a jolt," he explained without apology.

He was giving her a jolt right now with his perverse interest in her, with the clarity of a memory that surely held no significance to him. She'd been seventeen, fighting what she then saw as an unfair weight problem, trying to look more like her model-slim sisters. Impossible task.

She'd been born with a different bone structure and no matter how thin she got, the natural curves of her body denied her a boyish figure. Away from the repressive influences of her family, she'd grown into the woman she was always going to be, voluptuously curved, but not grossly so for her height. She was taller than average, though even in high heels, she found herself half a head shorter than Richard Seymour, looking up to him, which she suddenly resented.

"Well, Richard," she drawled, turning away to start down the path to the ornamental pond, "let me tell you I don't need your approval for who or what I am. In fact, your opinion—good or bad—is irrelevant to me." Which put him in his place in *her* world.

He laughed as he fell into step with her.

Leigh found herself clenching her hands at his amusement. She sliced him a totally unamused look, wishing he would take his disturbing presence elsewhere.

He grinned. "I have missed the black blaze of those incredibly expressive eyes."

Missed? Had she really made such a strong impression on him all those years ago? Or was he attempting to flirt with her, now that she "looked good"?

She frowned over the questions as he walked on with her. The black suit she'd bought for the funeral was figure-hugging. She didn't favour layers of shapeless clothes that made her look fat. Apparently Richard liked her current shape. As for her eyes, Leigh simply accepted them as part and parcel of her coloring—matching the blackness of her hair and toning with her olive skin. She had a slightly long nose and a wide, very full-lipped mouth, and she'd come to accept them, too. Since her face had filled out, the features she'd despaired over looked more right somehow, in keeping with the rest of her.

Certainly she no longer felt like *the ugly duckling* she'd always been in the Durant household, though she could never be counted as a blonde beauty like her older sisters. Ruefully she remembered her one desperate attempt to dye her hair blonde. Total disaster. Like everything else she had attempted in her teens in her hopeless need to fit some acceptable mould. She hadn't known then she was a cuckoo in the nest and cuckoos couldn't turn into anything else.

"I have no doubt you have no need of *my* approval, Leigh," Richard picked up, apparently determined on teasing her out of her silence. As she glanced at him he added, "There wouldn't be one red-blooded male who didn't approve of you."

Sex! Leigh wrenched her gaze from his and walked faster, inwardly fuming over this shallow view of her. She was more than just a lush body that a lot of men fancied. But then men like Richard Seymour probably didn't want a woman with a mind or a heart. Taking sex as needed was probably his style.

In all the publicity and media speculation sparked by Lawrence Durant's fatal heart attack, the newspapers had made much of the fact Richard Seymour was not married—one of the most eligible bachelors in Australia—and Leigh wondered if he was as much a womaniser as Lawrence Durant had been, behind the respectable facade of his marriage. With his looks, Richard certainly wouldn't lack choice.

Was he now thinking the same of her? He was wrong,

if he did. She hadn't even cared to sample the chances that had come her way. Somehow an internal barrier went up the moment any man started getting too close to her. As for desiring them...she'd often wondered if desire was linked to trust and that was why she couldn't feel it. Maybe one day she would meet someone she could really trust to love her as she wanted to be loved.

"Are you happy in the life you've made for yourself?"

The apparently artless question snapped Leigh out of her private reverie. Danger signals flared in her mind. Give anything away to a man like Richard Seymour and somehow he'd use it against her. She'd had too much experience of that process in the Durant household to be offering any information about herself.

Keeping her *expressive* eyes fixed on the path ahead she answered, "Reasonably," in an even tone, then turned the question back on him. "What about you? Are you happy with what you've made of yourself?"

He laughed again, though there was more irony than amusement in the sound this time. "You know, no-one's ever asked me that question."

Of course. Brilliant success didn't exactly invite any such doubt. "Perhaps you should ask it of yourself?" she drily remarked.

"Perhaps I should," he agreed even more drily. "Though I can't say it's ever been on my list of priorities. I've always thought happiness an elusive thing, not easily captured and even more difficult to hold."

Unlike wealth and power.

"Then why ask me about it?"

"Oh, I guess I was really asking if you've found a relationship you find satisfying."

He dropped the question so casually, the impact came in slow motion. Leigh's first reaction was it was none of his business. Then his previous comment about the approval of "red-blooded men" started to rattle her. Did he fancy a quick fling with her while she was in Sydney? Was this why he'd followed her out here...to ascertain availability and charm his way into her bed? Did he see her as old enough for him now?

The idea was outrageous, yet oddly tantalising. Leigh was tempted to play him along, just to see if it was true. "No, I haven't. At least, not as satisfying as I would wish," she answered honestly, then slid him an assessing look as she added, "But I didn't come home for you, Richard."

It was a mistake to look at him. He instantly locked onto it with a piercing intensity that pinned her eyes to his. "Am I not one of the ghosts you wish to lay to rest?"

"Why would you think so?" she retaliated, disturbed by the wild quickening of her pulse.

"Because you hated me so much."

He was raising the ghosts, deliberately and too evocatively for Leigh's comfort. "Wouldn't you, in my place?" she snapped.

"Yes. But there was nothing I could do to change your place, Leigh. You had to do it yourself. Which you did. Yet I wonder if all those negative feelings towards me—the bitter resentment and the black contempt—still linger on?"

He *was* getting to her, digging around in her head and heart, and she didn't want him to. Realising she'd paused to counter this attack on her feelings, Leigh got her legs moving again, chiding herself for falling into the trap of letting him focus the conversation on her. She tried to switch it back on him.

"I can't imagine it matters to you."

"It does. Very much."

"Why?" she demanded, inwardly refusing to believe him. She would not—*not*—allow herself to be vulnerable to what Richard Seymour thought or felt about her. She'd been down that painful track, wanting *him to shine* for her, but he hadn't.

"I wasn't your enemy," he answered simply. "Your hatred was blind, Leigh. As much as I could be, I was your friend."

Hardly *a friend*, she thought with a violence that startled her. Let it go, she berated herself furiously. Just let it go and set him aside, right out of your life.

"I don't view you as an enemy, Richard," she said as dispassionately as she could. "I don't think I did then, either. Not personally. If you hadn't been the favoured protégé, someone else would have won that place, and been used in the same way to show off my father's dissatisfaction with me."

"I didn't enjoy my place in that particular game, Leigh."

She couldn't stop herself from seething over how he had conducted himself, even though he might not have enjoyed it. "You didn't walk away from it," she tersely remarked.

"As you say, it wouldn't have changed anything," he answered easily. "Lawrence would have found someone else. Someone who might have joined in the game with him, making it worse for you."

In all fairness, she couldn't accuse Richard of aiding or abetting the cruel baiting that had gone on during the

mandatory-attendance Sunday luncheons in the Durant
mansion. She remembered him diverting the conversation into other topics, taking the focus off her, but she'd
hated him for that, too, feeling he pitied her.

She'd wanted him—willed him—to stand up and fight
for her, though Lawrence would never have tolerated
that from him. With an older, wiser head on her shoulders, she could see that now, but at the time...

She took a deep breath, trying to clear herself of the
burning turmoil Richard Seymour could still stir.
Applying cold hard reason, it was possible to agree with
his point of view. He may well have meant to be *a friend*
to her, as much as he could, within the parameters of
retaining his position.

"Well, thank you for thinking of my feelings," she
said, trying to be fair and wanting this highly unwelcome
contretemps finished with. "As it happens, I don't hate
you any more, and you're not a ghost I need to lay to
rest."

"Good!" He sounded relieved.

His response nagged at Leigh. Why did he care what
she felt? Unless, of course, he did want to bed her, and
ghosts wouldn't be good in that scenario. But was that
really likely? She was no longer sure what was likely
with him. He kept on walking with her, seemingly deep
in thought, and she couldn't shake the feeling all his
thoughts were focused on her.

They reached the ornamental pond. Wanting to reduce
any sense of gathering intimacy with a man she could
have nothing in common with beyond the memories of
imprisoned hours together in the long-ago past, she sat
down on the wide sandstone blocks which formed a flat
platform on top of the pond's circular enclosure and

trailed her fingers through the water, making the fish dart into flashing movement, their luminous colours catching the light.

So beautiful, Leigh thought. Did they know they were prisoners, bought by the wealth of Lawrence Durant for his casual pleasure? Would freedom mean anything to these fish, or would they be lost in a world beyond this confinement? They were well fed, but being well fed wasn't everything. It was good to feel free. Yet even away from this place and all it represented, Leigh knew she was still emotionally tied to it, which was why she'd come back, hoping for...what?

It looked like she was only messing herself up again.

"I'm glad you came back, Leigh."

The soft intonation made the comment sound very, very personal. Leigh instantly steeled herself against its warming effect. If she started wanting too much from Richard Seymour, bitter disillusionment would surely follow. Any closeness with him had to be dangerous. As it was, she was acutely aware of him standing barely a metre away. That distance didn't feel far enough.

"I needed to be here today," she answered flatly, still watching the fish. "The funeral made Lawrence's death real...the coffin...the cremation...ashes to ashes, dust to dust. He doesn't have the power to hurt me any more." *And I won't let you do it, either,* she added resolutely.

"Your mother and sisters...from what I saw, none of them ever stood up for you. Do you expect that to be different now?" he asked, the soft tone projecting a caring she wouldn't let herself believe.

He hadn't stood up, either, though Leigh had to concede he had done more than the others to stop Lawrence's games. On the other hand, as an outsider, he hadn't been personally subjected to them. She wasn't the only one in the family who'd suffered verbal abuse. It had a repressive effect on all of them.

"I don't know if it will be different," she answered honestly. Suddenly and fiercely wishing for some open honesty from him, she lifted her gaze for direct confrontation. "Lawrence pulled the strings then. It looks like you pull them now. So what do you want, Richard? What is this conversation about? You'll do much better with me if you don't play games."

He cocked his head slightly, assessing the strength of that statement. His eyes held no warmth whatsoever. They were coldly calculating and Leigh sensed a ruthless gathering of purpose. When he spoke, there was no preamble, no dressing up with persuasive intent, just the bare bones of what he'd been leading to from the very beginning of this encounter.

"I want to marry you, Leigh."

CHAPTER THREE

LEIGH stared at Richard Seymour, too stunned to really believe her ears, but her eyes didn't pick up any messages that changed what she'd thought she'd heard.

He was watching her with intense concentration, waiting to weigh her reaction. His body looked relaxed but she could feel tension emanating from him. More than tension. Will-power was beaming out of those compelling blue eyes, asserting absolutely serious intent and firming up the wobbly ground inside her mind.

There was only one question to ask so she asked it. "*Why? Of all the women you could choose to marry, why me?*"

His mouth curved into a half-smile. "I could give you many reasons, Leigh, but since they're mostly from my point of view, I doubt you'd see them as valid."

Valid!

She laughed. Couldn't help herself. The situation was so wildly improbable, a sense of sheer hysteria bubbled out of her. King Richard wanting Cinderella as his wife? It might be understandable if he was madly in love with her, but that idea was as far-fetched as his proposition.

Leigh couldn't resist pursuing it, her eyes dancing a challenge as she asked, "Just give me one of those reasons, Richard. One I might be able to believe in."

His eyes seemed to twinkle knowingly at her as he said, "We're fellow travellers on a road that started a long time ago. Who else will understand what went into the journey?''

A straight stab to the heart, killing any urge to laugh and instantly evoking a sober and vehement reply. ''I got off that road.''

''Did you?'' he softly challenged. ''Not quite, Leigh, or you would never have come back.''

''I've explained why.''

He nodded. ''I listened, and what I heard is it's not finished for you. You're still seeking...'' He paused a moment, his eyes boring into hers. ''...justice.''

He was crawling into her mind, plucking on heartstrings that did yearn for what had never been given.

''What better justice can there be now than to balance the scales...with you taking all that was taken from you?'' he suggested with a terrible, insidious appeal to the darkness deep inside her. ''I can give it to you, Leigh.''

She wanted to look away, to escape this awful intrusion into her private soul, yet if she did, he would know he had hit truly and the vulnerability was there to be played upon. The darkness was not good. She'd tried to escape it, hating how it blighted her life. She realised now she had come back to confront it, make it go away. But how could marrying him turn it around? Wouldn't it be more of the same?

She'd been right about not giving him information to use against her. He was too clever at reading it. He wouldn't have succeeded Lawrence Durant if he wasn't both diabolically clever and ruthless. And she hadn't forgotten how the game was played. Hiding the hurt defeated the victory. She kept her gaze firmly on his and turned the darkness back onto him.

"Let's cut to the real point, Richard. I don't believe you *want* to marry me, so marriage to me has to have a purpose. What advantage is there in it for you?"

He laughed, completely disarming her for a moment, and his eyes danced at her in open admiration, disarming her even further. "I don't suppose you'd believe me if I said I love you," he tossed at her, moving closer to the sandstone rim of the pond, then lifting a foot onto it, leaning forward, resting his arms on the bent knee.

The pose brought him effectively closer to her, setting up an intimate togetherness while still respecting her personal space. And suddenly there was a sizzle in his eyes that set all her nerve ends twitching.

"But don't think I don't *want* you, Leigh," he said in a low purring voice, stirring even more havoc inside her. "There's nothing about you I don't want, including your blazing directness, which I find more refreshing than you could ever begin to believe."

Her heart was pumping so hard she couldn't think of a word to say. Her mind was jammed with sexual signals. And the terrible part was she couldn't push them out. There was a dreadful fascination in this crazy physical response to Richard Seymour. She remembered how his presence had always tied her in knots when she was a teenager. She hadn't recognised it then as sexual attraction. But now...

Did he know?

Did he *feel* it?

Sheer panic kept her silent.

He was not the least bit perturbed by her lack of response. He went on talking with easy confidence, knowing that she understood what he was spelling out. "You were supposed to be the son to carry on Lawrence's name and dynasty. And you paid one hell of a price for not being that son. What you don't know—yet—is he never lost the obsession of having his own flesh and blood carry on from him.''

''But that's impossible now,'' Leigh murmured, struggling out of her distraction.

''No, it's not impossible…if he has a grandson with the right capabilities. And Lawrence thought of that before he died. Thought of it and planned it.''

A grandson! It was sickening. An innocent little baby boy created for Lawrence Durant's massive ego, life and goals all rigidly mapped out before he even started living. As hers would have been if she had been the right sex and the right material for moulding into the right monument to a man who didn't deserve any kind of monument.

''Did he pick out the name, too?'' she asked in savage disgust. ''Mine was supposed to be Leigh Jason. The Jason part was dropped when I turned out to be a girl.''

''Lawrence,'' came the dry reply.

''Of course. One Lawrence gone. Another coming up.''

Something infinitely dangerous and determined flashed through the clear blue of his eyes. ''He can't reach that far from the grave, Leigh, and his purpose can be defeated.''

She was tantalised by the brief glimpse of something she didn't know—a force driving him that went beyond her previous judgement of his character. ''Go on,'' she urged.

''I was the one who took your designated role, insofar as I met the expectations he would have had for his son. My much publicised position as his successor is not ironclad. It is provisional to my fulfilling the terms of his will.''

''Which are?'' she prompted when he paused, although she could guess what was coming, and another painful emptiness yawned inside her.

His mouth curled into a mirthless smile. ''If I marry one of his daughters and produce a son, I get the necessary percentage of company shares which will make my position as his successor unassailable.''

The right material wedded to the Durant genes.

Hence the proposal of marriage.

Except she couldn't be the chosen one...never the chosen one.

There was one huge flaw in Richard Seymour's selection of her as his bride, and Leigh wasn't the only one who knew it. Her mother certainly did. Her four sisters might very well be aware of it, as well. They'd tell him soon enough, if it served their interests, and the evidence of her own observations pointed that way.

All five of them undoubtedly knew the contents of the will. Whomever Richard chose to marry would be sitting pretty in the world they knew. It explained why her mother and sisters had been so focused on courting his favour and not paying any attention to the return of the prodigal daughter. It was the same old sick game, sucking up to power.

Leigh found her gaze had dropped to the leg Richard had propped on the sandstone platform. The fine woollen fabric of his suit trousers was pulled taut over a strongly muscled thigh. Her mind fuzzed over an image of how he might look naked, all that male power energised by desire, wanting her...

Another fanciful dream turned to dust, she thought,

feeling the same old ache of disappointment Richard had always left her with. If she told him the truth he wouldn't want her, not as a wife. Even if he still fancied her— the woman she was now—she couldn't allow anything to come of it, knowing he would inevitably choose to make one of her sisters his bride. Best to cut it dead right now.

She dragged her gaze up and kept it levelled on his as she delivered her rejection. "The answer is no, Richard. I won't marry you."

Then to emphasise the matter was closed, she was up on her feet with her back turned to him and heading towards the steps that led down to the next terrace, away from him, away from the house that had dominated much of her life, away from the family who cared more for what it represented than they'd ever cared for her.

"Why not?" Richard shot after her.

She waved a dismissive hand without glancing around. "You have four other daughters to choose from. You just struck out on me, that's all."

"I don't *want* any of the others," he declared vehemently.

She shook her head over the black irony of that statement and kept on walking, down the steps to the summer-house which presided over the terrace of rose gardens. She could hear his footsteps following her and fiercely wished he'd leave her alone.

It was so perverse of him to choose her ahead of the far more suitable daughters, the beautiful blonde accomplished socialites with the right blood in them, only too eager to snap him up and grace his arm, his bed, and his bank balance. Felicity, Vanessa, Caroline, Nadine...such pretty, feminine, classy names.

The impulse to shove one truth she'd had to accept down Richard Seymour's throat made Leigh pause by the summer-house and cast a derisive look at him. He was already at the foot of the steps and striding towards her.

"You know, Richard, most people don't get everything they want. You may not be used to that but I'm sure compromises sometimes have to be taken, even in your world."

He kept on coming. "You can have everything you want from me, Leigh."

The strong conviction in his voice clutched at her heart, but only for a moment. He wasn't offering love. He probably didn't know what love was, any more than she did. The sheer sweep of his extravagant promise suddenly evoked another wild laugh, peeling into a wind that carried it away from her as swiftly as it arose.

It didn't stop him. His eyes didn't waver from hers, determined on burning away her scorn and supplanting it with possibilities that could breed hope. But there *was* no hope.

"It's very simple, Richard," she said flatly. "Regardless of what you can give me, I can't give *you* what you want."

He came to a halt, barely a metre away, totally unperturbed by her claim. His eyes challenged it with ruthless intent as he said, "Because you're not Lawrence Durant's daughter?"

Shock reverberated through her. "You know?" The words spilled from her lips before she could catch them back. Had he guessed or had he pushed her into admission? His proposal made no sense if he *knew*. A churning turmoil of shame and pride robbed her of any movement as he stepped towards her, a mesmerising satisfaction written on his face.

''I knew the day I first met you, Leigh. You didn't belong to Lawrence, not physically, not mentally, not emotionally. No bond at all and nothing of him in you. Nothing.''

It wasn't proof, she thought, but he went on, shattering that thought.

''Lawrence confirmed it when you went away and I suggested someone should be hired to keep track of you in case you were in need. 'She's my wife's child, not mine!' was what he said, then swore me to silence on the subject. A proud man like Lawrence didn't care to have it known that you weren't his.''

The power of his total self-assurance held her still, though her heart was pounding wildly and tremors of shock were still running through her.

''Legally, you are his.''

''No.'' Her voice sounded hollow but the words had to be said now. ''He disinherited me when I left.''

''He made no provision for you in his will, Leigh, but nowhere is there a claim that denies you are his child. And since Lawrence was cremated today, there can be no DNA tests to prove you aren't. I can marry you in good faith with the terms of his will.''

Instinctively she fought against the relentless beat of his logic. ''My mother could name my real father.''

A grim little smile curled his mouth. ''It's not in her best interests to do so.''

The manipulation of wealth! Leigh's hatred of it spurred her to argue. ''What makes you think my real father wouldn't come forward if he saw money in it?''

That killed the smile. Yet, even more disturbing, his

eyes seemed to soften with sympathy. "It won't happen, Leigh," he said quietly. "Your mother paid for him and his family to go back to Italy before you were born. From the date of their departure, I'd say he knows nothing of you."

"Go back to Italy?" she picked up in bewilderment.

"You didn't know he was Italian?"

She shook her head. On the terrible night she had learnt Lawrence Durant was not her father, her mother had refused to reveal the true circumstances of her birth. The argument between Lawrence and his wife had raged over her head, and had more to do with financial arrangements than the infidelity that had brought her into their world. They had forgotten her in hurling threats at one another. She'd simply slipped away, packed her things and left.

Italian...well, that explained her colouring. There weren't too many blonde Italians. It probably explained her non-boyish figure, as well. The only Italian actress she could think of was Sophia Loren, whose curvaceous femininity was legendary. Leigh supposed a hot-blooded Italian lover would have made a tempting contrast to Lawrence Durant, but her mother had hardly been wise in having a child by him, risking the possibility of producing the cuckoo Leigh had turned out to be.

"He was the gardener here at the time of your conception," Richard explained.

It shocked her into speech. "A gardener? My mother took a gardener as her lover?" It seemed unbelievable. Her mother was a dyed-in-the-wool snob who invariably disdained to notice what she considered the lower classes.

"He had four sons, Leigh."

Ah…the logic of it was instantly crystal clear. No escaping *that* connection. A man who fathered sons was precisely what was wanted when four daughters had been delivered and a son was required.

Leigh closed her eyes, revolted by the calculation that had gone into her conception…the payment that had been made for a service rendered. No doubt, if there'd been ultrasound scans done all those years ago to determine the sex of the baby, the pregnancy would have been terminated and she wouldn't even be alive today. Her mother had probably gambled on having a child that took after her in looks and colouring. No wonder she'd been *unwanted*. She represented failure in every sense.

"How do you know all this, Richard?" she asked, raising lashes that felt unnaturally heavy, but needing to see the answer in his eyes.

"I made it my business to find out."

"Why?" A weary, aching cynicism prompted her to add, "To ensure there was no wild card that could upset your plan?"

"There was no plan when I set about getting the information. That was six years ago, Leigh."

She frowned, realising the terms of the will would only have been revealed on Lawrence's death. "Then what use was it to you?"

His serious expression was softened by a touch of whimsy. "Oh, I thought one day you might like to know who your real father is."

"You did it for me?" She shook her head incredulously, unable to believe such altruism from a man who clearly calculated everything.

"We have more in common than you think," he said wryly. "I was not the child of the man my mother was married to. I bear his name but I'm not his child, and I knew it very early on.''

Leigh was dumbfounded. There'd never been a whisper of anything scandalous in his background. Another private family secret? Then it burst upon her that he knew what it felt like...travelling the same road...and he'd seen it all along in her...a fellow traveller.

''The truth of such a situation is not easy to deal with and a name can become important,'' he went on. ''Your father's name is Mario Vangelli. He and his family live in Naples. I can give you the address should you ever want to visit.''

Vangelli...Richard was right. It *was* good to have a name instead of a blank. ''What about you?'' She eyed him curiously. ''Did you find your real father?''

''Yes. He was married to someone else. They had a family. He didn't know I was his son and I didn't tell him.'' His expression hardened. ''As with your father, it was just seed sown that he walked away from.''

Paid to walk away from in her case. ''I wouldn't feel right about visiting, but thank you for telling me about him, Richard. It is better knowing than not knowing.''

He nodded, an understanding in his eyes that shared the scars of being a bastard child who didn't belong to the marriage of either parents.

''I might never have come back,'' she mused. ''You might have got that information for nothing, Richard.''

He shook his head. ''Information is always useful.''

Cynicism returned in a swift bitter sweep. It was information he could have used against her mother, or Lawrence, for that matter. ''Of course,'' she drawled. ''Knowledge is power.''

''And you were always going to come back,'' he continued without so much as a ripple in his cast-iron confidence. "When you felt ready to."

"Lucky for you it was now or you would have had no choice but to propose to one of my sisters," she mocked.

"Luck has nothing to do with it. If you hadn't come I would have gone to you."

Her heart contracted. He really did want *her* above the others. "You would have had to track me down," she pointed out.

"I've kept track of you all along, Leigh. As soon as I knew you had gone, I acted to ensure you were safe, and stayed safe, wherever you went and whatever you did. There wasn't one day of these past six years that I haven't known where you were, and been assured you were managing by yourself. I knew what flight you took out of Broome, where you stayed in Perth, and what time you arrived in Sydney last night. And I knew you would be here today."

It shook her, more than any of the previous shocks he'd delivered. Or perhaps it was the culminating effect of all of them. "You had someone spying on me?"

"No, not spying. Just checking that you were coping on your own, not in trouble, not in need of help. There was absolutely no interference in your life, Leigh, nor in whatever you chose to do."

"Why did you do it?" she cried, still appalled at having been so comprehensively watched over.

It came again, that brief flash of something deep and dark and dangerous behind the crisp blue of his eyes. "Because I cared. And no one else did." Even his voice carried a note of ferocity, suggestive of feelings he hadn't quite kept under control.

Leigh tried to focus on it but Richard distracted her by moving closer, lifting a hand and touching her cheek, soft fingertips grazing her skin, raising electric tingles. "Think, Leigh," he commanded, the powerful impact of his eyes increased by the knowledge he had of her. "You came, looking for some portion of justice…"

That was true.

"Marry me…and you'll have what your mother sacrificed you for…what your sisters covet. You'll have all that Lawrence denied you and more. What greater justice than to take what you were born for…"

Her head whirled with his words, all of them striking such painful places.

"I hand you the keys to the whole Durant empire, everything Lawrence acquired in his ruthless drive for power…"

To the exile, the spoils, she thought wildly.

"…and no one will scorn you again, Leigh, or treat you in a contemptible manner. As my wife, you will be my queen, in every sense."

As long as I give you a son.

There was always a price for the pot of gold.

"I want you as my queen, Leigh."

The low throb of his voice was like a drumbeat on her heart.

"Only you can satisfy me. Only you. We're two of a kind, Leigh. You and I."

And that mesmerising message blazed from his eyes as he moved closer, an arm sliding around her waist, taking possession, the hand on her face suddenly cupping her chin, holding it tilted, and she knew he was going to kiss her, knew he meant to seduce her to his will, but somehow she didn't want to stop him.

Her entire being was quivering with anticipation.

CHAPTER FOUR

LEIGH held her breath at the first brush of his mouth on hers, the contact so tantalisingly gentle, it took all her concentration to absorb each shift of pleasurable sensation. It wasn't a *taking* kiss. She would have fought it if he'd tried to blitz her with dominant strength. The relief of this controlled exploration allowed her to relax and let the urge to know flow freely.

She had blocked him out all these years, coupling him with Lawrence Durant, yet today she had been forcefully reminded that her hatred of Richard had been fed from the fierce wish for him to act differently. To her teenage mind he'd had the strength to fight her father, to stand up for her, to be her champion, and he hadn't done it. Not how she'd wanted it done, not enough to satisfy the bitter churning of needs inside her.

Could he give her satisfaction now?

Would he?

The feathery caresses teased her into responding, and no sooner had her lips softened and parted than the light pressures changed to a deeper searching, and she felt moving through her a great swell of yearning for the promise of everything...everything she'd ever wanted and could ever want.

Had the normal flow of such feelings been somehow locked up around Richard Seymour? Was this strange shifting inside herself the release of barriers that had been subconciously focused on needs *he* should have fulfilled?

Her mind and body were in such a whirl of inner chaos, she wasn't aware of lifting her arms. The instinct to press closer, to hold on to *this* moment of reckoning, to see it through as far as it went, swept her hands around his neck. His embrace instantly tightened, moulding her body to the hard length of his, and his mouth engaged hers in a far more passionate intimacy, stirring a sensual storm that spread like wildfire.

The heat of it banished the cold emptiness of being unloved and unwanted and ignited a hunger that craved everything she had missed out on. She revelled in the hungry ravishing of her mouth, exulted in every bit of the physical contact, the squashing of her breasts across the muscular breadth of his chest, the exciting pressure of his arousal, the straining of rock-hard thighs against hers. He did *want* her. It felt as though he was reaching out to her with every fibre of his being and the thrill of it was too enthralling to stop.

It was he who broke off the all-consuming flow of desire, suddenly throwing his head back, dragging in air, breathing so hard his chest heaved, bringing a rush of sensitivity to her breasts and stirring an intense frustration at the abrupt halt to what he'd started. She stared at him in confusion, seeing the tension on his face, not understanding anything except he'd stopped kissing her.

He moved the hand he'd curled around her head, touching her sensitised lips, tracing them with his fingers. Her daze cleared enough for her to see the glitter of triumphant satisfaction in his eyes as he spoke.

"It feels right, doesn't it, Leigh? The time has come for *us*."

Control, she thought. He wants to control this to suit him. Just as Lawrence Durant would. Never again would she submit to that. Never! The sweet, warm chaos he'd wrought inside her welded into a savage bolt of rebellion.

He'd run everything *his* way, following her out here, feeding her information, capitalizing on the chemistry between them. Well, she wouldn't let him control this. He wasn't going to mastermind when and how she got to satisfy herself about him.

All these years of spying on her, knowing where she was but not coming to her, waiting for her to come to him, thinking he could manipulate what he wanted of her, pressing buttons he had the power to press…oh, no! It was *her* turn to press the button!

"If it feels so right to you, Richard, what's wrong with *now*?" she challenged.

"You want *now*?"

The flare of raw desire in his eyes shot a turbulent mix of fear and elation through Leigh. What was she inviting, goading from him? The challenge had been a vengeful impulse. She hadn't stopped to think of the ultimate end of what she was laying on him, and he didn't wait for a reply.

He scooped her with him as he stepped to the door of the summer-house, opened it, and whirled her inside. By the time Leigh's feet steadied on the floor, the door was closed and she was pressed against it, and his mouth was delivering another rush of warm pleasure that felt very right, so right she held his head to hers, wanting his kissing to continue, kissing him back in a fierce need to fill herself with the warmth he generated, to keep the cold out.

Tautly muscled thighs lent supportive strength to hers as his hands roamed over her body, their touch hot and excitingly lustful as they felt her curves, reaching around the width of her hips to stroke the round slopes of her bottom, clutching them to press her closer to the source of his heat, the hard thrust of it liquefying her stomach, and he kissed her with all the raw intent of what he wanted, promising it would be all she wanted.

But would it? This had never happened to her before. She didn't know the end, had no experience of it. Maybe it was wrong, but she was caught in a force of her own making and she didn't want to break out of it.

Let him show her. Let him be the one. And if the promise wasn't fulfilled, she'd know then, wouldn't she? So she kissed him back with all the fire he'd lit in taking her this far.

Hands sliding to her waist, spanning it possessively, moving to unbutton her suit coat, parting it, and she was glad she hadn't worn a bra, only the silk teddy softly cupping her breasts, allowing firm palms and fingers to cup them so much more satisfyingly, making them feel lush and incredibly sensual and deliciously desirable.

Fingers sliding under the silk, kneading, caressing, exciting, lifting…then his mouth tore from hers, head swooping down, and she felt the bare peak of her breast hotly enveloped and this was a different kissing, hard suction pumping the most piercing pleasure through her, and her own fingers buried themselves in his hair, tugging and pressing, driving the action on, wanting the exquisite arc of sensation to keep vibrating through her.

She'd never felt anything like this before. Was it him? Was it the raw vulnerability of the day making it more than it would normally be? Was it her…giving up the fight she'd been fighting all her life, letting sheer reck-lessness take over? She didn't know and didn't care…savagely didn't care.

She was barely aware of her skirt being pushed up, but she felt his hand moving between her legs, making a space, moving past where her stockings ended to the bare skin above, to the hot moist apex of her thighs, his thumb hooking apart the studs that held her teddy in place.

Then the barrier of silk was gone and his touch made the arc complete, a touch that echoed the same pulsing rhythm of his mouth, so that everything inside her quiv-ered with the need for more and more of this unbeliev-able feeling.

She was melting. She threw her head back against the door in a blind seeking for something solid. It knocked her into opening her eyes, a last snatch at some outside reality. It was dark in the summer-house, the shutters closed against the winter wind, making it a secret, pri-vate place. No one could see what was happening to her. She didn't want to see herself, only to feel.

She shut her eyes tight, welcoming the darkness, giv-ing free rein to the darkness inside her, a wild, whirling chaos that revelled in the sheer wantonness of savouring all that Richard was doing to her. *Time for us,* he'd said, but it was really time for her…the first…and maybe the only time.

And she wanted it. Her whole body was screaming for absolute fulfilment. A wild, guttural protest burst from her throat when his mouth released her breast, but then his lips were covering hers again and his tongue promised the invasion she craved, and suddenly it wasn't his hand between her thighs. Something else was sliding down the intimate folds of her flesh, something hard and strong and purposeful, and every nerve end zinged with a sharp, intense awareness of it.

An arm around her waist, lifting her, swinging her. She clutched his back. Then soft cushioning underneath her and the hot spearing of his flesh, stretching a place that had never been stretched, her hands raking his back, urging him on, a hesitation from him and a hoarse command from her, "Do it!" She didn't want control from him. No control. This was her doing, not his. Her decision, not his.

And he did as she demanded, the brief pain of a barrier broken swallowed up by the fullness of a plunge that reached to the epicentre of need and pinned her to a new explosion of sensation, shock waves of it unfurling, overwhelming all that had gone before, then tide after tide of sweet pleasure with the rush of him filling her, withdrawing, and coming again and again, an ebb and flow that engaged her whole body in the rhythm of a different life where she was not alone, not empty, not set at a distance from everyone else, because *he* was with her, inside her, and she could feel the melding with him in every cell of her body.

And finally, he spilled his strength into her and he could do no more. There was a brief sense of ecstatic harmony before he lifted himself away from her, slowly, carefully, and for some reason she didn't mind the parting, still entranced with the feelings swimming through her, more languorously now, yet warm and lovely and infinitely comforting, because this could never be taken away from her. She had it in her keeping no matter what the future brought.

Her first time…amazingly with a man she'd never believed she'd be intimate with...yet it *had* felt right...with his knowing and understanding so much, the sharing of a past that coloured everything. Richard... Richard Seymour...showing her how it was. Or how it could be between them.

She lifted her lashes enough to see what he was doing. While she still lay in listless abandonment on one of the cane sofas, he'd fixed up his clothes, all very much together again as though nothing untoward had taken place. He opened the camphor chest that served as a table surface beside one of the armchairs, picked out a packet of paper serviettes, broke them open and came back to her, gently padding the tissues and cleaning up the aftermath of her torn virginity.

"Are you hurting, Leigh?" he asked softly.

"No," she answered, struggling to control her inner recoil from what he was doing...so matter-of-fact, almost clinical...bringing her down to earth with a shocking thump. The wild emotional chaos that had led her to this...this messiness...had also robbed her of dignity.

Best to let him get it over with, she argued to herself, fiercely wishing she had lost her virginity in other circumstances. But to whom? Only Richard had made her feel as though it was right. Except now, he was in control again, more in control than ever because she had given him these liberties with her. Somehow she had to stop him from taking a whole lot more because it might not be right at all.

His mouth curved into a self-mocking little smile. "Not quite the way I would have taken my bride, had I known you were a true bride."

"Bride?" Her heart catapulted around her chest. Letting him be the first didn't mean she had to join her whole life to his. "I haven't said I'll marry you, Richard," she quickly reminded him, instinctively fighting any sense of commitment that would give him power over her.

He threw her a dark, intense look. "You will."

She wasn't sure if that was certainty or resolution. He was distracting her, stroking her thighs, making them quiver again. He leaned over and kissed her stomach, a long warm lingering kiss, reminding her of the deep, inner connection that had been forged. But it wasn't the answer to everything, Leigh thought frantically. Not *everything*.

He tugged down her teddy and smoothed her skirt over her nakedness. He bestowed sensual kisses on her breasts, too, before tucking them back in their silk casing. "You are an incredibly beautiful woman, Leigh," he murmured huskily. Then his mouth was on hers, a sweet tingling sealing of a memory...or an assurance this was only a beginning, not an end.

"Ready to move?" he asked.

"No. You go," she urged, desperately needing a break from his company so she could sort out the confusion in her mind. She wasn't sure of anything right now, except she'd done this amazing thing with him and she had to think through the consequences of it.

"Not without you, Leigh," he replied swiftly, determination flashing through the caring in his eyes.

"You're the one who will be missed," she argued, instantly backing away from letting him order her around.

"I want you with me." A categorical statement.

She shook her head, the fear of being manipulated

rushing through her. "I'm not ready to take that stand with you, Richard."

He frowned. "I have no intention of making some public announcement, Leigh. I just want…"

She pressed her fingers to his lips, her inner agitation too great to listen to any more persuasive words. "Let me be," she pleaded. "I want time on my own right now."

He didn't like it. She watched the conflict between purpose and an awareness of moving too far too fast, and saw the decision to compromise even before he spoke. "Have dinner with me tonight. I'll come to your hotel. What time suits you?"

He knew her hotel.

The hunter, Leigh thought again.

But he couldn't take away her right to choose.

There was so much to think about…and still to do. The memory of why she'd come to the funeral sliced through the muddle in her mind. She'd wanted a sense of family again. It probably suited Richard to discount any relationship she might have with her mother and sisters, but Leigh couldn't dismiss them so easily. She'd come here today to be with them, not him, and regardless of all he'd said, she still wanted to know if she meant anything to the people who had shared most of her life.

"You did want this with me, Leigh," he said, his eyes focused intently on her expression.

"And I don't regret it," she assured him, forcing a smile to release him from any concern over recriminations on her part. Nevertheless, marriage was an entirely different question and she was not about to be pushed on it either way. She needed to know more of Richard Seymour, more than the glimpses she'd seen this afternoon. "Dinner tonight is fine," she decided. "Make it eight o'clock."

"Good!" Relief and pleasure in his eyes.

"I'll see you then," she pressed, slowly and rather tentatively swinging her legs off the cane sofa and sitting up to encourage his departure.

He shot her a quick scrutiny, then nodded as though assuring himself there was no mistake about her intentions. "We are right together, Leigh," he stated decisively. "Don't let anything your mother or sisters say distort that truth."

She didn't agree or disagree, not wanting to prolong this encounter with him, but as she watched him leave, the thought ran through her mind that everyone held a different truth within themselves, and finding it could be difficult, let alone expressing it.

She wasn't sure of Richard's truth.

She wasn't sure of her own...at least not where he was concerned.

One thing she was sure of...having been hit by a shattering range of different perceptions this afternoon, Leigh wasn't about to make hasty judgements about her family. Perhaps as a teenager she'd been too self-absorbed to see or comprehend the pressures on their lives. It was impossible to know what really went on inside other people unless they showed it. She'd never had the faintest idea that Richard had no birthright to the Seymour name.

He closed the door behind him, making the summerhouse dark again, dark and private. Light did filter down from the sky dome at the central peak of the roof, enough to see by, though the grey day made it dim.

Leigh looked around her, recognising all the furniture,

a little surprised it hadn't been changed. Though hardly anyone used this place, she reminded herself, recalling how it had provided a handy escape for her when tensions were running high, a private bolt-hole where she could count on not being disturbed.

A perfect place for secret intimacy, Leigh thought, smiling ironically over its handiness to Richard at the critical moment. Then the thought struck her with heart-stopping force.

Was this where *she* had been conceived...her mother with the Italian gardener?

Her hands instantly flew to her stomach. No...her mind screamed. Frantically, she numbered the days since her last period. Seven. Only seven. She was surely safe from pregnancy. The time of fertility would have to be further on from this. Relief rolled through her. If Richard was counting on a baby to turn her into his bride, he was in for disappointment.

Though he couldn't have calculated on impregnating her, could he? Not beforehand. He hadn't used protection, but going through with this intimacy hadn't been his decision, and he couldn't have known she wasn't using something. Until he'd realised she was a virgin. He had hesitated then...so definitely no premeditation.

Another roll of relief...followed by a strong wave of resolution.

She was not going to repeat her mother's life, having baby after baby in pursuit of the desired son. The sex of a child should never mean that much and no way would Leigh let it mean what Lawrence Durant had made of it. A child should be loved for its own sake.

Was there any love for her...just a scrap of it somewhere? She needed to spend time with her mother and sisters. Surely now with Lawrence gone, the real truth could emerge, without any fear of a backlash.

Then tonight…

Yes, she wanted to be with Richard tonight. She wanted…needed…him to show her more of himself…to make what had happened between them this afternoon more right.

If that was possible.

CHAPTER FIVE

THE Durant mansion finally emptied of guests...except for Richard Seymour. To Leigh's frustration, her mother hung onto him, insisting he stay and have coffee with the family. Her sisters were clustered around him like an entourage, eagerly adding their pressure to the invitation. Which he accepted, plunging Leigh into a torment of doubt about his intentions.

His words to her in the summer-house came flooding back... *We are right together. Don't let anything your mother and sisters say distort that truth.*

Was he deliberately staying on to protect what gains he thought he'd made with her? She had evaded being near him since she'd returned to the house, needing to regain her composure before facing her family in the privacy she'd been longing for. And now he was depriving her of it!

Wasn't her promise to meet him tonight enough, she thought in a burst of angry resentment. Or was he playing more than one hand, careful not to offend her other sisters in case one of them had to be his second choice? After all, he had no guarantee she *would* consent to his plans.

Leigh tried to set her turmoil aside as she trailed behind the others, heading for the more intimate lounge room. Whatever his purpose, Richard couldn't stay indefinitely. She simply had to wait out more time.

She wished one of her sisters would fall back and

hang onto her arm, or simply say something to her, at least give some hint of how they felt about her turning up again. The sense of aloneness was somehow worse now than when she had lived here. Was she being deliberately ostracised or was it up to her to take some initiative?

Leigh fought past a host of inhibitions and quickened her pace to catch Nadine, who at twenty-six was closest to her in age. "Can we have a talk, Nadine?" she asked, touching her arm in appeal.

"Not now, Leigh." She wrinkled her nose and tossed her artfully streaked and tousled blonde mane. "Bad taste, isn't it, turning up today?"

Leigh was rattled by the accusation. "I didn't think anyone would mind."

This earned a scathing look. "Playing Cinderella in public. Where on earth did you get that suit? In a bargain basement?"

Her clothes offended? But Richard had said she looked good. Was it really so obvious they were relatively inexpensive? Leigh could feel her cheeks burning. She hadn't meant to play Cinderella. Though compared to Nadine, who was poured into a soft black leather suit with calf-length boots to match, she probably did look...*cheap*.

"Now see what you've done, holding me back?" Nadine hissed at her as they entered the lounge room. "Felicity has snaffled Richard."

Her very elegant oldest sister was drawing him into sharing a sofa with her.

"Why don't you just disappear again, Leigh? No one wants you here."

Stunned by Nadine's hostility, Leigh hesitated. Her

sister flounced forward and commandeered the coffee service which had already been set out. She was full of sweet smiles for Richard, asking him what he'd like.

"Don't just hang there, Leigh," her mother reproved. "Come and sit down."

She indicated the armchair which was fairly close to the one she had chosen at the other end of the room. Leigh felt a surge of relief. At least her mother was prepared to welcome her company, now that her hostess role was virtually over.

As she skirted the sofas which her other sisters had claimed, she reminded herself Nadine had always considered her a nuisance, especially when she'd been asked to "look after her little sister." With both of them being adults now, she had thought it might be different. However, it seemed Nadine still harboured a nasty streak, especially when her self-interests were crossed.

Leigh sat down and offered a grateful smile to her mother but Alicia was no longer looking at her. She was keenly observing the scene with her other daughters and Richard. Leigh was left with the uncomfortable impression that she had been neatly removed from it, being placed in this particular armchair. Minutes passed, and her mother didn't so much as glance at her. This further evidence of being ignored was deeply deflating. Nevertheless, she resolved to wait it out.

Nadine brought her mother a cup of coffee, wiggling her derriere as she walked and bending over so far her short skirt rode up to give a provocative view. Except Richard wasn't watching, which gave Leigh some ironic amusement. His attention was focused on Felicity who had one arm hooked along the backrest of the sofa so she could idly brush his shoulder with her fingertips as she engaged him in conversation.

Felicity, the first-born, had always been "The Princess." She had a porcelain beauty; smooth, pale, almost translucent skin, china blue eyes, flawless features and ash-blonde hair, wound into a gleaming French roll today. Tall, with long graceful legs, she wore a superb coat-dress in fine wool crêpe, with satin collar and cuffs. To the teenage Leigh, Felicity had been the perfect model of the unattainable. She was still perfect at thirty.

Leigh's gaze drifted to Vanessa who was now twenty-nine. She had kicked her shoes off and was languorously sprawled on the chaise-longue, her more curvy figure displayed in black lace. Her hair was more a wheat colour, shoulder-length, and a glorious mass of waves and curls. Her eyes were blue-grey and heavy lidded, giving her a slumbrous sexy look, and her full-lipped mouth was pouting in displeasure at being pushed to one side by her more polished sister.

Both Felicity and Vanessa had married wealthy men while Leigh had been living here. She'd been ruled out as a bridesmaid at their weddings. Black hair would look wrong in the photographs. Not that the photographs were on show any more. Neither were their husbands. Divorced, her mother had curtly explained when Leigh had remarked on their absence at the funeral.

Caroline had grabbed the end seat of the sofa adjacent to where Richard sat. Her yellow-blonde hair was styled into a sleek, ear-level bob and she looked very sophisticated in a black velvet suit. She had a coltish figure and her features were thinner than her sisters', sharper. She had a sharp tongue, as well, Leigh remembered. Did that account for her not being married at twenty-seven?

Nadine sat down next to Caroline, having overlooked Leigh in her coffee serving. So there they were, all four of her sisters, all available to Richard and bent on attracting his attention. Did they want him or did they *need* him? Leigh wondered, struggling to suppress the needs he'd stirred in herself.

Being ignorant of the full contents of Lawrence's will, she had no idea what had been settled on his wife and daughters. Lawrence might have been mean enough to attach provisional clauses to their bequests, pulling financial strings since he could no longer manipulate personal ones. If this was so, she was far better off out of it and not tied to anything. At least she felt free to arrange her own future as she liked.

The Cinderella tag wormed its way into her mind again. Her black suit had been on a bargain rack in a Perth department store, and certainly didn't feature a designer label. Her plain court shoes were not Italian, unlike her real father, she thought with secret irony. She was now used to living on a budget. Her sisters weren't.

Her home life and her companions at the exclusive private school she'd gone to in her teen years had given her a force-fed education on desirable labels. Even though she'd been out of that one-upmanship game for some years, Leigh could still identify the distinctive styles.

Her mother, Alicia, was definitely wearing a Chanel suit, very smart and subdued. Felicity's coat-dress was undoubtedly a Carla Zampatti creation. Vanessa's lace had to be a Collette Dinnigan design. Caroline's velvet was unmistakably Trent Nathan. The leather Nadine favoured was probably from Saba.

Leigh knew she was looking at thousands of dollars

before even beginning to assess the cost of shoes, hats and handbags. Not that it mattered to her. It was simply indicative of a very wealthy life-style which all of them probably wished to maintain. Image, she knew, was important in the lives they led.

Richard could certainly keep them in the manner to which they were accustomed. Yet for all their efforts to snatch and hold his attention, as far as Leigh could see, he was totally impartial in his manner to them; polite, attentive, yet very self-contained. Was he keeping his choices open, Leigh wondered, finding herself hating the thought.

She wanted to be *special* to him.

Yet why should she be?

The question of why he'd asked her first began to nag her. Was he bored with her sisters, having known them longer? Did he see her as the easiest one to manage? Was he simply swayed by sexual chemistry? She squirmed a little, remembering the highly volatile nature of their coming together in the summer-house.

Wanting...was that the key element?

She tried to look at him objectively, needing to work out what was really driving him. As though sensing her scrutiny, he shot her a quick, enigmatic look, then deliberately set his coffee cup and saucer down and rose to his feet, targeting her mother with an appreciative smile.

"Thank you for your hospitality..."

"You're welcome to stay to dinner, Richard," Alicia swiftly interposed.

"It's very kind of you, but I'd rather take my leave now," he replied firmly.

Felicity leapt to her feet. "Time for me to go, too. I'll accompany you out, Richard."

He frowned at her, then pointedly transferred his gaze to Leigh. "Aren't you forgetting you haven't seen your sister for six years?"

Leigh's heart squeezed tight. She didn't want him to order what wasn't worth anything unless it was freely given. Though in the next instant she realised even *his* opinion on her behalf was not going to count.

"Oh, Leigh..." Felicity trilled a dismissive laugh. "What on earth would we have to talk about after all these years apart?" Her eyes flicked to the black sheep, chilling in their disinterest. "We never did have anything in common, did we, sweetie?"

The awful condescension kept Leigh silent.

"That may be different now, Felicity," Richard said in a silkily dangerous tone. "Why don't you stay and find out?"

Leigh clenched her hands. Of all the times she'd wanted him to be her champion, he chose now, when it was totally inappropriate. Or was he deliberately underlining the emptiness he knew was here, making her know it, too?

"What for?" Felicity argued, shrugging off the suggestion. "Leigh will probably be gone again tomorrow."

Vanessa sinuously unfolded herself from the chaise-longue and hooked her arm around Richard's, batting her eyelashes at him flirtatiously. "Why not come back to my place for dinner, Richard? I'm sure Leigh only wants to talk to Mummy."

He shot a hard, purposeful look at Leigh. "Thank you, but I have other plans, Vanessa." He gave a general nod around the company as he extricated his arm. "Please excuse me, all of you."

Her sisters watched his departure with grim-faced displeasure. None of them had made the impression they'd wanted to make on him and he was removing the opportunity to further their own ends.

It suddenly struck Leigh that Richard had stayed to keep them all together. For *her*. Just as he was leaving them all here. For *her*. Giving her what she'd wanted. As he'd promised. Her heart fluttered wildly at this evidence of his caring. Or was it another calculated move, showing her that what she'd wanted from her family was not here for her? That was already miserably obvious.

The moment the door was closed behind him, Caroline swung her head around to glare at her mother. "Honestly, Mum, couldn't you have fobbed Leigh off to some other time?" she demanded critically. "Richard has always had a soft spot for her."

A soft spot? Was there some heart as well as purpose in his proposal?

"So how do you think it would look to him if I'd done that, Caroline?" Alicia retorted wearily.

Leigh's heart twisted with even more misery. Politics. No caring for her at all.

"What do you mean…a soft spot?" Felicity snapped, looking incredulously at Leigh.

Caroline snorted derisively. "If you weren't so damned full of yourself, you would have noticed how Richard always took the heat off Leigh whenever Dad had a go at her in front of him. Usually he asked you a question, which you probably found flattering, but he was really protecting our poor little done by sister."

That much was true. Leigh recognised it now.

Felicity's chin lifted haughtily. "Richard *was* interested in me. He's always been interested in me."

"Oh, don't put on your airs and graces with us," Vanessa sniped. "He was nothing but polite to you. No sparks at all." She targeted Leigh with a mean, narrow-eyed look. "And just why have you been hovering around all day, like a black crow waiting to pounce? What's your game, Leigh?"

"A slice of the estate if she can get it," Nadine slid in sneeringly. "Look at her! Probably raided a charity shop for those clothes."

"She's got no chance of breaking the will," Caroline declared, pushing herself up from the sofa. Again she addressed Alicia sharply, "Might be worthwhile paying her to get out of here, Mum. She could spoil our pitch."

"Don't be ridiculous, Caroline!" Vanessa jeered.

"Didn't manage to vamp Richard into going to your place, did you?" Caroline whipped back. "Ask yourself why, Vanessa." She pointed at Leigh. "He was considering her!"

All four sisters turned to glare at her.

Felicity looking down her nose... "You really don't belong here, Leigh."

Nadine spiteful... "You were disinherited."

Vanessa mocking... "I can't believe you're a threat, but I'd prefer not to have a distraction. The sooner you disappear again, the better."

Caroline ruthless... "We don't need you. Just get out, Leigh, and stay out."

Having delivered that judgement Caroline stalked out of the room, followed by the others in quick succession. Leigh watched them go, too sickened to raise any protest. In a way, she supposed she had thwarted their desires to snag Richard's attention and hold it, but no reasoning in the world could ease the pain of their cold and callous rejection of her return to their midst.

She wasn't wanted.

No one cared about her.

No one was the least bit interested in her.

The cuckoo had flown away and they had probably all thought *good riddance.*

Into the silence of devastated hopes came her mother's voice, tired and frayed. "What do you want, Leigh?"

Leigh was still looking at the door Felicity had shut so decisively behind all four of her sisters. Half-sisters, she reminded herself, though there was no consolation in that brutal fact. It took a concerted effort to look at her mother, who had probably only stayed to find out if her unwanted fifth daughter meant to cause trouble.

Alicia's face was taut, her eyes biting in their disapproval. A leaden weight descended on Leigh's wounded heart. It was more of the same, even with Lawrence dead. There was no place for her here. Never would be. The pattern had been set long ago and no one saw any reason for it to change.

"What do you think I want, Mother?" she dragged out, mocking herself more than the woman who'd given birth to her.

"Why don't you tell me?" came the wary reply—a reply that gave nothing away—a reply that put a cold, impersonal distance between them.

Leigh couldn't bear to keep looking at her. She knew, beyond a shadow of a doubt, her mother was expecting her to ask for a share in Lawrence's estate. Her gaze wandered idly around the room—a blue and white room that had no warmth in it, just furnishings and pieces of art that cost a lot of money, flagrant exhibitions of buying power for others to admire and envy. There was no heart in it, no heart anywhere in this ostentatious mansion.

"Did you think of me at all in the past six years, Mother?" she asked, wanting to know if she had been missed, if only a tiny bit.

"Naturally, I thought of you," came the too smooth answer. "I hoped you were happy in your choice to make a life for yourself."

While she dissociated herself from it, Leigh thought, probably relieved to have "her mistake" removed so it wasn't a constant thorn in her side.

"Did you worry about me?"

A slight pause, then a slowly chosen reply. "I respected your choice, Leigh. I felt sure you'd contact us if you were in need."

Which required no action on Alicia's part, none at all. Not that Leigh had expected any *worry* over her disappearance at the time. Remembering back, she realised the truth of her position in the Durant family had been laid bare then. It was time and distance that had raised hopes for something else, a different interpretation of actions and non-actions.

"Did you wonder how I survived, kept myself going without your help?" she asked, determined on being absolutely fair before making a final judgement.

"Well, you obviously did or you wouldn't be here now."

The dry intonation goaded Leigh into looking her mother in the face again. "You don't care, do you?" she accused flatly. "You have no interest whatsoever in what I've done, where I've been, how I managed."

An impatient grimace. "You always had the option of coming home, Leigh. No one banished you."

Home to the kind of mental and emotional abuse her mother had never tried to stop? Leigh had wanted to believe the neglect and indifference was defensive, done out of fear of drawing Lawrence's wrath. But she couldn't believe that now.

"I was eighteen, Mother," Leigh reminded her. "In shock. Disinherited because you admitted to having me by another man."

No comment.

The silence heightened the memory of that dreadful night, the hate-filled revelations that had poured over her head because she had dared to stand up for herself and appeal to both of them for a fairer deal...her mother screaming, "You drove me to it, Lawrence, with your constant harping on a son."...Lawrence jeering, "And you thought a cuckoo would do?"

On and on it had gone...the contempt, the recriminations, the wounding, neither of them caring what she felt...the object of their personal battle...the object who was mangled between them as they tore into each other...the object of failed ambitions, thus being forever offensive to them.

Yes, she had understood it then.

Yet still she searched her mother's face for some hint of conscience about her. "When you discovered I was gone, did you think I was in a fit state to make my own way?"

Alicia's eyes hardened. "It was *your* choice. I had my own battles to fight at the time."

"So you didn't worry about me. I was—let us say—one less problem to deal with."

"You were always a problem, Leigh," was the terse reply.

"Much easier to be rid of me."

"Don't put words into my mouth," Alicia snapped.

Leigh couldn't let it go. "I don't suppose you reported me to the police as a missing person," she pressed.

"Don't be absurd! Lawrence would never have allowed it.'

"Perhaps you hired a private investigator to check that I was not in any trouble."

As Richard had...Richard declaring he'd done it because he'd cared...the only one who cared...

Alicia sighed, impatient with the inquisition. "I expected a call from you if you were in trouble." Her tone was loaded with exasperation.

"What if I was in no position to call, Mother? Did you worry about that?"

"Oh, for God's sake, Leigh! What are you going on about? You're here, aren't you? Safe and sound?"

No thanks to you or any member of my family, Leigh thought bitterly. Her gaze ran derisively over the Chanel suit. "I was just thinking that what you spent on the mourning outfit you have on today would have paid a private investigator to keep tabs on me for a while...if you'd cared enough to worry about me."

Alicia instantly leaned forward, pouncing on what she understood better than anything else. "Right! So you think you're owed a chunk of money and that's why you've come, now that you don't have to face Lawrence for it."

For several moments, Leigh's revulsion was so strong she couldn't speak. Her stomach churned violently. Her mind exploded under the sheer weight of all the burdens it had carried and whirled into the darkness of a world without love, the darkness of deep and abiding injustice. She wasn't aware of forming the words that spat out of that darkness. They came of their own accord, pieces of emotional chaos that had been gathering inside her all day long.

"Wrong, Mother! You can't pay me off...as you did my real father. And I won't disappear for you."

The eager satisfaction was wiped out. All colour drained from Alicia's face. "What do you know of that? Why do you bring it up?"

Ah, the triumph of doing some shattering herself! The darkness gained ground from it. Her voice instinctively copied Richard's silky dangerous tone. "Oh, that's just between you and me, Mother. We keep scandals buried in this family, don't we?"

Alicia sat back, adopting a pose of impervious hauteur. "Are you threatening me, Leigh?"

Suddenly it was easy to laugh. The madness of her hopes was really funny. Here she was, being seen as a threat and she'd come as a beggar for affection. "Not at all," she spluttered in wild amusement. "I came here today to find out where I stood with you. And with my sisters. Now I know."

Her mother looked totally bamboozled.

Leigh smiled at her as she stood up to take her leave. "Goodbye, Mother. I find I don't want to have anything more to do with you. Or your other daughters."

She started towards the door. Her legs were shaky. She willed strength into them.

"Where are you going, Leigh?" Hard suspicion in the question shot after her. No belief at all in the last farewell.

"To my hotel," Leigh answered, enjoying the light carelessness in her voice. It was good to show she could match the non-caring she had met.

"What do you intend to do?"

The answer came to Leigh, the beautiful perfect answer, pushing out of the darkness and shining with the glorious purity of justice. She stopped and half-turned, wanting to beam it straight at the mother who had always put ambition first. Alicia should really appreciate this. It was, after all, the ambition she held dearest at the moment.

"I intend to marry Richard Seymour."

The shock this decisive declaration raised was deeply satisfying.

"What?" Alicia croaked incredulously.

Leigh smiled. "He chose me, Mother. Not Felicity, not Vanessa, not Caroline, not Nadine...*me*. And I shall marry him as soon as it can be arranged."

On that triumphant note she left, shutting the door on the Durant mansion and everyone in it.

CHAPTER SIX

THE hours between throwing down the gauntlet to her mother and the eight o'clock deadline with Richard Seymour churned past for Leigh. From time to time the voice of sanity tried to drag her back from the brink...

You don't need this. You've made a good, normal, stable life for yourself in Broome. You can walk away, put it all at a distance again and never look back.

But overwhelming that voice in fierce, rebellious waves came a deep, soul-driven cry for justice...

All these years...the loser, the rejected one, the despised one, the one worth nothing. Why shouldn't she be the winner for once? Why shouldn't she take the prize? She'd always wanted Richard to be her champion. Let him be that now, openly, unmistakably, not just having a soft spot for her, but standing beside her, fighting anyone who cast any slur on her. *Her husband!*

The time has come for us, he'd said. So what if that was linked to dancing on Lawrence Durant's grave together! The kind of pact he'd offered her was grounded in sharing a common background. Who else would ever know her as he did, understanding the loneliness, the sense of separation from people who'd led more normal lives?

The plain truth was she'd been living a fiction of normality in Broome, a veneer of stability. Her darkest inner truths lay here, probably bound up more with Richard Seymour than anyone else. But she couldn't let him know that because he'd use it to get what he wanted. A hunter used everything to get what he wanted and she had no illusions about that side of Richard Seymour.

Ambition came first with him. It would be foolish to fantasise any really special feeling for her. Even though Richard had shown more caring towards her than anyone else, it had always been caring at a safe distance. He'd been very discreet about *being her friend*, and Leigh had no doubt he'd been even more discreet about keeping tabs on her, ensuring no harm came to him from his *caring*.

All the same, *she* was his first choice in the marriage stakes. Which had to mean something positive towards her, more positive than anything he felt for her sisters. Leigh comforted herself with that thought even as she realised she mustn't make too much of it.

She had to keep her mind straight on this. In agreeing to marry him, she didn't have to give him her head on a plate. No-one was ever going to take absolute control over her life. She wouldn't submit to another Lawrence Durant. Richard had better understand that. She had terms, as well, terms he had to respect if they were to share a future together.

What she needed was a plan of action…something firm she could hang onto…something that would show Richard she was purposeful, too, not just a pawn in his game to be manipulated as he willed. A wife was more than that. The need to be more than that to him welled up in her and wouldn't let go.

Somehow she managed to harness her erratic thoughts long enough to work out what kind of understanding she required from him in this marriage. She had priorities, too, and getting control of a financial empire wasn't one of them. She wouldn't be forced into having baby after baby after baby, just to get a son. And if Richard started abusing her rights as a person in any way, nothing would keep her with him. She wouldn't allow him to hurt her like that.

Despite this fierce bout of reasoning, when his knock came at precisely eight o'clock, Leigh was swamped by a sense of panic. It took all her will-power to get a grip on herself, to open the door. She stood back a little, just looking at him...this man she'd decided to marry.

He hadn't worn a suit, though the clothes he'd chosen could probably go anywhere; royal blue skivvy, grey leather jacket, grey slacks. The casual look didn't change anything. He still emitted the same charismatic power of knowing what he wanted and having the unshakeable will to pull out all stops to get it. She felt her skin start to burn as his laser blue eyes raked her appearance, assessing what it meant, how he could use it.

She hadn't dressed for dinner. She had no intention of dining with him, nor even talking with him beyond establishing what was to be done. She was afraid that any further intimacy with him at this point could weaken her decisions. Better to avoid it.

Her hair was still wound up and pinned into a rather messy topknot from the long hot shower she'd taken, and the oyster-pink satin wraparound covered a slip-nightie in the same colour. She was ready for bed, but not with him.

"I don't want dinner, Richard, and I don't want sex," she fired at him point-blank, forcefully defensive in struggling to deny the panic. "There are a few things to be arranged between us and that's it," she went on, amazing herself with the firm tone of her voice. "You can come in on that understanding."

He nodded, shrewd enough not to make any comment as he stepped into her room. Leigh shut the door and stayed by it, ready to let him out again the moment she was finished with him. Despite the resolution—the plan—seething through her mind, his actual physical presence stirred a host of vulnerabilities she didn't want to feel, didn't want to examine, either. This meeting had to be about promises, made and kept.

"Have you had any second thoughts about choosing me to marry?" she demanded, wary of making a fool of herself.

His gaze was fixed on her travelling bag which lay on the bed, unzipped, the suit she'd worn today folded neatly on top of the rest of her things which she hadn't bothered unpacking. He swung around slowly, noting the jeans, T-shirt, windcheater and underclothes she'd set on a chair, ready to don in the morning. The hotel room was very basic, which was all Leigh could afford. Richard missed nothing in it, clearly assessing the situation before facing her.

"I want *you*, Leigh. No-one else," he answered simply, his eyes searing hers with a blaze of desire that set every nerve end in Leigh's body twitching.

Her stomach contracted, her toes curled, her heart shot bolts of heat through her bloodstream, and her mind momentarily lost its focus. The sheer impact of that look pressed her back against the door, as though she was his prey, feeling cornered. Her hand clutched the doorknob, instinctively seeking a defensive weapon.

"Don't you take one step towards me, Richard!" she cried, wildly challenging his intent, despite her decision to take him as her husband. She was *not* going to be a victim in his scheme. Nor would she be seduced to his will.

He remained where he was. "You have the floor," he said, gesturing an open invitation that reduced any sense of threat, yet still there was a simmer in his eyes that let her know the desire was temporarily harnessed but very much alive and kicking.

At least they had that going for them, Leigh recklessly reasoned. What they'd done—felt—in the summer-house wasn't a one-off thing. It could happen again now if she let it, but it wouldn't resolve what she needed resolved.

"I'll marry you, but I have conditions," she blurted out.

The tensile spring in his body eased. "State them," he said equably.

"*You* make all the arrangements."

His eyes narrowed slightly. "You don't want to plan a wedding?"

Without a mother or a father or anyone who would be interested in her being a bride? How could he even imagine it? For a moment, Leigh's mind went totally blank. The idea of a *wedding* hadn't occurred to her, only the fact of a marriage between them. If he wanted *a wedding*…no, she would have to stay here for that to be managed and she recoiled from being anywhere within reach of her mother and sisters until this marriage became fact.

"Plan whatever suits you. I don't care," she declared, turbulently rejecting any wish for a public celebration.

She had no-one to share it with, and that bare truth only emphasised the lack of any real connections. Even her friends in Broome were more congenial acquaintances, sharing interests but nothing deeper than that. She couldn't imagine any of them going to the expense of flying across the continent to her wedding. They'd wish her well and let her go, maybe remembering her occasionally.

"Just leave me out of it until our wedding day, Richard," she said decisively.

Then she would have *him*, for better or for worse! *He* hadn't let her go. All these years watching over her...suddenly Leigh felt good about that. She wasn't *nothing* to Richard.

"So your family is not to be involved?" he said, watching her keenly.

Her chin went up in defiant pride. "I don't consider I have a family any more."

No comment. In his eyes was the knowledge of what she'd been through with her mother and sisters this afternoon, not sympathetic knowledge, more an assessment of how deeply it had affected her, and Leigh hated his understanding of her stance.

It was shaming, painful, yet in this awful, intimate sharing of emptiness and darkness, there was also a strange consoling that no-one else could give. He *knew*. He knew precisely where she was coming from...the injustices she had suffered, the rejections, the wiping off as of no account to anybody.

It provided a kind of kinship she doubted she'd find with any other man. Whether that was a good or bad kinship, she didn't know. What it did was take the edge off the sense of aloneness she'd felt all her life.

"You don't have any preference regarding how we get married?" he asked quietly.

Her mouth twitched into a mocking little smile. "It does need to be legal." His proposal was based on legalities so he should appreciate that point.

"It will certainly be legal," he assured her, his own mouth quirking, yet there was a flash of something dark and dangerous in his eyes as though she'd struck a core of secret purpose, beyond anything anyone knew about him.

A convulsive little shiver ran down her spine but she resolutely ignored it. Everyone had a secret self. As long as they respected each other, this marriage probably had as much a chance of working as any other.

"I'm booked on flights back to Broome tomorrow," she announced. "I'm not staying here, Richard. I have business to see to if I'm to shift my life to Sydney. I presume you can see to whatever documentation is required."

He nodded. "I trust you will be back for the wedding."

"The day before," she promised.

"And you intend to be my wife, living with me?" His eyes probed hers with merciless intent.

"Yes, but I don't intend to be a baby machine for you," she stated fiercely. Never, in a million years would she repeat what her mother had done. Not for anything or anyone.

"At least one child, Leigh," Richard barrelled straight back at her.

She took a deep breath and determinedly challenged him. "If we have a daughter first and you respond badly, I'll leave you."

A glimmer of very strong feeling flashed into his eyes. "Any child of mine will be precious to me."

There was a strong edge to his voice, too, instantly recalling to Leigh the circumstances of his birth... another cuckoo, perhaps shunted to one side because he didn't belong as he should. Or was she grasping at straws, needing to feel reassured that her decision to marry him would not lead to an intolerable situation?

"Having a daughter instead of a son will prolong the time you don't have full control of the company," she reminded him.

"I don't intend to stand still in anticipation of the terms of Lawrence's will being fulfilled, Leigh. Others might...I won't. The Durant company will be mine, one way or another."

Ruthless purpose suddenly emanated from him, and Leigh was forcefully struck with the realisation there was nothing soft about this man. He was hard, through and through, committed to a course nothing was going to stop. A very dangerous man.

Had Lawrence Durant recognised that or had Richard hid his hand from his mentor? Leigh suspected the latter. His choice to marry her was a blatant flouting of Lawrence's will. A victory over Lawrence, he'd called it this afternoon. What other victories did Richard have planned?

"So marrying me is only a ploy in whatever game you're about," she put to him, keenly watching his expression.

His eyes crinkled in amusement. "More than a ploy, Leigh. A step that needs to be taken. It also pleases me to marry you."

Pleasure curled her stomach. It was a struggle to keep questioning him. "Personal, as well as business?"

He smiled his heart-mashing smile. "On many levels, very personal."

Even as everything inside her squirmed and pulsed with treacherous excitement, Leigh fiercely told herself it would be stupid to let herself become too vulnerable to that smile. There would always be a part of Richard Seymour he'd keep to himself—the part Lawrence Durant had found so admirable—and she didn't really want to know that part.

So long as he let her be the person she was, they could coexist, couldn't they, sharing what they did share? She needed to feel a *kinship*, to have some sense of belonging to a kind of continuance instead of a blank nothing.

Still smiling, his eyes caressing her with a warmth that threatened to melt her will-power, he said, "Your passion always appealed to me."

"Passion?" Leigh queried, trying to fit the word to the teenager he'd known.

"You radiate intensity, Leigh. Always have. And I hope, always will." His smile tilted musingly. "Maybe from your Italian heritage."

It was a new thought. Leigh instantly wondered how much she took after her real father. Apart from temperament, which she supposed could be passed on genetically, there was the creative side of her nature. Gardeners could be creative. She thought of her pottery enterprise in Broome, which wasn't exactly lucrative, but she loved working with clay...the shapes and colours, the tactile pleasure of it.

"Any more conditions?" Richard prompted.

"Yes. One more. I want to go on with my pottery. You must know about that from your surveillance on me."

He nodded. "Once you're my wife, we'll choose a property that suits both of our living requirements. You can have a kiln built. Whatever you like, Leigh. I have no objection whatsoever to your pursuing your art during the day…"

He started walking towards her and there was no more giving in his eyes, only an intensity of purpose that encompassed her in a relentless grip. "…but the nights are mine," he said softly. "Understand that, Leigh. The nights are mine."

Leigh could feel herself trembling, whether in fear or anticipation she didn't know. Having screwed her mind to the sticking point of laying down her conditions, she simply hadn't thought of how he saw their life together, beyond the legalities that had forced his hand. Except…his hand wasn't really forced, was it? Hadn't he implied the marriage was more a *sleight of hand* while he pursued his own agenda?

He reached her while she was still in a whirl of confusion. He didn't touch her, but he was so close, she found herself holding her breath and her temples were drumming from her wildly accelerated heartbeat. She couldn't tear her eyes from the glittering intent in his.

"Are we agreed?" he asked softly, and even his voice affected her physically…sexually…

"Yes," she whispered.

"I don't take kindly to being made a fool of, Leigh. From the moment I leave this room, I'll be acting on the word you've given me tonight, on several levels, all of them important to me. Your word is your bond. No second thoughts. Total commitment. Is that understood?"

For a moment the gravity of the phrase—total commitment—shook her resolution. Then she hastily reminded herself Richard had accepted all her conditions. As for sharing his bed every night, once she was his wife, how could that not be acceptable, given the lust they seemed to arouse in each other? She didn't have the experience to know if something so physical lasted for long, but it felt like a positive factor.

"We're agreed," she affirmed with as much strength as she could muster.

He smiled and his eyes suddenly danced with wicked provocation. "Is a kiss to seal our bargain permissible or is the *don't touch* command still in force?"

A kiss...why not? Just to make certain it truly did feel right, a taste of what was to come. Realising she was still clutching the doorknob, Leigh released it and lifted both hands to the broad shoulders she was trusting to carry her decisions through.

With her permission implicit, Richard didn't wait for words. He swept her against him and there was not a trace of seductive intent in his kiss. It was hotly explosive, claiming her mouth in a passionate drive to take all she would give him. It was exhilarating, and deeply, deeply satisfying, feeling his desire pouring into her, knowing it was real and true, feeling her own desire rush to meet it, join with it, exult in the merging.

It was a powerful promise of exciting pleasure to be shared with him and Leigh was left dazed by it when Richard pulled away from her. He touched her lips with his fingertips in a gentle salute...or was it a sealing of his imprint inside her?

"I'll look forward to our wedding night," he murmured, his voice husky with sweet satisfaction, his eyes glowing with an inner vision that centred on her...as his…when there would be no pulling back from taking all he wanted.

He left, taking her consent to their marriage with him. More than her consent, Leigh thought dizzily, her commitment. And she wouldn't go back on it. He might be a dangerous man in many ways but he'd left her with one unassailable conviction. There was no other man for her. Never would be. Richard Seymour owned part of her soul that no one else could.

CHAPTER SEVEN

LEIGH sat on a rock, watching her last sunset at Cable Beach. Or maybe it wasn't her last. Who knew what the future would bring? Tomorrow she would fly to Sydney. The day after she would marry Richard Seymour and start another life, very different from this one, she imagined.

She'd disposed of most of her pottery. All her bills were paid. Everything she wanted to take with her was packed away in storage, ready to be sent on when she had a firm address. Friends had given her a farewell luncheon party today. Her ties to this place were virtually cut now. Only a few clothes and personal toiletries were left to be put in the luggage she would carry tomorrow.

Her gaze drifted down the long stretch of firm sand. All sorts of vehicles—cars, four-wheel drive wagons, small trucks, bikes—were parked along it, facing the water. Music was playing from portable stereos. People had unloaded foldaway deck chairs and picnic tables. Cold drinks and nibbles were being consumed. The mood was one of happy relaxation. It was an evening ritual in Broome, coming to watch the sunset at the end of the day. The news of the world could wait. Here, nature commanded first viewing.

A string of camels carried tourists on a slow amble along the water's edge, their rhythmic, swaying movement almost hypnotic. No hurry. No stress. Just the sight of them injected a calm pleasure. Leigh doubted she would feel any calmness tomorrow, but she was committed to facing whatever came with Richard...facing and dealing with it.

Six weeks it had been since the fateful night of giving him her word. The very next day at the airport terminal in Sydney, she'd been paged to meet a jeweller who had measured her ring finger. People sent by Richard had flown to Broome with papers for her to sign, a prenuptial agreement, documents that were meaningless to her. She wasn't after his money. The jeweller had come, too, bringing her a magnificent solitaire diamond engagement ring which must have cost a fortune. Tomorrow she would put it on.

But tonight...this time was just for herself. She watched the luminous yellow sun changing to red as it started to dip into the ocean. There were no clouds to reflect its colour. The sky was a soft lavender, the water a silvery aquamarine. It was beautiful, peaceful, the freshness of the air making everything feel clean and good, far, far away from any sense of pollution. A simple life this...and she was giving it up for what?

To balance the scales?

To heal what never had been healed?

Or to have Richard Seymour?

All three, she thought, but mostly the last. And where it would lead she didn't know. It was a journey she had to take, for good or ill. Only then would she know. There was no point in thinking about it. Doing it would tell her whether it was worthwhile or not.

The sun slipped to a mere sliver of burning red on the horizon, then was gone. The light changed, colours fading, the final setting of the day. The setting of six years of being alone, Leigh thought, standing up to walk away...walk towards a commitment of living intimately with a man who probably meant more than he should to her, the man bent on taking Lawrence Durant's throne in the financial world.

He was waiting for her.

The flight to Sydney had landed on time, exactly 12: 15 PM, which gave her the afternoon to do some necessary shopping. Leigh reached the top of the escalator leading down to the hall where carousels circulated incoming luggage. She expected someone to meet her. Richard wouldn't leave her wandering around, wondering where to go next. Every move from here on would be meticulously planned to achieve his purpose. Even from afar she'd felt the relentless beat of his will.

But still she wasn't anticipating his presence at the airport terminal. It was like being suddenly hit by a bolt of energy. Her heart skipped a beat. Her gaze was literally tugged to where he stood by a set of exit doors, a mobile telephone held to his ear, but his eyes were fastened on her, eyes that telegraphed such concentrated power, Leigh felt he was claiming her, body and soul.

Her feet must have automatically stepped forward onto the escalator because it was carrying her downwards. Richard tucked the mobile telephone into the breast pocket of his suit as he strode across the hall, clearly aiming to be at the foot of the escalator the moment she stepped off. Momentarily relieved of having to perform any action at all, Leigh watched him as intensely as he watched her.

This was the beginning of their future together. She had been marginally aware of the mantle of leadership he wore on the day of the funeral. Perhaps it had been more muted then, in deference to the public mourning of Lawrence Durant. There was no possible mistaking his air of command now. This man she was about to marry evoked the feeling he could and would take all before him, invincible and...*untouchable*.

Which put Leigh's defences on electric alert.

"Hi!" she said with a controlled little smile as she reached floor level.

"Hi!" he replied, his eyes dancing both amusement at and appreciation of her restrained approach to him. "I'm glad you're safely here."

She nodded. "It's good of you to break your busy schedule to meet me in person."

He laughed, his whole face radiating a delight in her that scrambled her strong sense of caution. He caught her hand and drew her along with him towards the baggage carousels, his eyes still twinkling, putting a ridiculously happy flutter in her heart.

"It would be very remiss of me not to welcome my trump card, Leigh."

Even that remark—centred as it was on his business goals—failed to dampen the rush of treacherous pleasure in being linked to him. The warmth and strength of the hand enfolding hers sent tingles up Leigh's arm. All she could think of was this was the start of not being alone.

"So you still need me," she half-mocked, trying not to show how vulnerable she was to his touch.

"Need and want," he answered, his gaze flicking momentarily to her mouth, lingering long enough to shoot heat through her bloodstream.

Leigh scooped in a quick breath. "I thought it was only the nights you wanted with me," she said drily.

''Ah, that was a minimum requirement. I didn't mean it to be a limitation.''

Danger bells rang in her head. She looked sharply at him, acutely aware of his taking power. ''What if I don't want more of you?''

He shrugged. ''You say so.''

''And you'll respect that?''

''Absolutely. I see our marriage as being about mutual agreements, Leigh.''

The assurance eased the tightness in her chest. Richard wasn't a tyrant like Lawrence Durant. Not once had he pushed beyond any line she'd drawn. There was no reason not to trust his word.

Noticing he was veering towards the exit doors, she quickly said, ''I have luggage to collect, Richard.''

''It will be collected and delivered to the hotel. I've booked a suite for you at The Regent. I'll take you there now.''

Leigh didn't protest, realising that hanging around at an airport, waiting for luggage to be unloaded, would be a waste of time to Richard. He'd collected *her*. She could probably take such an unnecessary courtesy as a compliment. It certainly indicated a personal note of caring that went beyond calculated profit. That was reassuring, too.

As they emerged from the terminal, a stretch limousine drew into the kerb of the sidewalk, right in line with the exit doors. Richard moved straight to it, opened the back door for her, and in the space of a few moments they were both seated in spacious luxury, behind privacy-tinted windows, and on their way into the city.

''Great timing,'' Leigh couldn't help commenting.

Richard gave her a quirky smile. "The driver was cruising. I called him in."

The mobile telephone. Of course. Efficiency plus. "Do you ever leave anything to chance, Richard?" she asked curiously.

"One can always be surprised by chance. Your flight could have crashed. The limousine could have been blocked. No one can control everything, Leigh."

"Only as far as it's humanly possible," she teased, sure in her own mind he would plan to cover all fore-seeable contingencies.

"Even the human factor can be unpredictable," he answered wryly, reaching across to pick up her left hand, his thumb brushing the ring on her third finger. "I didn't know what you would like. I wondered if you'd prefer a different stone to the traditional diamond."

It amazed her that he'd spent time considering her wishes. She had imagined him simply ordering what he thought appropriate. "You could have asked," she murmured, her voice husky from having to pass a wayward lump of emotion.

The eyes he lifted to hers were very blue, directly challenging. "You were emphatic about being left out of whatever arrangements I wanted to make. It's a bit late to be changing your mind about that, Leigh."

"I'm not. I didn't really care about an engagement ring. If it pleased you to choose this diamond, that's fine by me," she rushed out, feeling weirdly chilled by the sudden emanation of tension from him.

"Then I trust you won't suddenly start caring about the rest of the arrangements I've made."

"I said I'd go along with them and I will."

"Thank you for the reassurance." He smiled his satisfaction, visibly relaxing.

Battle won, Leigh thought. But what battle? She took a deep breath and asked, "What is the plan for tomorrow?"

"The wedding director, Anne Lester, is to meet us at the hotel. She'll take you through everything," he answered matter-of-factly.

Leigh gulped. "A *wedding* director?"

"Not my area of expertise. I hired a specialist."

"You mean we're having a *real* wedding?" Leigh could hear her voice climbing.

He nodded, his eyes glinting with some deep inner relish that had nothing to do with her. "Two hundred guests."

Dear God! He intended to parade their marriage in front of everyone he considered anyone! This was not a private sealing of a personal bargain between them. It was a public flaunting of the Seymour/Durant connection, positively spotlighting it. But for what purpose? Surely it was totally unnecessary.

"Why?" The word shot out, demanding reasons.

His face took on a flintlike hardness and there was not the slightest grain of giving in his eyes. "Because that's the way I want it."

Leigh swallowed hard. There could be no argument about this. She'd given him a free hand. He'd taken it, with a vengeance. "I'll have to buy a wedding dress," she said weakly, shock still thumping through her and panic beginning to shoot out fluttery tentacles.

"I chose one for you."

"You...?" The thought of Richard combing through bridal boutiques boggled her mind.

"I told Anne Lester the style of dress I wanted for you and she presented me with a selection from which I chose," he explained.

"What if it doesn't fit?"

"I believe a fitting is arranged for this afternoon. There'll be time for alterations. The wedding is scheduled for four o'clock tomorrow."

"In a church," Leigh said numbly, mentally crossing off the register office she'd anticipated.

"St. Andrew's Cathedral."

"The reception?"

"The ballroom at The Regent."

All top class! Leigh's mind whirled over the spectacle Richard was determined on. It would probably be the wedding of the year, featuring one of Australia's most eligible bachelors and *the bride of his choice*. In every sense, Leigh wildly added, even to the dress!

"You didn't ask my sisters to be bridesmaids," she fired at him, recoiling from any passive acceptance of that particular "socially correct" appearance.

"No. You will walk alone down the aisle to me."

She heaved a sigh of relief.

"But they did accept their invitations to our wedding, so they will be there as guests," he warned, watching intently for her reaction to this circumstance. "So will your mother."

Inwardly Leigh bridled at the sheer hypocrisy of her family attending a wedding they'd have no desire to celebrate. She really didn't want them there. The vengeful satisfaction she might have felt in their witnessing her marriage to Richard had slipped away from her in the past weeks, her thoughts more on a future with him than scoring off her mother and sisters.

Strangely, she realised they didn't really count any more. In that sense, she supposed it didn't matter if they were there. And there was a certain black irony in their being trapped by their own values into attending a wedding of this social magnitude.

All the same, they were bound to hate it, having to watch her being *the star* while they were relegated to the pews, onlookers, her half-sisters wishing they were *her*, the mother of the bride a mere guest, denied her natural duties, having denied Leigh any *natural* mother love.

In a way, it was justice—an eye for an eye kind of justice. Still, Leigh could have done without them beaming ill will at her while she went through with the ceremony Richard had planned. She looked wonderingly at him. Had he thought this scenario would give her an appropriate measure of much-needed satisfaction for the injustices done to her?

"Why did you invite them?" she asked, wishing she could read his mind.

"Many reasons…"

Foolish to think anything would be simple with Richard. She could sense the complexity of motives tumbling around in his ultra-clever brain as he selected the one he didn't mind her knowing.

"…mostly because I wanted them to see you as I see you."

It surprised her into inquiring, "How *do* you see me, Richard?"

His eyes glittered with the triumph he envisaged. "My bride, my consort, my queen…and homage will be paid to you."

A fierce pride threaded his voice and Leigh wasn't

sure what had dragged it forth, a need to have her shine
for him, or a need to have his power recognised and
acknowledged, even through the wife he'd chosen. Then
he lifted the hand that wore his ring, and pressed a hot,
lingering kiss on her knuckles, his eyes holding hers with
a long simmering blast of raw intent to have and to hold,
and Leigh was thrown into quivering confusion.

Need and want, he'd said to her.

She felt the same—*need and want*—and whatever else
Richard Seymour did, he brought her alive in ways that
made the past six years feel like a long dormant period
where she'd ridden in the shallows, a skimming existence that didn't really experience life at all. She had the
sense of being tugged towards heights and depths, an
inevitable flow birthed in dark underground currents that
swirled through both their lives.

"Should I ask how you see me?" he mused teasingly.

Did it matter to him? Leigh suspected it was quite
irrelevant as long as she fitted into his scheme.
Nevertheless, it would be interesting to have his reaction
to her view.

"The hunter," she said, without preamble or explanation.

It tilted his head and she imagined a multitude of
thoughts racing through it. His expression gave nothing
away. In his eyes was a serious weighing.

"You don't feel trapped, do you, Leigh?"

"No. I know I can walk away if I choose to. There
is no way you can trap me, Richard."

"Then why *the hunter*?"

"I'm not the end goal," she answered simply. "I
don't know what your end goal is but you're hunting it,

and I'd say you've been hunting it for a long, long time.''

"Other people might say I was merely ambitious,'' he blandly remarked.

There was more than ambition behind his ambition, Leigh thought. She'd seen it in his eyes several times, though she couldn't say what it was exactly, only an impression of a dark burning passion that knew no limits in its drive for satisfaction.

She shrugged. "You asked me how I see you.''

"So I did. And your reply was...unpredictable.'' He eyed her with keen interest. "I wonder how many surprises you have for me, Leigh.''

"Perhaps enough to stop you from taking our marriage for granted,'' she tossed back at him, feeling a thrill of exhilaration in having dealt a card he wasn't expecting from her.

He laughed and kissed her hand again, more lightly this time, his eyes flirting. "A wife to be reckoned with. A fascinating prospect.''

He was playing games to cover the truth chord she'd hit. Leigh felt almost dizzy with a strange exultation. He wasn't *untouchable*. Maybe, within the intimacy of their marriage, she would come to understand him as well as he understood her. A fascinating prospect, indeed.

The limousine turned out of the stream of traffic, alerting them both to its arrival at the private driveway up to the hotel entrance. Leigh was glad she had worn her good black slacks and the matching tunic top. The hand-painted scarf she'd fastened around her neck added a bit of distinction. The rock on her finger added more, she assured herself. Entering this hotel as Richard Seymour's fiancée suddenly seemed rather daunting, especially with a wedding director about to steer her through whatever was planned.

The limousine came to a halt. A doorman sprang forward to open the door. Richard alighted and stood by to help her out. The doorman greeted both of them by name and ushered them into the foyer, pointing out where Miss Lester sat, waiting for them.

A very svelte blonde in a smart red suit rose from one of the armchairs grouped in the centre of the foyer. She came forward, smiling, determined to please Richard Seymour, regardless of what she thought of the woman he'd chosen to marry. Leigh estimated her age as late thirties as she came closer, a woman of style and experience.

Richard smoothly performed introductions. "Leigh, this is Anne Lester. Anne, my fiancée, Leigh Durant."

"I'm delighted you're here at last," Anne poured out, offering her hand as her warm brown eyes generated appeal. "I just hope I've got everything right for you."

Leigh pressed her hand lightly and poured back assurance. "I'm sure you've done a superb job. I'm grateful to have it all taken care of."

"It has been a rather unusual assignment, without any input from the bride," Anne commented with a gleam of curiosity.

"Oh, I'm sure the groom's input made up for it," Leigh replied, smiling at Richard to show there was no disagreement.

He curved an arm around her shoulders, hugging her lightly as he smiled back. "I'll leave you in Anne's hands now. I'll call you tonight. Okay?"

"Yes."

Again his gaze dropped to her mouth and she knew

he was tempted to kiss her but he didn't. "Tomorrow," he murmured, and left her with that breath of promise.

She watched him stride back across the foyer to the doorman who stood ready to facilitate his exit. Richard commanded attention as naturally as he breathed. She wondered what kind of boyhood he'd had, and what would be in his heart tomorrow as he stood at the end of the aisle, watching her walk to him, the woman he'd decided to take as his wife.

"You've certainly got yourself a man there, Miss Durant," Anne Lester said admiringly.

Leigh swung her gaze back to the wedding director. An ironic smile tugged at her mouth. "I didn't get him. All this is his idea. I simply said yes."

"But you surely want him." It was said impulsively, out of puzzlement, and almost instantly discretion took over. "I do beg your pardon. I didn't mean to get personal."

Leigh couldn't help laughing. It really was an absurd situation…the prince and the ugly duckling. Nevertheless, it was obvious she needn't feel intimidated by Anne Lester or anyone else in this hotel. The label of Richard Seymour's fiancée lent her automatic respect.

"Well, let's get on with the process of turning me into a swan for him," she said, suddenly feeling quite light-headed. The die was cast and Richard expected to be proud of his bride. "Do we go up to the suite he booked for me?"

"Yes. I…uh…this way to the elevators. I have the key."

Anne Lester was clearly flustered, worrying about having put a foot wrong in what she undoubtedly saw as an extraordinary situation.

"Don't worry about it," Leigh soothed as they set off together. "I know most women would consider Richard a prize. And I do want him." She slid Anne Lester a twinkling look. "But mostly because he wants me."

"Ah!" said the older woman as though a light bulb had gone on in her head. "Well, I've never seen a groom so keen to have everything right for his bride. I do hope you'll approve, Miss Durant."

"The only consideration is that Richard approves," Leigh told her drily. "He's paying the bill."

"Yes. Yes, of course," came the somewhat dazed reply.

The cost of this wedding would mean nothing to Richard, Leigh thought. She wondered if the publicity of it would help his business manoeuvrings in some way. Or was it a strictly personal thing?

Pride...vengeance...satisfaction.

One thing she did know—it wasn't a celebration of love.

And sadness crept into her heart.

No love for Leigh.

But at least Richard needed and wanted her, she fiercely told herself, and that was more than she'd ever had from her family. She would not let them spoil her wedding tomorrow. She would pretend they weren't there. After all, they wouldn't be there...not for her. Only Richard would be there for her.

Only Richard.

CHAPTER EIGHT

His queen...

Leigh stared at the reflection in the full-length mirror, hardly believing the bride she saw was herself. Had Richard envisaged her like this when he chose what she was to wear? She remembered her sisters' wedding dresses—wonderful frothy confections with beaded lace bodices and sleeves and hooped skirts—making them look like fairy-tale princesses. But this...the whole look was incredibly regal.

The dress was medieval in style with a heavily boned damask bodice to mould her curves with amazingly sexy emphasis. A small stand-up collar, trimmed with gold piping, hugged her shoulders and dipped down to high-light the heart-shaped edge of the gold embroidered panel which ran down from her cleavage to a point below her navel. The long sleeves were tightly fitted to her elbows from where they widened to long cuffs embroidered with gold. The fluted crêpe skirt hugged her figure to mid-thigh before falling in graceful folds to allow walking room, and at the back was a sweeping train which also featured a design of gold piping.

Around her neck was a simple gold chain but it suspended a diamond that more than rivalled the size of the diamond in her ring. Diamond earrings glittered on her lobes, and to top it all, a gold tiara, holding a veil that completed the bridal picture, framing her hair and providing a filmy foil for the striking style of her dress.

The front section of her hair had been drawn up and rolled into a high chignon to hold the tiara. The rest of it had been fluffed out to fan across her bare shoulders before tumbling down her back.

Her face glowed as it had never glowed before, a tribute to the beautician who had worked on it, subtly playing up her eyes, putting colour in her cheeks and painting her mouth a brilliant cherry red.

"No pastels for you with your dark hair and olive skin," she'd said. "We go for a dramatic effect."

Drama...yes, that's what this wedding is, Leigh thought, the king getting his queen. She hoped she could carry off the part Richard had ordained for her once she was on stage. It was a very scary prospect, now she was fully dressed for it. She wasn't used to being a star.

"Your bouquet." Anne handed it to her, a glorious arrangement of cream roses with deep gold centres.

"Did Richard choose this, too?" Leigh asked, lifting the bouquet to smell the rich scent of the blooms.

"Yes. I suggested sprays of little orchids but he insisted on roses."

Their first kiss in the rose garden...had he remembered that? Did the roses signify anything, beyond the fact it was a flower that men had been brainwashed into thinking of? It was probably foolish of her to try to find meaning in everything.

"I must say they do set off the dress," Anne remarked appreciatively.

"Yes," Leigh agreed, telling herself that was the only meaning the roses had, completing the image Richard wanted her to have. Although roses were a kind of homage.

The telephone rang. Anne picked up the receiver, listened, said, "Yes," and hung up. She smiled at Leigh. "The car has arrived and it's time we were leaving. Are you ready to go?"

Leigh took a deep breath and looked distractedly around the suite. Everything had been tidied up. It had been like a railway station throughout the day, people coming and going, delivering things, doing her nails, her hair, her face. Visitors had commented on the magnificent view of Sydney Harbour from the big corner windows. It had been wasted on her, but tonight...tonight she would return to this suite as Richard's wife, and maybe she would look at the lights and wish for real romance.

Was she ready?

Her heart cramped.

She stared at her reflection again. Better to be a queen with a king than a lonely cuckoo. And she'd given her word.

"Yes. I'm ready," she said firmly, ignoring the nerves attacking her stomach.

"You look absolutely stunning, Leigh," Anne warmly assured her. "I don't think I've seen a more beautiful swan."

It evoked a wry laugh. "Just goes to show what experts can do. Thanks for all your work and care, Anne."

"It's been a real pleasure." She grinned. "You're a model bride. No tantrums. No arguments. Not even a show of nerves."

"I'll probably start shaking at the church. In fact, we'd better get this show on the road before I start shaking here."

The car was another stretch limousine, but white this time and decorated with white and gold satin ribbons.

Every little detail seen to, Leigh thought, as Anne helped to arrange her on the back seat. It was good to have someone riding with her, taking care of everything with the knowledge and experience of having done it all before, even if it was a paid wedding director. At least she didn't feel hopelessly alone on this last ride as the unwanted Durant daughter.

The driver timed their arrival at the cathedral to precisely four o'clock. Anne insisted Leigh wait in the car until guests who were still arriving or lingering outside were all directed inside to their seats. Apparently there were ushers hired to do this and one of them signalled the all-clear when it was accomplished.

The process of getting out of the car was carefully orchestrated by Anne so that nothing became disarrayed. The walk to the cathedral was slowly paced, although Leigh's heart was galloping. Once inside, Anne positioned her in line with the main aisle and set about arranging the train of the dress and the veil to her satisfaction.

A pipe organ was playing a hymn and a boys' choir was singing but the sound floated past Leigh's ears. There seemed to be a drum roll in her mind and her hands were trembling uncontrollably. She hoped her legs weren't going to get wobbly at the critical moment.

The hymn ended. Anne stood in front of her, assessing her arrangement, nodded her approval, held up her hand in a signal to someone, then gave Leigh one last smile. "Perfect. Hold it there for a few beats of the wedding march then set off nice and slow, right down the centre line of the aisle. Just aim for Richard. Looking at anyone else might make you veer or put you off balance. Okay?"

"Yes," Leigh whispered, her mouth and throat suddenly dry.

She wished she had a father to hold her arm. It was awful, being on her own, no-one to lean on, no-one to guide her, no-one to shield her from mistakes in front of all these people. But her father lived somewhere in Italy and she'd walked alone all her life so she could do it once more, couldn't she?

Aim for Richard, she repeated to herself, hoping it would have the effect of a calming mantra. She desperately needed tunnel vision because she could see pews filled with people in the nave of the church, people who would undoubtedly crane their heads to watch and appraise and wonder about the bride—the Durant daughter who'd dropped out of sight six years ago. Curiosity and envy and probably considerable pique would be aimed at her, but she couldn't let herself think of that.

Aim for Richard...

The beginning of the wedding march seemed to boom from the pipe organ. Anne moved aside, counting beats with her hand. "Go!" she instructed, and Leigh's foot jerked forward. Get the rhythm right, she screamed at herself. Centre line. Richard at the end of the aisle...a long, terribly long aisle. Movement on either side of her. A blur of faces. Mustn't look. Only at Richard. Gaze steady on him...step, pause, step, pause...

Then he smiled at her, and somehow his smile made everything easier. It was like a beacon drawing her on to a place of safety. Richard would look after her. All she had to do was reach him. She smiled back, her head high, shoulders straight, determinedly maintaining a slow regal carriage, wanting him to be proud of his bride.

The chosen one...that's what I am, she thought. Not a cuckoo, not a cast-off, not a reject...*the chosen one*.

The people in the congregation floated past. Only when she neared the end of the aisle was her awareness caught by the two women who flanked the front pews; on the left her mother, dressed in lavender, on the right...was it Richard's mother in pale apple green? She felt both women staring at her, emanating strong emotions, demanding attention that tore at her composure and tripped her heart into a faster beat.

Not now, she fiercely told herself. This was *her* moment, hers and Richard's. Let the mothers of the bastard children who were getting married today witness and acknowledge that. She wouldn't let either of them beat at her consciousness...mothers who'd visited the consequences of their own sins upon the children who'd been born from them.

Then Richard was holding his hand out to her and sanctuary was within her grasp. She was holding the bouquet so tightly, it took her several moments to unfasten her fingers. Placing her hand in his brought a hot jolt of reality.

He'd spoken to her on the telephone last night—checking there were no problems—but she had not been with him since he'd left her with Anne Lester. In the intervening time, their wedding had somehow gathered a level of fantasy, but his physical touch, the warm flesh and blood contact, brought Leigh thumping down to earth.

This was it!

He was taking her hand in marriage.

From this day forth...

And suddenly she couldn't meet his eyes. Her heart

craved love and she knew she wouldn't see it there. This
was a stage show. All the props were in place and the
play would go forward and reach its inevitable conclusion. It would be a triumph for Richard. It should be for
her, too. She mustn't let it feel hollow. He *was* the man
for her.

The minister, a tall, grey-haired man, garbed in ornate
vestments, stepped forward to perform the ceremony.
There was a rippling rustle of movement as the congregation settled down. Around the altar were magnificent
arrangements of creamy roses and massive candelabra.
Stained-glass windows shed beams of coloured light.

"We are gathered here today…"

Leigh did her best to concentrate on the words, resolutely holding panic at bay. She couldn't quite keep her
voice from shaking when she repeated each phrase of
the marriage vow. Richard spoke his in a warm mellif-
luous tone, as though he relished the words.

"…love, honour and cherish…"

Leigh closed her eyes and willed it to come true. Love
was not part of their agreement but maybe it could grow,
given enough encouragement. They were honouring
each other right now, so that was not in question. But
cherish… Leigh yearned to be cherished. If Richard
could view any child they had as "precious," might that
feeling overflow onto her?

She heard the minister asking if anyone knew of a
reason why they should not be wed, and Leigh's breath
caught in her throat. Would one of her sisters leap up
and denounce her as not a true daughter of Lawrence
Durant?

No one spoke.

She breathed again, castigating herself for the wild

concern. Of course, Richard would not have risked any blot on this shining hour. One way or another, he would have covered all contingencies. Nothing would stop the hunter.

He slid a gold ring on her finger. She didn't have one for him. Irrelevant anyway. Hunters didn't need to wear rings. They used them to get what they went after and hold it—whatever was necessary for a successful hunt.

"I now pronounce you man and wife."

The pipe organ boomed forth again, filling the cathedral with uplifting sound.

The minister smiled at them. "You may now kiss the bride."

The boys' choir started to sing "Song of Joy."

Richard's arm swept around her waist, gathering her in to him with an arrogant panache that signalled his mood of joyful triumph. *His wife*—a major step towards fulfilling the terms of Lawrence's will achieved, especially sweet since Leigh was *his* choice and would never have been Lawrence Durant's.

Leigh felt a major fluttering of nerves. The deed was done, for better or for worse. She had no idea where it would take her now and the fatalism that had brought her this far suddenly sprouted fronds of fear. Intense waves of vulnerability quaked through her.

"Look at me, Leigh," Richard murmured.

She had to…had to see…

Facing the truth was better than fretting.

She'd given herself into the keeping of this man and she had to know if all her instincts had been right…or wrong!

In almost paralysing dread, she lifted her gaze, expecting to be hit by a searing blaze of victorious possession. Yet it wasn't so. In his eyes was a soft, caressing tenderness, as though she was a waif of the world he'd taken under his wing. And her heart moved, not in shallow flutters, but deeply, gratefully, feeling he meant to take care of her in whatever ways he could.

He bent his head and his lips grazed softly over hers, making them quiver with the sense of caring he imparted. She didn't think of it as gentling a frightened creature so the show could go on as he wished. To her it was a taste of heaven…on her wedding day.

CHAPTER NINE

THE photography session was intense, mixed as it was with a mini press conference. Once Leigh and Richard arrived back at the hotel, the official photographer Anne Lester had hired was promptly joined by a battery of others from newspapers and magazines. Accompanying them were social reporters who shot their questions between poses.

Leigh was amazed and deeply gratified by the answers Richard gave, virtually denying the marriage had anything to do with business, portraying instead a highly romantic bond between them.

"Leigh chose to make a life of her own away from the Durant interests, but I never lost contact with her.

"In my mind, she was always going to be the woman I'd marry. It was only a matter of waiting until she was ready.

"I first met Leigh when she was fifteen. She was special then. She is even more special now."

He said it all so charmingly, so convincingly, smiling at her as though it was absolutely true, Leigh almost believed it herself. She was so touched by everything he projected, her own answers were influenced by his.

"There was never anyone else for me. Only Richard.

"I left home because I felt a need to become my own person. Richard is so strong, I wanted him to respect my choices.

"This is very definitely the happiest day of my life."

And Richard topped that by declaring, "Leigh and I belong together. It's as simple as that."

A love-match.

Leigh was so exhilarated by this *public* story, she didn't feel nervous at all, standing beside Richard at the entrance to the ballroom, greeting the guests and receiving their good wishes as they streamed in. Richard introduced each one to her, and if they had some important business connection to him, he mentioned it in passing. Social acquaintances didn't rate this particular attention. They tended to gush past. Window-dressing to Richard's success, Leigh thought. Only business associates really mattered to him.

Their families lingered behind everyone else. Whether this was prearranged by Richard and Anne Lester, Leigh didn't know. Her happy, relaxed mood lost some of its buoyancy as Richard introduced his mother, who was not accompanied by a husband. She *was* the lady in apple green, her features very similar to her son's, though her eyes were dark brown, not blue.

"Superbly executed, as always, Richard," she commented, a sardonic tilt to her smile.

"Thank you," Richard returned drily. "My wife, Leigh...my mother, Clare Seymour."

No natural chit-chat between them.

"I'm very pleased to meet you, Mrs. Seymour," Leigh rolled out with a welcoming smile.

She was subjected to a weighing look that questioned, far more than it congratulated her on becoming Richard's bride. She could almost feel the unspoken words... *Do you know what you've taken on?* and was tempted to say... *Yes, I do, because I've been there, too,* but she held her tongue, intuitively aware of wounds that had never been healed in this mother-son relationship.

"Richard has walked alone for a long time," came the slightly rueful remark. "I admire your bravery in marrying him."

"Oh, Richard has never been anything but kind to me," Leigh replied with confidence. "That makes it easy to be brave."

"Kind?" She glanced back at Richard as though it was a totally foreign word to be attached to her son. Then she forced a smile at Leigh, murmured, "Good luck, my dear!" and moved on.

It was an unsettling little contretemps, striking home to Leigh that Richard's mother certainly didn't believe in a love-match. But did she know Richard any better than Leigh's mother knew her? Had she ever been concerned about the heart of the cuckoo in her nest?

Leigh brushed the speculation aside as Richard introduced her to his two older brothers and their wives. So he had been the youngest in his family, too, she thought, as she received their good wishes, which also seemed somewhat constrained. Sibling jealousy, she wondered? They were shorter than Richard, barrel-chested, thicker in the neck and brown-eyed. Very much their father's sons, Leigh surmised, wherever he was. They were followed by two teenage girls, Richard's nieces, who artlessly enthused over the wedding and thanked their uncle effusively for inviting them.

It was a nice little moment, quickly eclipsed by the procession of Leigh's sisters. Caroline led them. Nadine took the opportunity of giving Richard a resounding sister-in-law's kiss as Leigh faced her sharper-tongued sister.

"I'm glad you came, Caroline," she offered politely.

"We had to, didn't we?" came the mocking reply.

"No. It was entirely up to you."

It earned a pitying look. "Wake up, Leigh. The master speaks. We jump or pay."

Was she being nasty or actually stating the truth of the situation? There was no time to question. Nadine took her place. "Well, you have managed to do us proud today," she drawled, envy in her eyes. "Quite a touch of class, little sister."

"Thank you, Nadine."

"Amazing!" Vanessa pronounced. "Truly amazing!"

"A swan?" Leigh couldn't resist suggesting.

It floated over Vanessa's head.

Felicity, coolly elegant as always, leaned forward to express wistful doubts. "I do hope you can keep this standard up, Leigh. Richard will expect it."

"I'll try not to let him down," Leigh drily replied.

Finally, the confrontation with her mother. Despite expecting nothing, Leigh felt her heart twist with mangled hope as Alicia Durant paused to gaze with what looked like rueful admiration at her youngest daughter. She shook her head as though bemused by the situation.

"The ultimate twist," she murmured. "You won't believe this, Leigh, but I find it curiously sweet." In a quick, oddly touching gesture, she reached up and gently stroked Leigh's cheek. "You weren't born for nothing, after all."

Leigh found herself too choked up to make any reply. She'd been born to be Lawrence's son. Now she was the wife of Lawrence's substitute son. Was the failure now seen as a success?

Alicia's hand dropped away. Her mouth tilted in a wry

little smile. "*My* child. I wish Lawrence was here to see it. You are a triumph, Leigh. I hope you play it well." There was a tinge of regret in her voice as she added, "Much better than I did."

Approval? After all these years? Leigh felt torn by it, attached as it was to her marriage to Richard. Was it only this that gave her worth in her mother's eyes? Or was there some different feeling behind that suggestion of regret?

Alicia headed off before Leigh could sort through her confusion, before she herself had said a word.

"Are you okay, Leigh?"

She jerked her gaze up to Richard. "Fine! An interesting comparison—your family and mine."

His eyes sharply scanned hers. "A problem for you?"

"Did you force them to come, Richard?"

He shook his head.

"Pressure them?"

He smiled sardonically. "Wild horses wouldn't have kept them away. There was no pressure applied, believe me."

What he said made sense to her so she did believe him, though Caroline's comment still niggled.

A band struck up and a singer gave an emotional rendition of "I've Finally Found Someone" as Richard led Leigh past the tables of seated guests to the centre of the ballroom where part of the dance floor remained clear. He drew her into his arms and danced with her, just the two of them in front of everyone while the beautiful lyric was played through.

"Did *you* choose this song?" she asked him.

He grinned at her. "Of course. I chose everything. But you, first of all, Leigh."

Her heart turned over. He was giving her all the romance she could have wished for, and if he didn't feel it in *his* heart, he was certainly performing wonderfully for her sake. Or was it a matter of pride for him? She couldn't tell and didn't care at this moment. She loved him for making her *his queen*.

The whole reception was superbly orchestrated. They sat at a table with the people Richard obviously most trusted, very close aides in the power structure he'd built within Lawrence's financial empire. They were comfortable with him and their wives were warm and friendly towards Leigh, putting her at ease. They didn't know her but it was certainly the diplomatic move to make with the boss's bride, and she was grateful for the lack of any tensions.

The music played by the band set an uplifting mood, the food served was excellent, French champagne flowed, and the speeches made were flattering and funny. Leigh was lulled into feeling good about everything. She even forgot Caroline's snipe about Richard until she crossed her sister's path on the way to the powder-room.

"Caroline, wait a moment!" she cried impulsively, reaching out to hold her arm.

"The bride commands," came the derisive reply.

"Don't be like that," Leigh pleaded. "I just want to know what you meant by suggesting Richard forced you to be here."

Caroline rolled her eyes. "Come on, Leigh, you know how it works."

"Please...tell me."

"He's the sole executor of the will. He can hold up probate as long as he likes. In the meantime, we dance to his tune," she clipped out impatiently. Hate-filled frustration flashed out at Leigh as she added, "Your tune, too, now, I expect."

"No!" Leigh vehemently denied. "I will never play Lawrence's game."

"Well, good for you!" Her expression slid into flippancy. "Doesn't change anything, though, does it? Richard holds the power and the purse-strings."

"Did he say he would hold up probate on the will?"

Caroline shrugged. "He's Daddy's man. Par for the course."

"No, Caroline. Richard is his own man," Leigh declared with utter conviction. He wouldn't have married her otherwise.

"Tarred with the same brush," her sister mocked.

Was it true? Leigh wanted to deny it. Richard had categorically stated he hadn't pressured anyone into coming. Caroline was assuming he would follow her father's pattern of behaviour, but that wasn't necessarily correct.

"I don't know about probate, but I'll speak to Richard about your inheritance," she said resolutely. "Perhaps he could arrange an advance on it."

"At what price?" Bitter mockery this time.

It instantly struck Leigh how deeply the scars of Lawrence's influence on their lives went, not only for her. It coloured the thinking of all her family. She gently squeezed her older sister's arm. "No price, Caroline, I swear. It's over…what we all went through. You can make your own choices without fear. Start living the life you want to live. There's no-one to stop you, not me, not Richard, not anyone. You're free now."

Her eyes filled with confusion. "I don't understand. Why did you marry Richard?"

"Because I love him."

"Love?"

Caroline stared at her as though there was no way she could grasp that concept, and Leigh herself was surprised that such words had tripped off her tongue. Had the fantasy of their wedding become real to her?

"I would like us to be true sisters, Caroline," she rushed out with urgent intensity. "Not pitted against each other. Could we try that?"

Glazed eyes looked back at her. "You're a fool, Leigh. Richard is a shark. He obviously chose you because you're a pushover, no-one to get in his way."

"That's not true!"

Caroline's focus sharpened into pale blue daggers of scorn. "Blind stupidity! Better learn to play the game or you'll be the loser again." She gave a wild laugh. "Love! My God! What a joke!"

She broke away, chuckling derisively as she headed back into the ballroom. Leigh watched her, suddenly frightened of the caring Richard was drawing from her. Could she trust him with her heart?

She'd married him.

He was her husband but he wasn't her keeper.

She still had choices. She had always had choices. It was only a question of having the will to exercise them. Today she was Richard's bride because she'd chosen to be, and she was going to do her best to make their marriage work right for both of them. It was wrong to let Caroline's cynical view taint what there was between them. Richard had earned her trust, hadn't he?

So far, a fearful little voice in her mind answered.

Give him the benefit of the doubt, her heart urged.

Keep giving it until you know some other truth with absolute certainty.

And it was that thought she took back into the ballroom, that thought she carried up to their hotel suite, that thought she nursed as she faced him alone…on their wedding night.

CHAPTER TEN

DESPITE all her inner reasoning, Leigh felt almost sick with nerves as she preceded Richard into their suite. They were out of the public spotlight now, and she truly didn't know what truth would emerge in private. How much of their wedding had been *real* to the man she had married, how much had been play-acting to his chosen gallery, how much a manipulation of forces she couldn't even begin to guess at?

A few lamps had been left switched on, lending a soft, romantic glow to the room. She spotted a silver ice bucket containing yet another bottle of champagne waiting for them on the table, along with two flute glasses and a silver dish of strawberries. In an attempt to hide her growing tension, she waved to them and lightly remarked, "We haven't finished celebrating?"

"Just about to begin," he answered, his voice a sensual purr of anticipation.

Her heart skittered. She set her bouquet on the table and swung around. His coat and vest were already off, his cravat dangling, and he was flicking the studs on his dress shirt apart. He grinned at her, his eyes twinkling wickedly. "I thought we might need some refreshment from time to time."

The nights are mine.

Their marriage bargain leapt in Leigh's mind and jangled her nerves even further. Which was silly, she frantically reasoned. She wasn't a virgin. He'd done this with her before. She'd wanted him. Still did. Why should tonight be different? He hadn't really meant *all* night, had he? Not all night, every night. What if it *was* different?

"You can let your hair down now, Leigh," he said teasingly. "In fact, I'll help you. That tiara might be tricky."

He left his shirt agape and strolled over to her, standing very close as he unfastened the clips in her hair. She was hopelessly distracted by the scent of his bare skin, male and musky, seeming to pulse with an animal vitality. Having freed the tiara, he tossed it and the accompanying veil onto the nearby sofa, then started working the pins out of the topknot it had encircled.

"You carried everything off magnificently," he murmured appreciatively.

She took a deep breath, trying to concentrate her mind away from the physical sensations he was arousing with the soft massage of his fingers through her hair. "Were you worrying I might fail you?" she asked, wanting to understand what was going through his mind.

"No. Not even Lawrence could crush your spirit. Why would I worry that anything else might?"

"You did rather throw me in at the deep end," she said wryly.

"You're a survivor. Like me."

Was she? As he ruffled the coiled tresses into tumbling loose, she stared at the pulse beat at the base of his throat, feeling as though she was about to be caught in a rip tide and swept wherever it took her. Then his hand was under her chin, tilting it up, and she lifted her lashes, needing to see what he felt. His eyes blazed into hers, but it was more an intense probe for knowledge than a desire to take and possess.

"Is this the happiest day of your life, Leigh?" he softly asked.

The fear of giving him too much power over her clutched at her heart. "Am I so very special to you?" she retorted, instinctively challenging him back.

"Yes," he answered simply.

"Then my answer is yes, too."

His eyes softened, darkened. "I didn't want you to ever feel you'd lost out on a proper wedding. No more losing out, Leigh. Not for either of us."

She had never once thought of Richard as a loser. His mouth covered hers before she could comment, and he certainly didn't kiss her like a loser. With sheer seductive mastery he cleared her mind of any coherent thought and kept it under siege with a flood of sensation. Leigh was right back in the summer-house, feasting wildly on the passion he ignited, not wanting it to stop, her response begging for more and more, her arms instinctively winding around his neck to hold him to her, keep him locked into the exciting flow of feeling he generated.

She was barely aware of him unfastening the bodice of her wedding dress. Only when he eased his mouth from hers to murmur, "Let me take it off, Leigh," did she realise the tight fit was no longer tight. Her arms slid from his shoulders as he stepped back, drawing off the sleeves. The boned bodice was shaped like a corselette, no need for a bra. As it was lifted away, Leigh was acutely conscious of her breasts being freed and fully naked to Richard's view.

Still dazed by the desire already stirred, she simply

stood there, eyeing him with aching vulnerability as his gaze fell to her exposed body. She felt her nipples tightening as tension screamed through her again. Did he like what he saw? A frenzy of uncertainty stormed through her mind. In the summer-house she'd been semi-covered, not completely bare, and the heat of the moment had made such worries irrelevant. But now she was committed to living with him, night after night...

A slight shake of his head...what did that mean? His lips curved into a soft, sensual smile. He lifted his gaze to hers and to Leigh's intense relief, his eyes bathed her in hot admiration. Her stomach unknotted and started rippling tremulously again. She was still desirable to him.

"I've been envisaging you like this these past six weeks," he said huskily. "Lush, womanly breasts... even more beautiful than I imagined."

Tingling heat raced over her skin and a surge of pleasure rolled through her mind. Richard had been looking forward to having her as his bride, thinking of how it would be tonight. This part of their marriage wasn't business at all. Not one bit. It was very, very personal.

And she was glad he was standing back from her so she could watch *him* as he stripped off his shirt, revealing a broad, tanned, muscular chest. It was amazingly hairless for a man with such thick black hair. His skin gleamed like smooth satin, a tactile invitation that instantly accelerated Leigh's heartbeat.

"You're beautiful, too," she said, her voice a mere whisper, awed by the magnificent physique of the man she had married.

He laughed, a joyous ripple of exhilaration. "Take your skirt off, Leigh. I want to see all of you."

Her hands moved automatically to obey his command, any shyness she might have felt banished by the totally captivating fascination in watching him discard the rest of his clothes. He was so aggressively male; the taut flat stomach, the strength of his thighs, and most of all that part of him which she had already felt inside her but not seen until now. Its rampant arousal told her his desire was very real and intensely physical.

Despite the terribly compelling distraction of seeing him stripped of clothes, Leigh had managed to step out of her skirt and rid her feet of shoes. Her fingers were fumbling with one of the suspenders on her garter belt, its fastening buried in the band of lace around the top of her white stocking, when Richard spoke, drawing her gaze back to his.

"Leave it! You look incredibly erotic, just like that."

"But…" *He was completely naked,* was on the tip of her tongue. Somehow the protest was rendered meaningless by the blaze of raw desire in his eyes.

"I'll take them off," he asserted gruffly, moving in on her, scooping her so hard against him her breasts were crushed to the hot vital wall of his chest, which swelled and eased as he emitted a huge sigh. "You feel even better than you look…everything a woman should be," he said with exultant pleasure, then kissed her again, his mouth invading hers with a hard, driving eroticism that stoked a raging need for every intimate connection possible between them.

The thick roll of his erection pressing against her stomach was in the wrong place. Blindly urging a more appropriate shift, she lifted herself onto tiptoe, rubbing herself provocatively against him and returning the fierce possessiveness of his kissing, uninhibitedly impatient in her wanting.

Richard's hands glided over every curve of her back, seeming to revel in the indentation of her spine, the smallness of her waist, the soft round cheeks of her bottom. Then to her intense satisfaction he cupped them and lifted her, swinging her with him to the bed, lowering her onto it, bending over her, kissing her breasts, feeding excitingly on them as he unfastened her garter belt.

It was a shock when he drew back from her, standing upright at the foot of the bed...until he propped her foot on his thigh and proceeded to unfasten her stocking and roll it off, slowly, stroking an electric sensitivity along the bared flesh of her inner thigh, behind her knee, down her calf to the sole of her foot. He removed her other stocking with the same sexy, mesmerising procedure.

Leigh found herself holding her breath, her whole being focused on his touch. With the garter belt removed, he peeled off the remaining lacy G-string, leaving her as naked as he was and everything inside her quivering with anticipation. He parted her legs, his fingertips skimming up exquisitely tingling skin. Then to her profound astonishment, he leaned over and his head hovered over the intimate apex of her thighs and he was kissing her *there*!

She half reared up from the bed, her hands scrabbling at his hair to get a hold and lift him away, but when her whole body was struck with piercing streams of the sweetest, toe-curling pleasure, she fell utterly limp, gasping incredulously as her entire nervous system seemed to clench and unclench with ecstatic delight. Impossible to imagine such intense waves of sensation. They swamped her, owned her, and kept building. She squirmed, moaned, writhed, lost every shred of control over herself, and then she was tearing at Richard's hair, begging for release because she couldn't bear it any more.

The very next instant, it seemed, he was surging up, over her, an arm hooking under her hips, lifting, poising, and she felt him pushing forward, filling her with a glorious solidity that answered all the wild craving inside her, and tears of gratitude gushed into her eyes.

"Yes," she sobbed. "Yes..."

"Yes," he echoed, soothing her with kisses as her muscles convulsed around him in blissful delight, and there was an exultation in his voice that echoed through Leigh, arousing the same feeling.

"My wife," he murmured.

My husband, her mind sang.

And the primitive swell of mutual possession was swiftly and beautifully reinforced as they moved rhythmically together, revelling in the physical bonding. There were many intense pleasure peaks for Leigh, so many her body seemed to roll from one to another until gradually they merged into a constant sea of ecstasy and it didn't matter at all that Richard stayed in control, giving her this incredible experience.

He was wonderful, so generous in his caring that she enjoy this with him, making her feel she was everything he wanted in a woman—in his wife—and she felt he was drawing out the wanting because it was just as magical to him as it was to Leigh...this deeply sensuous affirmation of their union.

Eventually it occurred to her that she wasn't really doing anything active for him, just deliciously luxuriating in what he was doing with her. Her arms felt heavy but she lifted them so she could graze her fingertips over the smoothly bunched muscles of his shoulders, slide her palms over his nipples in a gently rotating caress, stroke her nails down over his stomach.

The sharp intake of his breath caused her to look up. His eyes were glittery, staring wildly at her, and suddenly his body bucked into a driving force, and her heart leapt with mad elation as she felt the fierce tension sweeping through him.

New strength poured into her legs and she rocked him into a faster rhythm, faster, fiercer, her hands clawing his back in the need to push him to that same exquisite brink of no return he'd taken her to much earlier. A guttural cry broke from his throat as he tipped over it and joined her in sweet release, sharing the sheer blind ecstasy of floating together on waves of fulfilment.

With a deep sigh of contentment he lowered himself, gently covering her body with his, impressing flesh to flesh on each other, his forehead resting lightly on hers. She hugged him to her, loving him, loving all of him. His arms burrowed under her waist, hugging just as possessively as he rolled them both onto their sides. For a long time they simply lay entwined, content with closeness, their bodies humming with a harmony neither felt inclined to break.

Leigh thought how lucky she was, sure in her own mind that not many men would be as exciting and considerate as Richard. She could not have dreamed of a better lover. He was perfect for her. If this was to be the pattern of their nights, she certainly had nothing to complain about.

She felt prompted to acknowledge how good it had

been. "Thank you for making it so incredibly wonderful for me, Richard."

He sighed, his warm breath wavering through her hair. "That was how I meant it to be…for our first time."

Leigh smiled. His concern that everything be right for her—their wedding and this night—made her even happier. "We might not have got to this second time if I hadn't felt right about the first, Richard," she informed him, letting him know she had no regrets about what had happened in the summer-house.

He stirred, moving slightly away so he could smile at her, his eyes gleaming quizzically. "It did count then?"

"Oh, yes. I might not have agreed to your proposition otherwise," Leigh readily confessed. "For all your arguments, and I won't say there wasn't some strong persuasion in them, marrying you still meant sharing a bed with you."

He grinned. "Well, I'm glad you were satisfied."

"And you?" Leigh felt compelled to ask. "Are you satisfied with me, Richard?"

The grin broke into an elated laugh. "*Extremely* satisfied. I now have everything I want within my grasp. Including you, my darling." He sobered and indulgently stroked her nose. "I think champagne is called for at this point."

He gently extricated himself from her, rolled onto his feet and headed towards the table, moving with the lithe easy grace of an athlete in superb condition, confident in his nakedness, confident about everything.

A little niggle intruded on Leigh's pleasure in him. Was she really *his darling*, or was he simply delighted with her for falling in with his master plan…the means to his end? Once again she cautioned herself against getting too starry-eyed with Richard. On the other hand, she wasn't about to sour what they had together with the kind of bitter cynicism Caroline had shown tonight.

"I can't promise you a son, Richard," she reminded him, intently watching for his reaction to that truth.

He smiled as he lifted the bottle of champagne out of the ice bucket and wrapped the serviette around it. Still smiling, he glanced back at her. "It won't matter if we don't have a son, Leigh."

His blithe attitude threw her into confusion. She sat up to scrutinise him better. "Isn't that why you married me...to fulfil Lawrence's will and get control of the company?" she put to him bluntly.

He popped the cork and shot her a look that seemed to dance with secret amusement, but it was so brief she wasn't sure. He proceeded to fill the glasses as he answered her. "Our marriage is what we make of it, Leigh. Don't let anything else concern you. Getting control of the company is my business, and I don't want to talk about business tonight."

Neither did she. Though the thought she had in the limousine yesterday slid back into her mind. Richard left nothing to chance, nothing he was able to control. A convulsive little shiver ran down her spine. He'd controlled their wedding, controlled their wedding night...

Stop it! she fiercely berated herself. Everything was fine, wasn't it? She had no reason to fear anything with him. Richard was not *tarred with the same brush* as Lawrence Durant. He *cared* about her. Why else would he want to please her so much?

Because she'd be easier to control under the persuasion of pleasure, easier to manipulate to *his* will. *A pushover!*

Agitated by these thoughts which she savagely told herself were influenced by Caroline's warped view, Leigh sat up, instinctively hugging her knees for comfort. Why shouldn't she take what Richard said at face value? There was absolutely no reason not to, at this point. And she wanted to.

He replaced the bottle in the ice bucket, picked up the glasses and swung around, his gaze targeting her again. She had a brief impression of intense purpose encompassing her. Then it was diluted by a whimsical smile.

"You look like a teenager, sitting there like that."

"Well, I'm not," she returned lightly.

"No, thank God! I waited a long time for you to grow up."

"You *weren't* waiting for me," she scoffed, though secretly wishing she could believe it.

His eyes teased as he handed her a glass. "You'd be surprised how many times I was tempted by the passion you projected, Leigh, wanting to feel it differently."

"So now you have." She sipped the champagne, trying desperately not to show his banter could be deeply meaningful to her.

"And very addictive it is," he purred, setting his glass down on the bedside table.

Leigh's heart started to gallop as he stretched out beside her, his thigh brushing hers, reawakening a highly electric sexual awareness of him. He lifted the long thick tresses of her hair and ran his fingers through them.

"I want a child, Leigh," he murmured, a low throb of yearning in his voice. "You're not using a contraceptive, are you?"

"No." She'd considered it part of their marriage bargain that she would get pregnant as soon as possible.

"It doesn't have to be a son."

Surely it made it easier for him if it was. Easier on both of them.

"Neither you nor I have ever had a real sense of family," he went on.

Was that where he felt he'd lost out? She certainly had, and the idea of making a family of their own was suddenly very appealing.

"I want a child with you. It would be a child who would never feel rejected, not by its mother, nor its father. A loved child."

His words flowed through her, grabbing her heart...a loved child...a wanted child... "Yes," she whispered, and saw him stir, growing excited by the thought, arousing excitement in her, too.

She leaned over him and placed her glass on the bedside table. She didn't want any more to drink. She wanted...

Richard paused her where she was. "Straddle me, Leigh," he commanded, his eyes promising more pleasure, and Leigh needed no further encouragement.

As she settled herself over him, her heart pumping wildly at the prospect of feeling all she wanted to feel again, he guided her positioning so he could slide into her, slowly, prolonging the sensation of an exquisite journey to the innermost depth of her, and when he was there, he cupped one of her breasts and drew it to his mouth, drawing so strongly on it she felt an arc of almost searing desire linking to her womb.

A child, she thought, tears prickling her eyes. A family of their own...hers and Richard's...and it felt so right...so beautifully right, there was nothing to fear.

Nothing at all. Richard wasn't like Lawrence Durant. He would be a real father and she would be a real mother…and she hoped they were making their child this very night.

CHAPTER ELEVEN

THEY honeymooned on Norfolk Island, an isolated haven of tranquillity in the Pacific Ocean, a beautiful jewel of nature that was so far from glamour and glitz, Leigh was amazed at its being Richard's choice. Yet it was the perfect place to relax; no crowds, no frantic traffic, and glorious scenery—green valleys, towering cliffs and the magnificent Norfolk pines adding their distinction to the landscape.

Richard had rented a holiday cottage, nestled in the woods above Kingston, with glorious views of Creswell Bay and out to sea. It offered them every private convenience and comfort they could wish for, including a spa house.

They weren't *on show* here, much to Leigh's relief, and they could do as they liked, when they liked, with no unwelcome intrusions. It quickly became apparent this was precisely what Richard wanted since they spent most of their time naked, both in bed and out of it.

The days were long, lazy and intensely sensual. Leigh revelled in the intimacy, the almost constant state of sexual arousal where a mere look or touch could set her heart racing. It seemed to her pleasure-drenched mind that everything was as perfect as it could be between a newly married husband and wife. They were very much in tune physically and Richard was always ready to indulge her in whatever she fancied.

Having the convenience of a hired car, they spent the

occasional morning shopping in the one small town that served the island's population, the occasional afternoon stretched out on the pretty beach at Emily Bay, swimming in the crystal blue waters of the lagoon.

Sightseeing was more incidental than planned, but Leigh decided they should take in some of the history of the island. She had no idea—not the slightest premonition—that her interest in it would lead to rupturing the happy bubble of harmony she'd been living in with Richard.

Norfolk Island had once been an infamous penal colony where convicts had been offloaded from ships and left under a cruel authority to live out their lives as they were ordered. It seemed to Leigh a terrible irony that this beautiful place had been used as a prison, but browsing through the museum made it depressingly apparent how effective it was.

"No escape but the sea, poor devils," she murmured, reading the account of one rebel's fate and wondering if drowning had been better than living under such an appalling regime.

"Yes, it tends to put one's own life in better perspective, doesn't it?" Richard commented.

Leigh pondered this very valid point as they moved on to walk down the hill to the ruins of the pentagonal prison where the convicts had been housed. The neat Georgian cottages they'd been forced to build for government officials still stood in Quality Row, and were still lived in by those who provided professional services to the islanders, but there was little left of the prison, more a grim reminder of what had been here.

Six men to a cell, Leigh had read, and the outline of the cells showed how small a space they had provided.

She couldn't imagine how six men could be crammed into them for sleeping. No privacy. No comfort. Tempers frayed by the enforced closeness.

She sighed over the miseries they must have suffered and ruefully remarked, "I guess you couldn't call Lawrence's mansion a prison. Not like this. But it did feel like one, all the years I was growing up."

"You made good your escape from it, Leigh," Richard answered, glancing at her with warm approval.

Her curiosity was suddenly piqued. "What about you, Richard? What was your childhood like?"

He shrugged. "Lonely."

"You have two brothers," she prompted.

"Who weren't any more company to me than your sisters were to you," he retorted sardonically.

Leigh recalled his mother's slightly incredulous response when she'd said Richard was *kind*. It stuck in her mind as she asked, "Were they unkind?"

"Not particularly. Mostly I was ignored."

She heard a curt note creeping into his voice and sensed he didn't want to talk about that period of his life, but Leigh couldn't resist the urge to know more about him. "Why was that so?"

"They were older. No common interests. They went to live with their father after he divorced my mother. They had no time for me. It's just the way it was," he said dismissively, the curt note stronger now.

Leigh could feel herself tensing up because of it, but she persisted, determined on filling in his background, wanting to understand what had driven him to be where he was now. "How old were you when the divorce happened?"

"Seven."

"And you stayed with your mother."

"Not exactly. I was placed in a private prep school."

"A boarder?"

"Yes."

"At seven?"

"Out of sight, out of mind," he recited cynically.

"Why?"

He gave her a chillingly grim smile. "My mother considered I'd ruined her life. She fell pregnant to the man she wanted, except he had no intention of divorcing his wife for her and promptly dumped her when she suggested it. Then the convenient husband she did have divorced her when he found out I wasn't his."

"Was that when you learnt about your real father? When you were seven?"

"Yes."

Leigh was appalled at a child of seven suffering through the kind of scene she'd been so devastated by when she was eighteen. At least she'd been old enough to leave and survive by herself. Richard had been put away.

"Was the prep school like a prison?" she asked quietly.

He paused, staring off into the distance, past the prison ruins to the rocky shore and the sea beyond. Had he longed for escape, Leigh wondered?

"It wasn't too bad," he answered slowly, "for those boys who could excel at sport. And academically. It was a matter of getting to the top of the pecking order." Again the chillingly grim smile. "That kind of achievement was respected by everyone: staff, pupils, and most pupils' parents."

Leigh didn't have to ask if he had excelled. It was

written in his physique and in his current achievement, being at the helm of the Durant financial empire. She imagined he'd been a king at whatever schools he attended. University, too. She understood now the air of self-sufficency, the control he kept, the drive to have complete mastery over everything in his life.

"Why did you ask your mother to our wedding?"

He turned back to her, his eyes hard and glittering. "Because she's my mother, whether she wants to be or not."

A love-hate possession? Strange how neither of them could quite let go of the women who'd given birth to them. Something deep kept insisting there should be a bond, however tenuous it might be.

"Why do you think she came?" Leigh asked, remembering the note of antagonism, even of bitterness in Clare Seymour's comments.

His mouth twisted. "Because she takes a perverse satisfaction in the position I have attained."

Like her own mother.

A gathering sense of oppression weighed on Leigh's heart as they walked on towards the stone arch of the Hangman's Gate, one very stark part of the prison still standing. The haunting sense of blighted lives in this place added to the sense of her own life and Richard's having been blighted by others' ambitions.

At least Richard had risen brilliantly from the rejections that could have stolen his sense of self-worth, yet he'd been scarred, too. His need for family was just as deep as hers. She wondered if she was already pregnant. If not, it wasn't from a lack of giving it every chance.

She slid Richard a quizzical look. Was that in his

mind every time they made love? Did his pleasure in her have determined purpose behind it?

"What now?" he asked, catching her gaze on him.

The question popped out. "How do you plan to get control of the company if we don't have a son?"

"There are ways and means," he answered offhandedly.

"Tell me one of them," she insisted.

"Just leave it to me, Leigh."

She caught his arm, halting him, her eyes pleading with his. "I don't want to feel guilty about having a daughter. Please, Richard...I want to know."

He frowned. "There is no reason for you to feel guilty. We're married. We'll have a child. That shows intent to fulfil Lawrence's terms and whether it's a son or daughter won't matter. I'm the sole executor of the will."

Leigh frowned. Caroline had thrown the fact Richard was sole executor at her, as though it wielded power that could affect her family. But how? She shook her head. "I don't understand. How can that work for you?"

"It doesn't concern you, Leigh."

She would not be brushed off, not on this point. "I want it explained to me," she demanded stubbornly.

He grimaced in exasperation. The flicker of annoyance in his eyes sank behind a hard, ruthless shield. "Very well. Lawrence's will cannot be probated until its terms are fulfilled. Your mother and sisters cannot collect their inheritance until the will is probated. Which means, in the normal course of events, they have to wait...and wait..."

He bit out the word with grim satisfaction, and Leigh

caught the impression of a deep and abiding hostility towards her family that he'd never even hinted at before.

"...until such time as we do have a son," he went on in a tone of almost bitter relish. "Which may be never. And given your mother's experience of having five daughters, they all have a very strong appreciation of *never*."

Leigh struggled to fit his words and attitude into some kind of comprehensible context. "Doesn't that mean *never* for you, as well?"

His mouth curled and there was contempt in his eyes as he answered, "Sooner or later, your sisters will get impatient for their inheritance. I'm inclined to think one or other of them will sell me the proxy votes of the shares they can't touch. As the sole executor of the will, I'm in a position to make them that offer."

Leigh's mind whirled with everything Caroline had said...the implications...the assumptions...

The bride commands...the bride who might or might not have the son whose birth would release all their inheritances.

We dance to his tune... Your tune, too, I expect.

Sole executor...holds the power and the purse-strings.

At what price?

"Will you give them a fair deal?" she blurted out with painful urgency, almost panicking at the thought Richard might manipulate the situation meanly. If he really was *tarred with the same brush* as Lawrence Durant, she would not—could not—live with him.

He cocked a surprised eyebrow at her. "Scrupulously fair."

The terrible turmoil eased slightly.

"I wouldn't want to leave room for any legal come-backs," he added drily.

Pragmatic. And holding unassailable control. It was frightening...that relentless streak in him...yet there was really nothing for Leigh to criticize. Lawrence had made the abominable will, not Richard, and the act of marrying *her* had already undermined it, to which she had agreed.

Justice for her, Richard had persuasively argued, but somehow Leigh now suspected Richard had his own, very personal vision of justice in mind...the something dark and dangerous she'd seen flashes of on the day of the funeral. All her self-protective instincts were quivering as she stared at him, because what she saw was *the hunter*, stripped of the guise of caring lover.

He stood straight and tall and very still, but there was a lethal air about him that made her heart quake. Ready to strike whatever had to be struck, she thought, feeling the banked energy in him as though it were an electric force, ready to zap out and neutralize. A deeply in-grained pride was stamped on his face and the blue eyes were laser-sharp, probing hers with almost clinical detachment, looking for weaknesses, sensing all was not right with her.

"Why are you concerned about your sisters?" he asked. "Did they ever give you any caring?"

"No," she conceded.

His whole expression hardened. "They stayed in their father's household for what they could get out of him. They're still parasites, hanging on to get more out of him. Let them go, Leigh. As they let you go."

He was right. She knew he was. She just couldn't feel

that ruthless. "Is that how you feel about your brothers?"

He shrugged. "They didn't leech off their father. Both of them have established their own lives. I respect that. Your sisters have done nothing I could respect. Nothing."

"Perhaps your brothers' father didn't crush all sense of self-worth out of them," she argued. "Lawrence liked having slaves to his will, Richard."

"You weren't a slave to his will," he retorted tersely. "Your sisters saw the advantage to themselves in sucking up to him and took that road."

"Maybe they saw that road as the only way to survive."

"The easiest road," he scorned. "They didn't bother trying to get a self-supporting job. They stuck to the fat of the land that Lawrence provided. And any one of them would have married me to ensure the fat continued."

Leigh couldn't deny it, yet in a way she understood the mind-set of her sisters, brainwashed from childhood to barter for *the fat* which was held up to them as the be-all of life. They had *worked* for what they'd got out of Lawrence, and paid for it, too, in the loss of heart and soul that might have made them fight for something different.

"You don't know what it was like for them, all those years before you came on the scene," she pleaded, disturbed by the revelation of his deep contempt and wanting to lessen it. "The difference between me and my sisters was my mother never sided with me. Which left me isolated," she explained. "My sisters were encouraged to pander to their father. It was what they were taught, trained to do. Don't blame them for what that did to them, Richard."

He looked incredulously at her. "You defend them? When they wouldn't so much as lift a finger for you?"

She wasn't sure why she was fighting their cause, only that Richard's view of them was merciless and she knew—who better?—there were mitigating circumstances for how they had behaved and the choices they'd made.

Her eyes fiercely challenged his reading of their situation as she answered him. "As lonely as you might have been in your boarding schools, you had autonomy from a very early age to make what you could of your life, without interference, without the kind of mind punishment Lawrence handed out. Don't judge my sisters, Richard. You didn't live their lives."

"No, I didn't," he conceded with a mocking twist. "Perhaps isolation was better. For both of us."

She stared at him, knowing he was hiding much from her, just as he'd hid his contempt from her sisters with a layer of surface charm. None of them knew what he thought of them. She didn't really know what he thought of her, underneath what he projected to gain his purpose. Sexual attraction was certainly a given. That could not be faked. But what else was real? What was truly lodged in the heart and soul of Richard Seymour?

Then he smiled and the shifting sands of their marriage gained some solid ground, because surely he couldn't fake the warm appreciation he was beaming at her.

"You are an amazing person, Leigh." He stepped forward, lightly grasping her upper arms, and the warmth in his eyes sizzled into desire. "Let's get out of this depressing place. Go back to the cottage. I can think of much more pleasurable things to do.''

His hold on her suddenly evoked his words from their wedding night... *I now have everything I want within my grasp. Including you, my darling.*

Leigh barely controlled a convulsive shiver. She allowed herself to be led by him because there was really nowhere else for her to go, and his hug around her shoulders was comforting as they walked to the car. She didn't want to feel alone...isolated. It was easy to lose herself in the mutuality of the physical pleasure they shared, and she needed that right now, needed it badly.

Much, much later, lying together on the bed in their cottage, Richard propped on his side, his face relaxed in an expression of happy satisfaction, Leigh once again felt hopeful that something good could be forged with their continued intimacy. Her husband was a very complex man, but she hoped to reach past all the guarded layers, given time.

A whimsical smile curved his lips as he gently stroked her stomach. ''Do you suppose our child could have been conceived, Leigh?''

''Well, if you're potent and I'm fertile, I don't see how we could have missed,'' she said drily.

He laughed and leaned over to kiss where his fingers had grazed, then trailed kisses lower and lower, making Leigh catch her breath in anticipation of what he meant to do. But before her mind was mashed by the sweet pleasure that drowned all thought, it formed a fierce prayer...

Please, God, let our baby be a boy!

A son would end Lawrence Durant's hold on all their

lives. Richard would have what he wanted—ultimate control—and her mother and sisters could go free. Then maybe their marriage could begin to encompass all she desperately needed from it.

CHPATER TWELVE

"WELL, quite clearly, it's a boy," the technician declared, manipulating the green dot on the scan screen so
that Leigh could see, beyond any doubt, the sexual definition of the baby in her womb.

Relief swept through her like a tidal wave. No more
anguishing over having a daughter and how that would
affect everything. She could relax now, and look forward
to the birth of her baby. Having a son shouldn't mean
so much, but there was no escaping the fact it did to
her, if not to Richard.

For the past four months, ever since her pregnancy
had been confirmed, it had been a struggle, telling herself over and over that their child was to be welcomed
and loved, regardless of its sex. She had a great deal
more empathy now for her mother who had delivered
five daughters, each one of them denying her the mental
and emotional release that a son would have brought.
There was a lot of truth in the old saying... walk a mile
in your brother's shoes before judging him.

Of course, the baby still had to be safely born, but the
scan had assured her his development was perfectly on
track, everything normal, and she'd had no problems
with her own health apart from a slight queasiness and
fatigue, natural side-effects of her pregnancy. So long as
she took reasonable care, in another four and a half
months, the terms of Lawrence's will would be fulfilled,
finally ending his tyrannical rule.

A son...hers and Richard's son...and while it would be Lawrence's *legal* grandson, there was no genetic connection whatsoever to the man whom she could only think of as a sadistic egomaniac. She was glad there was not one drop of Lawrence Durant's blood in her child.

"You can get dressed now, Mrs. Seymour," the technician said, switching on a light to assist the process. She smiled at Leigh. "I hope that having a son is good news for you and your husband."

"Yes, it is. Though he wouldn't have minded a daughter," she added fairly.

"Maybe next time," the technician commented indulgently.

Next time! Leigh couldn't look beyond *this time*! One thing she would make certain of...there would be no more babies until she saw what Richard was like as a father. As a husband, he shared every intimacy with her in bed, but the intricate workings of his mind were still a mystery to her.

It was as though he boxed his life in separate compartments and he only gave her entry to those he considered part of their relationship. He was very adept at blocking her out of no-go zones. Sometimes she picked up things about him at the parties they attended, but he always brushed off her questions when they went home, making love to her so distractingly, Leigh was diverted from trying to know him in other ways.

However, he was a concerned father-to-be, very protective of her pregnancy, and it was wonderful she now had absolute confirmation that all was well. As soon as she left the medical clinic, Leigh pulled from her handbag the mobile telephone Richard had insisted she have with her at all times. It was almost noon and the

February summer heat was fierce so she quickly stepped into the shade of one of the trees along the pavement to make the call.

It was only necessary to press one button as Richard had put his office number in the computerized memory in case of emergency. While this was not an emergency, Leigh was eager to share the results of the scan, and she didn't think he'd mind her interrupting his work on this occasion. If it had been a girl, she might have needed time to work through her feelings before telling him, but a boy...she was smiling as the call was answered.

"Mr. Seymour's office. How may I help you?" a woman's voice rattled off.

"This is Leigh Seymour, Richard's wife. I'd like to speak to him."

"Oh!" A short surprised silence, probably caused by the fact Leigh had never called his office before. "He's in a meeting right now, Mrs. Seymour. Just a moment while I put your call through to the boardroom."

"If it's an important meeting..."

"No, no...you have top priority. I do hope there's nothing wrong," she added in somewhat of a fluster. "I'm buzzing him...he's picking up...Mr. Seymour, your wife is on the line."

Richard's voice burst into her ear, curt and concerned. "Leigh, what's the problem?"

Bemused by the fact that Richard had obviously instructed his secretary that any call from her had *top priority*, Leigh was slow to reply, her mind digesting the amazing fact that she and their baby were more important to him than any business.

"Leigh!" Richard called with urgent intensity. "Where are you? What's happened?"

A smile grew from deep inside her. "I'm fine, Richard. So is the baby. I just thought you'd like to know it's a boy. We're going to have a son."

"A son?" He sounded stunned. "How can you be sure?"

"I've just had a scan." A sudden surge of pride put a ring of triumph in her voice as she announced again, "It's definitely a boy."

Silence for several seconds. Then slowly, reprovingly, "A scan was scheduled and you didn't tell me?"

Guilt wormed through her pleasure in the news. She probably shouldn't have kept the scan appointment from him. It was just that she'd felt she'd cope better with the outcome, if she had some time to get used to it before facing Richard with the sex of their child.

"I didn't want to talk about it," she confessed.

He sighed. "I would have liked to be there with you, Leigh."

His disappointment made her even guiltier. It had been wrong, excluding him from the experience of seeing their child for the first time. "I'm sorry, Richard. It would have broken into your day and..." She faltered, thinking she was breaking into his day right now without the slightest compunction. Her decision to be on her own had been a selfish one, not considering his feelings at all. "I have a video of the scan. You can watch it tonight," she rushed out in hopeful appeasement.

"Ah!" Relief and pleasure in the sigh.

"He's perfect. Everything's as it should be," she assured him, anxious to give the information he would have seen for himself if he'd been with her.

"That's great, Leigh! Great!" More warmth in his voice now. "It really shows he's a boy?"

"No question. I've just come out of the clinic. I thought you'd like to know straight away."

"Yes. Thank you."

At least she'd done right about calling him, Leigh reassured herself. "I'll let you get back to your meeting now."

"A boy..." he repeated as though totally bemused by the thought...not excited, not triumphant, simply bemused.

The sex of their child really hadn't mattered to him, Leigh thought. A son did not represent an extension of his ego, as a son would have been to Lawrence Durant. Richard was not *tarred with the same brush.*

Buoyed by the hope of a happy family future, Leigh eagerly said once more, "You'll see him tonight."

"Yes...tonight..."

She could hear the smile in his voice and it put a light zing in her heart as she said, "Bye now," and disconnected the call.

Walking down to the basement car park, Leigh reflected on the two sides of her husband's character. He could be just as tender as he was ruthless, gentle...strong, warm...chillingly cold.

In company, he maintained a charming politeness that was never broken by any circumstance—the perfect guest, the perfect host. His social skills were as streamlined and polished as she imagined his business skills were. Yet Leigh knew his mind was working on two levels, superficially satisfying other people's requirements while sifting everything they said and did for information that might be useful to him.

She had learned this from the comments he occasionally dropped to her once they were alone. Sometimes she hugged these little confidences, telling herself they proved Richard trusted her enough to reveal his inner thoughts. Other times she worried over what he didn't tell her, aware he kept a great deal to himself.

Nevertheless, in other areas, she couldn't quarrel with his generosity, especially where she was concerned. Like her car, she thought, as she reached it. Anything she fancied, he'd told her. Cost no object. She could have been zipping around in a Porsche or a Ferrari, but she couldn't see herself transporting pottery or picking up essential materials in a sports car. She'd stipulated a wagon, and he'd insisted she have the Mercedes-Benz ML320, the best on the market.

She settled herself in the driver's seat, thinking this ultra-safe vehicle was much more practical for transporting a baby with all the baby paraphernalia, too. Smiling at the prospect, she drove out of the car park and headed for home, taking the road which led to Rose Bay where Richard had purchased the house Leigh had instantly fallen in love with.

It was ultra-modern and north-facing, with every room that overlooked the bay featuring a wall of glass which gave unrestricted views and allowed light and sunshine to pour inside. A happy, friendly, welcoming house, Leigh had thought, and still did, completely the opposite in style and atmosphere to the highly formal and formidable Durant mansion. And situated on the other side of Sydney Harbour, too.

The white walls and tiled floor had given her a free rein in choosing whatever colors she liked in the furnishings. Bright cheerful colors, she thought with satisfaction. Nothing muted or neutral. Maybe it was her

Italian heritage coming out but she liked a sense of positive vibrancy in a room.

All in all, the past four months had been highly eventful, with Richard delivering his half of their marriage bargain, and she delivering hers. It seemed so long ago now that he had first shocked her with his proposition, but it had only been August last year. They'd been married in the first week of October and Leigh had to concede she had little to complain about and much to be grateful for.

Richard was a kind and considerate husband. A fantastic lover. She had a glorious home. What had been the conservatory at one end of the house had been remodelled to serve as a studio for her, with a top-of-the-line kiln built in that most potters would die for.

Everything she'd left in storage at Broome had now been installed. An interior decorator had done all the legwork in finding and acquiring the furniture and furnishings Leigh fancied. House staff had been hired to do the cleaning and the cooking and the gardening. Leigh had plenty of free hours to work as she liked, and was currently dabbling with a crystalline effect in the glazing process, hoping to create a new range of pottery.

Richard had given her back a very privileged life, far more privileged than the one she'd led in the Durant mansion because everything was tailored to her needs and desires. Yet still she craved the sense of being loved, unconditionally loved. Material riches didn't fill that need. And the estrangement with her family was unlikely to be ever bridged.

Since she'd been living in Sydney again, she'd seen Felicity and Vanessa at social events, a first night at the opera, the opening of an art show. Apart from saying a polite "Hello!" that was the only contact she'd had with any of her sisters. Not that she sought contact but it never felt right, being so alienated from them.

In acquiring the designer clothes expected of Richard Seymour's wife, she had once run into her mother at a Double Bay boutique and impulsively suggested they have coffee together at one of the nearby coffee-shops. Her mother had agreed, though Leigh soon realized it was more from curiosity than any thought of trying to start a new relationship with her.

"Are you pregnant?" Alicia had asked directly, once they were seated at a table.

"Yes, I am," Leigh had answered, aware that it might be a relief for her family to know a child was on the way, a child that might release their inheritances.

It evoked an ironic smile and the comment, "Richard wastes no time." Then she'd looked askance at Leigh. "You are aware he's every bit as ambitious as Lawrence was."

"Is he?" she'd countered, not prepared to accept such a sweeping statement.

Alicia had sat back and in a detached way, mused, "I wonder if it will eat up your life as it ate up mine."

Their whole conversation—such as it was—had left Leigh with many disturbing trains of thought which she'd tried to banish, adding up all the evidence that Richard was not in the same mould as Lawrence, and her life was not going to run along the same lines as her mother's.

Occupied by these thoughts, Leigh was barely aware of the trip home. Turning automatically into her drive-way, she was jolted by the realization she had arrived without any memory of how she'd traveled here.

Berating herself for not paying proper attention, she garaged her car, but her mind was still revolving around her mother's life. Once inside the house, she went straight to her studio where privacy was assured and put through a call to Alicia Durant.

"Leigh?" her mother asked, a perplexed note in her voice, as though she couldn't imagine why her fifth daughter wanted to speak to her.

"It's not going to be the same, Mother," Leigh asserted. "I've just had a scan. The baby I'm carrying is a boy."

Silence. Leigh's satisfaction in announcing this incontrovertible fact was short-lived. It didn't really prove or disprove anything.

"I see," Alicia drawled. "Does it give you pleasure to ram that down my throat?"

Again Leigh was thrown into guilty confusion by the response to her news. "No!" she cried. "I just wanted to…" She faltered, tongue-tied. How to explain the desperate need to be clear of the past? To tread new ground?

"Share your happiness?" her mother supplied mockingly.

"No," Leigh answered on a desolate sigh. "I don't suppose I can ever expect that. Just tell Caroline, would you?" she asked dully. "And my other sisters. My having a son means they'll be able to collect their inheritances soon after the baby is born."

Tears pricked her eyes. She put the telephone receiver down as the prickling turned into a gush, and fumbled her way to a chair, helplessly surrendering to a huge churning of emotion. Accepting the way things were was only sensible. Her mind acknowledged that. Yet sometimes the hurt couldn't be suppressed. She wanted a mother. She wanted a father. She wanted siblings she could turn to. She wanted Richard to love her. Why couldn't she be *right* for somebody?

Eventually the deep wallowing in misery passed. In rocking herself through it, Leigh found herself hugging her stomach and remembered her baby, the tiny live human being she'd seen on the scan screen, all scrunched up in her womb. A new life would start once her baby was born. She *would* have love. Mother love, if nothing else. And she'd make everything wonderful for her child. He'd never feel deprived of what truly mattered.

Having pulled herself together, Leigh went upstairs to the master bedroom suite, gave her tear-stained face a good wash, tied back her hair, changed into a pair of stretch shorts and a loose T-shirt, then headed downstairs again to lose herself in work for a while. Shaping clay was always soothing.

Her stomach, empty and unsettled, told her to eat, regardless of a lack of appetite. The baby had to be considered. She made a detour to the kitchen where their cook and housekeeper, Rene Harper, was putting away a load of food shopping.

"Ready for lunch, dear?" Rene asked, her cheerful disposition and motherliness beaming at Leigh, who had chosen the rather plump, middle-aged woman above other applicants for those very reasons. She had instinctively liked her, and the liking was more important to Leigh than impressive references.

"Don't worry about me, Rene. I'll just grab a sandwich and a glass of juice."

"I bought some nice avocados. They're very nutritional, you know. Good for the baby."

"Okay. I'll have one of those, too."

She told Rene about the scan as she ate, and the housekeeper emanated delight in the news, chatting on about the charms and characteristics of little boy babies. The conversation put Leigh in better spirits, and on her return to the studio, she set about molding clay with positive enthusiasm.

The afternoon wore on. A knock on the studio door jolted Leigh from her concentration on the vase she was shaping. The clay collapsed on the wheel and she turned towards the interruption with considerable vexation. "What is it?" All staff had been told her hours in the studio were sacrosanct.

The door opened and unbelievably, Rene, waving apologetically, ushered in *her mother*! "Mrs. Durant insisted..."

Leigh rose from her stool, her hands still dripping wet clay, and stared in stunned disbelief at the elegant figure of Alicia Durant, pushing past the housekeeper. Once inside the studio, Alicia stopped still, her gaze distracted by the display of pots and vases on shelves and pedestals. When she looked back at Leigh, her eyes looked as stunned as Leigh felt.

"*This* is what you do?" she asked, a thread of awed respect in her voice.

"Yes," Leigh managed to get out, her throat tight, her chest tight, her whole body tensing up. She nodded a dismissal to the housekeeper. "Thanks, Rene."

The door closed.

Alicia stepped slowly over to a pedestal which held a tall vase in shades of blue which were enhanced by the crystalline effect Leigh had been experimenting with. "Your work?" she asked, touching it as though coveting it.

"Yes."

"It's beautiful." She shook her head. "Truly beautiful."

Doubly dazed by such unexpected appreciation, Leigh could only utter a weak, "Thank you."

Alicia proceeded to walk slowly around the room, examining all the pieces, occasionally touching. Leigh had no idea what was going through her mother's mind, why she'd come, what she intended by this unheralded visit. Nervously, she wiped her hands on her work apron, watching and waiting until her mother had completed her tour. When Alicia finally faced her again, it was with a look of weighing a new assessment.

"I don't know you at all, do I?" she said, seemingly more to herself than Leigh.

"You didn't want to." It was the plain, unadulterated truth, spoken with stark simplicity.

"No, I didn't," Alicia acknowledged. "You were a desperate act that didn't work, Leigh. Most of the time I couldn't even bear to look at you. It was a relief when you left. I've been thinking about it all ever since you called about the baby."

"I'm sorry. I didn't mean to crow over you...or distress you." Leigh heaved a sigh and searched to express her own feelings. "The last time we met, you drew parallels. It frightened me." She looked at her mother in anguished appeal. "I need my life to be different."

Alicia nodded. "I'm glad it's a boy for you, Leigh. I really am. You didn't deserve what you got from Lawrence and me. I hope Richard treats you well."

"Thank you."

"As for the conditions of the will, I made sure Lawrence provided well for me, independently of his life or death," she stated sardonically. "Felicity and Vanessa are quite well set up from their marriages. However, your news will be some relief to Caroline and Nadine. I'll let them know."

"Please…Caroline made reference to it at my wedding."

Alicia made a derisive sound. "She would. She hated Lawrence probably more than you did."

Leigh frowned, not having known that. "Why?"

"Because she's bright and smart and thought she should be the one to take over from him. He scorned the idea. A woman stepping into his shoes?"

Unthinkable to a man like him. "Why did you stay with him, Mother?" Leigh asked, wanting to understand Alicia's choice when it couldn't have been a happy marriage for her.

Her mouth tilted with irony. "Oh, he was powerful and exciting and challenging, and any other man would have been less. I just wasn't prepared to let him go." She eyed Leigh with a wry knowingness. "I imagine you feel the same way about Richard."

Did she? Leigh had never put her feelings in those terms, yet her mother's words—*any other man would have been less*—certainly struck true.

"Right to the end I wanted Lawrence," Alicia went on, her eyes glazing slightly, focused inward. "I look back now on all I did to keep him…what was gained and what was lost…and realize how obsessive I was about it. Maybe it was a sickness…"

She paused, expelled a long breath, then looked ruefully at Leigh. "Do we really have choices? Or are they driven onto us by a complex array of forces?"

It was a very thought-provoking question. Leigh remembered Richard's comment about her choosing to leave home, taking nothing more from Lawrence, but there had been no consciously made choice in her escape from the life that had turned into a traumatic nightmare. She'd run because *she had to*, driven away by the unfaceable. Even her choice to marry Richard had been influenced by many emotional forces.

"Why did you come here, Mother?" she asked, curious about this choice. It didn't feel awkward to ask. The frank conversation invited it.

Alicia shrugged. "No doubt you'll think it strange after all these years of indifference, but I suddenly wanted to know you, Leigh." She made a self-mocking little smile. "Rather too late for the mother-daughter act. Impossible, I would think, for either of us to carry that off. But I would like to get to know the person you are."

Leigh stared at her mother, hardly believing her ears. The offer to bridge some of the gap between them was like a rainbow at the end of years of rain. Afraid it might disappear, Leigh rushed to meet her halfway, cautioning herself at the last second not to sound emotional. "I'd like that, too," she said as casually as she could. "Getting to know you, I mean."

"I'm not a very nice person," Alicia warned.

"I'm interested." Leigh offered a whimsical little smile. "You're still my mother."

"Yes. I am that," she drily conceded. "Perhaps we could meet for lunch in a week or two. Go shopping for baby things."

"Why not? Give me a call when you find it convenient."

"A boy." Alicia grimaced and shook her head. "I would have given my eye-teeth for a boy."

Leigh was instantly sympathetic. "I felt that way this morning before I knew."

Alicia's eyes suddenly warmed. "It's good to be able to talk to you like this. Without recriminations."

She didn't want guilt, Leigh thought. Then, who did?

"So, we can take it from here," Alicia said with a sigh of satisfaction. "I'll leave you to your work now."

"I'll see you out," Leigh offered, starting to undo her apron.

"No. I'll find my way." Her mother walked over and lightly touched her arm. "Thanks, Leigh. I'll be in touch."

And Leigh suddenly felt too choked up to reply. It wasn't a loving touch but it was a reaching out to her. There was no lingering, no further words. Her mother walked briskly to the door, opened it, stepped out, and closed it behind her. Yet Leigh was left with the sense of a much more delicate door opening, different from the one she had given up on, but very appealing all the same.

She took off her apron, no longer interested in working. She wandered over to the sliding glass doors that opened to the garden and stepped outside. A new start, she thought, breathing in the fresh, slightly salty air from the bay, enjoying the breeze wafting through her hair. Her hand lifted to her stomach, tenderly feeling the tight little mound that held hers and Richard's son. A new start for all of us, she resolved.

From now on she would be more open with Richard and encourage him to be more open, too. Feelings should be expressed, not hidden where they gathered too many other meanings and fed on doubts and worries. She wanted to know more about his choices, where he was really heading and what was driving him.

The hunter...

Tonight, she promised herself. Tonight she was not going to hold back from seeking the answers she wanted.

CHAPTER THIRTEEN

"FOR the mother of my son," were the words at the top of the note accompanying the flowers. Leigh's heart lifted every time she glanced at the beautiful arrangement of dark red roses. She'd carried it up to their bedroom so she could keep looking at it while she dressed for the celebration dinner Richard had booked a table for. The scent of the perfect blooms seemed to fill the room, adding more intoxication to the thought...red roses for love.

"Home at six-thirty," he'd written, and it was almost that now. She'd been getting ready ever since the flowers had arrived, but hadn't used the time efficiently, her mind excitedly playing through scenarios of how she and Richard would spend tonight. Her fingers fumbled with the tricky catch on the gold chain with the heart locket that set off her dress, then finally got it right.

She'd deliberately chosen the red, rather clingy dress which skimmed her curves but had a loose enough fall over her tummy not to show the slight bulge there too much. It was buttoned through from the V-neckline to the hem, which made her feel sexy, readily accessible to Richard's touch. She'd left her long hair loose, easily touchable, as well.

Having slid her feet into gold sandals, dabbed perfume onto her pulse points, smelled the roses once more, she hurried downstairs to the home entertainment room to ensure the scan video was ready to play. It was going to look amazing on the huge TV screen Richard had chosen.

No sooner had she satisfied herself that all was as it should be, than she heard the powerful engine of Richard's Jaguar, and raced to the front door to greet him, knowing he would leave the car outside, ready to transport them to the restaurant. He reached the door before she did, opening it as she entered the foyer, and she stopped, taking stock of the man she had married, the father of her child.

Would she do anything to keep him?

And the answer was...probably yes.

"Do I pass?" he asked, cocking one eyebrow quizzically even as a confident grin broke across his face.

She laughed. "Oh, I think you'll do."

"Good! And may I say red becomes you."

He closed the door and in two strides, had her swept into his embrace and very securely held. His eyes scanned hers, checking for an unguarded response as he asked, "You're happy it's a boy?"

Her smile was straight from the heart. "Very happy. And thank you for the lovely roses."

"My pleasure," he said warmly, then carried even more warmth to her mouth, kissing her long and deeply, making her feel loved even though he didn't say the words.

Maybe he would later tonight, Leigh thought, her heart dancing with hope and her body zinging with desire as she led him eagerly to the entertainment room to show him the video image of their son. She picked up the remote control from the coffee table and snuggled up to Richard on the sofa before pressing the play button. He curved his arm around her shoulders and lightly squeezed as the first picture of their baby flashed onto the screen.

Leigh reported as well as she could remember what the technician had pointed out to her. Richard looked totally enthralled by what he was seeing, not commenting at all. She pressed the pause button when the scan was directed at the genital area.

"There…you see?"

Richard grinned. "Well, he certainly has the right equipment for a boy." His eyes sparkled pure wickedness at her. "Built like a bull."

She punched him playfully. "That's all you men think of…potency and performance."

"Hmm…" He carried her down on the sofa and plucked at her top button. "I think my potency is proven, but I'll have to admit performance is very much on my mind."

"We're going out to dinner, Richard," she reminded him, not really caring if their departure was postponed.

"And it must be said anticipation heightens the pleasure," he murmured, bending to kiss the valley between her breasts before slowly refastening the button. His eyes simmered with promises of pleasure as he added, "A slow escalation is in order. Champagne, lobster, tropical fruit…"

"Not too much champagne," she warned. "Not good for the baby."

"Just a sip now and then to put tingles on your tongue."

He was doing it again, Leigh suddenly realized, making her so sexually aware of him and herself, other things faded into insignificance. But did it really matter tonight? It was an occasion for celebration. Why not simply enjoy it? She would still be married to him to-morrow and the next day and the next. Plenty of time to infiltrate his defenses and get closer to the man he kept to himself.

Leigh happily nursed that attitude for the next couple of hours. They went to Doyle's at Vaucluse, famous for its seafood. Richard flirted with her the whole time, charmingly, provocatively, seductively, and Leigh basked in his undivided attention, both laughing and al-most squirming with delight at his turning their dinner into a very sensual feast.

The lovely French champagne did tingle on her tongue. It tingled all through her. The lobster was tender and superbly flavored, not needing any sauce to enhance it. The tropical fruit accompanying it gave a delicious contrast of tastes.

So engrossed were they in each other, neither of them had given any notice to the other patrons in the restau-rant, not those arriving or those already seated. It sur-prised both of them when Clare Seymour stopped at their table and greeted them with the words, ''Well, you two seem to be having a good time together.''

''Mother...'' Richard frowned, his gaze darting around to spot where she'd come from. ''...I presume you're here with someone?''

''A friend's birthday.'' She waved at a table where three other ladies were seated, watching curiously.

''I hope you're enjoying your evening, Mrs. Seymour,'' Leigh offered with a smile, uneasy with the tension that passed between mother and son.

Clare Seymour directed a rather thin smile back at her. ''You seem to be celebrating something, too.''

''Yes,'' Leigh agreed, and seeing no harm in imparting the news, added, "we found out today that the baby we're expecting is a boy."

The thin smile took on a derisive twist. "So Lawrence gets his grandson." A steely blue gaze turned to Richard. "Quite a coup for you, although no doubt you engineered that, as well."

"I can hardly direct nature, Mother," he said sardonically. "Now if you don't mind…" He nodded towards her table. "…you are interrupting a rather special evening."

His mother ignored the hint. "It must give you a lot of satisfaction to have accomplished what your father didn't…in *his* marriage bed. And it's your very first child."

"That's enough!" Richard commanded, his face losing all trace of relaxed geniality.

"Five daughters," she jeered, then swung her gaze back to Leigh. "No, of course. Only four. Richard couldn't have married you if you'd truly been Lawrence's. He's rather fixated on legality. Marriage to a half-sister would be too questionable."

Leigh froze. Richard couldn't have married her if she'd been his half-sister? Then Richard had to be…Lawrence's son! It was Lawrence Durant who'd been Clare's lover…Richard's father…

"For God's sake! Keep your bile to yourself!" It was a savage hiss of fury from Richard who was up on his feet, his face thunderous.

Unabashed, his mother turned and patted him on his shoulder. "I congratulate you, my dear! Such remarkable efficiency in carrying through your master plan. I hope Lawrence is turning in his grave. Writhing in it, actually. Getting his taste of hell for spurning what I could have given him.''

Richard gripped her arm and forcibly lowered it. ''All through my boyhood years, I paid for your silence, Mother,'' he bit out in a low seething tone. ''I promise you, it will be *you* who pays if you ever break your silence again.''

The threat was so palpable, it instantly sobered Clare Seymour. Richard released her and she headed back to her table of friends with a very stiff spine...the imparter of news that held no joy and brought no joy...leaving devastation in its wake.

The expression *being turned to stone* equated fairly well with what Leigh felt. Her eyes still had the ability to see, but the rest of her had become a leaden weight, totally lifeless.

''Leigh...''

She didn't want to look at him. The moment she looked at him she would start studying his features, finding traces of similarity to his *real* father. Like his eyes. Were they the same color blue as Lawrence Durant's? What about the cut of his chin? Now that she knew...

''Leigh...'' He sat down, leaned his forearms on the table, head thrusting forward, urgent intensity emanating from him.

She folded her hands in her lap and sat very still because bad things were clustering around her, bad, bad things, and maybe they wouldn't hurt too much if she sat still and tried very hard to contain herself, keeping her gaze lowered, focused on her hands so that everything else could be shut out. Even Richard's voice could be shut out if she concentrated hard enough.

She remembered doing this at her father's table when

she was little. Except he wasn't really her father. He was Richard's father. Funny to think she'd been born to be *the son*, and there'd been no need for it. The son was already born. He'd been fathered with the wrong woman, that was all. So silly, really, that Lawrence hadn't been informed of it. Then this wouldn't have happened. No need. No need for any of it.

Though her mother wouldn't have liked it. No. Maybe her mother would have kept trying for a son anyway, still using the Italian gardener. But Richard wouldn't have had to marry the cuckoo in the nest to get his natural inheritance if he'd confronted Lawrence with the truth. Control of everything would have gone directly from father to son. She would have been left completely out of it.

The solitaire diamond sitting on the third finger of her left hand winked up at her. Her engagement ring. Wedding ring beside it. The only Durant daughter he could marry, the only one who wasn't a real daughter. *The bride of his choice.* What a terrible lie that was. She was his only choice to get what he wanted, what he must feel he had every right to.

It was as her mother had said this afternoon...not really a choice at all, more a decision driven by a complex array of forces.

Nothing to do with love.

Or being special.

The *only* means to the end...that's what she was to Richard. And a hunter always took whatever means was available to get what he wanted.

A hand grasped her arm, urging her up onto her feet as the chair she was sitting on was tilted back. "We're going home," a soft gravelly voice said.

Home...where was home? Where the heart is, her mind answered, but her heart was all minced up and Leigh doubted it could be put together again. Nevertheless, her body got steered out of the restaurant, the arm around her waist making sure she moved along with it. The next thing she knew, a car door was being opened in front of her and she was being lifted onto the passenger seat and strapped in.

It didn't really matter where she was taken, Leigh reasoned. The bottom had dropped out of the world she'd thought she had. Once again she just didn't belong to anyone or any place. She was adrift...alone.

No, that wasn't quite right. There was the baby. Lawrence's grandson. She moaned in anguish at the thought of her child bearing any part of Lawrence Durant's genes.

"Are you all right?"

The sharp concern from the man who had done this to her, without conscience or caring, sheared through the defensive cocoon of shock and snapped something inside Leigh, letting forth a blaze of fury that energized her whole body. Her head jerked towards him and words seethed off her tongue.

"No, I'm not all right! I'm all wrong, Richard. And I doubt I'll ever be right again, thanks to you and the way you've used me."

He glanced at her, a quick blast of focused power. "What my mother said is irrelevant to us."

"Irrelevant!" Leigh heard the shrillness of her voice and fiercely brought it down. "Like hell it's irrelevant! Don't take me for a complete fool, you bastard!"

He gave a harsh laugh. "Oh, yes, I'm a bastard. And if I'd ever told Lawrence I was his bastard son, he would have made capital out of it, so if you think the truth would have ever served me well, forget it, Leigh. Start remembering Lawrence as he was! How he was to you...the bastard daughter!''

''I wasn't *his* flesh and blood! You *were*!'' she shot back at him.

''Do you think he wanted a son who could match him? Beat him?'' he retaliated with biting derision. ''Lawrence would have taken as much pleasure in keeping me down under his heel as he took in putting you down, Leigh. That was the nature of the man. Only in remaining an outsider could I force him to respect me.''

She hadn't considered this perspective. It rattled her hastily formed conviction that Richard should have revealed himself. She kept her mouth shut while she thought about his view of his position. What he'd said was probably an accurate reading of Lawrence Durant's character. Would Lawrence have wanted a son capable of competing with him, or would his egomania demand the son be lesser than the father? Add on the illegitimacy of the son and Lawrence would have undoubtedly taunted him with his lack of any legal rights to anything.

''He would have seen it as weakness, Leigh, my telling him I was his son,'' Richard stated with ringing certainty. ''A son wanting something from his father. A leg up. Concessions. An easy road to the top. He would not have assessed my abilities fairly. As it was I had to constantly challenge him to win every piece of ground I took over from him.''

Yes, she could see that. But... ''You didn't have to work for him, Richard,'' she said bitterly. ''With your abilities you could have done anything, gone anywhere.''

She saw his knuckles whiten around the steering wheel. "He was my father," came the taut reply. "I'd known that since I was seven, Leigh. Lawrence Durant, one of the most powerful, wealthiest men in Australia...my father. Do you think I could forget that? Put it aside? Leave it alone?"

An angry sound grunted from his throat. "All those days when parents came to watch their children perform at school, to take them out, to give them treats...I thought of him. I thought of how his other children— the children by his wife—were getting the attention and privileges of being his *legitimate* children."

His half-sisters! All four of them...Felicity, Vanessa, Caroline, Nadine...his half-sisters, getting *the fat of the land*, while he got nothing.

Leigh suddenly saw it very clearly...Richard's drive to get *everything*...one way or another. She even understood it, but it didn't make anything better for her. To him, she was just one more tool in his armory to attain the end he'd aimed for. A contingency plan to his master plan.

"The course was set a long time ago," he muttered, and she remembered again the dark, dangerous flashes of passion from him, the sense of ruthless purpose that would not be diverted.

"And I'm a victim of it," she said, feeling hopelessly drained of any significance as a person.

"Not a victim," Richard retorted sharply. "A partner."

Sheer outrage at his duplicity tore through her, spitting the words, "A partner usually knows the plan."

"You did know it," he asserted. "I spelled it out to you the day of Lawrence's funeral."

"Ah, but you failed to tell me the critical part, didn't you, Richard? That I was the only one you could marry. Not *your choice*! *The only one* who could do the trick of bypassing Lawrence's will for you."

He thumped the steering wheel in angry frustration. "Don't tell me that didn't appeal to you, Leigh, because it did!"

Her own anger surged. "You haven't got a clue what appealed to me, Richard Seymour. You never bothered to find out. All that ever mattered to you was I serve your purpose."

"That's not true!" he cried vehemently.

"Liar!" Leigh fired at him just as vehemently.

"I have never lied to you. Never!"

"I'd like to hear how you reason that one to yourself," she scoffed. "Put in a little grain of truth and then it's not a lie? Is that how you do it, Richard?"

"I have *not* lied to you," he grated between clenched teeth.

Leigh scorned any reply to such blatant mendacity. She sat in grimly seething silence as Richard drove what little distance remained to be traveled. It gave her a savage satisfaction to know he was not so coolly in control of the situation any more, directing play as *he* wanted it, but the way he had manipulated her kept stinging like a swarm of hornets.

The moment the car was halted in their garage, she was out of it and into the house, getting away from him as fast as she could without running. Pride forbade running. Naturally he followed. The hunter didn't let his prey go unless he was convinced his chances of containing it were lost. Except he'd slipped up, and slipped up beyond any chance of putting damage control in place.

The bride of his choice!

That was the worst lie...making her feel special...more attractive to him than any of her sisters...*his* sisters whom he couldn't marry. No wonder he hadn't *wanted* them.

She headed up the stairs in a fury of rejection of every nice thing Richard had ever said to her. Sweet persuaders for getting his own way and keeping her blind to it. Caroline was right—a pushover! Trapped by her own vulnerability into believing—hoping—Richard could give her what she most wanted.

It was a joke! The blackest joke of all!

She reached the top of the stairs and paused to fling the gauntlet down at her cheating husband who was just starting up them. "I am not sleeping with you tonight. Nor any night to come. Find yourself somewhere else to bed down because I will not be your...your *patsy* wife any more!"

He looked up at her with a grimly set face and kept coming. Leigh stalked off down the corridor, reached their bedroom, opened the door, stepped inside and slammed the door behind her to punctuate her decision. This was *her* house. It was part of their unholy agreement, and she saw no reason she should end up with nothing when she'd provided him with the inheritance he'd coveted. He could find himself another residence to live in!

She kicked off her shoes and stormed over to the dressing-table, wishing she could tear off the gold chain with the heart locket, but knowing she needed the mirror to see how to work the tricky catch. She was literally shaking with rage and found it impossible to concentrate on the task.

Then the door opened and Richard stepped into the room.

"Get out!" she screeched at him.

He ignored her demand. With a calm arrogance that incensed her even further, he closed the door behind him and stood in front of it with the air of an immovable force.

"I said get out!" Leigh raged, and with violent passion she picked up the beautiful arrangement of red roses and hurled them at him. "Take these with you! They're a lie, too!"

But he didn't go. He didn't move at all. He stood there, determination carved on his face, a relentless strength of will emanating from him, reaching out and winding around her, trapping her in its force field.

"I let you go twice, Leigh," he said quietly. "I will not let you go now. Apart from what there is between us, you are carrying my child, and I will not be cheated out of having my son. Nor will I allow him to be cheated out of having his father."

CHAPTER FOURTEEN

THE father of her child...

Somehow the reminder of Richard's paternity and what it meant to him knocked the rage out of Leigh. She just stood there, staring at him, trembling from the turbulent passion expended while between them shimmered the commonality of their childhoods, both of them cheated of a mother's and a father's love.

Her mind was hopelessly torn. Could she really justify shutting Richard out of their lives on the grounds that *her* love would be enough for their child? A son needed a father, and not just in name. A name wasn't enough. Not nearly enough. God knew both Richard and she were painfully aware of that...the lack of any caring support, the emotional deprivation. And he had told her—told her from the beginning—any child of his would be precious to him.

No use telling herself that was a lie. All the evidence pointed to its being the truth; his caring over her pregnancy, his disappointment at not being with her at the scan today, his enthralment in seeing their baby for the first time this evening. She knew intuitively that all the years of Richard's lonely life would have built a deep resolution to do the very best by any child of his, in every way there was.

"I'm sorry you're so distressed by what my mother revealed," he said gently.

Out of her misery shot a question that hadn't been

answered. "Why didn't *she* tell him? You might have had a father taking an interest in you."

He grimaced. "Pride. My mother took the attitude that since he didn't want her, he couldn't have me. It was a silent revenge, but one that I believe has given her considerable satisfaction over the years."

"So why tell me? Why come out with it tonight?"

"He's dead. No risk of any nasty comeback from him." His face tightened and anger burned in his eyes. "Though *I* shall certainly have something to say to her. She had no right..."

The bitter anger in him inflamed her own at his deceit. "No, she didn't have the right. But *you* should have told me, Richard. Been open with me..."

He shook his head. "I didn't want you to know. Ever. It would have affected how you saw me, how you felt about me." He expelled a heavy sigh. "As it's doing now, despite the fact I'm the same man you happily embraced when I came home tonight."

"No. That was the mask you put on for me," she cried in vehement denial of such a stance from him. "The real man is what I know now."

"So what is different, Leigh? A name I don't even bear? A name that haunted my childhood, as it did yours? A name I hate as much as you do?" He started walking towards her. "Don't let it drive us apart. It's a bond we share. It's a..."

"Stop it!" She thrust out her hands in a warning gesture as she backed away. "Don't you come near me, Richard." Her voice shook with the violence of her physical recoil from him. "If you try to touch me I'll fight you tooth and claw."

He halted near the foot of the bed, yet Leigh felt

crowded, panicky. She grabbed onto the sidepost of the head of the bed, not that it provided any defense against the power Richard emitted, but it did lend her some physical support and she needed it. Her legs felt weak, her knees in danger of buckling.

Richard frowned. "Surely you know I wouldn't hurt you, Leigh. Not in any way."

"You have hurt me!" she hurled back at him. "You lied...and I believed you. You must have known I wanted to believe you, and you fed me what I needed to hear..." Tears blurred her eyes. "...what I needed..."

She choked. The hurt went bone-deep, soul-deep. Impossible to even begin to express what he'd done to her with his lies.

"I didn't tell you everything about myself, Leigh, but I never once lied to you," he insisted quietly, using a calm, soothing tone that agitated her even further.

"You deceived me. You know you did, making me think you liked me best." That was the cruelest cut of all and she would bleed forever from it.

"I did like you best," he softly claimed. "There was no deceit whatsoever in saying you were the bride of my choice."

"You couldn't choose my sisters so there was no choice," she snapped, hating him for trying to refute what was so painfully obvious.

"I wouldn't have wanted them even if I could," he persisted. "I wanted you, Leigh. I always wanted you."

"No...no...no," she howled, frustrated by the relentless beat of his replies. "You didn't choose me for *me*! Who I am...what I am as a person...didn't count!"

"Yes, it did. It most certainly did," he said with intense fervor.

It made Leigh scream, "Don't lie to me! I was the only one who could get you where you wanted to be."

"Yes! The only one," he finally agreed, his voice riven with a passion that tore along her nerves. "Because where I wanted to be was *with you*!"

"That's not true! Not true!" she cried, frantically refusing to believe him because it meant too much and she couldn't bear him twisting the truth any more.

"*With you*, Leigh," he repeated, his eyes blazing at her, projecting a furnace of feeling as he went on, "*with you*...and laying all Lawrence Durant stood for at your feet, to have or dismiss as you chose. *With you*...in the role you wanted me to play before it was time to do it...your champion. *With you*...for the rest of our lives. That's where I want to be!"

She stood poleaxed, dumbfounded, her heart quivering in some profound vacuum that made no sense to her, but he was tugging at it. Dazedly she watched him break into pacing the floor, gesticulating at her as he pumped out more of his feelings in a turbulent torrent of words that did more than tug at her heart.

"You *are* the only one for me. The only one there's ever been in any meaningful sense. It was *you* who drew me to Lawrence's Sunday lunches, not him. I felt an instant bond with you, Leigh, for all you were only a young teenager. I came to protect you. I came to block him. I sat there, willing you not to be crushed, to keep holding to your inner sense of yourself, and when you finally left that household, I felt so proud of you, I went around for days, inwardly cheering, 'She's done it! She's broken free! She'll make it on her own now!'"

He paused, a strangely haunted look in his eyes, some inner conflict working through him. His mouth made a resigned grimace. "It was all I could do to stop myself from going after you then."

"Then?" Leigh echoed incredulously, barely able to get the word out, her mind shattered by his outburst, the eerie answering of dreams she'd secretly nursed and never voiced to him. How could he know them? Had she been so transparent?

He was shaking his head. "It would have been wrong to try to connect with you then." His eyes flashed that conviction at her. "You connected me to Lawrence."

Yes, she had. Her father's man. But he wasn't, and had never been Lawrence's man, and what he said about his feeling for her... her memory clicked back to the day of the funeral...a fellow traveler, he'd said. A fellow traveler on a road few people could know or understand...a bond...

"You needed to be away from it all," he went on. "Needed to find your own road to take. And time...time to grow into the person you were capable of being."

Looking back, Leigh realized the truth of what he was saying, yet for him to have thought it all out back then, when she had run away...had he really?

"I hired the private investigator so I wouldn't lose you. It was also the best way of ensuring you came to no harm. Then I set a search in motion for your real father, thinking he might be someone you could go to, someone who might want to acknowledge you as his daughter, but that didn't prove to be the case."

He paused, appealing to her for understanding. "I would have put you in contact with him, Leigh, if I'd thought he'd be of any help to you. But he was in Italy and I couldn't see good consequences for either side. It seemed best to leave it alone until such time as the knowledge of his circumstances wouldn't add to the hurt you were already carrying.''

Her throat was too constricted by a lump of emotion to make any reply. She had been so suspicious of his motives and here they were, laid out so clearly, how could she doubt his empathy with her situation, his wish to help?

He frowned, recollecting himself. ''I didn't expect Lawrence to die. Another year…two at most…I had the moves planned to take control out of his hands.'' His gaze lifted again, targeting her with a depth of yearning that reached right into her soul. ''I would have come for you then. Would have courted you with everything I could offer.''

And would have swept her off her feet, Leigh thought, dizzied by the sheer obsession of the vision that had encompassed her. His words on their wedding day… *In my mind, she was always going to be the woman I'd marry.* Not a lie. Not even a smooth line for reporters to pick up. The truth. The actual truth.

''Lawrence's death frustrated that plan,'' he went on, grimacing at having that eventuality rob him of his controlling hand. Again his eyes pleaded eloquently with hers…not the hunter…a man in need. ''And you came back for the funeral. No longer a teenager. A woman. A woman so beautiful, I literally ached to have you.''

She shook her head, realizing how hopelessly she had misinterpreted almost everything he'd said and done.

''It's true, Leigh. I swear it,'' he declared vehemently, misinterpreting her response. ''Yes, Lawrence's will came into play,'' he conceded. ''I wanted you to have it all. I wanted to give it to you. But most of all, I wanted you. I wanted you so badly, I used everything I had at my command to win you to me that day.''

In the garden, by the ornamental pool, Richard stating he wanted to marry her, saying… *I don't suppose you'd believe me if I said I loved you.* She hadn't believed it. Not for a moment. And these past four months together, she hadn't let herself believe it, would have doubted it even if he'd said the words, which he hadn't. Had he been waiting for her to say them?

''At the time, I didn't care why you agreed to marry me. You did. And I thought I could bind you to me…''

''With sex?'' Leigh queried, seeing how it must have seemed to him with her response in the summer-house, his concentration on that intimate aspect of their marriage. *The nights are mine…*

His cheekbones were suddenly illuminated by red heat, his eyes momentarily anguished. ''You responded to me. Every time. I thought it was the only certain way I had of reaching you, having you. But I did try to court you, Leigh. With the wedding, the honeymoon…''

His queen…

And roses…cream ones in her bridal bouquet…and today…she stared down at the broken red roses scattered across the floor…his pleasure…her torment…

''I thought having a child…our child…'' he went on, a deep throb of wanting in his voice, calling to her, telling her everything she had craved hearing from him, feeling from him. ''Please, Leigh…for him if not for me…don't shut me out.''

As he'd been shut out most of his life.

She dragged her gaze up, tears filling her eyes, spilling

down her cheeks. He was a blur but it didn't matter. He was there for her, would always be there for her.

"I love you, Richard," she blurted out. "I thought you didn't love me, that I was...I was nothing again. I'm sorry. I..."

He had her wrapped in his arms so fast, Leigh forgot what she was trying to say. She simply sagged into his warmth and was grateful for his strength because all she could do was hang onto him and weep onto his broad shoulder.

He held her tight, as she needed to be held...no letting go, ever...and there was such wonderful comfort in it...the sense of finally having found her home...where she belonged...*with him*...and all the years of loneliness were over...the pain of the past slipping away...and what had been forged out of that pain was this...their togetherness...unbreakable because it meant so much...so very, very much...to both of them.

Her tears kept flowing, like a dam burst of all the feelings she'd kept suppressed, the fears, the uncertainties, the hopes and doubts, the need to be strong and independent, to protect herself. They could be released, and released they were as Richard held her, rubbing his cheek tenderly against her hair, murmuring what he'd kept hidden in his heart.

"My life is nothing without you, Leigh. From the day I met you, you gave me a reason for being. A good reason. So many times over the years, I'd think...this is for Leigh. Then to have the reality of you since we've been married..."

His chest rose and fell in a sigh that whispered warmly over her temples. "Don't ever think you're nothing. You're everything. The light of my life. The joy. The

woman I love. With you I feel...*right*. Like all the missing pieces have come together. The empty spaces have
been filled by you. I don't know if you understand what
I mean..."

"Yes. Oh, yes," she answered, the words dredged
from the same soul-deep needs he fulfilled. And the well
of tears was gone, pushed out of existence by a surge of
well-being that carried an exhilarating sense of *rightness*.

She lifted her head to look into the eyes of this man
she loved and had wanted on so many levels. They were
open to her, clear blue windows, revealing all she needed
to see and know, no deceit, no manipulation, his desire
for her as raw and compelling as her desire for him.

Their mouths met in a mutual rush to taste it, feel it
as fully as they could...love unchained, flying free. For
all the pleasure they had taken in making love to each
other throughout their marriage, none of it matched this
coming together...this giving to each other of all there
was in them to give.

Long into the night they touched in all the ways there
were, expressing their feelings, confiding them, reveling
in them, completing an understanding that would spread
over the rest of their lives, a solid foundation on which
to build whatever kind of future they planned together.
All that really counted was that they would share it.

As they lay in contentment, stripped of every barrier
there had been between them, and Richard tenderly caressing the shape of the baby inside her, Leigh suddenly
remembered one of the terms in Lawrence's will and felt
an instant stab of rebellion against it.

"Richard?"

"Mm?"

"Do we have to name our son Lawrence?"

"No. This child is ours. And he's going to be himself." He leaned over and kissed her stomach just as a tiny foot skated under the surface of her tightly stretched skin. Richard grinned at her. "See? He's making his presence felt. An individual in his own right."

She laughed at his fatuous expression. "I thought it was stated in the will..."

"I can get around that," he said with such careless confidence, Leigh didn't bother pursuing the point.

"What names do you like?" she asked, happy to go along with his choice.

He shrugged. "Whatever you like."

"There are lots of names I quite fancy," she said, wanting him to suggest a few.

He gave her a hopeful look. "Then maybe we could have more than one child so you can use them up."

Leigh was happy to consider this now, certain Richard would be a wonderful father. "Mmm...just how big a family do you have in mind, Richard? Thinking of founding a dynasty?"

She'd meant it teasingly, but he instantly frowned. "No. Not that. Never that," he said emphatically, his eyes sharply scanning hers. "Don't mix me up with Lawrence, Leigh. Once I have control of the company, its holdings can be sold off if you'd like us to be free of it. I don't need any child of mine to step into my shoes."

"I know, Richard," she hastily assured him. "I wasn't lining you up with Lawrence." She smiled at him to show there was no shadow of comparison. "If I'm your queen, you're my king, and a king's family line is called a dynasty, isn't it? Except all our children can abdicate and do their own thing. Right?"

"Right," he affirmed, visibly relaxing again. Then he cocked a hopeful eyebrow at her. "*All* our children?"

"Well, I don't think our son should be an only child. That could be lonely for him."

"My thinking exactly." His eyes danced with delight. "A family of our own, Leigh. From beginning to end."

"Yes," she agreed, knowing what he meant. No child of theirs would ever feel unwanted or rejected, not belonging to anyone, not valued for the person he or she was. From the moment they were born they would be welcomed and loved by their parents, and that emotional security would spread over their lives, from beginning to end.

"It starts with us," Leigh murmured.

"We can do it," Richard said confidently, taking her in his arms again, cuddling her close. "We'll do it together, Leigh. A safe circle of love where they can grow into whatever they want to be."

"Is that the end you're aiming for, Richard?"

"With you, my love. With you."

He kissed her and Leigh knew it was true.

Taking wasn't what the hunt had been about.

Giving was the end goal.

CHAPTER FIFTEEN

IT WAS the biggest party she'd ever organized at their home and Leigh was delighted it was going so well. All the guests, both family and friends, appeared to be in high spirits, enjoying themselves. Of course, a christening party was a happy occasion, and their four-month-old son was a natural star. Better still, Lawrence's will had finally been settled, and the future lay open for new directions to be taken.

Leigh suspected the latter contributed to the congenial mood of her sisters, all of whom had accepted their invitations. It was doubtful she'd ever be close to them, but it was good to have their antagonism towards her lifted, letting her feel she was at least accepted by them as a desirable relation to have, even if it was only because she'd done right by them in having a son.

Or maybe they didn't see her as a thorn in their side any more. It was over a year since Lawrence had died. With his insidious influence removed and fading with the lapse of time, perhaps they were beginning to see through their own eyes. Both Felicity and Vanessa had seemed quite sincere in their comments to her.

"Lovely home, Leigh," Felicity had said admiringly. "Quite a striking use of color. Most unusual."

It would be to Felicity who had always stuck to a classical style, but it was nice that she wasn't critical.

174

"And the view is wonderful," she'd gone on, detailing what she liked.

It was a pleasant little conversation, as was the one with Vanessa.

"Gorgeous baby, Leigh. He's actually making me feel clucky." She'd looked coquettishly at the new man she had in tow. "Do you think you're father material, Jordan?"

"I shall only be used as your sperm bank if you marry me," he'd answered, obviously very keen.

"Oh, dear! He's putting the hard word on me, Leigh. I think he should prove he can be as besotted a father as Richard before I take him on as a husband. How else can I know what kind of father he'd be?"

Having had a father like Lawrence, Leigh could appreciate where Vanessa was coming from, but watching her sister and Jordan sparking off each other, she hoped everything would turn out well for them.

Richard *was* totally besotted with their son. Observing him now, carrying their baby around their guests, showing him off, one would never guess he controlled a financial empire. He was the epitome of a proud father, adoring his child and wanting everyone else to adore him. Which they should because he was adorable, Leigh thought, smiling over her own pride in their beautiful baby boy.

Having checked there were no hitches with the caterers, Leigh was making her way back to Richard's side when Caroline intercepted her.

"Got a moment, Leigh?" she asked, purposeful intent clearly on her mind.

Surprised, Leigh automatically answered, "Yes. What would you like?"

"To talk." An ironic smile took any spiteful edge off her next words. "If you can spare the time away from playing happy family."

Leigh sensed that Caroline was half-expecting a snub. She smiled to put her at ease, feeling no animosity at all towards her blunt-spoken sister, aware now of the life-long frustrations that had been carved into her soul. "I could do with a breath of fresh air," she said invitingly. "Let's go out to the patio."

Caroline relaxed slightly. "Thanks, Leigh. A bit of space would be good."

They strolled outside together, Caroline swiping drinks off a waiter's tray as they went. She handed Leigh an orange juice and kept a glass of champagne for herself. "Healthy stuff for you and fortification for me."

Leigh wondered why Caroline needed fortification but simply thanked her for the forethought of supplying her with the juice. She was off alcohol while breast-feeding the baby. They found an unoccupied garden bench just off the patio and sat down, ostensibly to enjoy a quiet drink together, although Leigh was acutely aware of her sister's tension. Caroline stared out at the view, sipped her drink, and without looking at Leigh, finally blurted out what was on her mind.

"I owe you an apology. I've been a pig to you and I'm sorry. You got it more right than any of us, Leigh, going out on your own. Got it right with Richard, too. All I can say in mitigation of my bitchiness is I've been screwed up for a long time."

Leigh took a deep breath. This was very touchy

ground. Slowly, softly, she said, "I hope it's better for you now, Caroline."

"Oh, I've got myself more sorted out if that's what you mean," came the wry reply. "I'm going to stop reacting to our dear departed father's rejection of my abilities and carve out a career of my own."

"What in?" Leigh asked with interest.

"Law. It's a challenge I can get my teeth into. And it leads to the corridors of power. I like power. I would have married Richard for it, but it's better if I go after it myself. I don't want it through a man."

Her mother was right, Leigh thought. Caroline was more her father's daughter than any of the others.

"You know, we're all better off that Richard chose you," Caroline mused. "It did set us free...like you said at your wedding...free to make our own choices, without fear." At last she turned her head and met Leigh's gaze full on. "Not that Richard would have chosen any of us," she said ruefully. "It was always going to be you, wasn't it?"

"Yes," Leigh acknowledged.

"And it is love. I can see that now. Not just you. Him, too. You've got it made together, haven't you?"

"That's how it feels, Caroline."

She nodded. "It gives me goose bumps watching the two of you. It's so different. So very different. No tension. Everything feel-good."

"I'm glad you don't mind..."

"Mind! I was wondering if you'd mind if I dropped in now and then. Just to remind myself how it can be. Visit with the baby for a bit?" she added hopefully. "I mean..." Her self-mocking smile held an apologetic appeal. "...I might develop a nice side, given half a chance."

"You'll be welcome any time, Caroline," Leigh said warmly, understanding all too well what her sister needed.

Her relief was palpable. "Thanks, Leigh. The baby's a real darling. I love it when he smiles. Makes my heart melt. Did Richard choose his name?"

"No. I did."

"Well, good for you! It's perfect. Alexander... Alexander the Great!"

Leigh laughed. "He doesn't have to be great, Caroline. As long as he's happy with himself. That's what I want for him. Richard does, too."

Caroline relaxed into a grin. "Well, you can count on this aunt to give him stacks and stacks of approval."

"Stacks," Leigh agreed feelingly, and they both laughed over their mutual understanding of that need. Healing laughter, she thought, and hoped it was a step towards a closer bond between them.

"What are you two cackling over?"

They turned to find Nadine making a beeline towards them, coming from the path that wound through the gardens.

"The lack of approval bestowed on us in times past," Caroline drily explained.

Nadine rolled her eyes as she came to a halt in front of them. "Why spoil a beautiful day with that miserable memory?" She half-turned, pointing back down the path. "Did you place those pots in your garden, Leigh?"

"Yes. They're part of a range I made for outdoor decoration."

Nadine's gaze swung back, a curious look of assessment in her eyes. "Mother said you did pottery. I must say you've got a terrific eye for picking the right spot for it."

"Thank you."

"You know, I never thought you were good for anything, Leigh. But you are."

The blunt declaration was so *Nadine*, Leigh didn't find it offensive. "I'm glad to hear it," she said.

"If you want approval, I'll give you lots of approval for your pots and urns and the way you've used them."

"That's very big of you, Nadine."

Caroline tittered.

Nadine frowned at her. "I'm not kidding. Leigh's really good at this. In fact, I'm planning to buy into a trendy gift shop, now that I've got the money. When it's all settled, I'd like to stock some of your stuff, Leigh. Could we do a deal on it?"

"I'm sure we could," Leigh readily agreed. "And I'm sorry I was such a pain to you when we were growing up."

"Well, you were an awful kid, always getting me into trouble. Then turning up and snaffling Richard. It was a bit much. I really fancied him. And damned if I could see what you had to recommend you."

"Call it chemistry," Caroline intervened sardonically.

"Guess so," Nadine agreed on a sigh. "Still working, too. Who'd have thought I'd ever see Richard Seymour a virtual slave to a woman and a baby. Speaking of whom…"

They all turned at the escalating pitch of a baby's cry in full demand. Richard was striding towards them, mak-

ing reassuring noises at his son who was not in listening
mode. Despite the comfort of his father's chest and the
patting that accompanied the soft baby chat, Alexander
arched himself against his father's hold and screamed
his lungs out.

Leigh leapt to her feet to meet them.

"What's wrong?" Caroline asked.

Leigh threw her a grin. "Feed time. When Alexander
decides he's hungry, he has a one-track mind."

"Feed time," Richard said, hastily bundling their son
into Leigh's arms. "One thing I can't do," he directed
ruefully to Caroline and Nadine.

Alexander instantly stopped yelling and started snuf-
fling around Leigh's chest.

"See? He can smell the milk," Richard explained.

Both women broke into laughter and starting teasing
Richard about the limitations of fatherhood. He was answering good-humouredly as Leigh headed inside to satisfy Alexander's needs. Rather than go upstairs to the
nursery, she turned down the hall to the studio where
she'd put in a rocking chair and a change table for day
use. Being at the end of the house, it was a quiet and
private place, even today with a party in full swing.

Finding her mother there was totally unexpected.
"Taking refuge from the party, Mother?"

Alicia smiled. "Not really. Just thought I'd take a
look at what you've been doing recently. Feed time?"

"Yes. Rather urgent."

"Mind if I stay?"

"Not at all."

Leigh settled on the rocking chair and quickly arranged herself to Alexander's satisfaction. Once he was

blissfully occupied, she turned her attention to her mother who had strolled over to the blue vase, still on the pedestal where it had stood ever since Leigh had created it.

"You haven't sold this," Alicia commented, touching it again as though she coveted it.

"Would you like to have it, Mother?"

"Oh, I'm sure you're keeping it because it's special to you, Leigh. I wouldn't take it…"

"As a thank-you gift for organizing the catering for me."

"Really?" She swung around, a look of sheer delight in her eyes. "You wouldn't mind parting with it?"

"No. I only kept it because it was my first success with that particular kind of glaze. If it gives you pleasure…"

"It's beautiful! I loved it from the first moment I saw it."

"Then it's yours."

"How kind! Thank you, Leigh. I'll treasure it."

Alicia chatted on about the more current pieces on the shelves while Leigh fed Alexander. Over the past year they'd established a comfortable relationship. Alicia readily handed out advice on where to shop and gave many good tips on being a successful hostess. She rarely opened up about her own personal life but showed a keen interest in Leigh's. Sometimes Leigh felt as though her mother was fascinated by a life she hadn't led, yet might have in other circumstances.

Alicia watched indulgently as Leigh changed Alexander's nappy. He was full of smiles again now, waving his little arms and making happy sounds.

"Amazing, all that black hair."

"Well, Richard and I both have black hair," Leigh reminded her.

"Yes. But he looks more like you, Leigh. His eyes are too dark to turn blue. People might talk of him as Lawrence's grandson, but he's really mine, aren't you, darling?" She leaned over and tickled Alexander's tummy and he blew bubbles at her. Alicia laughed. "Oh, it's going to be fun, having a boy in the family. And not one that has to be like Lawrence."

She sighed and smiled whimsically at Leigh. "You know, I would really like to enjoy a child. I wasn't much of a mother, but if you'll let me try being a grandmother…"

"You *are* his grandmother," Leigh assured her, smiling as she lifted Alexander and passed him to her mother. "Here! Waltz him out to Richard."

"And who's a beautiful boy, mm?" Alicia cooed as she did waltz her grandson out of the studio.

Leigh shook her head in bemusement. Time, she thought, had wrought changes in all of them. Looking back, she realized it had been very unrealistic to have expected the cloud of Lawrence's influence to lift from her family the moment he'd passed away. It might not ever completely lift but it was no longer a darkly divisive cloud. There was acceptance now. Even some tentative reaching out. Hope for something better.

Having tidied the change table and checked she was fit to be seen again, Leigh returned to the party in a happy buoyant mood, until she saw her mother, still holding Alexander, *and chatting to Clare Seymour.*

Tension instantly screamed along Leigh's nerves. Was

it all right? Should she break it up? Where was Richard? Her gaze darted around the crowd, trying to spot him, her mind awhirl with awful possibilities.

She didn't really *know* his mother, only that the situation between Clare and Richard had eased. He had gone to talk to her the day after the shocking revelation at Doyle's and Leigh had begged him not to use threats to force a maintenance of silence.

"Be open with her, Richard. Tell her how it's been for you. Tell her how it was for me. Make her see Lawrence wasn't worth wasting her heart on. That he's gone now anyway and there's no reason to hurt us. We didn't do anything to her."

But here Clare was, talking to Alicia, the wife she'd wanted Lawrence to discard…and while a *rapprochement* had been forged between mother and son, might not that old wound to Clare's pride pour forth pus?

Leigh's heart was hammering with fearful uncertainties when her gaze finally picked out Richard. A waiter, holding a tray of glasses head high, had momentarily obscured a view of him, but he actually stood only a couple of meters away from the two women and he was watching them. Leigh's wild pulse rate slowed as she saw that his face was relaxed. There was even a bemused little smile playing over his lips.

It had to be all right, she swiftly reasoned.

Richard would have intervened otherwise.

He must have convinced his mother to let the past go.

Relieved, Leigh hurried across the room, eager to be with the man she trusted to make everything as right as he could, within the parameters of human frailties. Long gone were the doubts about trusting her heart with him.

Richard had proved over and over again how safe that trust was.

Somehow he must have sensed her coming. His gaze swung to fasten on hers before she reached him and his eyes smiled his love for her, filling her with happiness.

His arm was outstretched, ready to gather her close, and Leigh nestled against his side with a sigh of contentment, reveling once more in the sense of belonging with him…Richard, her husband, the partner of her heart, her soul mate.

He dropped a kiss on her forehead and rubbed his cheek on her hair. "Our respective mothers seem to have found a positive interest in common," he murmured.

"Our son is the winner?"

"Our son will always be a winner," he declared warmly.

Leigh rested her head on Richard's shoulder and they both watched Alicia and Clare gazing down at Alexander with indulgent smiles on their faces.

What caused them to look up in unison and both spot Richard and Leigh viewing them together was inexplicable…some sixth sense?…a current of energy tugging at them?…a force of nature being reborn?…a maternal urge awakening?

Suddenly, unexpectedly, touchingly, it seemed there were two mothers, sizing up a son and daughter, and liking what they saw, liking what they represented, liking who they were.

Tears pricked Leigh's eyes, but she didn't cry. She looked up at Richard. His eyes met hers and she saw in them the same sense of something like a miracle…the rejection they'd lived with all their lives finally gone.

"It starts with us," he murmured.

"With love," she answered.

"And giving."

The deepest truth of love…giving. They knew it. And Leigh hoped all their family would. Because love was a gift and it was the one thing that should never, never be wasted or laid waste. It was the most precious thing of all.

* * * * *

Author's Note

Lawrence Durant is dead from page one of this story, yet as you have seen, he remained a driving force in the lives of everyone in it. Men of great wealth invariably exert power over others.

In the coming months, I invite you to King's Eden— a family empire built from a hundred years of pioneering enterprise, embracing a vast cattle station, mining shares in gold and diamonds, a pearl farm that produces the best pearls in the world, and an air charter business that brings tourism to the great Australian Outback.

This is the world of the legendary King family of the Kimberly, now ruled by Elizabeth, the widow of Lachlan, and their three sons—each a King of his own empire.

One by one, these men's hearts will be won by women who dare to challenge who and what the brothers are.

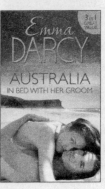

Discover more romance at

www.millsandboon.co.uk

- ❤ WIN great prizes in our exclusive competitions

- ❤ BUY new titles before they hit the shops

- ❤ BROWSE new books and REVIEW your favourites

- ❤ SAVE on new books with the Mills & Boon® Bookclub™

- ❤ DISCOVER new authors

PLUS, to chat about your favourite reads, get the latest news and find special offers:

- 🇫 Find us on facebook.com/millsandboon
- 🐦 Follow us on twitter.com/millsandboonuk
- ❤ Sign up to our newsletter at millsandboon.co.uk